UNDERSEA PRISON

Duncan Falconer

SPHERE

First published in Great Britain in 2008 by Sphere
Reprinted 2008

All characters and events in this publication, other than those clearly in the public domain, are fictitious and any resemblance to real persons, living or dead, is purely coincidental.

ISBN HB 978-1-84744-067-9
ISBN CF 978-1-84744-066-2

Typeset in Bembo by
Palimpsest Book Production Limited,
Grangemouth, Stirlingshire
Printed and bound in Great Britain by Clays Ltd, St Ives plc

Sphere
An imprint of
Little, Brown Book Group
100 Victoria Embankment
London EC4Y 0DY

An Hachette Livre UK Company

www.littlebrown.co.uk

Many, many thanks to Christine SS
and to Yorky for so much of the wet stuff

Chapter 1

Major Hillsborough, British Army Intelligence Corps, buckled into the rigid nylon seat of the Merlin troop-transport helicopter. A portly crewman sat by the open cabin door, chatting into his headset. The major was the only passenger; the other two dozen seats folded up against the bulkhead gave the cabin the vacant look of an empty biscuit tin. He couldn't hear a word the crewman was saying above the high-pitched whine of the engines and he leaned forward to look through the narrow opening into the cockpit where the co-pilot was talking into his mouthpiece while consulting a checklist and flicking overhead switches.

The view through the open cabin door revealed nothing but rough angular slabs of concrete: tall interlocking blast-walls that surrounded the helipad and large pebbles covering the ground to reduce the dust. The crewman slid the large door smoothly shut, muffling the higher and more irritating noise frequencies. These only got louder as the engine power increased and the heavy beast made a great effort to pull itself off the ground.

Hillsborough cleared his throat as he stretched around to look through the large square window behind his seat. The dust swirled under the thundering rotors, working its way out from beneath the pebbles. The old city beyond the camp's precast angular walls came into view. He had been in Afghanistan only a couple of weeks but that was long enough to acquire what was commonly known as the Kabul cough, an irritation caused by the fine grey dust common to the region. Locals described it as so fine that it could work its way through the shell of an egg.

The helicopter rose to reveal a view of the north-eastern outskirts of the city, the squat dilapidated sandy-grey habitats intermingled with shiny new metal warehouses owned by the UN, Red Cross and various Western food and hardware corporations. The craft slowly turned on its axis, giving Hillsborough a view of the rest of Camp Souter, the British Army Headquarters in Afghanistan, ringed by layers of imposing walls topped with interlocking spools of razor wire. A soldier stood in the doorway of the nearest sentry tower inside a corner of the wall, watching the helicopter as it climbed above him. The Merlin continued to turn and Hillsborough saw a massive Antonov cargo plane taxi along the runway of Kabul International Airport. A pair of military C130 transport aircraft were parked near a row of hangars, along with several Apache gunships and some Chinooks.

The chopper dipped its nose slightly as it powered ahead and Hillsborough looked beyond the airfield at a parched mountain range. He had to crouch in order to see the highest point of Khwaja Rawash, a craggy hill he had fancied spending a day walking up but had never got around to. He felt a tinge of guilt about the failed expedition and tried to console himself with the rationalisation that it would have been a pointless risk anyway. But this excuse was quickly negated by the initial justification he'd come up with for doing the walk alone in the first place – which was that he had about as much chance of being mugged on the coastline near Dover where he lived as he had of running into Taliban fighters in that deserted terrain. He knew that better than most since he was the Regiment's senior intelligence officer – or, at least, he had been until that morning. An aide from the Embassy had arrived unexpectedly in the operations room with a high-priority assignment that had to be carried out by someone who held at least the rank of major and Hillsborough was the only one available.

There was no shortage of men who would have jumped at the prospect of a jolly to London but Hillsborough was not one of them. He had climbed out of bed that morning, as he had every day since his arrival, looking forward to getting his teeth into his new appointment. It was his first senior command posting and having completed his handover from the previous IO the day before he was imbued with an invigorating feeling of his own importance. Now, suddenly, he was nothing more than a messenger carrying an important diplomatic package to Bagram Airbase where a plane was waiting to fly him to the UK. He had no idea what was inside the briefcase chained to his wrist and he didn't particularly care. This trip was a bloody nuisance and he already knew that he wouldn't be able to wait to get back to Afghanistan.

Hillsborough checked his watch, a shiny steel Rolex analogue that his wife had given him on his last birthday. Not more than twenty minutes, the pilot had told him. But Hillsborough displayed none of the sense of urgency and importance that the embassy attaché had ascribed to the mission. The man had not even given him a guesstimated return date and the worst-case scenario was that he could be gone for weeks.

The crewman sat with his elbows on his knees, supporting his large helmeted head while he stared at the floor as he did a rough calculation of his own. He had three days left of his tour of duty and his name was on the operations board under just two more scheduled trips. But since this particular excursion had been unexpected he wondered if he might not have to do only one of his planned trips because of it. At the end of the day it didn't matter, though, as long as in seventy-eight hours he was on that big beautiful C130 and heading for England. He could already taste that first pint in his local and hear the boisterous laughter of his mates at the bar.

Hillsborough sat back in his seat and concentrated on easing the tension in his neck muscles that had tightened since boarding the Merlin. He wasn't sure where the stress had come from, since he was generally a relaxed individual even on helicopter flights. He put it down to the anxiety of this unexpected and disruptive mission. He raised a hand to scratch an itch on his eyebrow, inadvertently pulling on the short chain attached to the briefcase, yanking it off his lap and forcing him to make a quick grab for it. Having something chained to his wrist was a new experience for him.

The crewman glanced at the major, wondering if he was nervous. 'You OK, sir?' he called out, leaning forward.

'What?' Hillsborough shouted back, unsure what the man had said.

The crewman was about to repeat himself when he changed his mind, reached above his head, removed a headset from a hook, unravelled the cable wrapped around the earpieces and handed it to Hillsborough who put it on.

'Be there in fifteen,' the crewman shouted.

'Yes. Right,' the major said.

The crewman shook his head as he touched his helmet alongside his ear and pointed to a small control box on the cable at Hillsborough's chest.

Hillsborough found the box and pressed a button on it. 'Yes. Thank you.'

The crewman gave him a thumbs-up and Hillsborough looked back out of the window to see the city already in the distance a couple of thousand feet below. A lonely black road directly below grew from the urban sprawl like a vine and passed below the helicopter. He turned in his seat to examine it as it weaved ahead across a vast, open, treeless land known as the Shomali Plains where half a dozen small villages or hamlets were spaced out on either side, some of them miles back from it. At the end of the plain the road snaked tightly up into a range of lumpy hills before disappearing short of the crest. What appeared to be some kind of ancient fortress came into view almost directly below: a hundred or so neatly spaced blocks of houses surrounded by a high rectangular mud wall. It appeared to be abandoned and Hillsborough studied it until it moved out of sight beneath him.

The Merlin banked easily when it neared the craggy hills, the highest crest a thousand feet above them. Instead of climbing the craft remained at the same height and changed direction once again to fly parallel with the range.

'Two vehicles, eleven o'clock,' said a scratchy voice over Hillsborough's headset. The sighting was on the other side of the craft and he looked away from the window at the crewman who was grabbing the handle of the large cabin door. With a well-practised sharp yank he slid it open a couple of feet. The wind rushed in and the crewman leaned out against it to take a better look, staring ahead of the helicopter.

'Seen,' the crewman said. 'Looks like they're static.'

'People climbing out, I think,' came a voice from the cockpit.

Hillsborough had an urge to unbuckle his belt in order to take a look out the door but immediately thought better of it. Helicopter crewmen could get testy about their passengers moving around the cabin without permission. Instead he took in the dramatic view of the hills that he had from his window. He had read many books about the British occupation of Afghanistan that had happened more than a century ago and he tried to imagine what it had been like for soldiers in those days: the oppressive heat and dust of the summers and the bitter cold of the winters. In many ways life for a rural Afghan had not changed a great deal since those times. Hillsborough wondered what the locals truly made of the Westerners and all their mind-boggling technology. Did they envy them or did they truly want to remain as they were? He was inclined to believe the former, suspecting that most so-called Islamic extremists were nothing more than political tools in the hands of men who could not otherwise vie for power.

'EVADE! EVADE! EVADE!' the crewman suddenly screamed. The last word had barely left his lips before the heavy machine jerked upwards, banked heavily over and dropped out of the sky on its side.

Hillsborough grabbed his seat in sudden panic as his stomach leapt into his throat and the briefcase clattered against the floor.

The crewman had had his suspicions the instant he'd heard the co-pilot sight the vehicles. They only increased as he watched several figures moving hastily around them. He had not seen much in the way of action throughout his tour other than the time when his crew had dropped off a Royal Marine fighting troop on a hillside during a battle taking place some distance away. The Yanks had lost two helicopters in those months, brought down by ground-to-air missiles, and it remained in the back of every crewman's mind each time he took to the air. The route from Kabul to Bagram was considered reasonably secure because of the relatively few numbers of attacks along it in the past six months. The wreckage at the head of the Shomali Plain of a US Blackhawk, shot down the year before, was a reminder to all that no helicopter was safe anywhere in this country.

The crewman had held himself back from hitting the panic button when he'd first thought he could make out the men taking something from the back of one of the trucks. He prided himself on his coolness and his caution against overreacting. But there was no mistaking the sudden flash from within the group and the instant cloud of smoke rapidly expanding behind it, the tell-tale signs of a launched missile.

The pilot had seen the threat and had initially increased power to pull the craft upwards, hoping to get above the missile's altitude limit. But after an instant recalculation he took the lift out of the rotors and banked the chopper away in an effort to gain downward speed and move out of the weapon's horizontal range. As he gripped the controls tightly, willing more speed into the lumbering beast, he knew in his heart that they would not make it. If the rocket was a Strela-7, rumoured to be the most common in use in the region, he needed to be over four kilometres away and above two thousand metres to stand a chance of evading it. He was short of both distances. They were in God's hands now.

The crewman could do nothing but squat in the doorway and stare at the head of the trail of smoke that twisted and curved towards them. The helicopter swung dramatically over onto its other side in an effort to shake its pursuer but the missile's computer nimbly adjusted the projectile's tail fins to compensate for the move. The smoke trail corkscrewed several times in a tight curve, cutting through the crisp, clean air as it homed in on the heat signature of the Merlin's red-hot exhausts.

Hillsborough did not know the nature of the threat but it was evident from the crew's reactions that the situation was a serious one. He put a hand to his seat belt to unfasten it in order to have a look for himself but then he remembered the helicopter crash drills he'd been taught, the fundamental rule of which was to stay strapped into the seat. If they landed he would want to get out of the craft as soon as he could and he focused on the open door in front of him, keeping his hand on the buckle in readiness. The crewman suddenly leapt from the doorway, throwing himself to the floor, and for a split second Hillsborough could see, in the bright sunshine outside, the instrument of their deaths as it homed in.

The impact struck above the cabin at the back of the engine compartment and the blast rocked the craft violently. A second later the fuel tanks ignited, exploding down into the Merlin's interior. The engines died instantly and the tail buckled as the chopper descended in a tight spiral, its nose dipping to lead its dive.

Hillsborough covered his face with one hand as flames engulfed him. The other was restrained by the chain, the briefcase having jammed under the seat. Even so, he managed to undo his seat buckle with his tethered hand and as he fell forward he saw that his body was on fire. He felt the scorching heat pour into his throat as he took his final breath.

'Mayday! Mayday!' the pilot screamed as he and the co-pilot pulled at the controls in a futile effort to get the craft's nose up. Then flames burst in from behind to fill the cockpit and as the men struggled blindly to release their seat belts the helicopter slammed into the ground.

Durrani followed the course of the missile with wide, anxious eyes, his heart pounding in his chest in excited expectation. As soon as he saw it strike and the side of the Merlin burst into flames he shouted for his men to get into the two battered pick-up trucks. He was first into the cab of the lead truck. Its engine was still running, and Durrani yelled again for his men to hurry as they scrambled for the back. Impatiently, he floored the accelerator and the wheels spun in the dry soil before they gained traction and shunted the vehicle forward.

Two of the men gave chase. One of them managed to grab hold of the tailgate and hang onto it, his legs racing at a speed they had never achieved before. Durrani only had eyes for his prey as it dropped towards the horizon. The truck picked up speed as he steered it resolutely across the rough terrain, doing his best to avoid the worst of its hazards. The man hanging onto the tailgate lost his hold after a desperate attempt to pull himself into the back and after sprawling briefly on the ground he scrambled to his feet and leapt into the back of the other vehicle.

Durrani watched the helicopter as it fell out of sight. A second later a mushroom of smoke and flame spouted into the air.

He sped towards it, desperate to complete the planned follow-up phase of the attack. His eyes flickered left and right – he was keenly aware that the road across the plain was a regular military route between Kabul and Bagram and that there was every chance that the attack had been seen by the enemy somewhere.

The trail of black smoke twisting into the clear blue sky was a fast-dissolving record of the doomed helicopter's flight path from the point the missile had struck to the Merlin's impact with the ground. Durrani fought to keep the rising black smoke in his sights but the dust blowing in through his open window was getting in his eyes.

Bright orange flames came into view as Durrani closed on the wreckage. He kept the accelerator to the floor as the pick-up bounced up onto a tarmac road and across it. He looked quickly in every direction, including skyward. If anything remotely military-looking came into view he would turn around and head towards the nearest village at the foot of the hills behind him, his only chance of escape.

The helicopter lay on its side like a gutted beast, its ravaged carcass burning, its rotors buckled, its tail broken off. The cabin and cockpit were fiercely ablaze and Durrani drove in a wide arc around it until he was upwind and away from the direct heat and smoke. He slammed on the brakes, slid to a dusty halt, opened the door and stood out on the sill to inspect his handiwork. His first thought was that it did not look possible that anyone could have survived. Prisoners were a bonus but rare in such attacks.

The other vehicle halted behind Durrani's but the men were more concerned for their own safety, anxiously scanning every quadrant of the horizon like meerkats. As far as they were concerned Durrani was putting their lives at risk by remaining in the area.

Durrani took a long and patient look, scanning the wreckage for anything of value. The destruction appeared to be complete and he was about to swing back inside his cab when something caught his eye. Several metres from the wreckage, lying on the scorched earth, was a twisted, broken body, as charred as the surrounding debris and clearly dead. But a small metallic object lying in the midst of the remains and reflecting the strong sunlight was impossible to ignore.

Durrani stepped down onto the ground.

The anxiety among the others increased as they watched their leader walk casually towards the wreckage. One of them called out that they should be going. The others quickly echoed him. Durrani ignored them, his stare fixed on the body. The wind suddenly changed direction and the searing heat from the flames struck him. He was forced to shield his face with his hands and move back several steps. The wind changed again and he saw that the glinting object was a chain attached to what appeared to be a small case.

Durrani moved in at a crouch and picked up the case, the attached limp arm in a charred jacket sleeve rising on the end of the chain. The metal handle burned him and he quickly dropped it. He drew a knife from a sheath on his belt, pulled the arm straight and dug the tip into the wrist joint, slicing through the sinews until the hand fell away. He looked for the end of the other arm lying awkwardly across the body's back and wiped the thin coat of carbon from the face of the watch to reveal the clear, undamaged glass, the second hand rotating beneath it. The watch was cool enough to touch and he pulled it off the corpse's wrist. He picked the chain up by using the point of the knife. The smouldering case dangled beneath it and, after a quick check around for anything else, Durrani headed back to his pick-up.

He climbed in behind the wheel, dropped the briefcase onto the passenger seat, slipped the scorched watch onto his wrist, put the engine in gear and roared away.

Durrani felt exhilarated as he looked around for the enemy, confident that they would not appear. He was wise enough not to celebrate until his escape was complete but seasoned enough to trust his senses. He bounced in the seat as the pick-up roared back over the tarmac road and headed for the safety of the hills and the villages that ran along the foot of it. Any doubts that he would fail to escape vanished. It had been a well-executed plan.

Durrani looked at his new watch, the shiny metal exposed where the carbon had rubbed off. His gaze moved to the case on the seat, the cracks in the charred brittle plastic exposing more metal beneath. He looked ahead again but the briefcase and its as yet unknown contents remained at the front of his thoughts.

Chapter 2

It was dark by the time Durrani entered the city of Kabul in his battered, dusty pick-up. He was wearing a leather jacket whose condition matched the vehicle perfectly. He was alone. On the seat beside him, concealed beneath a Tajik scarf, was a loaded AK47 with a seventy-five-round drum magazine attached. When Durrani had contacted his Taliban mullah to report the success of the attack and describe what he had subsequently found in the wreckage he was told to report to the mosque with his find as soon as the sun had set and to ensure he was protected. That meant he was to travel with bodyguards.

But Durrani did not like the company of others and avoided it even if it meant increasing his personal risk. He endured the presence of other men only when carrying out tasks he could not physically complete alone. In his younger days, during the fight against the Russian occupation, he had chosen to specialise in mines and booby traps because it was a military skill that he could develop alone. And to ensure he would always be employed in that role and to avoid being thrown into a regular combat company he had worked hard to become one of the best. In the process he'd gained a reputation for innovation and thoroughness, qualities that his peers felt could be employed in other roles – such as the shooting down of helicopters.

Durrani's desire for solitude was not a survival tactic in the usual sense although it had its advantages in that regard. He had been alone, except for a handful of acquaintances, since his early childhood. None of those few friends could ever have been described as close to him. He would not allow that. Durrani was living a lie that if discovered could give rise to dangerous accusations and lead to the loss of his head. He feared that if any got close to him they might somehow find out. One way of avoiding unwelcome scrutiny was to gain a reputation for being introverted. He had achieved this but it meant that he could never let his guard down. Success as a soldier bred jealousy and the need to remain enigmatic only strengthened as his celebrity increased.

Durrani was a Taliban – or, to be more accurate, he had joined their cause. The ranks of the Taliban were made up mostly of Pashtuns, the most privileged of the Afghan tribes, and he had been accepted as one of that ethnic group since his childhood. His claim to that heritage was not entirely valid. Durrani was actually half Hazara, a race considered by the Pashtuns to be no better than slave material. The Hazara were also Shi'a whereas the Pashtuns were Sunni. The Pashtuns were the largest ethnic group in Afghanistan and at one time had been considered the only true Afghans. The Hazara were not only different socially, tribally and religiously. They also looked very different: their features were distinctly Mongol – flat faces with flat noses.

Durrani's mother was Hazara and had grown up in Kandahar with her father who was a servant of a wealthy Pashtun family. They had lived in a hut at the bottom of the back garden and the Pashtun master's son, who was a year older than Durrani's mother, had spent his adolescence with her. When she had fallen pregnant in her mid-teens it had been obvious who was responsible and before the bump became too visible the girl's father threw her out of the city.

Durrani knew very little more about his mother's early life than that. He didn't know if her master's son had forced himself upon her or if they had been lovers. Durrani did not suspect rape, though. What little his mother did say about his father, when she eventually told Durrani that he was the son of a Pashtun, revealed no sign of malice or dislike and sometimes even displayed a hint of affection.

Durrani had no great interest in finding his father but even if he had wanted to it would have been impossible. He didn't know where the family had lived or even who they were. All his mother had revealed to him about their identity – it was something she was quite proud of – was that they were descended from Ahmed Shah Durrani, an eighteenth-century Pashtun king of Afghanistan. In the years leading up to the Russian invasion every member of that line had been considered a potential threat to the Communist Afghan government of the day. Those who survived assassination either went into hiding or fled the country along with the rest of the royal family and their relatives.

Durrani had been able to hide any visible evidence of his Hazara bloodline because he had not inherited the distinctive physical Mongol characteristics of that ethnic group. Instead, he had acquired his father's angular, long-nosed, lighter-skinned features. His mother had died of some illness when he was eight before he had developed any curiosity about his male parent. By that time they were living in abject poverty in Kabul in a small mud hut on the outskirts of a residential area at the foot of a hill occupied by an old British military fort that had long since been abandoned.

The memories of the day she died were now cloudy but Durrani remembered being very hungry and his mother lying on the blanket that was their bed, calling weakly for God to help her. God had not heard her: she eventually stopped making heavy and laboured breathing noises and her open eyes became still and unfocused. He shook her and asked her to wake up. When blood trickled from her lips and down the side of her mouth he knew she would never talk to him again. He did not look for anyone to help for there was no one. He could not remember ever talking to anyone else but his mother in those days and as far as he knew she had only ever talked to him – unless begging counted as talking to others. He remembered that his days with her included collecting water in a bucket from a tap and walking miles to get wood for the fire on which she cooked their paltry meals. Looking back it was hard to see how they had survived.

Hunger eventually forced Durrani to leave his mother's body in their dark, miserable hut and walk the streets of the city, ragged and unwashed, scavenging for something to eat. He remembered sorting through rotten food in gutters, competing for it with filthy dogs and cats, and sleeping in abandoned dwellings. Then one day – perhaps weeks later, he had no idea how long – he was literally picked up off the street and carried into a house by a man who turned out to be a schoolteacher. After nursing Durrani back to health the teacher placed him in an orphanage where he joined a dozen or so other children.

Durrani said his name was Po-po, his mother's nickname for him, but when asked for his family name he said, quite accurately, that he did not know. He might have told them what little he did know about his family but for reasons he could not fully understand at the time he was afraid to. His mother had never explained the complexities of race discrimination to him but he was aware that he and she had been different from the Pashtun majority and not in any positive way. Weeks later, after much badgering by the orphanage staff and the other kids, he finally muttered the only name he knew that linked him with his family. To his surprise the reaction had been most favourable, which gave him the confidence to stick with it.

One day a little girl with features similar to his mother's arrived at the orphanage. Durrani immediately went to befriend her but he was pulled aside and told by the other children to leave her alone because she was of a low caste. It was Durrani's first lesson in how Hazaras were considered inferior to the Pashtuns. The

Hazara children were often taunted by the others, treated like animals and made to act as if they were slaves. The schoolmasters did not appear to see anything wrong in it and only intervened when they saw the Hazara being severely beaten.

Durrani soon realised how imperative it was that he should never mention his mother's Hazara ethnicity. He became so fearful of the ramifications that his denial turned into a phobia. When walking the streets he would avoid eye contact with any Hazara he passed for fear that they might recognise him. A memorable exception was the day he saw coming towards him a young woman who looked exactly as he remembered his mother. He could not take his eyes off her until she was feet away, at which point he dropped his gaze and turned his back to her in case she really *was* his parent. He was afraid she might talk to him.

When the woman had passed Durrani he ran up the street as fast as he could and didn't stop until he found somewhere to hide. He did not feel shameful about his reaction. On the contrary, he was relieved at avoiding a close call. But he could not shake loose the memory of the girl's face and he gradually became confused about his mother's death, doubting whether she had actually died at all. The frightening implications of that were that if she was still living he could be exposed.

Since the day Durrani had walked out of his hut, leaving his mother's corpse inside, he had never returned to the area where they had lived. But a few days after seeing the Hazara woman in the street he was filled with the urge to learn if his mother really was still alive. The need to know was not based on any sudden longing to be with her again. His fear of being labelled a Hazara was now greater than any affection he had ever had for his mother. To avoid being seen he waited until the sun had dropped behind the mountains before making his way to the top of the hill that overlooked the area. He crept inside the old British fort and climbed the ramparts of the weathered but still imposing walls to search for the hut from afar. He could not find it where he thought it should have been. But after walking from one end of the fortifications to the other and back several times, identifying some vaguely familiar reference points, he came to the conclusion that the dwelling no longer existed.

Durrani remained on the battlements for many hours, gazing down at the huts and houses, the people coming and going and the handful of children playing where he used to, watching in case his mother should turn up. He left when it was completely dark and all he could see was the glow of kerosene lamps inside the houses, never to return to the place again. From time to time throughout his life, whenever he caught a glimpse of the old fort as he passed through the city, his thoughts went back to those days. The most vivid memory was that of his mother lying in the hut with blood trickling from her mouth.

So fearful was Durrani of being exposed as a Hazara that to maintain his security at the orphanage he decided to keep to himself, rarely talking to the other children. When asked about his family he shrugged and said he knew nothing other than that they were Pashtun.

Durrani was nineteen and working in a barber shop as a floor sweeper when the Russians marched into Kabul by invitation to support the beleaguered Communist government. He might have stayed in the city if it had not been for another orphan, Rog, a Pashtun boy Durrani's age. Rog was the only person in Durrani's life who he had allowed to get close enough to call a friend. When Rog one day declared that they should leave Kabul and join the mujahideen to fight against the Russian invaders Durrani experienced his first taste of the lure of adventure. It was an enticement that would subsequently tempt him many times. The following night he and Rog left the city together.

After several days of mostly walking, with the occasional ride on a truck, they arrived at a village in the hills outside Kandahar where Rog had a relative. Within a week they had joined a band of mujahideen.

Thus Durrani began a nomadic guerrilla existence that would span practically all of his next two and a half decades and end with his capture and incarceration in the most impregnable prison on the planet.

The pair were initially employed by the mujahideen as general dogsbodies: carrying ammunition, fetching supplies, cooking and washing. But after Rog was killed in a Russian helicopter attack along with a dozen others in the group, Durrani was handed a rifle and from that day became one of the fighters. A year later, while being treated for a wound and recovering at a training ground in the Hindu Kush mountains, he met a fellow soldier who had recently lost an eye, a quiet, tall, muscular man with an intense and unusually charismatic personality. His name was Omar and the next time Durrani saw him, a decade later, the man had become a mullah and also the leader of a powerful new force that would eventually become known to the rest of the world as the Taliban.

After ten years of fighting the Russians were eventually chased from Afghanistan and Durrani found himself pondering his future and how he was going to make a living. It felt strange to be considering a normal life after so many years as a warrior but it did not take him long to come to the realisation that he had no useful peacetime skills other than the ability to drive a vehicle. And so that was precisely what he did. He got a job as a taxi driver in Kabul, hoping eventually to own his own vehicle and go into business for himself. But the peace he expected to descend on Afghanistan with the end of the war against the Russians did not materialise: the battle for control of the country continued. It was not long before he was lured back into the ranks where he joined the rebellion against the Communist government that was still in power.

Durrani's involvement in the struggle was not motivated by any political loyalty. It seemed to him that the endless battles were for the personal gains of others and that Afghans were merely the tools of Pakistan, Saudi Arabia and the Americans. There was little remuneration other than what could be got from looting. But when he was called to join the fight he went because it seemed better than what he was doing at the time. He was a nomadic warrior purely for the sake of it.

Once again Durrani took part in the capture of Kabul, a new government was installed, and he went back to driving a taxi. During the brief period of calm a pretty young Tajik girl who worked in the taxi company's office came into his life. Durrani set his sights on marrying her. He planned to work hard enough to buy a car, set up his own taxi company and prove his worth to her. But Durrani was to have his heart broken only a few months later when the son of the taxi company's owner announced his intentions to marry the girl, who had accepted his offer. For her he was, financially, a far wiser choice than Durrani.

The failure of the new Afghan leadership to bring order led to the country breaking up into zones, each one led by its own warlord. The two most powerful generals were Massoud and Hekmatyer who both vied for ultimate control at the whim of the same old power-brokers: Pakistan and the US. Crime became pandemic and the general unrest led directly to the emergence of a new clan formed by a sect of Pashtun Islamic-fundamentalist students known as the Taliban. Their banner call was to rid the country of corruption, crime and greedy warlords and they quickly became very popular.

A combination of peer pressure, heartbreak, loss of confidence in the future and the subconscious need to find a purpose to his life saw Durrani leaving Kabul to join in this latest effort to bring order to Afghanistan. He also could not ignore an important characteristic of the Taliban. They were essentially a Pashtun organisation that, in the early days at least, were keen to return the old Afghan monarchy back to power. In such uncertain times it was wise to stick with one's own kind and so Durrani enlisted with the Taliban.

A couple of months later he took part in the battle for Kandahar and after a successful campaign found himself marching on Kabul once again. On his thirty-sixth birthday, a date he had chosen arbitrarily as he did not know his real date of birth, the Taliban took the capital and from there embarked on a crusade to liberate the rest of the country. Durrani approved of the harsh politics of his new leaders, having decided they were necessary to bring order to his war-torn country. Neither was he deterred by the level of brutality used by the Taliban in order to enforce its rule. However, the massacre of Yakaolang left him with scars that never fully healed. Yakaolang was a predominantly Hazara town that had shown the potential for resistance to the new rulers. The truth was that the people had not yet taken up arms against the Taliban but were used as an example to any who might be considering it.

Durrani, now sporting a long black beard, arrived at the town one afternoon along with several hundred Taliban and met up with a force of similar numbers made up of foreign fighters from Pakistan and various Arab countries. Their orders were simple enough: to systematically select every male over the age of twelve and execute him. During the next few days a festival of looting and slaughter took place. More than three hundred men and boys were shot or mutilated along with dozens of women and children who simply got in the way.

On the final day of the massacre the gang Durrani was part of burst into a house and on finding a young Hazara boy of the right age started to drag him outside to execute him. But the boy's older sister tried to stop them, directing her pleas at Durrani. He was standing in the doorway, unable to take his eyes off her

– her likeness to his mother was astounding. While pleading for mercy she walked towards him, her hands grabbing the front of her clothes as if she was trying to rip them from her body. She stopped in front of him and became suddenly calm, lowering her voice and talking to him as if she knew him, or so it seemed to him.

'Please spare him,' she said. 'He is just a boy. You know that. You must have sympathy.'

In the Pashtu language it sounded to Durrani as if she could see that he was one of them, one of her kind, a Hazara.

The other Taliban were watching the display as they held the struggling boy, looking between Durrani and the girl, something Durrani suddenly became aware of.

'Please,' she cried, stepping even closer to Durrani. 'You are not the same as the others. I can see that. Spare my brother. I beg you.'

She could see compassion in his eyes but had failed to recognise the overriding fear behind them. Durrani squeezed the trigger of his AK47 and shot the girl once through the chest. She fell back to the floor but managed to support herself on her hands defiantly, refusing to fall all the way back. Her brother wailed on seeing the bloodstain grow down the front of her dress. She never took her eyes off Durrani even as they filled with tears. She looked more like his mother than ever as death came to claim her, a trickle of blood on her lips. She raised a hand towards him as if she wanted him to take hold of it. Durrani wanted her to stop and the only way he could do it was to fire again. The second bullet killed her instantly.

Durrani's colleagues approved of the execution and pushed past him, taking the girl's brother outside. A few seconds later more shots rang out.

Durrani remained staring at the girl's body for a long time, a confusion of emotions swirling inside his head. He felt neither approval nor satisfaction. What he did feel was something that up until that moment in his life had been alien to him. It was guilt.

He left the house, walking past the limp body of the girl's brother hanging lifeless over the front-garden gate, and continued down the main street and out of the town. It was not so much because he was disgusted by what was going on but because he was lost inside himself, consumed by his experience in the house, wondering what was happening to him.

The memory of the girl remained with him for the rest of his life – until his very last breath, in fact.

The Taliban plan to control the whole of Afghanistan did not succeed. The fighting continued for years against the Northern Alliance until the bombing of the World Trade Center when it was the Americans' turn to invade the country. The Afghan weapons and strategies that had worked so well against the Russians were no match for US might and the Taliban were swept aside.

Durrani took to the hills and eventually escaped into Pakistan where he stayed for several years. He remained in the employ of the Taliban, for his own security as well as to earn his keep. Occasionally he was sent back over the border on sorties, gathering intelligence on US troop movements, sometimes getting into fights with American or Pakistan border patrols. Some of his comrades-in-arms joined the fight in Iraq but Durrani did not want to move that far from his country. Most of his compatriots believed that, as with the fight against the Russians, and against the British many decades before that, a protracted guerrilla campaign against the Americans would eventually see the Afghans victorious. But the Americans had also learned from those past campaigns and the Taliban found it far more difficult to operate in the same way they had under the Russian occupation.

A degree of order descended upon many parts of the country, Kabul in particular, but this time Durrani could not go back to being a taxi driver or live a normal life in any Afghan city. It would not take long before questions about his past were asked and so his only chance of survival was to stay among those like himself.

He often wondered what his life would have been like if he'd married the Tajik girl. It might have kept him from joining the Taliban, for one thing. But such speculation was pointless. The Durrani who had wanted to marry and settle down was very different from the one who always went to war and there was little left of the former one anyway. Durrani was under no illusions as to how it would all end for him. Thousands of men he had known had died, and all he could remember of them were blurred images of their faces over the years. One day he knew he would join them. He could not look forward to paradise either for he was not a devout Muslim. Deep down he did not believe in such myths. It did not make sense to him that a life devoted to death and destruction could be rewarded with everlasting beauty. He could imagine nothing after life, only dark emptiness.

Durrani drove along a dark narrow street with dilapidated single-storey homes on either side, the rooms illuminated by kerosene lamps or lonely bare bulbs. Grey water trickled from waste pipes onto sodden, crumbling concrete pavements strewn with decaying rubbish. His eyes glanced everywhere as he reached the rear entrance of a sturdy mosque in the midst of the squalor, the largest building in the neighbourhood. The side streets he had used for much of the way after entering the city were unlit and quiet but traffic was busy along the main road that passed in front of the holy building.

He pulled to a stop in a wet and muddy gutter, turned off the pick-up's lights and engine and sat still, his window open, waiting for his senses to grow accustomed to the sounds and shadows.

Durrani looked down at his wrist and the Rolex watch, now clean and shining, more to appreciate his treasure than to note the time. He had few possessions, only those he could carry. The watch was the prettiest trinket he had found in years and he hoped he would not have to sell it, for a while at least. He was curious about the engraving on the back. The next time he met an educated man who could read the language of the enemy he might ask what it said.

He lifted the Tajik scarf off the passenger seat to reveal his AK and the charred briefcase with the chain attached. He placed the case on his lap, the weapon on the floor and the scarf back over it. He wound up the window, checked that the passenger door was locked and looked up and down the street to ensure it was empty. He climbed out of the cab, locked the door, crossed the narrow road, stepped carefully between two parked cars to avoid the muddy gutter, crossed the pavement and passed through a small brick archway.

He entered a stone courtyard, immediately turned the corner towards a large wooden door and on reaching it he knocked on it. He turned his back on the door and studied the dark, silent courtyard that was surrounded by shadowy alcoves. A gust of wind blew a collection of leaves in a circle in the middle of the courtyard before scattering them into a corner. A bolt was loudly thrown back behind the door and Durrani turned around as it opened wide enough for a man with a gun in his hand to look through and examine him.

The man's name was Sena and Durrani had seen him before in the service of the mullah. He was tall and gaunt and, despite the gun, looked unthreatening. Durrani suspected the man had never fired a shot in his life and would probably drop the weapon and run if he were to kick the door open. Sena stepped back to allow Durrani inside, secured the door again, and led him along a corridor, holding the gun at his side as if it was a tiresome appendage. Two Taliban fighters lounged on the floor, staring up at Durrani. They were dressed in grubby black and brown robes and wore long black beards. Two AK47 rifles were leaning against the wall between them. Neither man made any attempt to shift his dirty sandalled feet out of the way as the other men stepped over them.

Sena opened a door at the end of the corridor and led the way down a short flight of stairs to the bottom where two more fighters stood smoking strong cigarettes – the small space stank of tobacco. Sena knocked on the only door on the landing and waited patiently. A voice eventually summoned them and Sena pushed the door open and stepped to one side, indicating that Durrani should enter.

Durrani stepped inside a long narrow windowless room illuminated by a lamp on a desk at the far end. The door closed behind him. Sena remained in the corridor outside.

The room was sparsely furnished: a chair behind the desk, two more against a wall and several cushions on a worn rug. A mullah, dressed completely in black, was replacing a book on a shelf behind his desk. He turned to face Durrani as the door was closed and he studied his guest solemnly. A moment later his face cracked into a thin, devilish smile. 'That was a good job you did today,' he said.

'It was my duty,' Durrani replied courteously.

The mullah's gaze dropped to the case in Durrani's hands.

Durrani stepped forward and placed it on the desk.

'You have not opened it?' the mullah asked as he put on a pair of expensive spectacles.

'Of course not.'

The mullah took hold of the chain, raised it to its full length, released it and turned the case around so the locks were facing him. A brief test proved that they were locked as he suspected. 'Sena!' he called out.

The door opened and Sena looked in.

'A hammer and screwdriver,' the mullah ordered.

Sena closed the door.

The mullah took a packet of cheap African Woodbines from a pocket, removed one, placed it in his mouth and offered the pack to Durrani.

'No. Thank you,' Durrani said.

The mullah pocketed the packet, dug a lighter out and lit the cigarette. He blew a thick stream of strong smoke into the room as he turned the case over to check the other side. 'It was British?'

'Yes.'

'How many dead?'

'I don't know. It was burning. One or two, perhaps, plus the crew.'

The mullah stared coldly into Durrani's unwavering eyes. He had known the fighter for many years, having first encountered him during the Taliban's capture of Kandahar. 'You look tired, old friend. Are you well?'

'I am well. You are kind to ask.'

'Would you like some tea?'

'Not right now. But thank you.'

The door opened and Sena returned with the tools. 'Open it,' the mullah ordered briskly, impatient to know the briefcase's contents.

Durrani placed the case on its side with the locks uppermost as Sena stepped beside him to assess the task.

'Hit the lock,' Durrani said. To the mullah, Durrani appeared to be as anxious as himself to see what was in the case. But in truth Durrani was merely irritated by Sena's sluggishness.

Sena was the mullah's clerical assistant and had been a servant of one type or another all his life. He was graceful, thoughtful and in no way technical and as he placed the tip of the screwdriver in the joint between the two locks every shred of self-confidence had drained from his expression.

'The lock,' Durrani said, a hint of irritation in his voice. 'Put it against the lock.'

Sena moved the tip of the screwdriver closer to one of the

locks, gritted his teeth and raised the hammer that looked a touch too heavy for him. Before he could bring it down Durrani snatched away the tools. 'Hold the case,' he snapped.

Sena gripped the briefcase, nervous in the presence of his master and this veteran fighter.

Durrani placed the end of the screwdriver on the mounting of the lock, raised the hammer and brought it down, splitting it. The case was not designed as a safe; its real security depended on its human escort. Another blow split the second lock as easily and the case popped, its top springing open slightly. Durrani would not be so forward as to open it completely himself and he turned it to face the mullah.

The mullah took hold of the briefcase and lifted the top fully to reveal the inside filled with foam-rubber pad tailored to fit. He removed the top layer of foam to reveal a thin manila file and several letters. He moved them aside and studied the rest of the contents: a grey plastic box the size of a cigarette pack neatly placed in its own little cut-out space.

The mullah decided to open the file first. It contained several white pages with typed paragraphs in English, a language which he could not read. He put it to one side and looked at the letters, each with a name on it. He placed them on the file, his interest now focused entirely on the grey plastic box which he removed from its mould.

He rotated it, searching for a way to open it, and dug a dirty thumbnail under a tab. As he prised it up he fumbled, almost dropping the box as it opened. A grey sliver, part plastic, part metal and the size of a small coin, fell out onto the desk. The mullah put down the box to examine the object that appeared to be a tiny technological device. He picked it up and studied it, with a deep frown on his face.

Sena was unable to resist leaning forward to have a look for himself.

The mullah opened a drawer in his desk, pulled out a magnifying glass and held it over the object to examine it more closely. The device had several gold contact surfaces on one side, similar to those on a SIM card.

The mullah had no idea what it was but the security surrounding it was evidence enough that the device was of significant value. He placed it back inside its box and rested it on the desk.

Durrani looked between the box and the mullah, wondering what his leader planned to do with such a find. The potential value was not lost on him either but how to determine that value precisely was beyond him.

'Leave,' the mullah said to Durrani. 'But do not go far.'

Durrani did not hesitate. The mullah was his boss and if he was to profit in any way from this find it would depend entirely on the mullah's generosity. Durrani headed for the door. Sena sprang to life and beat him to it. They headed back up the stairs, along the corridor where they had to step over the lounging guards again, past the entrance and to a room at the opposite end.

Sena opened the door. 'Make yourself comfortable, please,' he said, stepping back. Durrani entered the small stone room that contained a rug, several cushions and a little cooker with everything required to prepare a cup of sweet tea. 'Would you like some food?' Sena asked.

Durrani considered the offer. He had not eaten since that morning, before the helicopter attack, and although he did not eat very much when he did, priding himself on his ability to operate for days without sustenance, it was also a rule of soldiering to take food when the opportunity presented itself. One never knew when the next meal would come. 'Yes,' he said.

Sena bowed slightly and left the room.

Durrani looked around the cramped space. It was no larger than the one he was given to use by the mullah in a run-down house on the outskirts of the city on the Jalalabad road. He preferred sleeping outside under the stars, except during the rains and when it was exceptionally cold. But when staying in the city he opted for the better security. This room was more comfortable. It had a stone floor whereas his own dwelling's was earthen and always dusty. There were no windows, though; a naked bulb hung from the centre of the ceiling provided the only light.

Durrani crouched by the cooker to light it and make himself a cup of tea. He wondered why the mullah had asked him to wait but did not trouble himself with the question for long. Durrani took life very much day by day, hour by hour, and was as content sitting back and doing nothing as he was taking part in a battle. It seemed that while he was involved in one he looked forward to the other.

Sena soon returned with a metal plate of rice and chunks of succulent lamb placed on a large thin folded sheet of unleavened bread. After Durrani had eaten it he lay back on the rug, his head resting on a cushion, and within minutes had dozed off.

Durrani did not know how long he had been asleep when he heard the door open and saw Sena looking down at him. The servant immediately apologised for disturbing Durrani but explained that the mullah wanted to see him.

As Durrani followed Sena back down the corridor, stepping over the now sleeping guards and heading towards the staircase, he checked his watch to discover that it had stopped. Durrani shook it but the second hand did not move. He was dismayed and the malfunction was all he could think of as he followed Sena down the stairs. He tapped the timepiece several times and, as they reached the door, to his delight the second hand started to move again. He decided he should sell the watch at the first opportunity.

The door to the office was open and Sena stepped to one side to let Durrani in. The mullah was seated at his desk with another man leaning over it. They were talking in low voices as they inspected the device that was back out of its box and resting on a white china plate between them. The stranger, who looked the intelligent, well-educated type, was dressed in clean traditional Afghan garb made of expensive cloth. He was immaculate, his beard neatly cropped, and Durrani could smell his strong perfume even through the tobacco smoke.

As Durrani entered the room the man looked up at him through a pair of delicate wire-rimmed glasses. He said something to the mullah who glanced at Durrani, then back at him.

'I need you to do it here, in this office,' the mullah insisted.

The man's expression remained one of reluctance but he argued no further.

'Durrani,' the mullah barked as he got to his feet, studying his most trusted fighter as if making a final confirmation of a decision he had come to. 'You have been chosen for a special task. A most important task.'

Durrani looked at the stranger who was staring at him as if measuring him.

'This man is a doctor,' the mullah went on. 'He needs to examine you.'

Durrani could not begin to fathom what this was all about. A special and important task preceded by a medical examination was a bizarre combination, unlike any experience he'd ever had previously. 'I don't understand.'

'You will,' the mullah said confidently.

'Remove your robe,' the doctor said.

Durrani looked at him quizzically. He'd never had a medical examination before in his life and removing his clothing in front of a stranger like this was alien to him.

'We don't have time to waste,' the mullah said testily. 'Do as he says. That is a command.'

Durrani had been obeying orders of one kind or another all his life and during the last fifteen years they had been those of mullahs. To act without question was ingrained in him. He pulled off his robe to reveal a grubby sweat-stained wool shirt.

'And your shirt,' the doctor said.

Durrani unbuttoned his shirt, pulled it off his shoulders and held it in his hand as the doctor studied him from where he stood. Durrani was sinewy, without an ounce of fat on him, his taut muscles and large veins well defined beneath his tight yellowy-brown skin. He was also covered in a collection of interesting scars.

The doctor slowly walked around him, pausing to study the marks of some of the old injuries. He had no doubt that each of them had some kind of horrifying story attached to it. He was not wrong.

A series of deep gouges on Durrani's chest was the result of shrapnel from a missile fired from a Russian helicopter in the Jegay Valley in 1983. A round indentation on his right lat with a corresponding one on his back marked the entry and exit holes of a bullet that had struck him during his first assault on Kabul. A scar across the side of his stomach was from a cut given to him by a Pakistani fighter two days after the Yakaolang massacre when the man accused Durrani of cowardice. Durrani cared little for the man's opinions and was content to ignore him but the man took the lack of reaction as proof of his accusation and drew his knife to kill him. Durrani was not easily riled but a threat of death was sufficient to get his blood up. The Pakistani's thrust to Durrani's side was his last attack. Durrani sidestepped, knocked the man's arm away, closed the gap between them in the next instant, wrapped an arm around his assailant's throat and, while others looked on, crushed his windpipe, letting go only when the man had been dead a good half-minute. His back bore the chequered scars of dozens of lashes that he had once received from a Saudi troop commander who had accused Durrani of stealing loot he was not entitled to. During the next battle a week later Durrani bided his time and in the thick of the fighting he pulled the pin from a grenade and stuffed it down the back of the man's chest harness. No one suspected that the explosion and subsequent disintegration of the Saudi was Durrani's way of taking revenge.

'You have survived much,' the doctor muttered.

'He is my best,' the mullah said with some pride.

'Lie on the desk,' the doctor said. 'On your back.'

The mullah cleared the items off the desk and Durrani sat on the edge of it and lay back.

The doctor moved alongside Durrani, concentrating his examination on the fighter's stomach area. He took hold of the top of Durrani's trousers and pulled them down as far as his pubic hairs, prodding around his lower abdomen. 'It should not be a problem,' the doctor finally acknowledged.

'You must do it now,' the mullah said. 'Tonight.'

The doctor nodded and turned to get his bag from the floor in the corner of the room.

The mullah leaned over Durrani to look into his eyes. 'He is going to perform a small operation on you.'

Durrani stared up at him, unsure how to respond. But whatever was going to happen would happen and, as the mullah had said, Durrani would find out the reason behind it soon enough.

The doctor placed his bag on the desk beside Durrani and removed a bottle of lidocaine, a hypodermic needle, a scalpel, some gauze and a pair of rubber gloves which he pulled on over his hands. Durrani stared at the cracked smoke-stained ceiling and concentrated on detaching his consciousness from whatever was happening to him.

The doctor filled the hypodermic needle with the lidocaine and wiped a small area of Durrani's lower abdomen with an antiseptic swab. 'I'm going to anaesthetise a small area of skin,' he said reassuringly.

Durrani gave no response and did not flinch when the doctor pushed the needle deep into his flesh and squeezed out the contents of the syringe as he slowly withdrew it. The doctor then took a small plastic bag from his medical kit, placed the tiny device inside it, sealed it by winding thread tightly around the opening and dropped it into a bottle of betadine antiseptic solution.

There was a sudden flash of flame and Durrani's eyes darted to the mullah who was lighting up a cigarette.

The doctor picked up the scalpel and paused, the blade hovering over Durrani's stomach. 'How do you feel?' he asked. 'Are you OK?'

'You will not bother Durrani with a small cut, doctor,' the mullah said confidently.

The doctor looked at the deep scars on Durrani's torso and shrugged in agreement. 'You should not feel much anyway,' the doctor said. 'Perhaps a small burning as I cut into your muscle.'

Durrani exhaled slowly, wishing the man would stop talking and get on with it.

The doctor placed the scalpel against Durrani's flesh. Durrani felt a sting as the blade cut him and the doctor began a slight sawing motion. He could feel his blood trickling down his side and the doctor swabbing him with a piece of gauze. He raised his head to take a look. The doctor pressed a gloved index finger on the cut and pushed it in until it disappeared inside Durrani's body up to the second joint. Durrani decided it was too bizarre and went back to staring at the ceiling.

The doctor withdrew his finger, wiped the blood off it and produced a pair of tweezers from his kit. He removed the small plastic bag with the device inside it from the betadine and, opening the incision, placed the bag in the hole, pushing it all the way in with his finger. He took a fresh piece of gauze, wiped the wound clean, pushed the sides together and nodded to himself.

As he reached for a suture pack the mullah stopped him. 'No,' the mullah said. 'No stitches. It must look like an untended wound.'

'He must lie still for a while, then,' the doctor said.

'Tape it,' the mullah said.

The doctor suspected that the fighter would not have the luxury of resting at all. But it was none of his business anyway so he took a roll of tape from the bag, tore off several strips and placed them across the cut to hold it closed. He covered the wound with a large dressing which he taped firmly into place, returned his instruments to his bag and closed it. 'It's done.'

The mullah nodded. 'You can go.'

The doctor was about to pick up his bag when he had a second thought. He reopened it and removed a packet of tablets in a strip of foil-covered plastic. 'He should take these. Just in case there's an infection.'

The mullah took the pills and fixed his gaze on the doctor who read the clear message in his eyes. He left the room.

'Sit up,' the mullah said to Durrani when they were alone.

Durrani started to sit up, pausing as he felt a sudden pain where the doctor had cut him. He took his weight on his hands and pushed himself up the rest of the way. He examined the dressing – a bloodstain was forming at the centre – and eased himself to his feet.

'Get dressed,' the mullah said. 'It will stop bleeding soon. You've had far worse than that.'

Durrani pulled on his shirt.

'You are to go to Kandahar and then on to Chaman,' the mullah told him.

'Pakistan?' Durrani asked, buttoning up his shirt. Chaman was a well-known pass out of southern Afghanistan.

'You will be met at Spin Buldak and escorted across the border.'

'And then what?' Durrani asked.

'There is no need to trouble yourself with more information. You will be in good hands. What you carry in your belly is of great importance.'

All Durrani understood was that at the end of his journey someone else would cut him open once again, this time to remove what the doctor had placed inside him. The mullah was going to a lot of trouble to hide the device but he had to concede it was a smart way to ensure that it was not lost. If Durrani had a serous accident or was attacked and robbed, unless his body was completely destroyed the device could still be retrieved. 'I leave right away?'

'Sena will give you all you need. Money and food. You will travel with four of my men.'

'Would it not be better if I travelled alone?' Durrani asked, even though he knew the mullah would not agree.

'I know you like to work alone, Durrani. And it is not that I don't trust your abilities. You are the best of my mujahideen. But this time I need to know where you are every second of every hour. The men who travel with you will not know that you carry anything other than an important message inside your head. Not even those who you will meet in Chaman will know your true purpose. You will be taken to Quetta where you will meet great leaders of our cause who are expecting you. *These* men will know your purpose.' The mullah emphasised the gravity of his words with an intense stare. 'Durrani. I believe that whatever this is inside you is of great importance to us and to our cause.'

'It will be delivered,' Durrani assured him. He was flattered, despite his concealed indifference to the so-called cause.

'Sena,' the mullah called out and the door opened.

Durrani pulled on his robe, a streak of pain flashing through his gut as he raised the garment over his shoulders.

'Allah will watch over you,' the mullah assured him.

Durrani nodded. As he turned to walk away the mullah grabbed his arm and held up the packet of pills. 'Use these if you think there is infection,' he said.

Durrani took the packet and left the room.

The mullah went back to his desk, glanced down at the charred briefcase on the floor, pulled out his packet of Woodbines and lit one.

Chapter 3

Sumners walked into the security-conference 'bubble' on the sixth floor of the Secret Intelligence Service's London headquarters by the Thames and placed a file on a slender chrome podium standing to one side of a wide-screen monitor. Bubble was an obvious nickname for the multi-layered mesh-and-plastic module apparently suspended inside an ordinary room. It had insulated contact points with the floor, walls and ceiling and was protected by layers of various technical screens that prevented all forms of transmission, X-ray and vibration from escaping the module. In short, it was an anti-eavesdropping environment for top-security meetings.

While Sumners attached a memory stick to a USB port on the podium a man in a smart pinstripe suit who looked like a First World War general with his snow-white hair and matching handlebar moustache stepped up into the bubble. He paused in the entrance, planted the tip of his cane on the rubber floor and looked around as if unsure where he was.

'Good morning, Sir Charles,' Sumners said in a jaunty tone without pausing from setting up his presentation.

Sir Charles nodded grumpily. 'Am I early?'

'No, no, you're right on time,' Sumners said, producing the smile he reserved for his superiors.

Sir Charles looked at the four comfortable leather armchairs spread around in no particular pattern. 'Anywhere?'

'Oh, yes, anywhere you like.'

Sir Charles plonked himself into one of the chairs, exhaled

heavily, rested his cane against the side of the armrest, put on a pair of spectacles and perused a thin file he had brought with him.

A moment later another man walked in, younger than Sir Charles, lanky, highly intelligent- and sophisticated-looking with his cold eyes and very white skin.

'Good morning, sir,' Sumners said, with distinct gravitas and no smile. This time he paused for the newcomer and there was a hint of a servile nod too.

Sir Charles looked up at the man. 'Van der Seiff,' he said casually before going back to his file.

'Sir Charles,' Van der Seiff replied, a surgical precision in his tone as he selected a chair and sat down in it, straightening the razor crease in his trousers and ignoring Sumners altogether. Van der Seiff's nickname within the lower echelons of the SIS was 'The Spectre' but it referred more to the coldly calculating way he talked and moved than to his actual personality. His pale complexion might also have contributed to the phantom-like impression.

Sumners arranged some papers on the podium and checked his watch as another man entered the bubble. This new arrival looked downright scruffy compared with the others. His suit was clearly off the peg, the knot of his tie was too small and his worn shirt lapels were askew. But if a stranger was to form a lowly opinion of the man based on his clothing he would be making a great miscalculation. His eyes alone threw any negative assessment into confusion. At first glance they appeared weasel-like but on closer inspection they more closely resembled those of a shark.

His name was Jervis and he scrutinised the backs of Sir Charles and Van der Seiff before looking coldly at Sumners. 'This gonna take long?' he asked in a distinct South London accent that was nonetheless far more refined than it had been in his younger days.

Sir Charles and Van der Seiff did not look around at the man although it was clear from their reactions that they knew who he was.

'Hard to say, sir,' Sumners said, trying to sound matter-of-fact but unable to disguise his grudging respect for the man.

Jervis's gaze returned to the backs of the other two men. 'Mornin', gentlemen,' he said as if it were a mild taunt.

'Good morning,' Van der Seiff replied without shifting the direction of his stare, which was fixed ahead at nothing in particular.

Sir Charles gave a grunt without looking up from his file.

Jervis sat down in the armchair furthest from the podium. 'Don't suppose you can smoke in 'ere?' he asked.

Sir Charles frowned.

'I'm afraid not,' Sumners said. 'Apparently it can interfere with the bubble's instrumentation,' he added by way of an apology for denying his superior a chance to indulge his habit.

Jervis smiled thinly. He was well aware of the rules but liked to take every opportunity to rub the toffs up the wrong way.

Sumners busied himself checking various cable connections in order to distance himself from the tension-tainted atmosphere. The hostility sometimes displayed by certain department heads towards each other never ceased to perturb him. This was a particularly bad lot and he put it down to their extremely diverse pedigrees. Sir Charles was ex-army, Hussars, a retired general, very old school, tough as marching boots and a consultant to the Ministry of Defence and certain lords and monarchs. His brand of diplomacy and numerous highly placed contacts in Europe and America made him very useful in certain areas.

Unlike the other two, Van der Seiff had no military experience. On paper he was the classic brilliant Intelligence recruit: an Oxford graduate, fluent in French, Italian and Spanish with masters degrees in both classics and history. The abilities that placed him a notch above those with similar credentials were an extraordinary geopolitical vision, outstanding analytical skills and a cold, ruthlessly logical mind unhindered by emotion. Van der Seiff had been in MI for eight years and was currently with the Directorate of

International Special Services. He was tipped to go all the way to the top of the intelligence ladder.

Jervis was more like a common urban fox but with some very *un*common qualities. The events of his earliest years were shrouded in rumours, one of which gave him gypsy origins and another a criminal record. Strangely, all documentation of his life before the age of nineteen no longer existed, the result of either catastrophic bureaucratic failure on several levels or the work of a very senior government official. Jervis had found his way into the Secret Service through the army, signing up to the Intelligence Corps, the first documented proof of his existence. After a year training as an analyst in a camp outside Dover he volunteered for and was accepted on a posting in Northern Ireland. This was during the heyday of the campaign against the IRA, in the late 1960s and during the 1970s, and after showing great promise he was trained and eventually operated as a tout maker, one of the most dangerous jobs in the MI field.

It was during this period of Jervis's life that he began to display some extraordinary gifts. For example, he had a photographic memory and was able, after single and often fleeting observations, to quote countless vehicle registration numbers as well as each vehicle's make and colour. But his greatest skill was an ability to piece together seemingly unrelated or only remotely connected pieces of information. The sum of these talents made him a most useful operative. He was posted to London where his skills developed further and were applied to Cold War diplomatic counter-espionage with impressive results. After his success in piecing together a particularly complicated surveillance operation involving Russian mini-submarines and Eastern European diplomatic staff in Scandinavia he came under the gaze of the head of MI6.

Despite Jervis's rough edges he began to make his way up through the ranks. He was unlikely to see promotion above his current post but as head of 'special operations worldwide' Jervis had reached far higher than he could ever have originally expected. He had earned his position despite his reputation for mischievousness which some of his peers interpreted as disrespect. His high proportion of successes, however, ensured a long career ahead of him despite the misgivings of his many detractors.

The last man to step into the bubble was Gerald Nevins, department head of the South-Eastern European Section and Sumners's immediate boss. After a quick look around to see if everyone was present he closed the triple-skinned door and turned a locking lever until a green light appeared at one side, indicating the room was sealed.

Nevins ignored the remaining armchair and, looking quite solemn, chose to stand at the back of the room. Folding his arms across his chest he gave Sumners a nod.

'Gentlemen,' Sumners began and then took a moment to clear his throat, sipping from a plastic water-bottle he had brought with him. 'Pardon me.'

Sumners was an experienced briefer but had never before addressed a group made up exclusively of such senior personnel. When he'd been walking up the stairs from his office on the floor below he hadn't been able to help thinking how this was not just a briefing but a personal assessment. These sorts of things always were. They placed a person under the microscope, something which was very much a double-edged sword. Giving a briefing not only put on display a person's eloquence and ability to address their superiors comfortably. It also exposed organisational, analytical and presentation skills as well as conciseness of expression and general bearing. If a person made a hash of it, especially in front of such an eminent audience, it could have detrimental effects the next time their name came up for review. People always remembered bad briefings.

Success at this stage of Sumners's career was more important than ever to him. He did not possess what would be considered by his peers as the best of pedigrees and it was growing late in the game for him to make a significant step up the ladder. He was the son of a British Army colonel who was not from the right regiment and Sumners himself had not gone to the right university. Jervis might well be proof that pedigree was not everything but Sumners did not possess any of that man's extraordinary skills either. However, because of current world instability, specifically the threat from international terrorism, further promotion was not out of the question by any means. Years ago it had been not only a case of pedigree and contacts but also of dead man's shoes. But since 9/11 the service had expanded rapidly in all directions, with government funding increasing every year. There were many more senior positions opening up all around the globe and Sumners was in a good position to grab one of them.

He could only hope that his fate would not depend on the contents of this briefing, a fear that grew as he compiled the latest intelligence on the day's subject. If it did then his career opportunities would probably terminate immediately on completion of the presentation. In his opinion it was a God-awful mess and heads were undoubtedly going to roll because of it. On a positive note, though, that could only open up new positions which he might be able to take advantage of.

'Sorry for the initial alert two days ago and then the long wait followed by the short notice this morning,' Sumners said. 'Intelligence is still coming in but time is a factor and we have enough – er – info to get the ball rolling.' Sumners glanced at Nevins who was giving him one of his 'get on with it' looks.

'Right. If I can quickly bring us all up to speed regarding the various pertinent regional situation reports.' Summers cleared his throat again as he hit a series of computer keys on the podium. The wide-screen monitor came to life, showing a satellite image of Afghanistan. It continued zooming in on Kabul before moving to the open countryside north of the city, finally focusing on a scorched patch of ground with the charred wreckage of a helicopter at its centre.

'We have positively confirmed that the package was recovered from the wreckage by Taliban fighters immediately after it was shot down. All hard-copy files in the mission briefcase have now been declassified. All operations referred to in the documentation have been cancelled. I can also confirm that the memory tablet carried by the intelligence officer contained all one thousand, four hundred and forty-three British- and US-run indigenous agents and informants operating in Afghanistan and the Middle East – including Iraq of course.'

'Does the list include top tier?' Sir Charles asked.

'Yes, sir.'

'Maple, Geronimo, Mulberry?'

'All of them, I'm afraid.'

'Good God,' Sir Charles muttered as his jowls collapsed to put a seriously unhappy expression on his face.

'What level of personal details exactly . . . for the individual agents?' Van der Seiff asked.

'In most cases, pretty much everything: telephone numbers, addresses, emails, secondary contacts. Many of the attached notes include meeting points, dead-letter boxes and personal contact codes. Suffice it to say that if the tablet was decrypted it would provide enough information to identify every one of them.'

'How many can safely be expatriated?' Van der Seiff asked.

'I . . . I don't have those figures, sir,' Sumners said, glancing at Nevins for help and finding none forthcoming.

'I take it expatriations are in process, though,' Sir Charles said.

'No, sir,' Sumners replied.

'What?' Sir Charles asked, half turning to look inquiringly at Nevins without actually making eye contact.

When Sumners looked at Nevins his boss was already contemplating a response. 'Not at present,' Nevins said.

Sir Charles made the effort to sit forward so that he could turn his stiff old neck around enough to look at him. 'I take it you have an explanation.'

'That's one of the reasons we're all here – to decide if such measures will be necessary.'

'But we're talking about a lot of lives here,' Sir Charles thundered. 'Not to mention the exposure of other information if these people are captured and interrogated. It should have been the first thing to be put into motion.'

'First of all, it would be impossible to bring most of them in anyway. Some of them are on official wanted lists. Others would not be able to run without rousing suspicion. Many have families that cannot immediately be moved. Some are so deep we are unable to make direct contact with them – we wait for many of our agents to contact us when they can. Closing them all down would put us back decades. The repercussions of such a strategy are incalculable. We are, of course, preparing measures for such a course of action but we must first examine every other alternative. I have some suggestions. Perhaps you'll have some of your own,' Nevins added. 'Go on, Sumners.'

Sir Charles did not look confident.

'Excuse me,' interrupted Van der Seiff. 'At the risk of ruining the dramatics of this presentation, do we know the current whereabouts of the tablet?'

'Yes, sir,' Sumners said, miffed on the one hand at the sarcasm but relieved on the other that he could answer the question.

Sir Charles cocked an interrogative eyebrow while Jervis toyed with a packet of cigarettes as if he was only vaguely interested.

Sumners touched several keys on the computer's pad. 'The security case taken from the wreckage was broken open in the Kalaz Alif Mosque in Kabul where it was delivered the same day it was retrieved from the helicopter wreckage.'

The screen image dissolved to a satellite shot of Kabul before zooming in on a mosque surrounded by narrow streets in a densely built-up area.

'The senior mullah of the Kalaz Alif Mosque,' Sumners went on, 'is one Aghafa Ghazan who we believe to be the most senior Taliban resistance leader in Kabul.'

A grainy image of Mullah Ghazan took up a portion of the screen.

'The fact that Mullah Ghazan received the briefcase before anyone else would lend support to our assessment of his seniority. We have an informer in Mullah Ghazan's staff who witnessed the briefcase being opened. He accurately described the contents. The same informant also witnessed the tablet being removed from its case and inspected by Mullah Ghazan. In the early hours of the following day – the security case was brought into the mosque in the evening – a doctor implanted the tablet into a Taliban fighter by the name of Durrani.'

'You did say implanted?' Sir Charles asked.

'Surgically, yes, sir. In his abdomen. We don't have a photograph of Durrani on file although the Americans have a current image that we have requested through Camp Souter's int cell in Kabul. Durrani was then sent by Mullah Ghazan into Pakistan where we understand he was to hand over the tablet to senior Taliban or al-Qaeda personnel. We suspect the tablet was destined for members of ISI, the Pakistan Intelligence services, where it would have eventually been deciphered. However, fortune, in respect of that dilemma at least, was on our side. Before Durrani could make contact, he and his escort were captured by an American Special Forces patrol while attempting to cross the border. There was a brief firefight. Two of Durrani's escorts were killed and Durrani was taken into custody with minor injuries.'

'Do we know if Durrani was a specific US target?' Van der Seiff asked.

'We understand it was a routine border patrol with no specific orders other than to challenge those intent on crossing the border to avoid the frontier checkpoints.'

'I'm sorry for jumping ahead – it's the suspense thing again,' Van der Seiff said, his sarcasm tangible. 'Do the Americans know anything about the tablet?'

'We think not, sir.'

'Why do we think not?' Van der Seiff asked.

'We would've picked up indicators by now,' Nevins intervened, walking to where he could be seen without the others having to turn in their seats. 'Which brings us to the first issue. The minister would like to avoid the Americans finding out about the missing tablet if at all possible.'

'Obviously,' Jervis mumbled.

'You mean, this Taliban chap . . .' Sir Charles stumbled to remember the name.

'Durrani,' Sumners said.

'This Durrani chap is a prisoner of the United States military?' Sir Charles asked.

'That's correct, sir,' Sumners confirmed.

'That's a very dangerous game,' Sir Charles warned, frowning disapprovingly.

Nevins glanced at Jervis and Van der Seiff for any reaction but neither man was giving anything away.

'The minister does not have the right to risk that information falling into the wrong hands,' Sir Charles continued, haughtily. 'I mean, you say the Americans now have it, but if they don't know they have it who's to say they actually do, or that it can't be lost again, for that matter? If no one is controlling it then it could still end up in the wrong hands. The Americans would never forgive us. And I wouldn't blame them for a moment, either. Oh, no.'

'That's all understood, Sir Charles,' Nevins said, suppressing a sigh. 'We believe the tablet is still inside Durrani and, well, he's going nowhere for the time being.'

'Not the point, old man,' Sir Charles said. 'Doesn't the minister realise this could cost him his job, if it hasn't already?'

'Frankly, Sir Charles, the minister's job security is not our concern. What I *am* concerned about is the security summit meeting next week in Washington. A revelation like this will put the minister in a weak position with the Americans at a time when we can ill afford to be . . . In the simplest of terms, we need to get the tablet back or destroy it before the Americans find out about it. The reason we are all sitting here today discussing our options is because we have some. There is a window of opportunity to retrieve or destroy the tablet before we are forced to come clean with the Americans. It's an opportunity we are here to thoroughly explore. At this moment in time, no decisions have been made.'

'Playing with bloody fire even thinking about it, if you ask me,' Sir Charles mumbled.

Nevins wanted to tell Sir Charles that no one was interested in his opinions about the conduct of operations, only in his contributions towards their success. But he also knew that despite Sir Charles's doomsday reaction the old boy would give his all at the crease if his turn to bat came.

'Do we 'ave a plausible reason to ask the Yanks for an interview with Durrani?' Jervis asked, putting an unlit cigarette in his mouth just for the comfort of it.

'None that won't cause some bright spark to become suspicious enough to dig around,' Nevins said. 'The minister hasn't been particularly supportive of the American propensity for shipping prisoners, terrorist suspects or otherwise, out of countries without the express permission of those countries' sovereign governments and detaining them indefinitely for interrogation purposes. The hypocrisy of us suddenly asking to join in would raise eyebrows at every level.'

'Assuming that your bright spark is already digging around,

even routinely, what could he find out about Durrani's operation?' Van der Seiff asked.

'Durrani could be linked to the shooting-down of the helicopter and also to his master, Mullah Ghazan,' Nevins said. 'Let's assume the Americans know there was something of importance found in the helicopter wreckage. They know it was carrying a senior British intelligence officer. Let's even assume they know that what was found was brought to Mullah Ghazan in Kabul. Outside of this room and our intelligence staff in the Kabul embassy only four other men know the contents of the case: Mullah Ghazan, the doctor Emir Kyran, Sena – Mullah Ghazan's servant – and, of course, Durrani himself. Naturally, none of them know the significance of the tablet.'

'I take it that the servant, Sena, is the informer,' Van der Seiff said confidently.

'That's correct. But he works strictly for us. Doesn't like the Americans and would offer nothing to them. If they brought him in for questioning Sena's handler would be able to inform us.'

'Then the danger lies in the Americans questioning Ghazan and the doctor,' Van der Seiff said.

'Up to this moment they have not. We are monitoring the possibility. I believe, at this present time, the Americans do not know that Durrani is carrying anything inside his body. The tablet is non-magnetic and has such minuscule metallic properties that it cannot be detected by a regular scanner.'

'What about if they X-ray him?' Jervis asked.

'It would show up on an X-ray,' Nevins admitted. 'But we know it is not part of their standard procedure to X-ray detainees.'

'This is ridiculous,' Sir Charles scoffed. 'They probably have the damned thing already and aren't telling us.'

'That's why you're here, Sir Charles,' Nevins said, glancing at him with a chill in his eyes which he quickly warmed with a thin smile. 'If there's anyone who can sniff such a change in the wind, you can.'

'And if they have it?' Sir Charles asked, brushing off the ego stroking.

'We've covered that already,' Jervis said, barely hiding his irritation with the old soldier. 'The minister will be buggered.'

'He won't be the only one, either,' Nevins muttered.

Jervis smiled at the squirming that would take place throughout the organisation when this thing broke open.

'What if our American cousins ask us to contribute to Durrani's file?' Van der Seiff asked, staring into space as he often did when having such conversations.

'I don't see the point in addressing that until they do,' Nevins replied.

Those who did not know Van der Seiff might have expected him to take Nevins's response as lacking in courtesy. He did not. 'Are we prepared to add further lies to the original deceit? That is my question.'

'I know,' Nevins replied. 'I was asking for time to consider that one.'

It was unclear if Van der Seiff accepted the answer but the lowering of his gaze suggested he was not entirely pleased with it.

Jervis's apparent lack of serious interest in the topic was due to the fact that his area of expertise was operational planning and not diplomacy. He knew he would eventually have a significant part to play in this meeting otherwise he would not have been invited so he was anxious to be done with all this banter and move on. He gave his assessment: 'So the continued secrecy of this tablet depends on Durrani and those other characters not telling the Americans that he's carrying something inside his belly.'

'In a nutshell,' Nevins responded, eager to move on himself.

'Bloody marvellous,' Sir Charles grumbled. 'Now we're relying on Taliban terrorists to keep our secrets for us.'

Nevins wanted to tell Sir Charles to stop being so melodramatic but he continued to disguise his irritation.

'I take it everything's in place to knock off the doctor and the mullah,' Jervis said matter-of-factly.

'Of course,' Nevins said with equal callousness. 'If it's any consolation, what little information we have on Durrani is that he is regarded as somewhat special among the Taliban, hence him being entrusted with such an important mission. He doesn't seem the sort to give it up easily . . . And the Americans would have to know what they were looking for before they began searching for it.'

Sir Charles made a disagreeable harrumphing sound.

'Gentlemen,' Nevins declared, as if the word might clear the air. 'I would like to move on to the next phase of this meeting. I want us to examine the feasibility of getting close enough to Durrani to neutralise the tablet. Are we all in agreement?'

'Do we know where he is?' Jervis asked, displaying his characteristic impatience in the face of protocol, a habit at the root of his unpopularity among his peers.

'I'd like us all to move forward together,' Nevins said. There were some basic ground rules in this game that every man in the room knew well enough and Jervis was obviously trying it on. These meetings were recorded and anyone agreeing to proceed to the next decisive phase was also technically agreeing to favourably conclude the preceding one. In this case it meant approving the minister's request for time to consider an alternative means of retrieving the tablet and to delay informing the Americans. The important subtlety, and also the danger, was that the group would have ostensibly formally agreed to deceive their country's closest allies. If the group decided against moving forward to the next phase the request would not be given operational approval and it would be returned to the minister who would have little choice but to follow a course that would ultimately result in revealing the true situation to the Americans.

But there were some obvious as well as hidden dangers in that course of action. The arc of the swinging crushing-ball is predictable but the collateral damage caused by falling debris is not always easy to foresee. Heads would roll as a result of the action. On the face of it, as it had been laid out by Sumners and Nevins, the safest and most prudent course, for the group at least, was to decide against attempting to 'neutralise' the tablet. However, the reputation of the service was also at stake and that was no small matter. The British enjoyed the most enviable position when it came to international espionage on practically every level. For the group to accept the risk and move forward would take them into territory where the dangers were unknown. Still, one could not get a little pregnant in this business.

'I have another meeting I must attend,' Sir Charles said, getting to his feet. 'I'll see you later, Gerald. Van der Seiff . . . Jervis.'

Nevins and Jervis watched Sir Charles leave the room while Van der Seiff stared ahead as if he was unaware it was happening. One decision against might not be enough to close the case – depending on who made it, of course. But two would seal it. Now the only person Nevins could afford to lose had gone and he waited for one of the others to climb out of their chair and end the meeting.

Sumners resealed the bubble entrance and returned to the podium, unsure if he was to press on or not.

As the seconds ticked away neither of the two department heads spoke and Nevins grew confident that they would remain seated. He took a moment to consider his next move. He was not overly concerned about Sir Charles backing out. The old boy was the sort who could be revisited if advice was needed, even with a task that he had declined to approve. Few people knew that about Sir Charles but Nevins had known him for many years having served under him in MI6 in his earlier days. Van der Seiff and Jervis were the more important, for the time being at least. The operation to get a team close enough to Durrani was going to need Jervis's particular genius. And Van der Seiff would be essential when it came to political plotting, defending against repercussions and manipulating the players in the international arena.

The Americans were going to have to be played very carefully. They were old allies but had a severe sting in their tail if crossed. Britain's enemies within the US corridors of power would call it mistrust while its friends might understand it was all about saving face. Nevertheless, the hammer would fall, and hard. The danger of the tablet ending up in the wrong hands was a serious one and British Military Intelligence as well as the minister would suffer immensely as a result of their decision if it went wrong. Then there was the risk to the identities of the secret contacts on the tablet if they ended up becoming public knowledge. Pragmatic individuals within The Service would argue that its reputation was more important than the lives of a few wogs.

Fortunately for Nevins that was beyond his area of consideration. He'd been given the job of assessing the immediate options. He was not officially committed to going forward either, even if the others decided to proceed. That was the luxury of his position as the meeting director – for the time being, anyway. His final decision would depend on the ideas and suggestions of the two men in front of him. Van der Seiff and Jervis were the ideal pair to devise an operation of the complexity and subtlety required and were clearly curious to hear more. The prospect of an interesting challenge was probably the only reason keeping them in the room. If they could convince Nevins that it was possible to get to Durrani then he would go along with it. But despite his positive leanings, that would not be easy.

'Let's move on then, Sumners,' Nevins said. 'And since your flair for suspense is not appreciated why don't you cut straight to where Durrani is being held?'

'Yes, sir,' Sumners said, pursing his mouth in irritation at being the butt of Van der Seiff's sarcasm and striking a selection of keys.

A schematic diagram appeared on the screen. It looked like a hill containing dozens of engineered tunnels and compartments in various layers with a large portion of the excavation beneath ground level. As the schematic turned on its axis, showing plan as well as side elevations, more detailed illustrations were speedily created. A slender cord grew skyward out of the top of the hill, curving like a snake. When it reached a considerable height a large barge-like construction with several compartments began to take shape. Antennae protruded from it and it moved gently as if on water. A pair of cable cars left a floating platform and moved at a steep angle down to the hill on a system of heavy-duty wires. Machinery appeared in the lower hollows of the hill with conduits and hawsers fanning throughout the complex, some following the tunnels while others created their own ducts leading to dozens of small rooms in neat rows on several levels.

'Styx,' Jervis mumbled.

'That's right, sir,' Sumners said. 'The undersea prison. Destination of America's highest-category prisoners. And since the announced closure of Guantánamo it has also become a terrorist-detention centre.'

Van der Seiff glanced at Jervis who was grinning slightly. Jervis raised his eyebrows at him in a manner that suggested he thought the situation was becoming much more interesting.

'It's immediately obvious why the minister hopes that time may be on our side,' Nevins said.

'Durrani won't be going anywhere for a long time,' Jervis surmised.

Nevins looked at him as if he might not entirely agree with the comment, a sentiment that Van der Seiff appeared to share. Jervis caught the subtle flicker in both their expressions and narrowed his eyes. 'Why would that not be true?'

'There's a rumble in the jungle,' Nevins replied. 'Styx may be in trouble. Something's going on down below but we're not entirely sure what. It may be a combination of things. We initially assumed the problem was to do with rumours about the CIA using unconventional interrogation techniques. But it could be worse than that. Public interest in Styx has grown with the transfer of prisoners from Guantánamo Bay to the underwater facility. Human-rights groups, the media and political opposition groups are unhappy that they can't even get close enough to look through the bars.'

'Excuse me, sir,' Sumners interrupted politely. He had started off the briefing feeling a little nervous but Nevins's increasing encroachments on what he regarded as his patch were now beginning to irritate him. 'I can expand on that subject.'

'Go ahead. Go ahead,' Nevins said.

'Our analysts have prioritised their trawling for anything related to Styx and they've come up with some interesting threads. On the subject of interrogation, it would seem that the CIA receives a level of cooperation from the facility's civilian management. The deduction is that the interrogations, under the guidance of the Central Intelligence Agency, may involve pressure and therefore require the assistance of the prison's life-support and engineering staff. This ties in with other evidence that suggests there is a deeper and somewhat nefarious relationship between the Agency and the Felix Corporation that owns and runs the corrections facility.'

As Sumners talked he skilfully produced on-screen visual material in support of each topic. The resulting pictures had even Nevins's full attention.

'The Felix Corp is part-owned by the Camphor Group, an R&D subsidiary of Aragorn Oil. We've also picked up a thread of FBI interest in several executives of the Felix Corp. The Bureau has been conducting covert investigations of offshore accounts connected with the company. The circle begins to close with the evidence that there are connections between certain Felix Corp shareholders and Congress. To examine the relationship between these Felix Corp executives and the CIA I'd like to go back a few years. I'll be brief but I think it's useful to understand the genesis of Styx itself.

'The underwater facility was originally a NASA- and US government-funded research programme experimenting in the subsurface engineering of habitat, mining and agricultural environments. The Camphor Group was one of several smaller investors. NASA's main interest was the relationship between deep-sea and deep-space habitability. The Camphor Group provided funds and technology for the mining module. Early surveys revealed evidence of precious minerals. It was hoped a mine might provide a contribution to the overall costs of the research facility. Construction began in 1983 and the first habitats were occupied on a full-time basis four years later. I should add here that the project was given the security classification of "highly confidential" with security provided by the federal government. This kept media interest to a minimum. By 1993 some sixty personnel were living in the facility which was by then fifty per cent self-sufficient in breathable air, potable water and sewage recycling and was providing twenty per cent of its own energy from wind turbines and solar panels. Two babies were born in the facility,' Sumners added, clearing his throat and instantly wishing that he'd left out that particular snippet.

'Five years ago, in what was apparently a surprise move, NASA and the administration pulled their funding. The government agreed to provide the money to maintain the facility for a period of three years in the hope that an investor might be interested in the site. The pumps were kept operating and vital machinery was serviced. Before those three years were up the decision was made to pull the plug – no pun intended. It was then that the newly formed Felix Corporation stepped in with a surprise proposal. This was aimed at the US Department of Corrections and the intention was to provide the ultimate top-security prison. The idea was greeted with a mixed response. The Agency played no small part in seeing that the proposal received some heavyweight support, enough to see it pass in principle through the House of Representatives. It was awarded a probationary development licence. Technically Styx is still in that category but the first prisoners were interned within its underwater walls two years ago. It's unclear what number of inmates Styx was originally licensed for but it would seem the figure has in any case been exceeded since the invasion of Afghanistan and Iraq. One of the Felix Corp's proposals was to reopen the mine. The running cost of the prison is obviously much lower now than it was at the time of NASA's experiment and the small yield of precious minerals apparently provides five per cent of those costs as well as giving employment to selected inmates. It's the mine that appears to be the focus of the FBI's interest. After this briefing I'll provide you with a more detailed report of the corporate structure behind Styx and the relationship between Felix Corp and the Camphor Group with details of the FBI's investigation to date.'

'Interesting,' Van der Seiff said as he folded his arms across his chest and looked down at his feet extended in front of him. 'I was talking with one of our people in DC the other day. Styx has been popping up as a subject of concern in the White House for some months now. The Oval Office appears to be running its own independent inquiry. They must be concerned about the obvious political implications of an undersea Alcatraz as well as the questionable interrogation techniques taking place down there.'

'It's basically a Guantánamo Bay where outsiders can't get at it,' Jervis said. 'They'll weather the criticism. They'll keep that going for years – decades if they want to.'

'If the White House is conducting its own investigation,' Van der Seiff said, continuing his train of thought, 'it's because they don't want any other government agencies involved. That should provide us with some clues. I have noted for some time now how the White House has shown itself willing to act independently of its intelligence and judicial communities in a variety of arenas. It's no secret that the Oval Office has its own special-operations wing in the guise of "select Secret Service agents". It's also interesting that certain White House staff include people whose curricula vitae are more suited to black ops than to the administrative duties indicated on their payslips. I believe that if the White House decides to close down the prison they're willing and able to go against their various national security agencies.'

'The implications for us right now are how it affects Durrani's future,' Nevins said. 'We have to be prepared for the possibility that prisoners could be moved out of the facility any time soon. We may not get a warning.'

'What about the risk of Durrani removing the tablet himself?' Jervis asked.

'I think that's unlikely,' Nevins said. 'He's a tenacious, pragmatic individual, moderately intelligent and with a stubborn single-mindedness forged by more than twenty years of guerrilla warfare. His mission was to hand the tablet over to those he was ordered to and he'll do his best to achieve that goal no matter how long it takes. Unless someone with authority whom he knows and trusts can get to him and convince him to cut it out and hand it over he's going to hang onto it. It's his simplest and most obvious option. While he remains in Styx the chances of that happening are remote. That won't be the case if he returns to a more open prison on the surface . . . Now, do we have the time to get to him?' Nevins asked. 'Probably more to the point, is it possible?'

Jervis did not need to look at Nevins to know that the man was talking to him. He replied: 'Someone has to get into the prison before Durrani gets out . . . Breaking it down, we have two options: official entry and unofficial entry. "Official" means going in as an authorised entity. That means officially requesting to interview Durrani for some reason. Which will without doubt invite curiosity and surveillance by the Agency . . . *Un*official entry of course means getting someone inside the prison without the Agency being aware of that person's true purpose. That would be bloody difficult.'

'But possible?' Nevins asked.

'Nothing's *im*possible. It's all a matter of risk.'

'Risk to the person who goes in?'

'No,' Jervis replied, sounding as if he thought Nevins was retarded. 'Risk of compromise. Risk of failure. We won't know the percentages until we come up with a plan. I don't doubt we can get someone in. But the risk has to be worth it.'

'And what about getting out?' Nevins asked. 'The Americans say that's impossible. I'm inclined to accept that.'

Sumners wished he could suddenly be struck by a moment of brilliance and present an idea. But his initiative box was utterly empty.

'That might not be necessary,' Jervis said, thinking out loud. He looked at the others. 'The tablet only needs to be destroyed. That reduces the scale of the operation by half as far as I can see.'

Nevins nodded, feeling encouraged so far.

'I don't think this can be done without the help of the Americans,' Van der Seiff said.

Nevins looked at him quizzically. 'But isn't the whole point of this to do it *without* their knowledge?'

'I didn't say do it with their *knowledge*. I said with their *help*.'

Jervis smiled as if he had an inkling of where Van der Seiff was heading.

Nevins was none the wiser. But neither did he feel inferior because of it. The two men in front of him were among the finest in the world at this sort of thing but Nevins had his own specialities. 'You'll have to explain,' he said.

'They could help us get into Styx without knowing why we want to get in,' Van der Seiff said. 'We would provide them with a reason that satisfied their curiosities. Frankly, I can't see how we can do it without them . . . Jervis?'

'The loose ends,' Jervis said. 'It's the loose ends that would bugger us. I see where you're going. Yes. That would be quite sexy.'

'Sexy?' Nevins asked, feeling even more in the dark.

'There's a sniff there, and a cheeky one at that,' Jervis said.

Nevins shook his head, suggesting it was still unclear to him.

'You can smell a solution without knowing it,' Jervis offered.

'When can you give me something more tangible?' Nevins asked. A sniff was not quite sufficient reason for him to propose to the minister that they should go forward.

'Cheeky, yes,' Van der Seiff agreed, the slightest suspicion of a smile on his thin lips.

Nevins frowned. 'Sumners?'

Sumners looked wide-eyed at his boss and shook his head. 'I have no idea what they're talking about, sir.'

'I didn't expect you to. Is there anything else?'

'Nothing significant. The file is available for their eyes on the internal.'

'I need to make a few calls,' Van der Seiff said. 'Can we get together later in the day?' he asked Jervis.

'Sure,' Jervis said.

Nevins took a moment to consider the situation. 'OK. End of the day. Then let's see where we are.'

Van der Seiff got to his feet and smoothed out his suit. 'I take it you're going to clean up Kabul,' he asked Nevins sombrely.

'Of course,' Nevins said. 'That'll go in tonight even if we don't go ahead with the Styx op.'

Van der Seiff nodded and left the room. Jervis followed and Nevins indicated for Sumners to close the door again.

'What do you think, sir?' Sumners said.

'That'll depend on what they come up with.'

'And Kabul, sir? You haven't finalised your options.'

'I want pinpoint accuracy. No bombs. People have a terrible habit of surviving bombs. It has to look like a local hit. Local weapons. That's more to convince the Americans than anyone else.'

'And is that all of them, sir?' Sumners asked, innocently.

Nevins took a moment to consider the question. 'Mullah Ghazan and Doctor . . .'

'Emir Kyran, sir.'

'Yes. Not Sena.'

'I'll pass that on right away, sir,' Sumners said, heading for the door and out of the room.

Nevins put his hands on his hips as he walked over to the wide-screen monitor. He flicked a button on the keyboard. A dozen image windows appeared on the screen like a contact sheet. He touched one of them to expand it. The undersea prison filled the screen and he stared at the complicated diagram. It looked like an impossible task to him. But if Jervis and Van der Seiff said they had a sniff, well, that was good enough for him to wait until they got back to him.

He clicked off the screen and headed out of the room.

Chapter 4

Sir Bartholomew Bridstow sat alone in the back of the British Embassy's black armoured Lincoln Town Car perusing a newspaper through a pair of silver-rimmed reading glasses. His sharp old eyes looked above the small lenses as the vehicle stopped at the first security checkpoint on 17th and East Street in northwest Washington DC. The driver powered down the inch-and-a-half-thick window enough to hang out his pass while another security guard looked in the back. Sir Bartholomew smiled politely at him while holding up his own ID. The vehicle was invited to continue. It passed through two more gated checkpoints manned by members of the uniform division of the Secret Service, the last of whom directed the driver into West Executive Drive.

The Lincoln pulled to a stop outside the West Wing of the White House. As Sir Bartholomew climbed out he was met by a member of the Presidential office staff. The aide escorted him through the entrance where they turned immediately left and up a narrow set of stairs to the Vice-President's office.

Sir Bartholomew was escorted straight in.

Vice-President Ogden eased his heavy frame out of his seat and stepped from behind his desk, wearing a broad smile. 'Good to see you, Barty,' he said, extending his hand.

'You too, Frank.' Sir Bartholomew shook the VP's hand that was almost twice the size of his own.

'How's Gillian?' Ogden asked.

'At this very moment she's being dragged around Georgetown Park Mall by Senator Jay's wife.'

'Kicking and screaming, I'll bet.'

'No fear of that, I'm afraid,' Sir Bartholomew said, with a chuckle. 'Gillian could shop for Britain, I promise you.'

'Tea?'

'No, thank you. I'm not going to keep you long. It's very good of you to see me at such short notice.'

'Have a seat. I have a meeting in ten minutes. Is that enough time for you?'

'Ample. Ample.'

Both men sat down in comfortable antique armchairs, with a dainty coffee table between them The aide arrived carrying a tray, a jug of ice water and two glasses balanced on it. He placed it on the coffee table and headed back towards the door.

'Hold all my calls,' Ogden called out.

'Yes, sir,' the aide replied before closing the door behind him.

'So. What's on your mind?' Ogden asked, sitting back and shifting his bulk to get comfortable.

'The subject is Styx.'

Ogden nodded. 'OK.'

'You have three British subjects incarcerated in it.'

'Now, Barty. You know that's not a subject that right now you and I—'

'No, no, no,' Sir Bartholomew interrupted, smiling and gesturing dismissively. 'Allow me to start again,' he said, adopting a more appropriate expression. His smile disappeared. 'There are problems involving the prison.'

'Show me a prison that doesn't have problems.'

'Styx is not your usual prison and neither are its current problems. I've heard them described by some as merely problematic for your administration, downright serious by others.'

'Barty, we've known each other many years. We have what I

think is more than just a solid working relationship. You can be direct with me. But even as an old friend I'm not about to fill in any of the blanks for you.'

'I wouldn't play that game with you, Frank. To be honest, when I read the request from London I was unsure quite how to approach it. Still am, in fact.'

'I'm all ears,' Ogden said, making a point of checking his watch.

'OK. Well, I'll tell you how we see it and you can ignore me entirely if we're way off the mark and I won't be offended . . . The problems associated with Styx are heating up and when they boil over they're going to cause a substantial mess. Your administration succeeded in taking a lot of the heat out of the volatile issue of political prisoners and foreign terrorists imprisoned without charge with the proposed closing down of Guantánamo. Even if you're now in the process of hiding them all under the waters of the Gulf of Mexico instead. But that's all about to erupt like a volcano. I'm talking, of course, about the corruption within the Felix Corp prison management – the funnelling of money to private bank accounts, undeclared revenue from a mine which utilises inmates as slave labour, that sort of thing. Even more damaging are the Agency's questionable interrogation techniques – with the cooperation of the civilian prison staff, no less. It indicates a most unhealthy, possibly criminal relationship between the CIA and the Felix Corp while at the same time implicating certain members of Congress. One can only imagine what a congressional examination of that relationship would reveal. The leaks have already started . . . Now, of course I'm not here to tell you what you already know . . .'

'You're here to help?'

'What else are friends for?' Sir Bartholomew said, his smile back on his face.

Ogden's suspicions increased.

'Shall I continue?' Sir Bartholomew asked, unsure if he might have gone too far too soon. Personally, he would have preferred more time to prepare the field before setting out his troops. But London had insisted that he should make his way to the proposal as soon as possible. That meant by the end of this meeting.

'I've got a few more minutes.'

'You'd like to shut down Styx but you might run into some obstacles. If you try and point accusatory fingers the resultant inevitable mud-slinging could leave you as dirty as anyone else.'

Ogden stared at Sir Bartholomew, remaining poker-faced, waiting for him to get to his point.

'What if we could provide you with a good enough reason to shut the place down?' Sir Bartholomew asked.

The VP's expression did not change. As he saw it, he had two options at that stage. The first was to end the meeting politely there and then. The other was to acknowledge the existence of the problems and hear out the offer. The Brits didn't usually go to these lengths without being sure of their position and the ambassador did appear confident that he had something of value to offer. It would be timely to present the President with a solution, if the Brits indeed had one. Then there was, of course, the reason why the Brits were doing it – the pay-off. All things considered, though, Ogden didn't see a reason not to continue. Barty had not been far off the mark and the administration was prepared to pay a good price to see the back of this particular problem. 'I'm listening,' he said.

Sir Bartholomew smiled to himself. He was over the first hurdle. It would seem that the transcript he had received from London that morning was accurate. 'Time is a factor, of course,' Sir Bartholomew added.

'I'm interested to hear what you could do that we couldn't,' Ogden said.

'If we were to be of reasonable help in this matter, could we expect our three British subjects to be released into our custody?'

The Ambassador had to ask for a payment of some kind. Any demand could not be too greedy to risk scaring the VP off. But it had to be weighty enough to divert any suspicions.

Ogden knew Sir Bartholomew to be a shrewd old fox: after all, the Brit had been in the business twice as many years as himself. And the old boy was right about one thing. Time was indeed running out. 'Let's hear what you have to say first.'

'The PM would also like to make the opening address at the summit meeting next week.'

Ogden sat back with a smile. 'This had better be good,' he said. Ogden knew the President could not care less who opened the summit. Who spoke first was more important to the Brits than it was to the Americans and was probably just part of a strategy aimed at one of the other summit members. The three Brit prisoners were not such an easy issue. But, even so, Barty's price was paltry compared to the administration's gains if there was any substance to this offer. Ogden remained suspicious, though.

Sir Bartholomew was about to speak when a gentle knock on the door stopped him. The door opened just enough for the aide to stick his head through. 'Your meeting, sir.'

Ogden nodded to the aide who closed the door. His look conveyed to Sir Bartholomew that time was tight but he had the chair.

'We propose an escape,' Sir Bartholomew said.

'What?'

'An escape. Prove the prison is flawed and the President can immediately order a temporary closure to review security – which will, of course, become a permanent closure. Rather like Alcatraz.'

Ogden frowned. 'First of all that place is escape-proof. I've been through all the scenarios and, trust me, it doesn't get any tighter than Styx. Therefore you would need help from the inside. We won't get any cooperation from the Agency and we sure as hell can't ask the Felix Corporation to leave a door open.'

'Of course not. We understand that entirely.'

'So how the hell are you going to do it?'

'We'll manage.'

'You guys'll *manage*?' Ogden asked, unable to mask his cynicism.

'Hear me out. First, let me stress that if anything should go wrong at any stage of this operation you'll be protected from having any connection with it. I think that's a most important point to bear in mind. Let me give you the opening scenario . . . The White House will commission a private British company to carry out a survey of the prison's security. We will need a little help with aspects of the initial set-up phase but it's very insignificant and in any case it would be an expected detail in setting up the evaluation. Then we get a man inside – and he escapes. If it looks like the game is up at any stage we say it's just a part of the private security appraisal.'

'You're kinda missing one glaring point here, Barty. Styx actually *is* impossible to escape from. I've been down there. It makes Alcatraz look like a paper bag.'

'*We* don't think Styx is impossible to escape from.'

'Houdini's dead, Barty, and "Beam me up, Scotty" – you know, *Star Trek* – is fiction.'

Sir Bartholomew's smile was like that of a father to a naive son. The truth was that he had no idea what the operation entailed and, like Ogden, believed the prison to be as he described. But he was ostensibly a salesman and on a good day he could sell ice to an Eskimo. 'This private company will be getting a little bit of help, of course.'

'You mean your SIS will do the job.'

'One of those organisations, I suppose.'

'You're serious, aren't you?'

'I'm well known for laughing at my own jokes,' the ambassador said, no sign of a smile on his face now.

'So how are you going to do it?'

'The plans have not been finalised but I'm told the operations department is very pleased with what they've come up with.'

'I sure would like to see those plans . . . Look, I'll be honest, Barty. I can maybe buy someone getting in. I never saw a study on that because, well, who would want to? But getting out? No. Not without help.'

'Of course you can see the plans.'

'I would have to approve every phase.'

Sir Bartholomew sighed. 'Planning by committee is a recipe for disaster.'

'That's non-negotiable, Barty.'

'OK, but let these chaps get on with it. They *are* rather good at it, you know . . . And bear in mind that any interference by your chaps is tantamount to culpability. It would only compromise the authenticity of the independent survey.'

A frown wrinkled Ogden's forehead as he searched for pitfalls. 'How long before the plans are ready?'

'I'm told the latter phases are complete. The initial phase requires some input from your chaps.'

Ogden got out of his chair and went to the window.

'As I said, should anything go wrong at any stage . . .' said Sir Bartholomew.

'Yeah, yeah, we'll be covered . . . You guys just love your secret-service missions, don't you?'

'And you don't, I suppose?'

'You really think you can get a man inside that place and then out without assistance from the prison?'

'Me? No.'

Ogden looked back at Sir Bartholomew quizzically.

'I'm with you,' the ambassador said. 'I think it's impossible. But someone clearly thinks it isn't. Point is, you have nothing to lose by letting them have a go and quite a lot to gain if they should succeed – don't you think?'

Ogden looked back out of the window. 'Assuming the plan has some merit, which I doubt, how soon could this "independent survey" be ready to kick off?'

'I'm told within a week – depending on your contribution.'

'Do you at least have something for me to look at?'

Sir Bartholomew got to his feet, walked over to Ogden's desk, took an envelope from his inside breast pocket, opened it and removed several mugshots of a man. 'They want you to find someone in your criminal system who looks like this man. Any level of criminal will do, even a parolee. You have an estimated one point two million white males at various stages of the judicial process in this country. I'm sure you can find someone who resembles this fellow closely enough. I'm told it doesn't have to be a perfect match. Just close.'

The Vice-President took the mugshots. 'Who's this guy?'

'One of our chaps, I assume . . . Well,' Sir Bartholomew said, before placing the empty envelope on the coffee table beside the photographs. 'I'd better be off.' He held out his hand.

Ogden shook it as he looked into the old man's eyes. He smiled thinly as he watched the ambassador leave and then he looked down at the photographs.

The aide stepped into the doorway.

Ogden looked at him thoughtfully. 'Cancel the meeting. Call the President's office. I need to see him.'

Sumners was seated behind the desk in his small sterile office, reading a file on his computer monitor when there was a knock on his door. 'Come in,' he called out without looking up.

The door opened and John Stratton walked in. He was wearing a worn leather jacket and his hands were plunged deep in its cracked pockets. His hair was tousled and his face was covered in a dark stubble. His clear green eyes betrayed a cold contempt for the man in front of him.

Sumners looked up and his expression immediately darkened. The two men held each other's gaze for a moment, Stratton winning the competition easily. 'Would you mind shutting the door, please,' Sumners said, going back to his monitor and hitting several keys.

Stratton casually pushed the door closed and looked around the room, his gaze resting on the single pleasant aspect of it: a small window with broad horizontal plastic shutters that partially concealed a splendid view of the Thames. The bottom of the window was too high for Sumners to see the river from where he sat. The half-closed shutters pulled down on one side at a careless angle suggested the civil servant was hardly interested.

The only wall decoration was a world map and a picture of the Queen. There were no family photographs on the desk. Stratton knew Sumners had a wife, or at least had had one a year ago. He was the selfish, callous, pompous type who didn't bother with such trivial mementoes.

Sumners completed his typing and did his best to force a smile as he leaned back, determined to remain superior. 'I see you're still using the same tailor.'

Stratton studied the man he had grown to despise over the years, dismissing a curiosity he'd had before entering the room about whether Sumners had changed even remotely for the better since they'd last met. In Stratton's early days as a member of the operations section he'd seen Sumners fairly regularly, as often as one would expect to see one's SIS taskmaster in this business. That was about a dozen times a year in his case, which was more than most. But then, Stratton was used more than most in those days.

The last time he'd seen Sumners had been over a year ago during a mission neither man would ever forget. Sumners had been long overdue for a shot at the next rung up the ladder and his boss, unwisely in Stratton's opinion, had bumped him up to operational commander. But things did not go well, to put it mildly, and within a few days he'd been relieved of his position. The significant rift that immediately developed between the two men was due to the fact that Stratton had played a pivotal role in that demotion. As far as Stratton was concerned Sumners had deserved it. He had been exposed as inadequate when the going got tough.

Only a handful of people outside the secret operation would have known the facts, though – a select few at the very top. Stratton was probably the only one who knew all Sumners's shortcomings. Sumners was aware of that, too. He had been out of his depth and not only a threat to the operation's success but also to Stratton's survival, as well as that of others. Despite the mission's positive conclusion Stratton had not been invited to take part in another SIS task since then. He suspected Sumners had had a lot to do with that.

Sumners had gone back to the job he'd done prior to that operation which involved selecting operatives for tasks. Stratton had not expected to hear from the SIS again. It was why he'd been surprised when he'd answered his phone that morning to hear Sumners dryly telling him to drop by the office. It did not necessarily mean that Stratton had been summoned for a task but he couldn't think of any other reason why he would be invited to the SIS London HQ. If there *was* a task on offer, Stratton strongly suspected that his name had been mentioned by someone else, one of Sumners's superiors. Sumners must have found it painful to make that call.

'What've you been doing the past year?' Sumners asked.

'Usual stuff.'

'I understand you've been confined to the training teams these days.'

The snide implication was that even the SBS had tired of Stratton. He was beginning to think that was true. The routine of the training slot had been gradually eroding his morale. His commanders in the SBS had clearly become unsure quite what to do with him after his last outing in the USA. Stratton had needed to lie low anyway but instead of sending him away on remote operations somewhere they'd stuck him where they'd thought he couldn't do any harm. Initially Stratton had been relieved that he had not been kicked out of the service altogether. But within a few months he had begun to think that might have been the best choice. Ironically, the man who'd lifted his spirits out of the gutter that morning was the man least likely to. Sumners was one of the few people who knew there was nothing else Stratton would rather do than work for the SIS.

'I take it that you're fit?'

Stratton shrugged. 'Usual.'

'What about diving fit? I'm surprised you were medically cleared to dive after your chest wound.'

'I guess they know what they're doing.'

'Are you medically fit? I can check.'

Arsehole, Stratton thought. Sumners looked as if he was waiting for an opportunity to explode and vent some of his pent-up anger. Stratton didn't care. He even pondered on a comment or two he could make that might provide that trigger. He suddenly began to doubt this was a job offer after all. Sumners was looking far too smug. Perhaps the bastard had brought him in just to screw him about. 'If it was essential to the job I don't doubt you would have checked already.'

'Don't be impertinent,' Sumners snapped, his face flushed with anger. 'Remember this is a military structure and I am your superior – far and above, I may add, the rank of sergeant.'

'Colour sergeant,' Stratton corrected him.

Sumners stared at him while making an effort to calm himself. This wasn't like the old days when he'd had more leverage with his young bucks. Things had changed, even in the last year. The mandarins were taking more of an interest in lower-level decisions than they had before. He could not overlook the fact that his own position had been damaged by that damned operation in Jerusalem. He blamed Stratton for much of it but deep down he knew that he, Sumners, had lost control. Still, he had expected more loyalty from the man. That was unforgivable. The trust had been broken. If he had his way Stratton would never work for SIS again and certainly not under him.

But there was no denying that the man had carved himself a reputation, albeit a chequered one. He had fans in high places despite his many flaws. The only way forward for Sumners was to get himself another posting. New jobs were opening up all over the place. He needed to patch up the past, get a few feathers back in his cap, and then at the right moment apply for another position. This operation didn't help any, though. It seemed to him to be doomed to failure. His plan was to distance himself from it as much as possible, do the minimum required to see it through and ensure that he made no operational contributions to it. When the investigation into its failure was conducted his name would appear purely in a lowly coordinating role. The good news was that it could end up being the final nail in Stratton's coffin. A failure of such magnitude on the back of his American fiasco could be his ultimate undoing. Taking an even more brutal view, Stratton might not even survive it. That would probably suit everyone.

'You're under consideration for a task,' Sumners said calmly, suddenly feeling more in control. 'I don't think you're the ideal person, for a number of reasons. But we're hellish busy at the moment with most of our people on the ground – our best are certainly unavailable. You're not at the top of the pile any more, Stratton. As far as you're concerned you're lucky to be here at all.'

Sumners got to his feet, opened a drawer, removed a plastic

card and held it out to Stratton. 'Your key card. It'll get you from the main entrance to this floor and the secure elevators only. Let's go.'

Stratton took the pass and followed Sumners out of the room and down a corridor to a pair of elevators. Sumners placed a card into a slot, the doors opened and they stepped inside. Sumners pressed his hand against a glass panel. His fingerprints were scanned in a second but the doors remained open. 'Everyone who steps into this elevator has to have their hand scanned. It won't move otherwise. You're logged in for three days.'

Stratton pressed his hand to the glass. A second later the doors closed and the elevator descended. When it came to a halt the doors opened onto a brightly lit empty corridor. Sumners led the way to a door at the end and used his card and a PIN-code to gain entry. They stepped into a small empty space in front of another door that had a tiny red light glowing in its centre. Sumners waited until Stratton was inside and the first door had closed fully before he pressed a button on the wall. An electronic magnet locked the outer door and the red light turned green, accompanied by a soft click.

Sumners pulled the door open and they stepped through into a large gloomy room with a low ceiling that appeared to stretch to infinity in every direction. Stratton followed Sumners across the carpeted floor past untold numbers of cubicle workspaces, some of them like little islands of light. These were occupied while the others were empty and in complete darkness.

They arrived at the far end of the room where the ceiling rose up to accommodate an enormous plasma screen showing a colourful map of the world on whose edges appeared various calibrations and readings: satellite information, time zones, weather, daylight and night-time areas, and temperatures.

Three men were standing by a large low table, talking under a spotlight. Two of them were young and were dressed scruffily.

The other man, older and wearing a dark suit, had his back to Sumners.

'Excuse me, Mr Jervis,' Sumners said, stopping behind him.

Jervis turned to look at Sumners, a file in his hand. His weasel eyes immediately focused on Stratton.

'This is John Stratton,' Sumners said.

'How are you?' Jervis asked drily.

'Fine, thanks,' Stratton replied, wondering where he had seen the man before – his face was familiar. The two younger men were strangers to him. Both nodded a greeting that oozed deference. Stratton immediately labelled them as technicians of some sort. They did not look at all like operators. Apart from being young they both had a neophyte discomfort about them, as if they were overawed by the company and where they were.

'Paul and Todd,' Jervis said. 'Has Sumners told you anything about the job yet?'

'I just got here,' Stratton replied. Jervis's London accent reminded him where he'd seen the man before. Jervis had headed up a major Scandinavian operation against Russian mini-submarines years before when Stratton had been purely SBS. It had led to the shutting down of a serious hole in Europe's back-door defences through which the Russians had been ferrying spies, Spetsnaz special-forces infiltrators and information. Jervis looked pretty much the same as he had then – a little older, perhaps. It was his foxlike features that made him so memorable, plus his brilliance. He'd been one step ahead of the Russkis all the way.

'They'll be working the early set-up phases with you,' Jervis said.

Stratton's hope that he would eventually be working alone grew.

'I 'ope a year on your backside hasn't made you soft.'

Stratton's only reply was to stare at Jervis.

'You see that, lads?' Jervis said, a hint of a smile in his eyes. 'That's arrogance. I like a bit of that in my boys. Don't you,

Sumners?' he added, well aware that it would wind him up no end.

Sumners forced a smile of his own that quickly crumbled and fell apart.

'This is an unusual operation,' Jervis went on. 'Complex and with little time to put it together. It's an operator-driven task. Tell them what that means, Stratton.'

'I'll be figuring it out as I go along.'

'Unfortunately that means the more important parts,' Jervis said, his cheery tone gone. 'That's why you're back, Stratton. They'd thrown your card out of the company Rolodex. I'm the only one who voted for you on this. Just so happens my vote counts more than anyone else's. Don't let me down . . . You can go ahead,' Jervis said to Sumners as he handed him the file. 'Come with me,' he said to the other two men as he walked away.

Stratton was a little overwhelmed by the compliment. Over the past year his confidence in himself had slipped, along with his hope of being selected for an op again. It was a much-needed slap on the back and greatly appreciated. 'He's the ops director now, is he?' Stratton asked.

'Yes,' Sumners said, miffed that his earlier dressing down of Stratton had been entirely neutralised. He pushed a button on the side of the glass-covered table, illuminating several flat-screen monitors beneath the glass. The two men's faces reflected the various colours shining up at them. Each screen displayed a different image of the undersea prison. 'You heard of Styx?'

Stratton had heard the name but he couldn't place it. 'No.'

'They probably didn't do Greek mythology in that South London state school you went to,' Sumners said.

It was the clue Stratton needed. 'A river?' he asked, unperturbed by Sumners's dig at his education.

'So you *do* read,' Sumners said. 'Yes – a mythological river in Hades, between earth and the underworld. Dead souls were ferried across it. Well, it's no longer mythology. Today's Styx is the most secure prison on the planet.'

'Gulf of Mexico?' Stratton said, remembering reading something about it.

'It's the focus of this operation,' Sumners said, touching the screens to change the schematics. 'You'll have to study every detail of the place.' Sumners pushed the file over to Stratton. 'There's a list of data files. Read every one of them. You can use that cubicle there. The passwords and links are on the face page. Everything we know about Styx is there. It will become apparent to you that there's a lot we don't know . . . Those two young chaps with Jervis? Paul is the boffin and will help clarify any technical stuff. Todd is a communications specialist. Both show a strong aptitude for fieldwork and although they're not operatives they can be relied upon to be of assistance – in non-hostile situations only. You have a room booked in your name at the Victory. It includes breakfast. Lunch is in the canteen. You can expense dinner tonight up to twenty pounds as well as taxis to and from the hotel only. The briefing is tomorrow morning at eight. Be in my office by five to. Any questions?'

Stratton shook his head. He would know all he had to by the end of the following day.

'Tomorrow, then,' Sumners said and walked away.

Stratton watched Sumners go, pulled off his jacket, hung it on the back of a chair and opened the file.

Chapter 5

Nathan Charon sat playing cards with several other inmates in the recreation hall of the Cranston minimum-security prison on Rhode Island, New England. He was a handsome man in his thirties, with mousy hair, and was more sociable and unassuming than his rugged looks indicated. He was a bank clerk, or had been until his association with a small-time cheque-forging syndicate had been uncovered. Since he was not one of the organisers of the scam and was only a first-time loser he received a two-year sentence. With only two months still to serve he might well have completed it without undue drama but for one small accident of nature. He bore a striking resemblance to a man in a photograph that the British Ambassador to the USA had handed to the American Vice-President, that man being an English Special Forces operative called John Stratton.

'Ah ha!' Charon shouted as he dropped a running flush onto the table, much to the disappointment of the other players who watched as he scooped up the chips.

'Nathan Charon?' a voice called out from across the room.

Charon looked up, the grin still on his face, as he searched for whoever had called his name. When he saw the duty officer with one of the guards in tow approaching he got to his feet. 'Here, sir,' he said, grinning. 'Just fleecing these gentlemen of their cigarette coupons.'

The duty officer was not smiling as he stopped in front of the inmate and read his file one more time just in case he had got it wrong. But he had not and although it was one of the most bizarre orders he'd been asked to carry out in his career and undoubtedly an horrendous bureaucratic cock-up he reckoned it was a case of his was not to reason why. He had a job to do and he exhaled deeply before carrying on with it. 'You need to come with me, Charon.'

'Whatever you say, sir. Where we goin'?'

The duty officer licked his lips as he stared unblinkingly at Charon. 'You have a transfer.'

'Transfer?' Charon echoed. The odd expression on the officer's face warned him that all was not entirely well. 'I've only got two months left to do, sir. Where they transferring me to? Disneyland?'

The inmates at the table chuckled.

'Styx. Undersea,' the officer said dryly.

The chuckling ceased.

'That's very funny,' Charon said, grinning broadly and looking at his pals. 'You nearly got me goin' for a moment there, I tell yer.'

The officer's expression remained blank. 'You got twenty minutes to pack your sack before we leave.'

Charon's grin hung on in there but it was becoming a struggle. 'You're pushin' this joke pretty far, ain't yer, sir?'

'It's no joke,' the officer said. 'You can either go easy, or we can do it the hard way,' he said. The severe-looking accompanying guard took a step closer, a restraining system in his hands.

Charon's smile dropped off his face as his colleagues got to their feet and stepped back. 'I got two months left to do.'

'I don't make the orders, son. I got a relocation order here for you signed by the governor himself and no matter how weird it is – and I agree with you that it *is* pretty goddamned weird – I'm gonna carry it out. Now let's get going.'

'But I'm white-collar. I processed a coupla bad cheques. There has to be some kinda mistake.'

'I'm sure someone's sortin' it out right now. But until they do you're comin' with me,' the officer said, nodding to the other guard who came forward to join him. Together they manhandled Charon through the room.

'This is crazy!' Charon shouted. 'You can't put me in undersea . . . For God's sake! I wanna speak to a lawyer!'

A small fishing boat puttered over a rolling black ocean in a growing squall at a minute to midnight. The lights of Galveston Island on the east coast of Texas were little more than a faint glow behind it. The top of a wave broke over the bows and struck the front window of the wheelhouse that was only slightly roomier than a phone kiosk and looked as though it had been stuck on the deck as an afterthought. Paul stood inside, bathed in a fluorescent green glow, his hands gripping the wheel tightly, his eyes flicking between the darkness ahead and a radar tube at his side. Several blips blinked on the glowing circular screen with each sweep of the scanner, the nearest of them only a few hundred metres away. For a second he thought he saw an even brighter object on the periphery of the screen, mixed in with the rain and the rolling swell, and he maintained an unblinking stare on the same spot until it appeared again.

Paul leaned out of the open door, keeping a hand on the wheel, and was immediately pelted with rain and spray as he looked aft for Stratton and Todd. Both were wearing glistening yellow sou'westers and were dragging a heavy bundle to the stern. 'We're coming up on the perimeter buoy!' he shouted.

Stratton and Todd paused to squint at him, unsure what he had said.

'Perimeter buoy!' Paul repeated, cupping a hand around his mouth.

Stratton gave him the thumbs-up and crouched to carry out a final check on the contents of the bundle before clipping it shut.

It contained a mixed-gas partial re-breather diving system with extra-large gas bottles and a full-face mask, a set of extra-long glide fins, a digital depth gauge with a pre-programmed ascent schedule and depth alarms, a strobe system, a flashlight, an inflation jacket with an expandable bladder that could reach the size of a VW Beetle when filled and a transponder which he turned on. A small, intense blue LED light blinked slowly on and off and Stratton closed the flap of the bag and clipped together a single large buckle, yanking it hard to ensure that it was secure.

'How long will that set give you?' Todd asked, blowing through one of his clenched hands to warm it.

'Ten hours,' Stratton said.

'Is that how long it takes to decompress?'

'There's a couple of hours to play with.'

Todd shook his soaked head inside his yellow hood. 'First you have to swim and find this thing, then open it, turn it on, put the mask on and all that. It sounds impossible.'

'The toggles glow in water – that'll make it easy to find. One tug and the bag opens. The set's already pressured up. All I have to do is put the teat in my mouth and breathe.'

Todd remained unconvinced. 'And you've got to do all that on one breath.'

'The main umbilical's only thirty metres from the ferry dock,' Stratton said, attaching the end of a long nylon line to a strongpoint on the bag. 'I should be able to make that.'

'Without a face mask?'

'I can't miss the umbilical. It's a metre thick. This line'll be looped around the bottom of it. I find the umbilical, I find the line, I find the bag.' Stratton was running through the scenario in order to convince himself as much as Todd that it was possible.

'And what about your decompression stops? You have to hang about at certain depths for hours.'

'I'll be going up the umbilical, attached to it by the line. The depth gauge is pre-set to the dive stops. I simply tie myself off at each depth and wait. It'll be boring but it'll work.'

'You'll either drown or freeze to death.'

'It's a living.'

'You're bloody mad – with all due respect.'

'Truth is, if I have to depend on this lot to get out of there I'm screwed anyway.'

'I can't tell when you're joking or being serious.'

'I lost track years ago.'

'So why're we going to all this trouble?' Todd persisted.

'Every op has to have emergency RVS.'

'What?'

'Rendezvouses to head for if everything goes wrong . . . even if they're tough to get to.'

'Impossible, more like.'

'Don't dramatise. It irritates me.'

Todd looked apologetic. 'Sorry . . . You're right. It's not impossible – just very, very dodgy.'

'As long as it's *theoretically* possible it allows them to blame me if I don't make it.'

Todd looked bemused. 'Who?'

'Them who tell us what to do.'

'Sorry, I'm confused.'

'For us, on the ground, it's all about how we're going to do the job. For the suits who send us out it's all about win or lose, success or failure, blame and responsibility, medals and demotions.'

'But no one expects you to pull this off anyway. The person who ordered it will surely take the fall.'

'He'll take the blame. But then there's the blame and the *real* blame. If I screw up it'll be my fault . . . Check that line can pay out without catching on anything.'

Todd obeyed but remained puzzled. 'Then you're even more insane,' he decided.

'Perimeter buoy port side!' Paul called out from the bridge.

Stratton went to the side of the boat to see the large red metal buoy holding firm in the heavy sea just ahead. Below the flashing beacon was an illuminated sign warning anyone against trespassing beyond it.

'Less than a mile,' Stratton said, tidying up the bag and ensuring that all was ready. He peered into the darkness, the wind whipping at him, his oilskins flapping open noisily to reveal a black wetsuit beneath.

Todd joined him in the search, shielding his eyes from the swiping rain. 'You been doing this work long?' he asked.

'Breaking into prisons?'

'You know what I mean.'

'A bit.'

'Is that why you're so cynical?'

'No. That came early on.'

'I'd like to get the chance to be that cynical . . . I mean, working for who we do . . . I'm just a tech,' Todd said. 'One day I might get a chance to do a task . . . not like this, of course. I'd never do what you do . . . So how did you get to do this kind of stuff, anyhow?'

'I got a call one day.'

It was obvious that Stratton did not want to elaborate but Todd could not resist taking advantage of such a rare opportunity, standing beside a real operative who was actually responding somewhat to him. 'You're SF, I suppose.' He immediately felt uncomfortable asking the question. Prying into an operative's background was not advisable but he decided he had started so he was going to finish. 'Paul and I reckon you're SBS . . . only because this is a dive task and we know the SAS don't really do water – nowhere near as serious as this.'

Since the briefing a week before Todd had spent many hours with Stratton, sorting out equipment and going over the plans and countless procedures. The man was not exactly a chatterbox. They talked about nothing outside of the operation. Todd accepted that Stratton was on a different level – way above his – had different friends, and moved in very different circles. Nevertheless he felt comfortable with him despite how little they appeared to have in common. Stratton didn't make him feel inferior in the way so many other superior types in SIS seemed to enjoy. Stratton made his underlings feel as if they were every bit as essential a part of the team, which of course they were. The point was, he made them *feel* like they were. That was the difference. When they cocked up, as Paul had done by forgetting to pack the bundle's transponder, an essential element to Stratton's own survival, Stratton simply took the quickest and simplest course to correct the error without undue fuss. What was more, he made you feel just sufficiently bad about yourself to ensure that it never happened again. You wanted to work harder for him. It was the quintessence of leadership and Todd wondered if he could ever be like that one day.

'Sorry,' he said, filling the silence after his question. 'I get a bit carried away . . . Good luck, anyway.'

'You'll always need that . . . In fact, we might need a little right now,' Stratton said, looking towards the wheelhouse. 'Paul!' he shouted, banging on the side of the small cabin.

Todd wondered what had triggered Stratton's sudden concern and he peered into the rain-soaked blackness. He immediately saw the tiny lights breaking through the weather, a green and red one either side of a patch of white signifying it was a vessel of some kind, the red on the right-hand side indicating it was approaching.

Paul quickly stuck his head out of the bridge door to look ahead. 'I had short-range on. It just came on screen. It's big.'

'Is the support barge showing yet?' Stratton shouted.

'Dead ahead – three hundred metres. What do we do?!'

Stratton looked ahead as he thought, gauging the wind and water. 'Push over to port!' he shouted back to Paul. 'Make them follow us. Give it all you've got! They won't be able to turn as close to the barge as we can because of the sub-sea cables. Make a chase of it!'

Paul turned the wheel, the bows coming about sluggishly against the swell.

'Perimeter security?' Todd asked.

'Who else?'

'Do you think they'll shoot – if we don't stop, I mean?'

'We're about to find out,' Stratton said, squinting ahead. 'There's the barge,' he said, gauging the distances between them, the barge and the security boat as its glowing wheelhouse became clearer.

Several lights came into view dead ahead followed by the outline of an enormous black rectangular box, like a square island, so large and heavy as to be unaffected by the swell. They were crossing the tide which was against the security vessel, thus improving their chances of getting to the barge first.

'We're aiming too close,' Todd said, alarm in his voice. 'We'll be pushed into it!'

Stratton did not appear concerned as he watched the security boat, still gauging the distances. He banged on the wheelhouse. 'The anchor cables!' he shouted.

'I know!' Paul replied. 'I know what depth we have!'

Stratton was more or less confident that Paul knew what he was doing. He was a careful young man, inexperienced but nonetheless someone who paid close attention to detail. Stratton had checked the anchor-cable angles from the corners of the barge and expected Paul to have done the same, especially since he was the driver.

Paul swung the boat out at the last minute and steered a wide berth round the first corner of the barge. A large wave suddenly shoved them within feet of the massive structure but by that time they were past the submerged cable. The good news was that the security boat was now out of sight.

The barge was a welded and riveted rectangular mass of metal the size of a tennis court, an uninhabited automated service vessel for the prison, held in position by a series of cables anchored to the sea bed. It contained fuel, potable water, emergency oxygen supplies and back-up generators. A structure in the middle bristled with various types of communication antennae. Fixed atop a stubby gantry was a giro-stabilised satellite dish fighting to maintain its position. All the various pipes and conduits were channelled into a single umbilical cord over a metre in diameter that snaked down from the centre of the barge to the prison a hundred and fifty feet below.

The small fishing boat bobbed its way along the side of the barge, the top of which was several metres above Stratton's head. As they closed on the next corner Paul pushed the bows out to avoid the mooring cable he knew went down at a steep angle. But a heavy swell reversed the manoeuvre and the boat heaved over towards the barge. Stratton grabbed up a pole and held it at the ready as Paul struggled to turn the vessel away from the barnacled steel wall.

'We're going to hit as we take the corner,' Stratton called out. Todd searched around for anything he could use, found an old oar and hurried to Stratton's side with it.

As the boat reached the corner it was slammed into the side of the barge. The gunwales cracked loudly, several pieces smashing off. Stratton and Todd did what they could to push the boat off but their efforts were hardly effective. The boat scraped along the barge as the nose went past the corner. Everyone's thoughts went to the cable that was just below them. The wind and tide were running along the edge of the barge around the corner. As the midway point of the boat reached the corner of the barge the bows started to make the turn around it. It looked as if the boat was going to break in half but the stern suddenly pushed out to follow the corner around. As the stern approached where the cable was attached a huge swell lifted the boat up and completed its turn. The crunch of the propeller being ripped off by the cable never came and they shot down the side of the barge towards the next corner.

'Was that luck or what?' Todd shouted.

Stratton ignored him. They were going to need a lot more.

Running with the wind and tide did not make the steering any easier to control but Paul managed a wide sweep of the next corner before turning the bows tightly back in. They passed the corner and entered the leeward side of the barge where the wind was only half as strong and the sea was practically calm. Paul played the engines as he manoeuvred the boat to face the barge, holding position in the tide that was coming at them from beneath it.

Stratton was galvanised into action. He dropped the pole, removed his sou'wester and oilskins, looped the harness attached to a small diving tank over his back and quickly pulled on a pair of fins.

'What if the security boat comes before you get back?' Todd asked.

'Get the bundle ready! Now!' was Stratton's response. He pulled on a face mask, picked up a karabiner attached to one end of the coiled nylon line fixed to the dive bag, clipped it to his belt and leapt overboard. Todd looked over the side into the swirling black water but Stratton was already gone, the line unwinding rapidly and zipping over the gunwales after him.

Paul stuck his head out of the wheelhouse door. 'We're not close enough yet!'

'He's already gone. Get into the barge!' Todd shouted as he hurried to the bundle.

Paul yanked himself back into the wheelhouse and powered the boat ahead. A thought struck him that if Stratton couldn't beat the tide he might go under the boat and get chopped up by the prop. The thought no sooner entered his head when it was brushed aside. He had his job to do and Stratton had his own.

Stratton turned on a powerful small light attached to his mask and headed down to the bottom of the barge. As soon as he slipped beneath it the tide hit him like a wall and threatened to push him back. He battled against it, turning onto his back and at the same time jamming his fingers behind any barnacle or limpet to pull himself forward.

Approaching the umbilical from the leeward side was still the best option as far as keeping the fishing boat in one piece was concerned, but only if Stratton could get to it. He could make out the huge vertical pipe ahead and finned for all he was worth, sucking the air from the bottle as he increased to near-sprint mode. He was certain he could make it. The question was could he get back before the security boat challenged the boys. If not this phase would be a failure.

Stratton reached the umbilical – it felt like a fat conduit of rubber – and pulled himself around it, the nylon line following him. Once he'd got around to the other side the tide catapulted him back in the direction he had come.

A spotlight swooped across the small fishing boat and Todd looked up to see the top of the security vessel's superstructure above the barge heading towards them.

The nylon line continued to unravel down into the water and Todd wrestled with the heavy bundle to balance it on the edge. 'Come on, Stratton,' he shouted at the water.

The security vessel made a wide berth round the corner and came into full view. If the security boat caught Todd in its light the bundle would be exposed.

The light struck the rear of the fishing boat and made its way along its deck. Todd had to make an extremely serious decision but then quickly determined he had no choice. He heaved the bundle overboard and it dropped beneath the water as the powerful beam illuminated him.

'Cut the engines,' Todd shouted.

Paul wasn't sure that he'd heard Todd correctly and looked out of the wheelhouse as the security boat bore down on them.

'Cut them!' Todd shouted again.

Paul was in a mild panic, unsure what to do. Stratton was gone. Perhaps Todd knew something he didn't. He reached into the wheelhouse and turned off the power. The engines died, the dull droning replaced by the wind and rain whistling across the boat, which quickly began to drift. As it left the calm leeward side of the barge the wind and sea returned to play with it like a toy.

'STOP WHAT YOU ARE DOING AND STAND IN SIGHT WITH YOUR HANDS IN VIEW!' a voice boomed over a loud hailer as the security vessel powered towards them. Its fierce spotlight was blinding.

The security boat was a large cruiser of the type used by the coastguard and behind the bright lights Paul and Todd could make out men on the bridge wings and in the bows. They were carrying rifles. The big ship came alongside the little fishing boat and slowed abruptly, both vessels rapidly drifting away from the barge.

'YOU'RE IN A RESTRICTED AREA!' the voice boomed. 'STAND WHERE YOU CAN BE SEEN!'

Paul stepped from the wheelhouse with his hands in the air. Todd raised his hands too, looking towards the barge that was almost out of sight and wondering where the hell Stratton was.

'WHAT ARE YOU DOING IN THIS RESTRICTED AREA?'

Neither man answered, unsure what to say or do, despondency suddenly threatening to overwhelm them. All they could think of was that their boss was somewhere behind them in the sea and this entire operation was falling apart before it had even begun.

'Tell them we've a man overboard,' Paul said in a voice just loud enough for Todd to hear.

Todd wasn't sure whether to agree or not. He could see where Paul was coming from. It was concern for the man and not the operation. The question was, what would Stratton do, or want them to do? The answer was easy enough. 'No,' Todd said, squinting at the security vessel.

'Good answer,' Stratton said as he stepped from behind the wheelhouse, wearing his oilskins and yellow sou'wester. He put his hands in the air. 'Talk to them, Paul.'

Todd didn't look back but he was so pleased with himself, let alone with his boss, that he almost smiled.

Paul breathed a sigh of relief. 'We're truly sorry,' he called out in an Irish accent. 'We're a tad misplaced.'

'We've got engine problems!' Stratton shouted in his own version of the Gaelic twang.

One of the crew relayed the men's reply to the bridge.

'YOU WERE MAKING HEADWAY WHEN WE FIRST SAW YOU!' the voice boomed.

'Just runnin' with the wind, sir,' Paul shouted. 'Why'd we want to be in here anyway? Only tear our nets on all these cables, sure we would.'

'Can you throw us a line?' Stratton shouted. 'Tow us out of here?'

There was a long pause before the security boat's captain came to a decision. 'NEGATIVE. YOU'RE GONNA HAVE TO SOLVE YOUR PROBLEM YOURSELVES.'

Stratton and Todd went to the rear of the wheelhouse, opened the engine compartment and pretended to fiddle with the engine while Paul held the wheel.

'Thanks a bunch there, anyways,' Paul shouted.

'IF YOU ENTER THESE RESTRICTED WATERS AGAIN YOU WILL BE ARRESTED AND PROSECUTED!'

Paul made a gesture to signal that he understood and went back into the wheelhouse to give the impression he was working on their problem.

The security boat's engines roared and it pulled back as the fishing boat drifted away from it.

Stratton kept an eye on the cruiser as it held its position. The captain was clearly still suspicious of them.

'What about the bundle?' Todd asked.

'It's on its way,' Stratton assured him.

'You connected the ends? That's brilliant.'

'That was close,' Paul said, checking on them. 'How long shall we keep the engines off?'

'Who's idea was it to kill them?' Stratton asked.

'Mine,' Todd admitted, wondering if he was going to get in trouble.

'Good,' Stratton said.

A bell clanged and they all looked towards a perimeter-warning buoy a few metres away on the starboard side, a light swaying on the end of its short derrick as if it was a giant fishing float signalling a large bite beneath it.

When Stratton looked back towards the security vessel it had turned its flank to them and was still holding its position. 'Start her up.'

Paul entered the wheelhouse and a moment later the fishing boat's engine gunned to life. Stratton stepped inside to get out of the weather and Todd joined them, closing the door.

'Why were we speaking in Irish accents?' Stratton asked.

'Yeah, I was wondering that,' Todd said.

'I don't know,' Paul said, shrugging. 'I can lie better in Irish. Besides, everyone loves the Irish.'

'That was a crap Irish accent,' Todd said. 'You sounded more like a Pakistani.'

'Better than his,' Paul said, indicating Stratton.

'He's right, Stratton,' Todd said. 'Yours was rubbish.'

The two young men glanced at Stratton, wondering if they'd gone too far.

'Accents have never been my thing,' he admitted.

The others laughed. Stratton's face cracked slightly.

'He smiles,' Todd said, never having seen Stratton wear one before.

The two young men gabbled on, their tensions easing, and the sound of laughter rose above the chugging engine as the boat headed towards the glow on the horizon that was Galveston.

The bundle followed the curving umbilical down into the darkness, bubbles escaping from it as the pressure increased around it. A faint orange glow suddenly appeared below, the light coming from dozens of small windows and portholes in neat rows at various levels around a huge mound.

The bundle finally came to rest on a rocky ledge and hung by its line that went up and around the base of the umbilical where it disappeared into a massive concrete block. As the bundle settled it dislodged several rocks that cascaded down the side of the mound. The rocks dropped past one of the lines of glowing portholes, eventually disappearing into what could only be described as a thick layer of white water covering the seabed around the underwater hill like an impenetrable mist.

A face came to one of the portholes to look through the thick, grimy glass. It belonged to Durrani who was standing in a small cell in which a bed and a toilet bowl were the only furnishings. He was sure he had seen something fall past his window but after craning in every direction he thought he had imagined it.

Durrani stepped away from the window, went to the bed, picked up a copy of the Koran, sat down and began to read it. But, unable to concentrate, he did not get far, as was often the case. He dropped his head into his hands, stared at his feet in his worn sandals on the concrete floor and wondered, for the umpteenth time since arriving in the prison, if he would ever see his homeland or even the sunlight again.

Chapter 6

Congressman Forbes was seated behind a large oak desk in his sumptuous office on the first floor of the Rayburn House Building on Capitol Hill. He was editing a letter when his phone rang.

He picked it up. 'Congressman Forbes.' His pen went still in his hand as he recognised the voice. 'Yes . . . yes, of course. Where? . . . But . . . OK . . . No, I'll be there . . . Yes.'

Forbes replaced the phone, put down the pen and paused to collect his thoughts. He got to his feet, walked to a coat rack by the door, took his jacket off a peg, pulled it on and left the room.

His secretary looked up enquiringly as he passed her desk. 'I've got to go out. Be back in an hour,' he said as he left the office.

The congressman walked briskly along a shiny marble corridor, doors staggered along either side and adorned with ornate brass plaques bearing the names of various committees. He passed through an arched opening into a palatial hall where a staircase descended to a broad lobby. He skipped down the steps with a degree of athleticism, headed across the mosaic floor, returned greetings to colleagues without stopping and walked through the entrance into the bright sunshine.

Forbes stopped at the top of a broad arc of stone steps and scanned the panorama, starting from the Botanic Conservatory on his far left and sweeping across the manicured gardens in front of Capitol Hill. Halfway across he saw a man wearing dark sunglasses and a brown suit standing alone beside a groomed hedgerow and looking directly at him.

Forbes did not hesitate and walked down the steps, this time with a sense of caution. He crossed a footpath and deliberately headed in the opposite direction along the hedgerow from where the man was standing. When he reached the end he kept going at a casual pace. The man, who had followed Forbes down the other side of the hedge, was soon alongside him.

They continued in silence towards the Library of Congress until Forbes judged that they looked as if they had been together for the entire stroll. 'I'm assuming this is extremely important for you to meet me here of all places and without more than a minute's notice,' Forbes said without looking at the man, an irritation in his voice as if he were the superior of the two of them.

The man in the brown suit didn't reply as he casually looked behind them and to the sides whilst adjusting the glasses on his nose. Satisfied that they were unobserved he broke his silence. 'The feds are sending someone inside,' he said.

Forbes was perplexed enough almost to stop.

'Keep walking,' the man said casually. He was half Forbes's age and infinitely more composed.

'You mean Styx?'

'Where else?' the man replied dryly. Forbes was no superior of his.

Forbes's mind raced to calculate the implications of the statement. 'This isn't official. I mean, I've not heard anything,' Forbes said, unable to see the irritation in the man's expression.

'It's an undercover operation. They're making their move . . . It was only a matter of time.'

'You people said it would be years before anything like this could happen.'

'It *has* been years. Just not as many as we would've liked . . . We haven't been as nice to the feds lately as we should've. They're punishing us.'

'Just you? I mean, they're not investigating *us*, right?'

The man grinned and shook his head slightly, a gesture that Forbes also failed to register. 'You're the key to closing us down. You always were . . . They're investigating your offshore accounts.'

Forbes couldn't help pausing. The man continued and Forbes caught him up. 'Why're they sending in an agent? I mean . . . they . . .'

'To confirm what they already suspect . . . You can help us – the both of us.'

'How?'

'Give us more time.'

'More time?'

'They're sending in an agent – as a prisoner.'

'A prisoner?'

The man glanced at Forbes, irritated again, this time with the congressman's panic attack. 'He's on the next scheduled intake.'

Forbes stopped, unable to talk sideways for a moment longer. 'That's in a few days.'

The man stopped and faced the congressman. His eyes were invisible behind his dark glasses but the scowl etched into his acne-scarred skin was plain enough. 'That's right.'

'What . . . what are we supposed to do?'

'Stop him.'

'How?'

'How do you think?'

'I don't think I like your tone.'

'I don't give a damn.'

'Don't you talk to me like that, you son of a bitch. I'm not some CIA lackey. I know what we're doing here. Remember it was the CIA who approached me first, asking for my help in pushing forward the prison concept. I got myself on the congressional delegation trip to Guantánamo. I got onto the House Intelligence Committee so that I could push votes for you.'

'Oh, that's all correct. But we came to you only after we learned you owned a piece of the Felix Corporation and what you were planning for the old NASA facility. You already knew about the possible yield of the mine.'

'That's bullshit. The facility was built on legitimate concepts. The mine was a plus.'

'Is that right? The way I heard it was that a Felix engineer kept the potential mine yield from the various committees that oversaw the original NASA project . . . what, three years before the proposal of the detention centre?'

'It was you who corrupted it by introducing questionable interrogation methods.'

'And very successful methods too. We saved a lot of lives. You came into this deal a crook, Forbes, and we turned you into a patriot.'

'How dare you! No amount of money from that mine would even begin to compensate me for the risks I've taken for the Agency.'

The man didn't want to put Forbes over the top and softened his manner slightly. 'We still have a problem to take care of.'

'I want you to take that comment back.'

'Which one?'

'I am and always have been a patriot.'

'I'm sorry,' the man said, doing his best to sound sincere and almost making it.

Forbes knew it was the best he could expect and calmed down in order to think. 'Are you telling me it's over? The feds are making their move and so we pack our bags and leave.'

'No. We're not ready for that yet. You're going to stop that agent from getting into the prison.'

'I'll need the name. We can reverse him on a medical issue.'

'We don't know who he is.'

'Then how the hell do you expect me to stop him?'

'Use your imagination.'

Forbes stared at him, unsure quite what he meant. 'My imagination's not that good.'

'You've got people who have imaginations. We went to a lot of trouble to put them in the right places to help you in the event of situations just like this.'

'Mandrick.'

'For one.'

'What precisely are you expecting to happen?'

'There's over half a dozen men in the next intake. Since we don't know which of them is the agent we can't afford to let any of them get inside.'

'We can't turn them all away.'

'I know.'

Forbes struggled to think where the agent's line of thought was headed. When it eventually struck him his eyes widened in horror. 'You're insane.'

'It's the only way. There has to be a little accident before they get to the prison . . . The ferry – before it docks.'

'You don't get *little* accidents at those depths. Even the ones that start little end up big.'

The agent's smile was gone.

'That's going too far,' Forbes said, his voice quivering.

'Too far, congressman, is a distant star we haven't been to yet . . . You want to be a patriot. Nothing is too far when it comes to protecting this country, even from itself. You will block this move. There's a lot more road ahead. We like our little partnership. As always, you help us, we'll help you.'

'This is not cooperation. It's blackmail.'

'Blackmail is for civilians. We strategise. If Styx goes down before we're ready you'll go with it. Is that simple enough for you to understand? You hang in there and you'll get your villa on a mile of Caribbean beach with a little cottage at the end of it that your wife won't know about where you'll keep the little chick – Melissa? – currently living in an apartment you rent for her in Alexandria . . . You back out now and you'll sure as shit remain in the jail business, Forbes. Someone else's.'

The man started to walk away.

'If I go down you'll go with me,' Forbes growled.

'You don't even know who I am,' the man said without looking back.

Forbes stared after him with a scowl that quickly melted into an expression of utter anguish.

A prison transport wagon made its way along the San Luis Pass road from Scholes Field Airport, the sun rising out of the tepid waters of the Gulf of Mexico making a splendid view from the driver's window. There was no view for Nathan Charon and the prisoner seated opposite him, or the guard at the other end of the windowless cabin sealed off from the cab by a steel wall.

The prisoners were wearing crisp new white convict suits with light green stripes made up of small forks, the official inmate uniform for Styx penitentiary. On closer inspection the forks turned out actually to be mythological tridents, an attempt at irony by the uniform's designer.

Charon was staring down at his handcuffs, chained to his seat in utter disbelief at his predicament. The prisoner opposite, a bald-headed, grotesquely scarred beast was half dozing as the van shook gently.

Charon looked at the guard at the other end of the cabin who was leaning forward in his seat reading a magazine. 'Hey? . . . Hey?'

The guard sighed heavily. 'Give it a rest, will ya, for Pete's sake. You're driving me nuts.'

'You're the last person from the outside world who will see me before I go into that place,' Charon whined.

'Yeah, I know, you said – several times now.'

'Don't you care that you're taking part in this enormous travesty?'

'I'll get over it,' the guard said, turning a page.

'Doesn't anyone think it's just a little odd that a minimum-security prisoner with just two months left to do is being transferred to the highest-classified security prison on the goddamned planet?'

'It is kinda weird, ain't it?' the guard said, turning the magazine and holding it at arm's length to appreciate the centrefold.

'Kinda weird?!' Charon echoed, resting his head back against the van's internal wall with a bang. 'That's the final word, folks. That's what happened to good old Nathan Charon. Kinda weird, though. But hey – these things happen.' He dropped his face into his hands.

'It's gettin' old, Charon. One more word outta you an I'm gonna gag yer. Ya hear me?'

'Yeah, shaddap, Charon,' the other prisoner said without opening his eyes.

The vehicle suddenly shuddered violently, swerving slightly before rolling along with a rhythmic judder. The brakes were applied sharply and the dozing prisoner slammed his head painfully against the frame of the next seat.

The guard got to his feet as the vehicle came to a stop. He opened the small hatch into the driver's cab.

The guard sitting beside the driver turned to look at the cabin guard as he reached for the door. 'We gotta flat,' he said.

'Great,' the cabin guard sighed.

There was the sound of doors slamming, a clunking from outside, and a moment later the back of the van opened and the light spilled in, silhouetting the driver's-cab guard who was standing on the road. 'Get your ass out here, Jerry.'

'Technically, I ain't supposed to get out, Chuck,' Jerry said.

'Oh yeah. Well, *technically* you do, 'cause Harry's got a bad back and health-and-safety says I can't change the wheel on my own.'

'In that case we're supposed to call in roadside.'

'You wanna sit here for the next four hours?'

'I don't care.'

'Well, I do. Besides, we gotta have these guys delivered by twelve.'

'Who cares if they're a little late?'

'Don't screw with me, Jerry. I ain't in the mood. Get your ass outta there. I don't wanna hear anything more about it.'

'Who put him in charge?' Jerry mumbled as he lowered his oversize frame out of the back of the transport wagon and onto the road. A car cruised past with no others in sight as he joined his colleagues who were kneeling on the grass verge inspecting the flat.

'I still think we should call someone,' Jerry said, unwrapping a strip of gum and pushing it into his mouth.

'It's a flat tyre, not a broken axle,' Chuck said. 'You don't wanna get your hands dirty, fine. I'll do it.'

'Come on,' Jerry said. 'I didn't mean anything. I'm gonna help.'

'You don't have to,' Harry said, removing his jacket.

'I *wanna* help. Can we just forget I said anything?'

'We're all gonna help,' Chuck said, removing his jacket. 'I'll get the spare, you do the jack, you untie the wheel nuts. OK?'

Everyone agreed and set about their respective task.

Fifty metres from the side of the highway Stratton, wearing a pair of overalls, sat in among a dense crop of bushes, unscrewing a silencer from the end of a rifle barrel. He placed it in a box designed to house the weapon pieces and started to unscrew the scope. Paul and Todd, both wearing prison-guard uniforms identical to those of the guards in the prison van, sat a few feet from him. The two young men looked pensive in contrast to Stratton as they watched him place the final piece of the rifle in the box, along with an empty brass bullet casing, close the lid and fasten the clips. Stratton opened a small backpack beside him and removed what looked like an ordinary black tube-flashlight except for its unusual bulbous end.

'Speed they're going they should be done in about fifteen minutes,' Paul said in a low voice, rubbing the palms of his hands together, unaware of his nervous gesture.

'You ever used one of them before?' Todd asked Stratton.

'I haven't seen one in about ten years,' Stratton said as he pushed a test button on the bottom of the device that glowed green for a couple of seconds.

'It's that old?'

'Older. Works even better underwater.'

'SBS,' Todd said decisively, nudging Paul.

Stratton removed the bulbous rubber cover to reveal a thick fish-eye lens. 'They went on to develop a riot-control version but scrapped it because it induced fits in epileptics.'

'What if one of these guys is an epileptic?' Todd asked.

'He wouldn't get a job as a prison guard if he was,' Paul said.

'Good point,' Todd conceded.

'They've got the wheel off,' Paul informed them.

Stratton took a moment to ensure that his kit was organised and he had everything he needed. 'Glasses,' he ordered, taking a pair of dark brown goggles from the bag and putting them on.

Paul was wearing his around his neck and he pulled them over his eyes, tightening the elastic straps that held them firmly in place.

Todd took a long look at the device before pulling his goggles on. Stratton could feel the young man's eyes on him. Todd had hinted more than once the past few days about his desire to move up the ladder to hostile-field status. Part-way into an operation might seem hardly the time to do it to some but not to Stratton. It depended on the operative and he felt confident that Todd was up to it. He held out the device to him.

Todd looked at him in surprise.

'You want to do this?' Stratton asked.

Todd's mouth dropped open, a mixture of soaring excitement and apprehension. 'Seriously?'

'Your first lesson: when you're sure never hesitate unless it's part of the plan.'

Todd practically snatched the device out of Stratton's hand and then held it as if it was something precious.

'No doubts,' Stratton said, more an order than a question.

'None,' Todd said quickly in case Stratton took it back.

'The beam's forty degrees. You need to get within fifteen metres.'

'I know,' Todd replied, getting himself ready to move forward.

'You're not serious?' Paul asked, looking horrified.

'Watch out for cars,' Stratton continued, ignoring Paul. 'Let's not cause any collateral accidents.'

'You're going to let him do this?' Paul insisted.

'How long does it take to work?' Todd asked Stratton.

'Depends on the individual. Disorientation is almost immediate. Full incapacity can take up to ten seconds. Lasts about five minutes. But you can double-dose if need be.'

'This is madness,' Paul said. 'He's a tech.'

'Chill, Paul. I'm not going to kill anyone.'

'This is where it starts, though.'

'Bollocks,' Todd scoffed, getting to his feet but remaining in the crouching position.

'They've got the spare on. Let's go,' Stratton said.

Todd made his way forward, keeping low through the long grass, as Chuck reached under the truck to release the jack and the new tyre took the vehicle's weight.

Todd eased his way down an incline and through the foliage to the base of the slope that led up to the edge of the highway. The three prison guards had their backs to him as he moved into what he considered to be the ideal position, placed a finger on the trigger and aimed the device towards them. He suddenly couldn't remember if the target actually needed to be looking in the direction of the light or not. It seemed logical to him that they should. He decided not to take the chance – he'd wait for the guards to turn around.

Chuck pulled the jack out from under the vehicle, turned his back to the highway and looked directly at Todd who was partly exposed in an effort to get a clear shot. Chuck wondered why someone was in the bushes in the middle of nowhere pointing a flashlight at him.

Todd immediately recognised that his predicament was expecting all three guards to face him at the same time. Realising how unlikely that was, coupled with the fact that one of them had already seen him, he hit the trigger. A penetrating white light flickered from the lens like a powerful strobe.

Chuck immediately started trembling uncontrollably as the intense light penetrated his retinas. It was designed to pulse at the same frequency as brainwaves, upsetting the flow of information between the compartments and causing massive synaptic short-circuits. The other two guards began to feel odd sensations caused by the light bouncing off the side of the truck. They both turned to look at the source. Harry dropped immediately onto his hands and knees, unable to look away, fell onto his chest and remained still, apart from the fluttering of his eyes. Jerry, beginning to shake uncontrollably, had more resistance to the bombardment and reached for his pistol.

Todd kept his finger pressed firmly on the trigger, squeezing it hard as if the added effort might increase the beam's power. But the guard continued to pull his pistol from its holster.

Jerry raised the barrel of the weapon towards Todd although it began to shake violently in his hand. His knees began to buckle, his face twisting into a grimace as he fought to keep control. He could no longer see the man in the bushes as his brain filled with a white light which suddenly went out as he dropped forward onto his face.

Todd kept hold of the device, transfixed by the fear that he'd almost been shot. A hand gripped his wrist while another moved his finger off the trigger.

Stratton took the device, placed it into his backpack along with his glasses and climbed up the slope. He looked both ways along the highway to ensure there were no vehicles coming and crouched by the guards to check that their vital signs were OK.

Paul arrived, carrying the rifle case and looking flustered. 'That was lucky.'

'Be even luckier if you send the signal,' Stratton said. 'Put your caps on. Look like prison guards.'

Paul chastised himself for forgetting and grabbed his cellphone as he put his hat on. Todd joined him, fitting his own cap and looking seriously chuffed about the success of his task.

'This is Paul. Go, go, go,' Paul said into the phone.

Todd hurried towards the back of the wagon.

'Keys,' Stratton called out as he pulled a bunch from Jerry's pocket.

Todd halted and as he turned the keys were sailing towards him. He caught them and hurried around to the back of the wagon.

Charon and the other prisoner were sitting and staring down at him.

'How ya doin'?' Todd asked in an exaggerated American wise-guy accent that he could not help slipping into. He climbed inside the wagon.

A small van with the same prison markings on its sides arrived, pulled up behind the prison truck and two men in the same-style guard uniforms climbed out.

Todd pulled a syringe from a pocket, removed the sterile cap, plunged the needle into the scarred prisoner's leg and emptied the contents into it.

'Ouch! What the fuck's goin' on?' the prisoner cried as he struggled in his shackles.

Todd removed another syringe from the pocket, took off the cap and stuck the needle into Charon's leg. 'What the hell is *this*?' Charon exclaimed as his vision quickly began to blur. Then he lost consciousness.

Stratton climbed into the prison truck as the others unshackled the scarred prisoner and hauled him out, carrying him to the side door of the small van and putting him inside. Stratton pulled off his overalls to reveal his Styx prison uniform and sat beside Charon. One of the newcomers crouched in front of the two lookalikes in order to study them. 'Hold his head up, please,' the man said. Todd grabbed the back of Charon's head and held it upright.

The man opened up a well-stocked make-up artist's box and set about his work with agile precision. He gave Stratton a super-quick haircut to match Charon's. The colour match wasn't perfect enough for him and he sprinkled a little powder onto Stratton's hair and rubbed it in to lighten it. He compared the two men's faces back and forth, adding colour to eyebrows and complexions. The make-up man finally shook his head and frowned. 'His cheek-bones aren't as wide here as his are. I can't do anything about it.'

'Is the difference massive?' Todd asked, moving to where he could make his own comparison. 'He's right. It's noticeable. Your cheeks are slightly thinner than his,' he said to Stratton.

'By much?' Stratton asked.

'Enough,' the artist said.

'A tad, but noticeable, like I said,' Todd agreed.

'Mine need to be bigger?' Stratton asked.

'Yes,' Todd said.

'Hit me,' Stratton ordered.

'What?'

'Hit me. On the cheeks. Mess me up a little. We only have to fool these guards until they drop me off. The picture in the replacement file is me.'

'He's right,' Todd said, standing back. 'Hit him.'

'I'm not going to hit him!' the artist cried.

'You're the bloody make-up artist. You know where it needs swelling.'

'We never did thumping as a technique in make-up class.'

'Hit me, you little prick,' Stratton shouted at Todd. 'Now!'

Todd didn't hesitate a second longer and belted Stratton across his cheek. 'Well?' he asked the artist, nursing his sore knuckles. 'Bloody check it, then,' he shouted.

The artist looked at the blow, comparing it to Charon's cheek. 'I suppose it confuses the issue. Do the other side.'

Todd lamped Stratton on the other cheek and the artist inspected it. 'I suppose that'll do,' he said, and shrugged. 'It'll be better when the bruising sets in.'

'Get this guy into the van,' Stratton said nudging Charon and the men moved with urgency to obey.

Meanwhile, Paul climbed into the prison truck's cab where he found a metal box file. He sorted through the keys, found the one he wanted, opened the box, removed a file, checked that it was Nathan Charon's, replaced it with another identical file from his backpack and relocked the box.

He climbed out of the cab and put the keys back into the guard's pocket. The guard moaned and started to move.

Paul hurried to the back of the truck. 'They're coming round,' he said.

Everyone speeded the final tidying-up.

Stratton sat in Charon's seat and Todd shackled him in while the others piled into the van.

Todd took a last look around. 'Good luck,' he said.

'Get going.'

Todd was about to climb down when he paused. 'Thanks,' he said holding out his hand. 'Please come back in one piece.'

Stratton looked up at the sincerity in Todd's face. He held out his hand as far as the shackles would allow.

Todd shook it, dropped the keys on the floor, jumped down onto the road, hurried to the smaller van and climbed in. It sped away even before he had closed the door.

Harry pushed himself up into a sitting position and felt his head as he wondered what the hell had happened to him. Jerry rolled onto his back, his eyes flicking open, and stared up at the sky, trying to remember where he was. He suddenly sat up and looked towards the roadside foliage while grabbing for his gun.

Chuck sat up too, blinking his eyes rapidly to help bring them back into focus. 'What the hell happened?' he asked as Harry turned over onto his knees.

Jerry looked towards the rear of the truck, staggered to his feet and used the side of the wagon to help him keep his balance as he hurried around to the back. Stratton, unconscious, was slumped forward in his seat, the seat opposite him empty and the shackles lying on the floor. 'Shit!' Jerry exclaimed. 'We got a break!' he shouted as he moved out into the road to look in all directions.

The other two guards came to take a look. Chuck climbed inside to check on Stratton who moaned as he regained consciousness.

'What the hell happened?' Chuck shouted at him. 'Talk to me!'

Stratton took his time, pretending to gather his senses. The plan was to avoid talking to the current guards because they knew Charon's voice. He shook his head and acted dazed.

'What did you see?' Chuck insisted. 'Where'd Rivers go?'

Stratton continued to act stunned and shook his head, his eyelids drooping.

Chuck gave up and jumped back down. 'We gotta call this in,' he said as he headed for the truck's cab.

'Oh, boy,' Jerry sighed. 'Are we in the crapper.'

Chapter 7

Congressman Forbes sat in his office, staring at his phone. He was weighing his options, all of which looked grim. He had survived many a tight situation in his career but if there was a way out of this one he could not see it. The Agency had him well and truly by the throat and was tightening its grip.

Throughout his professional life Forbes had been an advocate of moderation when it came to the division of spoils. 'Always leave enough for others to fatten on' was one of his sayings. Sharing the profits along with the risks provided allies as well as scapegoats. He had never been greedy – not by his definition, at any rate. Styx was a way of making a tidy income, not without legitimate risk. His mistake had been in allowing the Agency to convince him they could mitigate that risk when all they did was to present him with greater ones. He had not seen the trap coming. The adventure had looked too good to pass on. Now, for his sins, he was faced with the grimmest choice he had ever had to make.

There had been life-and-death decisions to be made in the past but all of these had been in the name of national security. But this was purely to save his own skin. He *could*, he guessed, call it quits, suffer the consequences, the humiliation, the likely prison sentence and bring down a handful of colleagues with him. Better still, he could throw himself off a tall building. But that would take a type of courage that Forbes did not have. He loved life far too much and it was that same love affair that would make the final decision for him. The truth was that it had been made the instant he'd been faced with the ultimatum. This wrestling with his conscience was only a private show, a pathetic effort to convince himself that he was confronting a moral dilemma and therefore this was proof that he did in fact possess such things as a conscience and a moral sense. He had them, all right, but they were just not up to this level of testing.

Forbes stared at the ornately framed picture of his wife and two grown-up children in front of him, all smiles and confidence. It was more than enough to bolster his decision and compel him to get on with it.

Forbes picked up the phone, flicked through a notebook on his desk and double-checked the number before dialling it. The line buzzed rhythmically for several seconds before a voice came on. 'Mandrick? . . . Yeah, it's me. We have a problem . . . a big one. We've been offered a deal we can't refuse from our Agency partners . . . They've informed me we're to have an unwanted visitor . . . an undercover fed . . . Today . . . That's the point. We don't know who. That's why there has to be a terrible accident . . . The ferry, I think. Unless you can come up with something better. But it must be a success . . . This puts us into outer space on the risk chart . . . Can you handle it? . . . What do they say? They don't mind at all. They're the ones insisting on it.'

Pieter Mandrick was half American and half South African. Taking a man's life on the orders of a superior was nothing new to him but he had never received such a request from a civilian employer before and never for a hit that was to be carried out within the USA. And how he'd ended up as warden of the most controversial prison in the world was the story of a fascinating and circuitous journey.

His mother was from Brooklyn and had met his father while on a safari holiday in the Kruger Park. His father, ironically, was a senior prison guard who had spent the last ten years of his life as a shift commander on Robben Island, the notorious prison where Nelson Mandela spent most of his twenty-six-year incarceration. Mandrick had never had the slightest intention of following in his father's footsteps and as a young man would have laughed at the very notion of one day working in a prison, let alone running one. He grew up in South Africa, rather than the States, after his mother became attracted to the new lifestyle she encountered in her husband's homeland. She was not a fan of apartheid but neither was she strongly opposed to it. What she did appreciate were the two live-in maids who practically mothered her baby boy; they fed him, changed his nappies and played with him. That was in between doing every bit of housework including gardening, cooking most of the household's meals – and serving sundowners.

Mandrick was a born adventurer and after leaving university in the mid-1970s he was determined to find more action than the prison service could offer. Before his military conscription papers arrived he volunteered to join the South African army, which was only the first step in his plans. As soon as he could he attended the selection course for the 4th Reconnaissance Commando, a Special Forces unit based in Langebaan, and was accepted after passing with distinction. The unit was set up to perform maritime operations, a subject that interested Mandrick, and after joining the R&D submersible wing he piloted one of the unit's first swimmer-delivery vehicles.

Military life was for the most part enjoyable but after three years it had failed to deliver the adventure that Mandrick had joined up for. As luck would have it, as he was waiting in the HQ building to talk to his sergeant major about quitting the armed forces one of the clerks told him that his unit had just been placed on standby to go to Angola. They were to join in the fight against the South-West Africa's People's Organisation (SWAPO), a black guerrilla group fighting for Namibia to separate from South Africa. It was going to be a real war, a deadly guerrilla campaign and more of an adventure than Mandrick had ever hoped to experience. He was overjoyed. To make matters even more exciting, his introduction to the conflict was from the air when his section parachuted deep into enemy territory.

By this time Mandrick was a sergeant in charge of his own troop. Having shown his talents early on in the campaign, he was given a lead role in the raid to destroy the SWAPO headquarters in the heart of one of the most hostile jungles on earth. The opening battle for the HQ was the most brutal he had experienced and it would only get worse. In the latter stages, when his section found itself cut off from the rest of the unit, it came down to hand-to-hand fighting where empty guns gave way to knives and machetes that then gave way to clubs, fists and boots. By the end of it the black greasepaint he had used to disguise himself as a SWAPO guerrilla in order to get close to the compound had been washed away by blood – fortunately only a little of it was his own.

A few months after the war, while attempting to drink a litre of Scotch alone in his barrack room, Mandrick tried to recall how many men he had actually killed in Angola. But his mind was immediately swamped with images of machetes slicing into limbs, boots stomping on throats, fingers gouging eyes: scenes of carnage that assaulted him until he screamed for them to go away. He woke up a day later, lying in his own urine and vomit. The memories were still vivid and it took many years before they eventually grew foggy and their accuracy became uncertain.

In the mid-1990s he quit the military after turning down a full commission and went to America to visit his mother who had by now divorced his father. The trip was intended as a sabbatical that would last long enough for Mandrick to get his head together and figure out a plan for the future. But the weeks turned into months and he still hadn't discovered a firm direction. To help pay the bills he took employment in a local sports bar. He soon settled into a relaxed routine, although he was plagued by a permanent unease that prevented him from making any kind of long-term commitment to work or relationships. He blamed his disquiet on the political events taking place in his home country. Several options concerning his future that he had considered depended on him returning to South Africa but the growing revolt against apartheid and then the death of his father at the hands of a berserk prisoner influenced his decision to close that door and pursue a life in the USA.

Taking advantage of his mother's nationality Mandrick applied for American citizenship and the year it was granted, in the absence of anything more inspirational, and perhaps still motivated by a latent need for action, he decided to join the New York Police Department. He was not unduly surprised when he was turned down; he assumed it had a lot to do with his politically incorrect South African military background. But several weeks later something extraordinary happened that he later suspected was a result of his application – he had shown up on someone's radar. It was a mysterious meeting that would turn his entire life upside down.

Late one evening, as Mandrick left the bar where he worked, he was approached by a man who introduced himself as an employee of the United States Government. The man knew everything about Mandrick's past from the day he'd been born: his parents, his military background (including citations for bravery) and the operations he'd taken part in while serving with the South African Special Forces. Mandrick was invited to a meeting a week later which curiosity more than anything else urged him to attend. It took place in an innocuous sterile room in a downtown office block and was, to all intents and purposes, an interview conducted by three suited men who were also 'United States Government employees'. He was asked to keep the meeting secret although he was not told what kind of job the interview concerned and was denied any information that would provide a clue about the government department to which the men belonged. It seemed pretty obvious though that they were connected to the intelligence community.

A week later the mysterious man appeared again. This time he extended to Mandrick an invitation to take part in a personal evaluation. Mandrick was again left without a clue as to what it was all about but neither could he resist continuing with the mystery tour. A few days later, as promised, he received expenses money and travel details for a flight to a small airport in Virginia. On arrival he was met by a man who gave him a password that he had been briefed to expect and he was then driven without further conversation to Camp Peary near Williamsburg, otherwise known as 'The Farm'. It was his first solid clue that these mysterious men were employees of the Central Intelligence Agency.

After signing several confidential contracts and undergoing a fitness and medical examination Mandrick embarked on a week of private schooling. He was the only student in the class. Lessons included the part US embassies played in intelligence processing, agent contact and human-pipeline procedures, field-finance accounting, a basic medical course, clandestine photography and how to operate a sophisticated coded communications system that separated into several innocuous components that fitted into a shaving bag. On the last day he attended a briefing about his potential duties and where he was asked if he would like to go back to Africa and work as an intelligence gatherer and processor for his 'new' country.

Mandrick had then become an operative for the Central Intelligence Agency, although he was no ordinary NOC (non-official cover). Older than most new recruits, he had not gone through the usual agent-induction system at The Farm. His level of knowledge of Africa and his military jungle skills could not be learned in any school and his composure in life-threatening situations was, rightly, taken as proven.

He was given a month to set his regular life in order and prepare a cover story for his mother and a handful of friends. His explanation for moving abroad was that he needed a change and had taken a position in an American travel agency that was opening offices all over Africa. On arrival in Nairobi he was given time to acclimatise and to familiarise himself with procedures under the supervision of the US embassy's operations officer.

Two weeks later he was sent out into the region with the false identity of a road-construction engineer for an American contractor. His main theatre of operations was Uganda, Kenya and the Congo and his main task was to monitor the subversive activities of groups like the Allied Domestic Front and the Lord's Resistance Army. It was not as exciting as Mandrick had hoped but he embraced the role with enthusiasm and within a couple of years he had set up a comprehensive network of couriers and informants.

While carrying out one of his tasks, the processing and collating of information, Mandrick detected the presence of a home-grown, powerful, dark and disturbing influence that was acquiring an operational foothold in the area. But his efforts to get his superiors to take his findings seriously were doomed to frustration. The faction was at the time a relatively unknown group of Arab Islamic militants and only when the US embassies in Dar es Salaam in Tanzania and Nairobi in Kenya were blown up by them, killing more than two hundred and twenty people and wounding over four thousand, were his warnings vindicated. By then it was too late. To add to Mandrick's misfortune he himself was caught up in the Nairobi bombing, barely escaping with his life.

Mandrick was repatriated to the USA to recover from his minor wounds. After sitting at home for a month while waiting to be retasked he was informed, without explanation, that his services were no longer required.

A month later he received what at first appeared to be a severance package that would keep him comfortable for a year or so. But the messenger's parting comment suggested that Mandrick had not necessarily been dumped and was being held in reserve. It was a vague communication but enough to ease the feeling of rejection. Mandrick waited for the call that he hoped would come soon.

A year passed without a word and then one day, as if the serious inroads into his severance package had been monitored, he received a formal letter on headed notepaper from a company called the Felix Corporation. It invited him to attend a meeting at their headquarters in Houston. The way the message was worded, in a minimalist and coldly cordial manner, Mandrick assumed it was an NOC task. Without hesitation he packed an overnight bag and headed for the airport.

Mandrick expected to meet yet another party of anonymous faces in a sterile, nameless office that had been rented especially for the occasion. He was surprised to discover that the Felix Corporation was in fact a genuine company, and an affluent one at that. After being taken to a five-star hotel to freshen up he was escorted to the executive offices of the CEO where, among other senior members of the corporation, he was introduced to Congressman Forbes. The meeting began with lunch and the rest of the day was taken up with detailed briefings that included models and computer-generated images of a proposed undersea prison. The mine was not discussed in any great detail and was presented more as a remedial employment scheme providing, with luck, a nominal contribution to the running costs of the facility.

Throughout the day Mandrick wondered why he was there and figured that there would be a twist of some sort at any moment. At no time was he asked about his background or if indeed he had any level of experience in maritime technology or correction-facility management. Finally, back in the CEO's office, in a meeting where Congressman Forbes appeared to be the most influential force, Mandrick was asked if he would consider a position as assistant warden of Styx once it was built. Forbes outlined the basic remuneration package that included a house in Houston, a car, a generous expenses allowance and some handsome incentive bonuses.

Confused as he was, Mandrick was nonetheless nobody's fool. The whole business had the sniff of the Agency about it. How else had Felix Corp known so much about him – enough not to ask him any questions about his past life and achievements and yet to have such confidence in him? He had been recommended for the post by a covert authority highly placed enough for none of these men to question it and it was therefore wise to assume this influence implied a partnership of some kind. On the other hand, it was a legitimate appointment that he was being offered – or it appeared to be, at any rate.

A couple of weeks before the first batch of Afghan insurgents arrived the warden was suddenly relieved of his position. He was a highly experienced prison officer who had done an exceptional job in getting the facility up and running. Mandrick was handed the job as if that had been the plan all along. His role as assistant warden had been purely so that he could learn the ropes and take over as soon as the CIA's interests became a reality. Styx was not only a top-security prison far from prying and curious eyes. It was a CIA interrogation centre. And Mandrick was its guardian.

The most problematic feature of the prison was the apparently innocuous mine. It caused Mandrick more concern than the interrogation cells themselves. The prison itself was a going concern although its profits were not very big. But the mainstream revenue came from the US government and could therefore be accounted for. The mining department, however, had apparently 'discovered' a tidy vein of precious minerals and was turning over a considerable amount of money. The problem was that it was mostly undeclared revenue. This was the *quid pro quo* aspect of the deal. The minerals were a private bonus as long as the Agency got what it wanted. It was also their leverage. The arrangement was a minor one compared with the deals that the CIA made with major global drugs and arms dealers in the pursuit of international terrorists. Unlike the drug and weapons deals where thousands of lives were lost or ruined daily as a result, the mine gave a handful of American businessmen profits for their patriotism. Mandrick and the prison guards were also beneficiaries.

Before the rather desperate phone call from Congressman Forbes, in the great scheme of things it had all seemed justified. Mandrick had no problems sleeping at night. But the project had suddenly become considerably more sinister and dangerous. He was being asked to kill an FBI agent. Warning bells were sounding in his head.

Mandrick was in his own office seated behind his desk, a high-tech steel construction with a glass surface. A window made of thick, toughened glass behind him offered a view of bright lights attempting to illuminate a grey darkness. A little shrimplike creature scurried across the glass as a large fish cruised past in the background. The spacious domelike room was supported by steel girders set at intervals against the walls, arching to a central point in the ceiling. Rows of cabinets were sunk into the rock walls between the girders on one side of the room and across from Mandrick's desk a bank of flat-screen monitors displayed multiple views of the prison. Some of the monitors showed split-screen vistas while others flipped viewpoints between different cameras at intervals.

Mandrick climbed out of his leather chair and walked over to a complex communications console as he pondered the congressman's unusual and disturbing request. But even as he considered what course to take he was reaching for the internal phone system to start doing his masters' bidding. To ignore them would be to turn his back on his own future – perhaps worse. If the powers that be were prepared to kill an FBI agent to protect their interests then Mandrick himself was of little consequence. But it was not fear that kept Mandrick in line. He was made of more complex and sterner stuff. Since his earliest days he had enjoyed being a part of a team and, even though the Agency was a cold and distant master, he did feel like a small yet important cog in a big and powerful machine – and a winning one at that. He did not know precisely why the FBI agent had to be stopped but he was expected to carry out the order without question. It was the first real opportunity he'd had recently to self-examine his moral fibre. Now that he found it was indeed corrupt, what he'd initially believed to be a spasm of guilt when he'd received the order turned out to be merely a pause for thought before he obeyed.

Mandrick picked up a phone, punched in a series of numbers and held the receiver to his ear. 'Get me the manifest for the next in-transfer,' he said, his accent a cross between New York and somewhere else that few could guess at. 'Who's the transport officer for that serial? . . . Anderson? . . . I want Gann on it . . . Yeah, and send him to my office . . . Yeah, right away.'

Mandrick replaced the phone, pushed his fingers through his short tan hair and walked over to a detailed model of the prison facility.

A buzzer sounded and Mandrick glanced at one of the monitors showing two angled images of a large man wearing a lime-green tailored uniform and standing outside a door. The man looked up into one of the camera lenses, his expression blank, his eyes cold.

Mandrick took a hand-held remote from his pocket and pushed one of several coloured buttons on it. The sound of escaping gas lasted a couple of seconds as a thick rubber seal around a steel oval-shaped door shrank and, after a heavy clunking sound, the door moved back into the room like a filing cabinet drawer before pivoting open.

Gann walked into the room, a big heavy-boned man of distant Scandinavian origins. He was almost a head taller than Mandrick and remained standing by the opening like a barely obedient hound, staring at his master with an arrogant indifference that those who did not know him might have mistaken for insolence.

Mandrick pushed a button on his remote and the door closed with another clunk and a further escape of air as the seal puffed back up to fill the space around it. 'You'll be picking up the next in-transfer,' Mandrick said without a trace of drama.

Gann waited for an explanation. He was not particularly interested but was curious nevertheless about why the schedule was being changed.

'Didn't we have a problem with one of the ferries a couple weeks ago?' Mandrick asked, suddenly remembering.

'Number four,' Gann said.

'What was the problem?'

'The number-three relief valve in the main cabin. The seal needs changing. It leaks.' Gann's accent was soft: many thought he was from Chicago or Philly but no one knew for sure.

'Why hasn't it been changed?'

'It has a scheduled service next week. I guess they're waiting till then.'

Mandrick looked at Gann, gauging him as he often did. The man was a gift from Felix Corp, a special assistant. A thug, in other words. He hadn't gone through the normal vetting procedures and his personnel file was clearly a fairy tale. Gann was supposedly a former US Marine sergeant, an ideal pedigree for the prison service in which he had to look after the most desperate individuals in the world. Mandrick knew soldiers and Gann did not even begin to fit the profile. What Gann did for the company required a pedigree far more ominous than any that the Marines could provide. When they'd first met at the corporate offices in Houston, the day Mandrick was promoted to warden, Gann had been introduced as his key security officer. Forbes went even further, seeming to boast of some secret information when he said to Mandrick, *sotto voce*, that Gann would take care of any 'delicate situations'.

At the time Mandrick could not accurately imagine what that might entail but he got a taste within the first few days Gann was on the job when an inmate was caught stealing gems from the mine. The prisoner, an armed robber and escape artist from Leavenworth penitentiary who was serving three life sentences, had a partner in the guard force who was smuggling the 'merchandise' ashore. The inmate suffered a paralysing injury when a piece of machinery fell on his back and in that same week the guard was involved in a fatal alcohol-related traffic accident. When Mandrick had mentioned that the inmate could have died Gann must have thought he'd said '*should* have' because his reply was that a dead man attracted attention whereas one who'd had an accident and was recovering from his injuries did not.

It was a wise theory. Only one inmate had died in Styx since it had opened, an impressive record which helped protect it from outside scrutiny. But it did have an unusually high rate of injuries, the level of whose seriousness was often concealed. But as Gann so accurately pointed out, as in a war, the 'merely' wounded were hardly taken into account, no matter how serious the damage they'd sustained.

Mandrick had never personally ordered Gann to do anything unsavoury, nothing beyond the bounds of what a normal prison guard looking after category one-plus prisoners might be expected to do. That was indication enough that the man received his orders from someone else. Mandrick had no problem with that. They were all steering in the same direction. And this particular request was going to require a team effort. It was not only serious but technically complicated. Gann could not achieve success without Mandrick's assistance.

The order was also proof that Forbes received his orders from someone. It wasn't easy to get a congressman to become a willing party to a murder – and of an FBI agent, at that. Forbes wasn't a tough guy. Mandrick personally found him weak and pathetic. He was typical of the type: born to wealth and influence, carried through school, did his time in the army in an administrative role, thus avoiding Vietnam, and was handed his political career on a plate. Someone must have dangled him by his testicles over a pool of sharks to get him to do this.

'We have a problem,' Mandrick said in his usual calm, controlled manner. 'One of the prisoners on the next intake cannot be allowed to enter the prison.'

The printer on Mandrick's desk came to life and spat out a sheet of paper. Mandrick picked it out of the tray and glanced over it. 'Six prisoners . . . but we don't know which one is our unwanted guest.' Mandrick glanced up at Gann who was staring at him without a shred of emotion in his expression. 'Would the valve be enough, do you think?' Mandrick asked, knowing the answer but wanting Gann to get involved in the conversation.

'Everyone?' Gann asked, impressed. This was by far the biggest deal he had been presented with since taking on the job. Come to think of it, it was the biggest hit numbers-wise that he had ever been asked to carry out.

'It looks that way. We don't have the time to figure out who it is.'

Gann took a moment to absorb the request. 'I guess the valve would do it . . . with some added insurance.'

'Like what?'

'It would have to happen deep . . . close to the dock would be best but not too close. They'd have to be denied access to the escape suits, for one thing.'

Mandrick was satisfied that Gann was on the right track and would come up with a plan. He looked at the six names again, none of whom he had heard of before. Five would be collateral victims. Once again he was surprised at how easy it was for him to ignore the evil of the decision. Perhaps it was because they were all scum anyway. The list did not include their crimes – he would have to look at the files for that – but he didn't need to. No one got a ticket to Styx who wasn't a special-category prisoner. As for the FBI agent, the risk came with the job.

'We can't afford to screw this up,' Mandrick said, sounding like an officer even to himself. He did not particularly care what Gann thought about him. The man was an ape and needed to be reminded as often as possible of his place in the pecking order, even if his strings were usually pulled from somewhere way above Mandrick's own position. 'What about the other guard?' Mandrick asked. A minimum of two guards was required to ferry an intake of prisoners from the surface. Escape was considered impossible but this minimum was a procedural requirement in case there was a medical incident – like a guard becoming incapacitated due to a bad compression or something similar.

The prison's seventy-five guards were divided into three shifts. When the dark side of the system was designed it had been regarded as dangerous if not impossible to try and recruit only corrupt employees. However, applying principles learned from the infiltration of entire police forces by organised-crime syndicates, the compromising of key positions of responsibility could be coordinated. Once the necessary personnel were in place it was easy to recruit and then manipulate the lower ranks by using the basic motivating principle of greed.

The thinnest of smiles came to Gann's lips. 'Use Palanski.'

'Palanski?' Mandrick was unaware of any significant connection between Palanski and Gann. 'Why him?'

'He's a leak,' Gann said. 'He's been talking to a journalist. They've met a coupla times already. We've been wondering what to do with him.'

We? This was another reminder that Gann had sources and controllers that bypassed Mandrick's own authority. It had CIA written all over it. Mandrick showed no hint of surprise or disapproval. Palanski was a fool for going outside the corporation and deserved whatever he got anyway.

'They won't survive,' Gann said reassuringly, as if Mandrick needed convincing.

'That will be unfortunate,' Mandrick said, checking a screen on his computer monitor. 'Ferry four is officially operable.'

Gann knew nothing about Mandrick beyond his role in the prison. He suspected that the man might be weak. Treating him as a boss was an act. Mandrick was the warden but Gann did indeed answer directly to others and looked upon his official prison duties simply as a cover for his real purpose. Mandrick's cold willingness to be complicit in the deaths of so many people did, however, impress Gann. Mandrick obviously had to have some kind of background that qualified him for the position. But what Gann didn't know he didn't particularly care about as long as it did not directly affect him. 'It must be important,' Gann said, wondering if Mandrick knew more about what lay behind the plot.

Mandrick would not tell Gann the precise nature of the problem, that the victim was an FBI agent – it might even have negative implications if he did. This sabotage was a serious act of desperation and had 'endgame' stamped clearly right through it. The writing was on the wall.

Mandrick didn't want anyone prematurely jumping ship, not before him. If the feds were snooping around it was a warning that the party was coming to a close. The death of one of their agents might only accelerate it. But perhaps the end could be delayed, which was clearly what the Agency was hoping for. It suited Mandrick too. The mine was still generating cash while the CIA was extracting information from Taliban and al-Qaeda insurgents. All affected parties wanted it to go on for as long as possible.

Mandrick made a mental note to start putting together his escape plans in greater detail. 'We can afford to have at least one serious mishap, I suppose,' he said as he touched a button on his desk and another gush of air announced the opening of the door.

Gann smirked, wondering if Mandrick knew anything at all. He walked out of the room.

The door closed behind him with a clunk and yet another hiss of air and Mandrick looked once more at the names of the men who were going to die. He dropped the paper onto his desk, walked over to an antique bureau, opened it up and took out a bottle of fine Scotch. He poured himself a small glass and took a sip.

Chapter 8

The prison truck slowed to a crawl in order to negotiate a fat speed-bump, its chains and metal innards rattling as it lurched over it. Out of the corner of his eye Stratton watched the guard pull himself to his feet.

Jerry had scrutinised Stratton when he'd eventually climbed back inside the van after the police had arrived at the scene of the escape on the highway. The guard's expression conveyed his irritation with the prisoner for not being of any help to the investigators.

While a medic had cleaned Stratton's wounds and inspected his body for anything more serious a police officer had questioned him. For the most part Stratton just shook his head and mumbled how he had seen nothing. They eventually left him alone, unsure if he was telling the truth or simply protecting a fellow con. Stratton felt confident that neither of the guards was suspicious about his identity. They were preoccupied by their own problems and were also still suffering some minor after-effects of the strobe.

Before the police had arrived the guards had huddled outside the truck, trying to clarify the events leading up to the escape. They were worried about their descriptions of the strange hypnotic device and wondered if they would be taken seriously. Harry described a multicoloured flashing light while Chuck remembered the man in the bushes pointing something at them that was not a gun. Jerry could only remember feeling nauseous, followed by an intense paranoid feeling that he was going to die. It all sounded too much like science fiction.

The first thing the police did on hearing the story was to breathalyse all three of them and then take samples of their blood for testing. The cops eventually provided an escort for the rest of the journey while the investigation continued.

Stratton was pleased with how it had gone. He had successfully passed through the phase that many in the planning department had considered the greatest gamble – mainly because it had been left entirely up to the Americans who had failed to send through a photograph of Nathan Charon to confirm the degree of likeness between him and Stratton. Handing control of such an important segment of the operation over to any other outfit had always been going to be difficult but the Yanks had, Stratton reckoned, just about come through, with a little help from Todd's fists. So far, so good. The rest of the journey into the prison would be relatively straightforward.

The vehicle continued slowly around a tight corner before it came to a stop. The guard walked to the rear doors and waited beside Stratton. The outside latch was pulled aside with a heavy clunk and fluorescent light spilled into the cabin as the doors creaked open.

Jerry climbed out of the back and exchanged greetings with several men. Another guard climbed in and unshackled Stratton from his wrist and ankle chains. 'Let's go,' he said and Stratton got to his feet. 'Prisoner coming out!' he shouted and Stratton was helped down.

'Stand still,' Stratton was ordered as his feet touched the concrete floor surface inside a large hangar. A robust wire-mesh belt was fastened around his waist and his hand shackles were secured to it, in front of his stomach.

Chuck appeared from the front cab, holding out a box file. 'Here's his files,' he said to the handover guard who took the metal box.

'Hey, you managed to bring half of 'em home,' the handover

guard said sarcastically, much to the amusement of the others. 'Walk on,' he said to Stratton as another guard joined them.

Several more prison wagons were parked around the hangar, with clusters of guards standing around them, chatting and smoking. Stratton walked up a short flight of metal stairs onto a concrete platform and stopped in front of a heavy-duty steel door. The handover guard pressed a button on the wall by the door, a buzzer sounded inside and he looked up at a video camera. 'Come on, wake up,' he mumbled impatiently. Seconds later there was an electrical buzz followed by a clunk.

The guard pulled the steel door open and Stratton was led into a white room where a female officer seated inside a steel cubicle watched them from behind a thick glass window. The guard bringing up the rear closed the door behind them and a red light above another steel door on the other side of the room turned green. 'Walk on,' the female officer said over a loudspeaker.

The two guards moved Stratton towards the door, one of them in front, the other behind. The handover guard pushed open the steel door and they entered a sterile concrete corridor with a high ceiling. Halfway along they turned and entered a room with yet another heavy steel door already open.

Stratton was led to a metal bench that was bolted to the wall. When he sat down a chain attached to the bench was threaded through rings on his mesh belt and fastened with a lock. The handover guard left the room while the other stayed by the door, one hand on his holstered baton alongside a Mace dispenser, a zapper and a radio.

'You're gettin' booked in,' the remaining guard said in a Southern drawl. 'Gonna be a while. You need the can?'

Stratton shook his head.

'That's just fine,' the guard said, taking a toothpick from his pocket to service his tobacco-stained teeth.

Stratton remained in silence for almost an hour before the

handover guard returned to release him from his seat and lead him out of the room. The trio continued to the end of the corridor, their footsteps echoing, and through another door. They had to wait until the entry door had locked magnetically before the exit door was unlocked by an officer inside a bulletproof cubicle.

Stratton was ushered into another room where five male prisoners wearing the same uniform as him were chained to a long metal bench. Stratton was placed at the end of the row where he was secured beside a surly unshaven individual who ignored him.

An older guard walked in, carrying a clipboard. Judging by his demeanour he was the senior officer. He stopped in the centre of the room, planted his feet wide and addressed the group. 'Listen up,' he said in a gravelly voice. A couple of the prisoners sat up but the rest ignored him. 'You've arrived at Styx transfer point. Shortly you'll be moved to the dock where you'll board a boat that'll take you to the ferry platform. From there you'll commence the final leg of your journey. Did anyone have a problem understanding what I just said?'

A dirty-brown-skinned Latino inmate with a straggly goatee glanced up at the senior guard, a quizzical expression on his face.

'*Comprende*, Ramos?' the senior guard asked him.

Ramos shrugged to convey his ignorance, a malicious smirk on his face.

'Give Ramos the Spanish card,' the senior guard said.

One of his colleagues responded by walking over to Ramos and holding a plastic card in front of him. It had the requisite information written on it in Spanish.

'I take it you *can* read?' the senior guard muttered.

Ramos glanced over the card, shrugged again and muttered something that amused only himself. The guard returned to his position.

The senior guard walked to a steel door at the end of the room, reached for a small hatch at face level and opened it. He pulled a two-way radio to his mouth as he looked through the opening. 'Transfer room to dock . . . Transfer room to dock.'

'Dock reading you loud and clear,' a voice crackled over the radio.

'This is Perkins, senior watch. Those guys from Styx ready for transfer of six packages to the dock?'

'That's an affirmative. Officer coming up now.'

A look of irritation passed across the senior guard's face as he closed the hatch and turned to look at the prisoners. There was a deafening silence, one that Ramos chose to break with an extended fart.

'You fuckin' stink, Ramos,' said a large, muscular, tattooed neo-Nazi beside him.

'Shut it,' the senior guard said before Ramos could respond. 'You're still mine until you get on that boat and I ain't too pleasant if you get me riled.'

The other guards remained watching silently, their cold expressions reflecting their boss's threat.

A minute later a clunk signalled that the outer door had been unlocked. The senior guard checked through the hatch once more before unlocking the door on his side.

It opened to reveal a Styx prison guard in his tailored one-piece lime-green uniform. 'Hi,' the Styx guard said, a broad smile on his face that was destined to irritate anyone who saw it.

The senior guard retained his grim look as he checked his clipboard. 'You Gann or Palanski?'

'I'm Palanski.'

The senior guard handed Palanski a sheet of paper from the clipboard. 'You taking any of your stores down with you this trip? They're piling up all over my goddamned hangar.'

'Sorry. Not this time. I hear they're gonna be runnin' ferries all day tomorrow, shippin' stores.'

'They better be.'

Palanski smiled again as he finished reading the paper, took a pen from his breast pocket and signed the bottom of it.

'No matter how often I see that uniform I can't help thinking how cute it is,' the senior guard said mockingly.

His fellow guards grinned. There was a distinct one-sided animosity between the regular land-based prison guards and their Styx equivalents. The land guards resented the sizeable disparity between their perks and remunerations and those of the Styx custodians. The rumour was that with bonuses and special allowances the undersea guards got twice the annual pay of the land ones. It was also well known that, apart from the negative aspects of living under pressure at the bottom of the sea, the Styx amenities such as food and leisure facilities were of a far higher standard.

'It is kinda nice, ain't it?' Palanski replied, not remotely insulted. Indeed, the Styx guards were quite used to being needled by their surface colleagues. 'Designed by Ralph Lauren, tailored to the individual, breathable fabric for added comfort. Oh, and a real large wallet pocket inside the jacket . . . for extra-large wallets.' A wink finished off the rejoinder.

The senior guard's smirk turned into a scowl. 'Let's do it,' he said and stepped outside as one of his men took over his position and closed the door.

Stratton looked down the line of prisoners, a variety of disagreeable-looking individuals. The man beside him finally glanced at him but when Stratton met his gaze he looked away.

A few minutes later the door opened and the senior guard stepped back into the room while Palanski waited outside. The prisoner closest to the door was unshackled. 'On your feet,' the senior guard said. The prisoner was escorted out of the room and the door was secured once again.

Several minutes later the guards returned to collect the next prisoner and the process was repeated. Ten minutes later Stratton was the last remaining prisoner and the guards returned to unshackle him. 'On your feet.'

As Stratton stepped through the door and walked through a narrow low-ceilinged hangar he could smell the distinctive odour of ripe sea kelp and hear the distant cavernous echo of lapping water. A curtain of mildew-stained overlapping strips of opaque plastic hung from the ceiling across the width of the hangar. The escorting guard pushed through, holding it open for Stratton. The hangar continued for a short distance, the concrete floor meeting a flight of metal steps that led down onto a landing made of heavy steel girders. As Stratton walked along it he could see black lapping water through the chequered metal pattern of the flooring.

Up ahead, moored alongside one of several landing fingers, was a low, slender fibreglass passenger craft, its cabin and cockpit enclosed. Gann stood on the open aft deck, eyeing him coldly.

Stratton was led up a short gangway and onto the deck. Gann took hold of him brusquely and shoved him towards the opening into the cabin. Stratton ducked inside to find the other five prisoners already shackled to a long metal bench. Palanski was standing at the far end of the cabin, his back to a couple of pilots inside the sealed cockpit. Gann followed Stratton inside and after chaining him into his seat he went back outside to complete the exchange formalities with the senior guard. When he returned he shut the door behind him, leaving two guards outside on the aft deck pulling on life jackets.

Gann unhooked a handset from the wall and held it to his mouth. 'Clear to depart,' he said before returning the handset to its clip. His words were echoed over a speaker by the pilot and the engine revved loudly. A large door at the end of the hangar opened, pulled up into the ceiling, and the boat puttered through it.

'Should for any reason the boat develop problems and begin to sink a device at the end of the row might be activated that will release your chains,' Gann said. 'You notice I said "might".' He grinned. 'The mood I'm in right now it ain't gonna happen so do something to cheer me up . . . Under your seats you'll find life jackets. I'm supposed to show you how to put them on like I was an air hostess but you'll figure 'em out for yourselves if you need to. Anyone don't understand what I'm saying, then tough shit,' he said, looking at Ramos whose sudden smirk implied that he understood well enough. Gann smiled back for just a second.

The sun spilled in through the windows as the boat moved out of the hangar and the grey ocean took up the forward panorama. A prisoner said something to the one beside him and Gann walked down the narrow aisle and stopped in front of the offending talker. 'I'm gonna say this just once, fuckwit. No one talks on this boat except me . . . and Mr Palanski. You belong to me now. This ain't like the cushy little numbers you just left,' he said, addressing all of them. 'You have any complaints, you talk to me. Any problems, you talk to me. Just one word of advice, though. I don't like people talking to me. Got that?'

'Whatever you say, boss man,' the prisoner replied, sarcasm clear in his tone.

Gann slammed him brutally across the face with the back of his hand and leaned in even closer as if he wanted to bite the prisoner's face off. 'I said no talking – and no fucking attitude, neither. Now. You got any complaints?'

The man licked his split lip, tasting the blood as he looked at Gann with death in his eyes. But, wisely, he choked back his response.

'Learn fast. It'll keep you healthy in Styx. It's unhealthy enough down there as it is.'

The boat rocked in the swell but Gann did not grab hold of anything to steady himself, spreading his large powerful legs to maintain his balance.

Stratton could not see very much of the ocean outside from where he was sitting but he knew the ferry platform was only a couple of miles away. Gann brushed past him to take up his position by the rear door, his hand on his utility belt beside his baton and zapper, his other hand on his Mace dispenser, his stare fixed on the prisoners as if hoping one of them might give him an excuse to launch himself at them.

The ferry platform eventually loomed into sight as the vessel manoeuvred to enter a docking bay. It was an impressive construction, like the top section of an oil platform. The most prominent feature was a towering derrick with a dozen heavy cables passing over large wheels at the top before they stretched down at an angle into the roof of a building on the edge of the platform.

The cabin cruiser slipped snugly into its tailored dock and gently hit the bumpers at the end. Several platform guards, all wearing life vests over brilliant yellow jackets, secured the vessel into place, its gunwales level with the landing deck.

Gann opened the rear door and faced his passengers. 'I'm gonna unlock your chains and we're all gonna walk together in a line across the platform to the ferry housing. For those of you who think it might be risky on our part to have all prisoners walkin' at once even though you still got your hand chains, that's because there's nowhere to go from this platform – nowhere but down, that is. And you can either do that in the comfort of the ferry where you can breathe, or you can jump or get shoved off the side. Either way you're going to the bottom . . . I know you'll be surprised to hear I don't give a rat's ass which you choose. Anyone screws around I'll personally toss 'em over the side.'

Gann undid a latch at the end of the bench, took hold of a lever and pulled it up with some effort. Every prisoner's hand shackles were released from the bench between their legs although their hands remained chained together at the wrists. 'Stand up,' he called out and the prisoners got to their feet with a clatter of metal. 'Turn towards me.'

Stratton faced Gann's broad chest an arm's length away.

'Forward march,' Gann said as he stepped back through the door. 'Move it.'

Stratton walked outside and onto the short gangway.

'Keep going,' Gann said. 'Follow the guard.'

Stratton stepped off the gangway onto the wooden deck of the jetty, walked across it and up another steep gangway with a hinge at the top that allowed it to rise and fall with the ocean swell. He stepped onto the main platform, the sea visible through a steel-mesh floor, and followed the guard at an easy pace that allowed the others to catch up. The prisoners' ankle and wrist chains clinked behind him as they walked along a covered ramp that led to another platform connected by massive chains that allowed it to move independently of the docking section.

They approached the entrances to two hangars joined together, each with several thick wire cables coming down at steep angles from the derrick wheels and passing through openings in the roofs. A sign above the entrance to the left-hand hangar read *FERRY 1 & 2*, and above the right hangar *FERRY 3 & 4*. Stratton was directed towards an archway into the right-hand hangar.

Inside, the hangar was fully enclosed, the mesh floor limited to a central pathway with open water either side. A squat craft that looked like some kind of submarine occupied the right bay, while the left bay was empty. Thick, greasy cables entered through the hangar roof, one set dropping into the left bay and disappearing beneath the water, the other set crossing over the top of the squat vessel and through a complex series of wheels on a heavy framework rather like that of a cable car. As Stratton looked at the steel vessel, which was painted white with the number four stencilled in black on the top and sides, the blueprints he had studied in detail came to life in his head. There were four ferries in total, the conveyance method much the same as a classic cable system with a car at either end, both moving at the same time to counterbalance the driving mechanism and passing each other at the halfway point.

The ferries were identical, each with a safe operating capacity of fourteen persons. They were divided into two compartments: a larger main passenger cabin and a smaller section designed for emergency escape. Both compartments had escape hatches but only the emergency compartment had an airlock-tube system that allowed one person at a time to escape without flooding the entire compartment. The escape hatch in the passenger cabin was a standard maritime docking system that a rescue submarine could attach itself to prior to opening.

Massive weights were fixed to the base of the ferry to keep it in the correct attitude as well as to provide negative buoyancy. Along its sides were neat rows of high-pressure gas bottles that provided fourteen passengers with breathable air for up to twenty-four hours at a hundred and fifty feet of pressure.

'Stop there,' a guard called out and Stratton came to a halt halfway along the length of the ferry. The other prisoners shuffled to a stop behind him.

'Turn and face the ferry,' Gann called out as he walked down the line, his voice echoing.

The men obeyed, all looking at the vessel, in particular at the single open door that led into the main passenger compartment.

'You are about to take the last stage of your journey to Styx max-security pen,' Gann said. 'This may look like a submarine but it ain't. There are no pilots or crew. It's an underwater cable car controlled from the prison – unless somethin' goes wrong, then it can be controlled from here. There's a toilet on board but it ain't workin' at the moment so if you wanna go, say so now or do it in your pants 'cause once you're in your seat you don't get out of it until we reach the prison. We won't be serving any snacks or drinks, either. The journey'll take about twenty-five minutes. I ain't gonna go into the technicalities but it's as safe as takin' a bus ride. There's only gonna be me and Mr Palanski on board with you so behave yourselves. For safety reasons, if anyone should get outta line we have the legal right to use whatever we have at our disposal as a restraint to prevent putting other lives at risk. I love that legal right. I've got an iron bar inside and my idea of restraint is a crushed skull. So don't piss me off.'

Gann nodded to Palanski who stepped inside the vessel, remaining by the door.

'We're gonna go in one at a time, just like before, and you'll be secured to your seat,' Gann continued. 'Lead off,' he said to Stratton, who stepped towards the vessel's entrance. The man beside him began to follow and was grabbed harshly by Gann around the throat and held before his leading foot had touched the ground. 'One at a time, I said.'

The man choked, unable to grab Gann's hands because his own were secured to his waist-belt. Gann gazed into the man's reddening eyes before pushing him back into line.

Stratton was led by Palanski to the end of a back-to-back double row of metal seats fixed to the floor along the centre of the cabin.

'Sit down,' Palanski said. Stratton obeyed. The woven steel seat was cold. His hand chains were removed from his waist-belt and placed over a hook poking up through the metal seat. Palanski pushed the hook down into a slot in the seat until it clicked into place. 'That's a release mechanism,' he said. 'We can release you if there's a problem. But don't worry, there won't be.'

Palanski talked without any threat or cruelty in his tone, the good cop to Gann's monster. Stratton watched him walk back to the door to receive the next prisoner. It was the same dark surly-looking individual that Stratton had sat beside since joining the group and he watched as the securing procedure was repeated. When Palanski walked away the prisoner gave the hook a firm tug. It was immovable. He glanced at Stratton and they held each other's gaze for a few seconds. Stratton was surprised to see no real malice in his eyes, nor any sign of the cold macho aggression that the others naturally exuded. They were intelligent and without the torment that an incarcerated convict of his level usually possessed. Stratton wondered what his crime was. It was obviously a serious one to have got him a trip to Styx.

Stratton went back to studying the vessel, as much of it as he could see from his seat without stretching around too much. It was interesting to identify various components from the blueprints and those added since. The docking hatch was the same, almost directly above him with its interesting dual lock-and-hinge system designed to open either inwards or outwards. The interior of a regular submarine remained pretty much at surface pressure no matter how deep it descended, which meant the forces against the outer skin were always greater than those inside. The Styx ferries, however, were designed so that the internal pressure increased as it descended, constantly equalising with the outside pressure. For the return phase the pressure remained at the prison depth to allow slow decompression even as the ferry ascended. The ferry was therefore built to prevent it blowing open as opposed to the conventional imploding. Decompression could be carried out inside the ferry or, once on the surface, the vessel could be connected to a habitat chamber and the passengers transferred into it to decompress in more comfort.

The prison was kept at the same pressure as its depth which was an average of a hundred and fifty feet. There were a number of reasons for this, both security and structurally related. If the forces inside the structure equalled those outside (or were just fractionally lower, to be more accurate) there would be less chance of structural failure and fewer leaks. As for the security aspect, an escaping prisoner would have to decompress for hours or risk dying of the bends.

Stratton studied the door to the emergency escape room, hoping he might get a chance to look inside at some stage. From this point on he would have to constantly evaluate possible ways to escape from the prison despite the fact that it was not essential to the plan. His orders were to attempt it only once he had disposed of the tablet and ensured that there was no risk to himself or to others. He reflected on how stupid the 'no risk' part of those orders was. He was in the extreme-risk business. An escape would only give closure to the counterfeit aspect of the plan which was the 'independent evaluation' of the escape potential of the prison. It would be nice if Stratton could manage it all but no one was expecting him to get even close to that. But as long as he destroyed the tablet first he could make an escape attempt if he so desired.

Stratton decided that he would have a go for the adventure of it. His other option, the one most popular with the mission's planners, was that once he had successfully destroyed the tablet he was to give himself up. By doing so he would technically have failed as far as the evaluation was concerned but his real mission would have been achieved. The truth was that Stratton himself did not really expect to succeed in escaping. To do so certainly appeared impossible after he'd studied the plans and experienced the system thus far. But he still fancied the opportunity if it should arise even though he was less inclined these days to take the kind of risks he used to have scant regard for. He'd come close to dying too many times and the incidents were more than just vague memories. The emotions he had experienced during the worst of them were deeply etched into his psyche. It was as if he were two people: one eager to volunteer for any operation, the other warning of the consequences. He could have done with a little less of both.

A heavy clang yanked Stratton out of his thoughts and at the same time he felt the pressure change in his ears. He looked at the entrance to see Gann spinning the central wheel on the closed watertight doors. The action pushed out a dozen clips around the seal, squeezing it shut.

'You're soon gonna feel the pressure build in your ears,' Gann said. 'Sorry you can't use your hands to help relieve it if it hurts. If you get any pain wiggle your jaw or try to yawn. If that don't work then just sit it out. Your eardrums'll burst but that's not a problem. There's nothin' in Styx worth hearing other than me and I'll always make sure you know what I'm sayin' . . . Some pearls o' wisdom for you before we set off. From here on in you're gonna be under pressure, and I don't mean just from me. You're gonna be under *sea* pressure. That means the only way you can get outta the prison is by decompressing, which takes hours. Give you an idea how it works. If you somehow got outta the prison and floated up you'd be big as a Buick by the time you reached the surface. Course, long before you got there you'd explode into a thousand pieces. So if you did escape no one would know about it. A little piece of advice to add to that: if you piss me off too much or you're caught stealin' from the mine – you'll get to learn about that – or you're just a pain-in-the-ass troublemaker I'll see to it that you *do* escape. This ain't like no other prison on Earth. There's nowhere to hide, no way to escape, no one to run to if you ain't happy. No visitors, no lawyers, no press.' He glanced at Palanski who thought he saw something in Gann's look. 'We do our own cleanin', our own cookin', our own laundry. We even do some of our own equipment servicin' if we find out any of you are geniuses. And then we've got the mine for you to play in. What's up, Ramos?'

Everyone glanced at Ramos who was looking agitated. 'I don't like small spaces,' he said, his lips quivering.

'Ain't you spent most of your rat life in a cell?' Gann asked.

'Not at the bottom of the fuckin' sea,' Ramos mumbled.

'Don't worry yourself about it,' Gann said, amused. 'You'll soon be in an even smaller, deeper space.' Gann took a handset off the wall and put it to his mouth. 'Control, this is ferry four, come in.'

A speaker crackled for a few seconds before a voice broke from it. 'Ferry four, control hears you. That you, Gann?'

'Yeah. We're ready to push from the platform. That's six packs plus two guards, total eight persons.'

'Copy, you're ready to push, eight up. Stand by, ferry four . . .'

'Oh, I almost forgot the emergency procedures,' Gann said as he hung the handset back onto its hook. 'If in the event of an incident, like a fire or the cables snap and we sink like a stone' – Gann glanced at Ramos and others who were beginning to look uncomfortable, enjoying their unease – 'your chains'll be disconnected from your seats by me or Mr Palanski. Anyone panics or gets outta control I'll zap you or knock you out,' he said, pulling a zapper from his belt with one hand, a blackjack with the other and holding them up. 'Whichever, chances are you'll get left behind. I got no time for assholes. If we have to bale out you'll be directed to the emergency escape room through that door over there where your cuffs'll be removed and you'll put on escape suits and go to the surface one at a time.'

''Scuse me,' said the large neo-Nazi. 'Can I ask a question . . . please?'

'Since you asked so nicely,' Gann replied.

'I thought you said we'd be the size of a Buick if we go straight up to the surface.'

'That's only if we're down on the bottom of the ocean more'n a few hours. If that's the case we'll stay in here and wait to be rescued by a special sub.'

The prisoners looked at one another, mumbling their concerns and dissent.

'I said I'm the only one who talks,' Gann grumbled.

Everyone shut up, already conditioned to their guard's potential to cause suffering.

The vessel jerked heavily as the cables above began to move and there was a long creaking sound outside like the tearing of sheet metal. Ramos started to tremble violently, his breathing quickening. He pulled on his chain in the hope that it might disconnect from the hook in the seat. Gann walked down the row and stopped in front of him. 'I'm warnin' you, Ramos. You fuck aroun' and I'll zap yer.'

'I . . . I can't take this shit! Let me outta here!' Ramos shouted. 'I told 'em I couldn't go down to that place but they wouldn't believe me.'

Gann gritted his teeth as he held the zapper in front of Ramos's face. 'I'm warnin' you, wetback. Settle down.'

Ramos ignored him as if his only obstacle to safety was the hook securing his chain to the seat.

Gann pressed the button on the device and a bright blue and white spark connected the tips of the chrome terminals an inch from Ramos's nose.

But Ramos could not be deterred, his claustrophobia more powerful than Gann's paltry threat. 'Lemme outta here! I gotta get outta here!' he screamed. 'LEMME OUT!'

'Prisoner's outta control,' Gann called out, as if formally declaring the way clear for his legal solution. Without further hesitation he rammed the terminals of the zapper into Ramos's throat where it clicked loudly in time with the high-voltage pulses. The two prisoners on either side of Ramos leaned away as he howled and shook violently. A short zap would have sufficed but not for Gann. He held the device firmly against Ramos's neck for an age. Palanski cringed as he watched. Some of the prisoners found it amusing.

Ramos had gone silent by the time Gann removed the zapper, his body shuddering, his head back, eyeballs rolled up, tongue hanging out, foamy saliva dribbling from the sides of his mouth.

Gann leaned over the Mexican to observe him like a crackpot

indulging in an experiment. 'He's OK,' Gann declared, none too confidently. 'That's how they usually go.'

The vessel shunted again and this time there was a perceptible feeling of movement that gradually increased as the craft gracefully pulled out of its holding bay. As it left the guide tray it dropped, taking up the slack in the cables. Everyone experienced that lost-stomach feeling, to the point where several of the prisoners groaned.

Gann tapped Ramos on the side of his head, still unsure if he had done any serious damage – not that he cared much. He gave up and shrugged. 'You got the picture, guys,' he said, walking back along the row. 'No fuckin' around or you'll get the same.'

Stratton focused on a map board at the other end of the bench row. The ferry's position was indicated on an angled line marked at regular intervals like a metro map, except the lit beads were depth markers between the surface platform and the prison's arrivals dock. A bright green LED light indicating the surface platform extinguished and a blue one blinked on further down the line.

Gann stopped in front of a bank of valves and gauges that displayed the internal and external ferry pressures, air-storage volume, air quality, and the carbon dioxide, nitrogen and oxygen percentages of the air. He tapped a couple of the gauges, noting with satisfaction that the internal pressure was several pounds per square inch lower than outside. As he turned around to check on the prisoners his eyes drifted to the line of relief valves in the ceiling, three in total. A drop of water fell from one onto a prisoner's head, causing the man to look up curiously.

'Lemme know if that turns into a fire hose,' Gann said, with a wink.

The prisoner wasn't amused and looked up as another drip fell onto his face.

Gann walked to the front of the cabin to Palanski. 'Did you check the escape suits?'

Palanski was looking at Ramos who, although still in a daze, appeared to be recovering. He raised an eyebrow at the request. 'That's the senior man's job.'

'I only asked in case.'

'I can do it if you want.'

'Nah. I'll check 'em.'

Palanski moved aside. Like most of the prison guards, Gann intimidated him.

Gann unlocked the six dog hasps around the emergency escape room door. Stratton watched as he tugged at the handle, unable to shift it. Both men looked up at a gauge on the wall above the door. 'Fuckin' room ain't equalised,' Gann mumbled as he turned a valve beside the gauge that allowed air into the escape room. Seconds later the door popped slightly towards him and he turned off the valve and pulled the door fully open.

He stepped inside and as he turned to close the door he caught Stratton staring at him. Stratton looked away and Gann watched him a little longer before closing the door. Stratton looked back to see a couple of the dog hasps turn to secure it.

Gann went to a rack containing more than a dozen bright yellow packs with ESCAPE SUIT written on them in large letters. He took one of the packs, pulled open the seal, removed the bright yellow suit and draped it over the side of the rack. He opened a red box on the wall. Inside were a couple of small air cylinders. He removed one, checked that the contents gauge was green and that the full-face mask was secured to the end of its high-pressure tube. He turned the bottle valve, put the mouthpiece in his mouth, took a quick guff to ensure that it was working and placed it on the shelf beside the escape suit.

He faced the emergency escape tube which was basically a large pipe welded vertically to the ceiling and big enough for a man to crawl up inside. The bottom end, covered with a hatch, was just below his waist. He checked a gauge to ensure that the pressure inside the tube was the same as the ferry's and squatted to take hold of the hatch wheel. He turned it a couple of times and the heavy hatch dropped open on its hinge and returned almost all the way back up on a pair of robust springs designed to counter its weight.

Gann got onto his knees, pushed the hatch fully open against its springs and poked his head up inside to take a look at the narrow space that was illuminated by an internal lamp. A hatch covered the other end of the six-foot-long tube, the brass wheel at its centre wet with condensation. A breathing umbilical was secured halfway up and he crawled sufficiently inside to reach up and press the spring valve inside the teat. An instant gush of air revealed that it was working and he inspected the small collection of valves and gauges that operated the flooding system. Satisfied that everything was in working order, Gann manoeuvred his large frame out of the awkward space and got to his feet.

He looked around to make sure there was nothing else he needed to prepare for his murderous plan and took a deep breath to steel himself. This was by far the biggest job he had ever taken on.

He walked back to the door and unclipped the two dog hasps. When he pulled open the door his gaze met Stratton's again.

Gann stepped through the door, left it open a little and crossed over to Stratton. 'You got somethin' you wanna say to me?'

Stratton looked down, playing the passive-submissive card.

'Then stop lookin' at me. You ain't my type.'

Gann brushed past him and Stratton watched as he stopped in front of the route-marker board where a blue light put the ferry a quarter of the way to the arrival dock.

Stratton sat back in his seat, beginning to wonder if this operation had any chance of success. It was always easier to see where the cracks were from the outside. On the other hand, the inside was where the reality was. He had no experience of penitentiaries and, frankly, the level of security so far was significant enough to suggest the job was going to have to rely much more on chance than the briefing had allowed for. There were things about the ferry that had not been reflected in the diagrams he had seen. They were small but significant enough. The control panel was in a different location for one thing, and there were three relief valves in the ceiling when he was sure there had only been one on the blueprints. Stratton's knowledge of the layout of the prison was based entirely on plans that had not been updated in several years.

Then there was the total lack of information about the everyday routine life of the prisoners as well as the guard system. Procedures could change overnight, anyway. There were also the various unquantifiable characters who ran the place – such as Gann. Asinine prison officers were only to be expected but Gann was more like some kind of classic medieval dungeon guard more comfortable running the torture chamber than looking after the everyday welfare of an inmate. He could screw up the operation all on his own.

'Hey, leave that open,' Gann called out.

Stratton looked over to see he was addressing Palanski who was about to lock the door to the emergency escape room.

'But it's supposed—' Palanski began but was cut off.

'I said leave it open.'

Palanski walked over to Gann at the console. 'We're supposed to keep it closed while we're in transit,' he said in a low voice, as if he didn't want the children to see their parents arguing.

Gann couldn't have cared less what the prisoners thought. 'And I want it open, OK,' he said glaring at his colleague. And then, as if regretting his anger, he calmed down, mimicking Palanski's lowered voice. 'I wanna go back in there and check on somethin', OK? Between you and me I think one of the relief valves is sticky.'

Palanski looked up at the valve. 'This whole friggin' ferry needs a service if you ask me.'

'Go check on Ramos,' Gann said.

Palanski stepped back, glad that Gann had calmed down. He leaned over the Mexican whose eyes were heavily red-rimmed and looked as if he had taken a drug overdose. Palanski had no idea what he could do for the guy and so he made a meal out of checking him over.

Gann went back to the route indicator. The timing of the next phase was crucial. The ferry needed to be close to the prison dock but not too close. The dock was designed on a moon-pool concept. The ferry arrived from beneath, the cables rolling under a series of wheels before heading up inside at an angle. Once the ferry moved below the wheels it followed the cables and emerged as if from a pool inside an air-filled cavern. Gann's plan was to sabotage the ferry and leave the prisoners for dead before it arrived at the dock. But the prison maintained a rescue team on standby whenever a ferry was operating in case there was a serious incident.

Gann estimated he would soon have to commence the operation and as he checked his watch he experienced a touch of nerves such as he had not felt since his earliest days in the business of skulduggery. He glanced up at the leaking relief valve, a pivotal element to his plan, and then at the prisoners sitting in a row, wondering which of them was the reason they all had to die. It was obvious that things were not well with the prison but perhaps his mission would solve the problem. The man was not just a threat to the future of the facility but also to Gann's employment. This was a great gig for him, the best he'd had. It was more money than he had ever earned and he didn't want it to end.

It was typical of Gann that never once did he question if all the men had to die. It made perfect sense. He was used to following orders that would result in the injury or death of people whom he did not know. He was more interested in how he was going to succeed. Gann knew his place in the great scheme of things. He always did. He was not the kind of man who could set up a company or a criminal organisation by himself. But he made a good lieutenant. Working at Styx had given him levels of responsibility he had never before been entrusted with and tasks such as this made it all so much more satisfying. If there was anything he could do to safeguard his job he would.

Gann's introduction to inflicting violence on others as a means of gainful employment came at an early age, shortly after he'd left school in Toronto, the city of his birth. He became an 'enforcer', a glamorous title bestowed upon him by his first boss, a ruthless housing developer who specialised in turning low-class neighbourhoods into upper-middle-class luxury homes. Gann's job was to put pressure on owners who did not want to sell. This he managed in a number of occasionally imaginative and usually violent ways. Once the houses had been bought the tenants were evicted. Normally the sight of Gann stepping in through the door and telling them that they had to get out was enough. If not, creativity was called for.

The turning point in Gann's life came when a particularly tough tenant organised a group of friends to beat him up on the day he arrived to press his demand to vacate the premises. It was a serious case of misjudgement: several days later Gann followed the man to his place of work, approached him in an underground car park as he was getting out of his vehicle and beat him to death with an iron bar. At first Gann was worried, never having gone that far before. But instead of panicking he kept his nerve and rigged the murder to look like a mugging that had gone wrong.

A few months later Gann's boss was slain as the result of a private business disagreement and Gann was hired by a powerful loan shark in whose employ opportunities to improve his particular skills were plentiful. Gann's reputation grew and he became a freelancer on the books of several major collecting agencies, becoming involved in bounty hunting abroad in places like South and Central America. The next honing of his developing skills was his introduction to assassination, a trade he took to effortlessly with his first task: the strangling of an accountant who had embezzled money from a New York crime family.

Gann carried out a number of similar 'jobs' for the same people until one day things took a turn for the worse. He was picked up by the FBI just before a job and, convinced he was looking at several decades in jail, he agreed to turn state's evidence. As luck would have it, Gann managed to avoid imprisonment altogether due to shockingly poor management of the evidence against him. The feds, however, stuck with their witness-protection agreement and, armed with a new identity, Gann was free to start life over again.

Gann's big concern now, however, was how he was going make a living. The feds had been quite clear in their threats about what would happen if he went back to his old ways. But depression and desperation soon set in when he failed to find satisfactory employment and just as he was contemplating his first armed robbery he received a call from a man who knew not just his real identity but every detail about his past. This man had called to offer Gann a job utilising his particular type of skill but this time for a legitimate company. Gann was curious, to say the least, and agreed to take a meeting in Houston at the headquarters of an outfit called the Felix Corporation.

After a brief interview he was hired as a special-duties prison supervisor, a position that, although he had zero experience of such work, filled him with excitement at the thought of its possibilities. His responsibilities were left vague for the time being and he was placed on a handsome retainer for six months. During that time he attended courses on the duties of a corrections officer, followed by training in sub-sea environments. Gann arrived at the prison several months before the first inmate and spent his time familiarising himself with the jail's layout and procedures, its life-support systems and the ferry procedures. At the end of it he received his special-duties brief, which included giving every assistance to Mandrick, the new warden, as well as to the government agents who would be conducting prisoner 'questioning'.

Gann had matured greatly since his early days and, anxious to keep his position in a company that, in his eyes, showed great potential for his personal enrichment he made sure he did precisely what he was ordered to and did it as efficiently as possible. In the exclusive world of murderous lackeys, Gann was at the top of his game.

Therefore, when Gann was told it would be convenient if everyone in the ferry that day should die it was as good as done. He could also expect a handsome bonus at the end of the month.

Gann went to the communications set, surreptitiously unplugged the handset and put it in his pocket. He went to the control panel and pretended to study the various gauges while taking hold of an adjustable wrench attached to a chain fixed to the panel. The tool was used for turning tight valves. A screwdriver was similarly attached and he used it to prise open one of the wrench's chain links and disconnect it. He reached for the interior main air valve and turned it until it was fully closed. The needle of the interior pressure gauge moved very slightly to indicate a drop in cabin pressure. With the screwdriver he undid the screw that secured the interior valve handle, removed the handle completely and, using the wrench, bent the valve stem enough to ensure that it could not be turned by hand. He placed the wrench in his pocket.

The gauge indicated that the pressure was dropping slowly and Gann looked up at the leaking relief valve in the ceiling to see the flow of the dripping water increase. He could feel the sudden decrease in cabin pressure in his ears and as the leak became a steady stream the other two relief valves began to drip. The prisoners beneath wondered what this sudden shower was all about.

Stratton also felt the drop in pressure and looked up as Gann walked past him towards the emergency escape-room door. The three relief valves popped and sea water burst into the cabin as if from fire hoses, soaking the prisoners who shouted and struggled in their seats.

Palanski was as confused as he was alarmed. 'Gann!' he shouted over the sound of gushing water as his colleague stepped through the doorway into the emergency compartment. 'What the hell's happening?!'

'Looks like we got a problem,' Gann shouted back.

Stratton sensed something odd about Gann's tone. He looked between the control panel, the rapidly flooding vessel and the empty doorway into the escape room. The relief valves were designed to allow any increase in internal air pressure over a specific setting to bleed out of the vessel and not allow any water into the cabin if the pressures reversed. But all three valves had failed – which suggested they had been tampered with.

The frothy grey sea water had already filled the shallow sump beneath the flooring grille and was lapping around Stratton's feet. He instinctively pulled on his chains – they were fixed solid – while his mind raced to search for a solution to a situation that was clearly catastrophic.

Palanski hurried to the control panel to check the gauges. 'The pressure's still dropping,' he shouted to no one in particular. He reached for the inlet valve, only to discover that the handle was gone. He searched frantically for it, on the panel and on the floor. Unable to find it he reached for the wrench, only to discover nothing on the end of the chain. In desperation he tried to turn the valve stem with his wet fingers but it was impossible.

Stratton watched Palanski give up on the valves and look around in despair.

'Break the pipe!' Stratton shouted.

Palanski focused on him, a confused expression on his face.

'Break the inlet pipe! The one the valve's attached to!' Stratton yelled above the hissing water. The extreme gravity of the situation was horrifyingly stark. Stratton might have little experience with prisons but he knew a hell of a lot about submersibles and the dangers of them flooding under pressure. The situation had 'extremely serious' written all over it.

Palanski realised the prisoner was making perfect sense. If he could puncture the inlet pipe between the valve and the exterior air bottles it would have the same effect as opening the valve. But there was something else Palanski realised he could do in the meantime and his eyes went to a large red button near the door. He reached up and punched it in. An alarm sounded.

He grabbed up the screwdriver and began to force it behind the high-pressure air pipe in order to prise it away from the wall.

Gann appeared in the escape-room doorway wearing the yellow one-piece emergency escape suit, the transparent hood hanging down his back. The suit made him appear twice as big as he was. He waded through the cabin, the water already to his knees, and brutally grabbed Palanski's arm to spin him around. Palanski looked at him wide-eyed, confused by the escape suit.

Gann did not give his colleague a second more to consider the implications and brutally slammed him across the face. But Palanski was no slouch when it came to fighting and, driven by the added desperation of the situation, he surprised Gann by ripping free the screwdriver and bringing it down hard towards the man's face. Gann would have been skewered had the chain attached to the screwdriver not reached its full length and abruptly halted the tool's progress in mid-air, an inch from his eye. Gann did not hesitate and punched Palanski in the gut with a mighty uppercut.

Palanski bent over double but recovered enough to lunge at Gann with a mid-body tackle. Both men bulled down the row of prisoners. Gann only barely managed to stay on his feet, his back slamming into the steel wall of the escape room with Palanski still bent down in front of him. Gann took hold of Palanski's arm, spun the man around and, positioning the limb across the open doorway, slammed the steel door on it, crushing the elbow joint. Palanski howled as he grabbed at his injury and Gann slipped the wrench from his inside pocket and brought it down onto the side of Palanski's head. Blood streamed across Palanski's face as he fell into the water.

Satisfied that Palanski was no longer a threat, Gann stepped through the emergency escape-room door, took a moment to look back and glare at the prisoners, and closed it behind him.

Stratton watched the dog hasps, waiting for them to turn to secure the door, but they did not and the door opened slightly though he could see nothing inside.

The water continued to flood in through the roof. Every man knew this was the end if they could not free themselves. They fought with their chains, their wrists bleeding as the shackles cut into the flesh. They shouted, growled, whimpered as they fought in desperation for a way out of the watery coffin that they were trapped inside.

In marked contrast, Stratton sat almost still as the ice-cold water lapped around his waist. He had been through every possible escape scenario in his mind but any one of them depended on first getting out of the seat chains. He looked down at the only possible chance of survival that was left – Palanski, sitting in the water, his chin just above it, teetering on the edge of consciousness. 'Palanski!' he shouted. But the guard did not respond.

The two duty controllers in the prison OCR (Operations Control Room) sprang to life with the triggering of the shrill ferry alarm, both of them flashing looks at a blinking red light on the master control board. Beneath it were four route-indicator maps, each similar to the one on the ferry: a small blue LED light was flashing on the far-right map indicating that the number four ferry was five hundred metres from the prison dock.

The senior controller reached for a button on the console and pushed it as he leaned towards a slender microphone protruding from it. 'Ferry four, this is Styx control room . . . Ferry four, this is Styx control room. Speak to me. Pick up the handset and speak to me!'

When no reply came the controllers looked at each other, unsure what to make of the lack of response. The operations-control technology was sophisticated when it came to the general running of the prison but there were few sensory or diagnostic transmissions from the ferries, apart from indications of the vessel's depth and its progress along the cables. Since the opening of the prison there had never been a problem with the ferries apart from some minor incidents and the OCR relied on the communications system and standard procedures to monitor the craft.

'Ferry four, this is Styx control,' the senior controller said again, frustrated that it was all he could do at that moment to contact the vessel. 'Do you copy?'

The only sound from the speakers was the gentle hiss of the carrier wave.

'Still moving towards us,' the assistant controller said, an observation that his boss could make for himself. 'Maybe it's an electrical glitch.'

'The alarm sounds and there's no one on the end of the radio?' the senior controller said. 'That's good enough for me something's gone seriously wrong. Alert the standby divers,' he ordered as he strode across the room and reached for a phone on the main console. 'Call the surface dock. Tell 'em to launch the rescue boats and to start looking for escape suits . . . Mr Mandrick,' he said into the phone. 'OCR duty officer. I think we have a situation . . . it could be a serious one.'

★

Gann had intentionally left the emergency escape-room door unbolted because the room needed to flood if his evidence during the inevitable subsequent investigation was going to be believed. It was that post-incident phase of the operation that had caused him his only misgivings about this task. If it was discovered that the ferry had been sabotaged then any investigation would become a murder inquiry. A motive would have to be found, which could lead to a scrutiny of the goings-on in the prison. If the feds learned that Gann was possibly involved his past would come flying out of the closet and he would never see the light of day again. Gann had a lot riding on the prison's future, hence the personal risk he was willing to take to save it. Everything would be fine as long as the incident looked like an accident.

As he zipped up his suit and positioned the hood on top of his head he pondered the risks to his own survival one more time. He looped the strap attached to the small diving bottle over one shoulder and faced the emergency escape tube. Water was streaming in through the gap in the open door to the main cabin and had reached the opening to the tube.

Gann got down onto his knees, felt for the hatch under the water and pushed it open against its counterweight springs. He took a breath, dipped below the surface, reached up into the tube and pulled himself inside. The tube was dry and he could breathe the air. He climbed up into the narrow space like a grub making its way back inside its cocoon, pulled his feet out of the water and stood on the inside rim of the hatch.

The tube was a tight fit for a man Gann's size and he had not forgotten how hard it had been to reach down and close the hatch during his training course. It had become easier once he'd developed a few techniques. He reached down with a foot and kicked the hatch away as hard as he could. When it sprang back up he caught the inside wheel with his foot and held the hatch shut while stretching one arm down. With an effort, he managed to get a couple of fingers to the wheel, his face pressing painfully against the tube's sides, and, aided by his foot, he turned the wheel several times to screw the locking cleats into place. When the wheel would turn no further Gann wiggled himself upright, his head an inch below the wheel of the top hatch and a small built-in light that shone in his face.

He looped the air-bottle harness over his head, making sure that he knew where the mouthpiece and mask were on the other end of the hose and, by the glow from the small light, he found the breathing tube that was plugged into the vessel's air supply. He placed the mouthpiece between his lips, took a couple of breaths to confirm it was working and turned the flood valve in front of him. Water immediately began to gush into the tube and bubble up over his legs.

'Palanski,' Stratton shouted. If the threat of drowning didn't wake the guard no amount of yelling was going to. Stratton felt around with his feet and found one of Palanski's legs. He dragged it closer with his heel and stamped on it repeatedly. 'Palanski! Get back here! Wake up!'

Palanski began to choke as the water lapped over his mouth. He suddenly made a move towards consciousness as his eyes fluttered open and he fought to raise his head out of the water.

'Palanski! Concentrate! You have to get us out of here! The chain-release lever. Palanski!'

Palanski battled to get a hold of himself as blood continued to seep from the wound on his head. He looked around, suddenly conscious of the desperation around him. Men were screaming, pulling at their chains. One was praying loudly, begging God to forgive him for his sins.

Palanski made an abortive move towards Stratton. But when he put his weight onto his broken elbow he cried out as the pain shot through him like a bolt of lightning.

'Fight it, Palanski!' Stratton shouted.

The sudden pain seemed to help Palanski stay conscious and he appeared more focused as he locked stares with Stratton.

'The chain release,' Stratton shouted. 'Get us out of here.'

The guard pushed himself away from the bulkhead with his good hand.

'That's good. Keep coming!'

Palanski reached out and Stratton offered an arm for the guard to take hold of. Palanski pulled himself alongside.

'Under my seat. The lever. You know where it is.'

Palanski nodded, his breathing laboured, and shuffled around to face the end of the row.

'Come on, Palanski!' the man beside Stratton shouted past him. 'All you gotta do is pull that fuckin' lever.'

Palanski reached down and felt for the box and the small opening on the face of it. His face dipped into the ever-rising water as he reached inside the opening and then he appeared to give up.

'Palanski. We're going to die if you don't get us out,' Stratton urged.

Palanski looked dazed. 'Gettin' . . . a . . . breath,' he muttered. He winced against the excruciating pain, then gritted his teeth, took a breath and plunged beneath the surface of the water that was now lapping at the prisoners' chests.

Ramos, shorter than the others, was crying out as he struggled to keep his chin above the froth.

Palanski surfaced, choking and coughing. 'Can't . . . can't reach it,' he stammered.

'It's there, Palanski! You know where it is. All you have to do is grab hold and pull it. Forget the pain. You'll have years to remember it.' Stratton was becoming stressed, his mind chasing ahead to what little he could do even if he did get free of his chains. The first problem was going to be everyone else. If Palanski did release them there would be half a dozen men thrashing around in an ever-decreasing space. It didn't look good and Stratton was starting to try and come to terms with the fact that he was not going to survive this one. There was just too much to overcome. The water was now up to his shoulders.

A high-pitched scream made him look over his shoulder to see Ramos going absolutely frantic, yelling insanely as he forced his mouth up above the rising water as far as it could possibly go. The water began to pour into it and he spat it out as quickly as he could.

Stratton looked back at Palanski in time to see him take a deep breath and disappear below the surface. He watched the swirling space that Palanski had occupied a second earlier, knowing that he himself would soon be beneath the water.

Ramos was spitting and gurgling as the water finally covered his mouth. He stretched to take another breath and his eyes bulged as he held on to the last few precious seconds of his life. He shook violently as he made a final Herculean effort to free his hands and then the water covered his eyes. Bubbles broke the surface around Ramos's head and he went still.

Stratton looked up at the ceiling but what he was seeing in his head was the chain-release mechanism, having studied it and every other device in the ferry and the prison that had anything to do with escape. It was a ring-shaped handle inside a tube in a box, not the most convenient design, low to the deck, intended to prevent easy access by a seated prisoner. Palanski had to get close to the floor and reach inside before he could grip the ring and pull it towards him.

As the water touched Stratton's chin he put his head back a little. He was cold but that was the least of his problems. His mind singled out the smell of the sea, an indication of how tuned his senses had become as adrenalin coursed through his body. The shouting had all but ceased. Stratton wondered how many prisoners were already dead. Those that still lived were, like him, coming to terms with the approaching end.

The water reached Stratton's mouth and as he automatically stretched his neck and head up to hang on for as long as he could he felt his hands move up an inch from the seat, enough for him to forget his imminent death for a moment. He took a breath, dropped his head below the water and felt between his thighs for the hook in the seat. Palanski had not managed to pull the handle all the way and had only partially released the securing cable. Stratton yanked on it with all his remaining strength. It suddenly came up another inch and he unhooked his chains and burst to the surface. A second later the man beside him appeared, spluttering and gulping for air. None of the others, including Palanski, joined them.

All Stratton could think of now was that he'd been given a little more time, only seconds perhaps, and that he had to find a way to survive this. He believed in his theory that there was always a solution, the only limitations being his inability to find it.

The airlock door to the OCR hissed and clunked as it opened inwards and Mandrick entered. 'What's the situation?' he calmly asked the senior controller who was standing at the console looking at a row of monitors. A couple of them showed murky, poorly lit exterior images. A white blob in the distance was the slowly approaching ferry.

'We think it could be flooded,' he said, looking vexed.

'It's rolling heavy,' the assistant controller offered. 'The buoyancy's way off. See how low in the water it is? It's almost in the milk,' he said, referring to the bizarre white phenomenon that covered the seabed like a mist in that part of the Gulf.

'Anything from the surface?' Mandrick asked.

'Nothing. They say it's pretty calm up there. If anyone makes it to the surface they'll see 'em . . . It's gonna go into the milk,' the senior controller said, stepping closer to the monitor.

Mandrick came alongside him to scrutinise the monitors. 'It's still moving.'

'Slow but coming on.'

'How long before it reaches the dock?' Mandrick asked.

'Four, maybe five minutes.'

Mandrick looked at the other monitors, one of them showing the arrivals dock where two men dressed in thick wetsuits were hurriedly donning tanks, aided by other guards. 'If it *is* full of water it won't be able to surface in the dock. Isn't that right?'

'Yes, sir,' the senior controller acknowledged. 'It'll be too heavy. Soon as it comes beneath the pool we'll stop it. The divers'll open it up right away and get some air in there.'

'What's your guess?' Mandrick asked him.

The controller shrugged as he stared at the monitor. 'I don't want to even begin to.'

Stratton and the surviving prisoner faced each other, illuminated by a dim emergency light, their heads pressed against the ceiling, the water at their chins.

'Any ideas?' the man asked, placing his hand against the relief valve that was still letting in water in a vain attempt to stop it.

'Top of my list is the emergency escape tube. Or we can try and get air in here using the console.'

'I don't know anything about the console but I can check out the escape tube.'

'If you can get up inside it there should be a breathing hose.'

'I'll come back and let you know,' the man said as he took a deep breath and disappeared.

Stratton couldn't help thinking how a promise to return was not something he would have expected from a desperate prisoner. He headed along the cabin, the bodies of the dead men in their seats under his feet. He stopped above the console where high-pressure air pipes entered the cabin from the tanks outside and then he ducked below the water to search for anything he could use to break one of them. The escaping air would increase the cabin pressure and stop the leaks. It might even reverse the flooding to some extent. But all he could find was the empty chain that the wrench had been attached to. He broke the surface to find the air gap even smaller and grabbed the air pipe in the hope it was loose. But it was solidly fixed to the bulkhead and with no tools he would die trying to break it with his hands.

The prisoner resurfaced, choking and gulping for air. He looked for Stratton, saw him at the other end of the cabin and made his way over to him. 'The hatch is shut tight. I tried to turn the wheel but I couldn't even budge it.'

That meant the outer hatch was open. There was a hand-crank mechanism for closing the outer hatch but Stratton was not sure exactly where it was located. If they could close it they would then need to drain the tube before opening the lower hatch. To do that they would need to operate the control valves which were located somewhere on the side of the tube. They simply did not have the time.

'What's next on your list?'

'This is all I have left,' Stratton said, gripping the wheel that operated the hatch of the docking system.

'We take a breath, open it and then what?' the man asked.

'Follow the cables to the dock.'

'That easier than heading for the surface?'

'Depends how close we are to the dock.'

They held their lips to the ceiling as the water lapped at their cheeks.

'The valve's stopped leaking,' the man observed, his lips beside it.

'We've got enough air for another minute. We go or we stay,' Stratton said, gripping the wheel.

The man glanced at him. 'I'm going for the surface,' he said after some thought.

'Take your boots off,' Stratton suggested as he ducked below the surface.

The man followed Stratton's lead and they removed their boots and socks. When they surfaced they both gripped the escape-hatch wheel.

'Which way you going?' the man asked, unsure of his choice.

'The dock.'

The man thought about it some more and for a second he found the funny side of it. 'Decisions, decisions,' he quipped.

'I hope it's not your last,' Stratton said sincerely. 'Good luck.'

'Name's Dan,' the man said.

'John.'

'Good luck to you, John. Hope to see you again.'

They tugged at the wheel and it began to turn. Water seeped in through the seal, the flow increasing with each revolution of the wheel. Stratton took a final deep breath as the air gap disappeared.

Gann filled the narrow escape chamber, his eyes blinking in the murky water, air escaping from the sides of his mouthpiece with every exhalation as he heaved up the outer escape hatch. After the initial effort it opened easily and the remaining air in the tube combined with the bubbles escaping from Gann's mouthpiece and made its way up into the gloom. He looked up to see the ferry cables illuminated by the dim light from inside the tube and felt around his body for the air bottle attached to the nylon harness looped around his neck. He found the valve on the end of the bottle and followed the hose to the attached mask and mouthpiece.

Gann made ready to swap breathing devices. He hoped he had calculated the distance correctly and that he had enough air to get to the dock once he left the safety of the tube. But there was one major thing bothering him, despite the dangers of the moment, and that was Palanski.

When the time came to be questioned about his actions Gann had planned to say that the ferry flooded so quickly that he'd charged into the emergency escape room to organise the suits and escape tube while Palanski was supposed to free the prisoners. By the time Gann got his suit on the ferry was almost completely flooded. When he went back to find Palanski there was no sign of him and the water was already above the heads of the prisoners who had obviously drowned.

The big problem was how he was going to explain Palanski's injuries. He had never intended to give Palanski a beating. Palanski wasn't supposed to have attacked him. The only way that Gann could resolve this problem was to go back into the ferry to remove Palanski's body entirely. He could open the outer docking hatch and adjust his story to make it appear that Palanski had not unchained the prisoners as ordered and had in fact panicked and opened the escape hatch, killing everyone. There were a few holes but it was better than leaving Palanski's corpse inside the ferry. If he hurried he might be able to get away with it.

Gann took a deep breath, removed the mouthpiece attached to the escape tube and pulled the full-face mask over his head. Holding the top of the mask firmly against his forehead he exhaled through his nose in order to remove the water in the mask by forcing it out of the bottom. He managed to do this after a couple of breaths, having learned the technique in the diving course he had attended as part of his pre-prison officer training.

He pulled himself out of the tube but did not take account of the motion of the ferry moving through the water. As he emerged he was forced against the side of the hatch, which he grabbed in a moment of panic. He had not reckoned on how travelling at even a slow speed underwater could create such a force. He looked ahead to see if the dock was close, discovering in the process that the ferry was almost in the milk. It was like some strange underwater snow scene. He'd seen the strange substance from the prison windows but it looked even more surreal from this close. Above the white blanket in the distance was a collection of hazy lights; the ferry cables led to the largest cluster, which marked the entrance to the dock. He gauged it to be a hundred yards or so.

The force of the water suddenly decreased, indicating that the ferry was as usual reducing its approach speed. Gann then realised the ferry was actually going to sink beneath the surface of the strange milk.

He turned around to face the docking hatch when, to his utter amazement, a stream of bubbles began to escape from around its edges and it slowly opened. Gann's reaction was immediate.

Mandrick stood with the two controllers, staring at the images on the OCR monitors. The screens appeared to be split, the bottom half white, the top black, with a murky white ferry in the middle dropping deeper into the white section. They all saw the blurred images of movement on the top of the ferry just below the cable struts.

'Looks like someone getting out,' the senior controller said.

'It's the emergency escape hatch,' said his assistant.

'We're going to lose them in the milk,' the senior controller said as he grabbed the mike. 'Send in the divers. Now!' he shouted into the handset.

Gann pushed himself towards the figure coming out of the hatch. He had no idea who it was but that did not matter. No one could survive the ferry now, and not just because it was the original plan that every prisoner should perish. A survivor could accuse Gann of the sabotage. With the power of the water at his back he struck the man forcefully, wrapping his arms around him and hauling him from the opening. The momentum and the force of the water carried them along the top of the ferry and off the end.

Stratton was just below the other prisoner when he felt him shoot from the hatch as if snatched by something passing overhead. But there was not a second to spare to consider what had happened. He pushed himself free of the hatch and up towards the cables. The ferry began to slow to a crawl, cancelling any thoughts he'd had about simply hanging on and hoping he could last until it reached the dock.

He hit the cables and grabbed hold of one, immediately dragging himself forward. He could make out a dim light ahead and pulled for all he was worth. He kept telling himself that the dock was within his range and he could make it. But suddenly the light ahead disappeared and everything became murky white. Stratton immediately remembered the 'milk' that was known to surround the prison most of the year round. The cable had dropped into it, dragged down by the weight of the flooded ferry.

Stratton's lungs began to cry out for air. The lights had been a psychological hub, something he could have used to focus on and help blank out the pain. All he could do now was imagine them getting closer with each pull and simply keep going until he rose up into the dock or went unconscious.

He pulled in a rhythmic motion, one arm over the other, his legs trailing behind him. He fought the urge to increase the pace and concentrated on keeping the pulls firm and controlled. The last time Stratton had swum underwater for any distance had been many years before. Fifty metres was the distance he'd been required to swim that day, two lengths of the camp pool as part of a general diving-fitness test. And he'd had to collect a brick off the bottom of the five-metre deep end before finally surfacing. But on that occasion he'd had a chance to practise a couple of times. Even then he had only barely made it. This time he had the additional incentive of death – which had to be worth a few metres more.

His face began to tighten and the palpable increase in fear made him pick up the pace. He prayed the cable would rise out of the milk, which would mean he was very close. He wanted to see the lights again. They would give him hope for another few seconds. If not, this was it. Stratton was going to perish at the bottom of the Gulf of Mexico after all. For a split second, in desperation, he almost let go of the cable to swim out of the milk. But his cold logic kept hold of him and refused to give his hands the permission. The cable led to air and dragging himself was quicker than swimming. It was that or die.

But the urge to open his mouth and suck in anything to relieve the increasing pain of oxygen debt only grew. His face tightened further and felt as if it was going to explode. His arms pulled faster, all discipline gone now. His fingers tingled, his temples throbbed. He had seconds to arrive in the dock or he was finished. His lungs were on fire, his heart pounding in his chest like a drum. His mouth started to open and his grip on the cable loosened. There was nothing left, no more oxygen, his last drop of will-power. The carbon dioxide saturating his body demanded that he open his mouth, insisting he draw in whatever there was. He entered the state of madness that accompanies a total lack of oxygen and he stopped, released the cable and inhaled.

The spasms began and he fought to hold on to his soul. The white changed to dark and he could see a light ahead. And then suddenly it all went quiet and serene. The pain that had tightened his face and body had gone and he drifted like a spirit in space, as if he had already left the water, all human senses gone. He could see himself, knew he had passed into another place and he did not care. The power that drove his life had ceased. Stratton was dead.

Chapter 9

Mandrick walked out through the hissing airlock of the OCR as it closed behind him and headed along a broad steel walkway suspended inside a black rock cavern. The OCR entrance hissed again seconds later as the senior controller emerged from it at a pace calculated to let him catch up with Mandrick before he reached the top of a broad stairway. The cavern echoed with the clatter of their feet as both men hurried along briskly. The controller, wearing a slender headset over one ear, listened intently as he followed Mandrick closely along a lower platform to another airlock door. A small red glass screen required Mandrick's thumbprint which it analysed before turning green. As with just about every other door in the facility, any minor pressure difference on either side of it needed to be equalised before the air-seal was withdrawn and access permitted.

'The standby diver's brought in a body, sir,' the controller said, pressing the earpiece closer to his ear to help cut out the sound of vents and metallic clunking that filled the everyday air in Styx. 'And one more . . . alive . . . it's Gann, sir.'

The door opened and Mandrick walked through while listening to the operations controller but without making any form of acknowledgement. He needed to act like a warden who had just experienced the worst catastrophe of his career, dealing with the horror of half a dozen souls lost, not all of them inmates, while at the same time maintaining calm and control. But he was having problems acting the horrified-warden part – acting was something he had never been any good at anyway. Mandrick had other things on his mind. Now that the deed was done something else was disturbing him, a premonition he'd had shortly after accepting the order to neutralise the new arrivals. Whatever had been achieved this day was going to give birth to even greater problems. And greater problems usually meant having to formulate proportionately more drastic solutions.

The two men made their way down a short flight of broad steps cut into the stone and reinforced with steel and concrete. Vegetation grew down the walls, large clumps of it in places. At the bottom was a bulky, robust steel door made of layers of riveted plates and covered in a dozen coats of thick red paint that had failed to prevent patches of corrosion. The area had become noticeably more humid, the walls moist and covered in mildew, the rock ceiling dotted with stalactites that dripped onto their opposite numbers on the uneven rocky surface beneath the metal-grid floor.

'The ferry's come to a stop below the dock,' the controller reported as he moved ahead to open the door.

The door was an exterior access point and required a higher level of clearances as well as a series of preliminary safety and security checks.

'Senior OC requires access to gate four Charlie,' the controller said into his mike as he punched a code into a keypad on the wall. 'Release four Charlie dock primary.'

After a brief pause a heavy clunk came from inside the door. The controller checked the pressure levels on several gauges beside the door as part of a mandatory procedure before punching in another code. 'Pressures are equalised . . . Release four Charlie secondary.'

Another clunk and the controller grabbed a large wheel on the side of the door and, with a little difficulty at first, began to turn it. After a couple of heaves it practically spun around at only a light touch. When the dozen cleats that surrounded the frame were clear of the breaches the massive door moved perceptibly outwards as cold air rushed in through the seams. The controller gave it a shove to help the electric motor on the hinge and the door slowly opened.

Mandrick stepped through into a large cavern hewn out of the rock and reinforced by steel girders and concrete. Every surface seemed to be contaminated by some variety of kelp and mildew, some of the ceiling species several metres long. The two men paused on a steel-and-concrete landing facing a pool the size of a couple of tennis courts, its water gently lapping several inches below the edge. Four separate clusters of taut dirty-brown heavy-duty cables rose out of the water and passed over large wheels suspended from the ceiling before heading back down. A lone ferry was parked at the far end with the number '1' stencilled on its surface in places. The water looked black, reflecting the dark rock, although it was crystal clear. The doomed ferry was visible several metres below a placard on the wall that had the number '4' stencilled on it behind the strings of vertical cables. A diver was making his way around the ferry, a line attached to him, its other end held by a guard on the landing.

Mandrick looked along the landing to where a metal ladder curved from the jetty into the pool. Several men were gathered in a circle, one of them wearing a diving suit, a set of dive-tanks close by. The other men were prison guards, all bent over a body lying prone on the wet concrete. Standing back a little from the group was Gann, pulling off his bright yellow escape suit as he kept an interested eye on the group's activities.

Mandrick glanced back to the number four ferry below the surface and saw the cables wobble as the diver pulled on the side door with some effort. He looked ahead at the group of men and walked towards them.

Gann's gaze met Mandrick's for a second as he closed in. The diver was giving cardiac massage to the man lying on the ground, pushing down on his chest in a quick rhythm. A guard stood aside to let Mandrick enter the circle as the dripping-wet diver halted the compressions long enough to feel for the man's carotid artery. A guard kneeling the other side of the body looked into the diver's face for signs of hope. The diver showed none as he recommenced his pumping action.

'I can spell ya, Zack,' the kneeling guard offered.

'I'm OK,' the diver replied.

A guard arrived and quickly placed a mask over the body's mouth, turned on an oxygen bottle connected to it and squeezed a bag attached to the mask, filling the body's lungs.

The man looked dead to Mandrick. His eyes were slightly open, water was trickling out the side of his mouth and his only movement was caused by the diver's efforts. Mandrick was reminded of the first time he had given a man the same last chance for life. Three times he had gone through the process during his military days and had never won back any of them. All three had bled away beneath him. The diver was obviously a tenacious bugger, or something was inspiring him to hold on.

The man with the air bottle checked his watch. The rule in the prison for cardiac massage was eight minutes. Mandrick had done his three for about a minute each, not much more. He'd known the men were dead before he had started but he had continued anyway. He'd had the time and people were watching. Maybe that was why this guy was still doing it.

'Sir,' the controller said and Mandrick turned around to look at him. 'Diver's inside the ferry and it isn't good. He counts four prisoners and Palanski – all dead.'

Mandrick looked back at Gann to find the man staring at him. He looked as if he was asking him for some kind of acknowledgement. Whatever doubts Mandrick had had about Gann's insanity were gone. The man was deranged, to say the least.

'I think we got something,' the diver called out excitedly.

Gann's expression blackened as his eyes snapped to the man lying at their feet. The diver's fingers were deep into his neck to one side of his throat. 'Yeah – we got a beat,' he said. 'Weak but I'm sure of it. The gurney on its way?' he called out.

'Doc's on his way down,' the controller informed everyone.

'Way to go, Zack,' one of the guards said, patting the diver on the shoulder.

Mandrick glanced at Gann who was staring at the lone survivor. Mandrick's initial thought was what the odds were on him being the fed. Even if it was it would not be smart to kill him now. No matter how much of an accident it looked. It would seem far too suspicious. Mandrick's prime objective was survival and he did not want to do anything that implicated himself in too obvious a manner. He had pushed it way too far as it was. One man was easy enough to keep an eye on. And there was always the possibility that he had suffered serious brain damage.

'Anyone know his name?' the diver asked.

The senior controller flicked through his file of the incoming prisoners, pausing at each picture. 'Charon,' he said. 'Nathan Charon.'

'Come on, Nathan,' the diver said. 'You can make it. Breathe. That's it. All right. He's back.'

Stratton opened his eyes to see a chequered steel mesh with bright lights spaced at uneven intervals set into the ceiling behind it. Fatigue tugged heavily at his eyelids but he fought to keep them open. The feeling of utter exhaustion lay on him like a lead shroud and he wondered how long he had been lying there. He fought to remain conscious, trying to remember what had happened and how he had ended up in what seemed like a small, clean hospital room. He knew who he was and that he had been on a submersible cable-car heading for an undersea prison. But other recent memories appeared to be missing or fractured. He remembered the ferry flooding and his desperation to get out of it. From the point of leaving the ferry he was unable to piece together the snippets of sounds and images he retained into a coherent pattern of events. He could see the face of a man and hear his voice while water lapped around his neck. The face of another prisoner appeared and Stratton remembered opening the hatch with him. After that it was all a confused blur.

He wanted to look around the room to see if there were other occupied beds but his head felt as if it was bolted to the pillow.

Stratton could hear a tapping noise as if it was floating around in his head all alone. He was unsure if it was a memory or if it was really happening. As he fought to collect the jumble of images speeding through his mind the tapping seemed to get louder. He couldn't lie still any longer and, desperate for clarity, fought to activate the muscles in his neck and turn his head. He slowly rolled it to one side but his eyes would not readily refocus and he looked back up at the ceiling. The mesh was clear but when he turned to look at the room again it was as if his eyes were jammed and unable to adjust.

Fear crept through him as he suddenly wondered what other parts of him no longer functioned. He broke into a cold sweat at the thought of being an invalid and concentrated on moving his arms. They rose up off his stomach where they came into focus and he let them back down with a feeling of relief. Next he had to see if he still had his legs. With a supreme effort he raised his head off the pillow until he could see two ridges under the sheet going from his hips to small mounds at the ends of them. They moved from side to side at his will and he dropped his head back with another heavy sigh of relief.

Stratton began to scan the rest of his body with his mind, tensing various muscles and then relaxing them. Suddenly, the ceiling light he had been staring at was replaced by the face of a beautiful dark-haired woman looking down at him. Her complexion was pale, her eyes and lips dark within the shadow of the light behind her. He was sure she was real only because he could suddenly smell her, a fresh soapy aroma. It was odd because his sense of smell had never been particularly acute. Perhaps he had been reborn, or he was in heaven and this was an angel.

'You're back, then,' she said, without a trace of emotion, looking at one of his eyes and then the other in search of something.

Stratton could only blink up at her. The total absence of a smile or any trace of cordiality ruled out paradise.

'What's your name?' she asked. Her voice was soft but at the same time strong, and her accent was American.

Stratton started to open his mouth but found it difficult, his lips sticking as if they had begun the process of healing together.

The woman moved out of his sight to reach for something and when her face returned she put a straw to his mouth. 'Have some water.'

He took a sip, feeling the cold liquid pass through his mouth and down his throat like the first rains along a parched river bed.

'Do you remember your name?' she asked again.

A dim alarm throbbed inside his head as his training and years of experience warned him never to talk unless he was compos mentis. Then he realised he couldn't remember the answer to her question anyway. He knew his real name but he also remembered that he had a cover. The false identity was just beyond his reach. He thought he saw it flit across his mind but he couldn't get hold of it. He found the image of the man sitting in the back of the prison truck. He saw Paul and Todd. And then the name was suddenly there in front of him. Nathan Charon. Then it was as if the effort had triggered the bursting of a bubble of information inside his head as other elements of his assignment fell into place.

Stratton decided to ignore the woman's question until he had gathered more information on who she was and on his own situation. One of the most important questions he needed an answer to was whether or not he still had a mission. Where on Earth he was would be a good start.

He tried to bend his arm to bring it under his shoulder but what should have been a simple effort proved difficult. He felt eighty years old.

'You want to sit up?' she asked.

Stratton nodded. The woman made a poor effort to help him, unsure where to hold him. This suggested she was not accustomed to helping someone sit up in a bed. That seemed to rule out nurse or doctor as her job. She was wearing jeans and a sweatshirt, both clean but not the usual attire of a professional. As she gripped his shoulder he could feel her strength. She was slender but strong and athletic. Nothing about her was adding up yet.

She pulled the bedclothes away to allow him to slide his feet off the mattress and onto the floor. He was wearing a tracksuit that he did not recognise. His body ached all over. The discomfort reminded him of the time when he'd fallen halfway down the side of a snow-covered mountain in Norway after narrowly avoiding a small avalanche.

Stratton looked around, his ability to focus gradually improving. He realised he was actually inside a steel cage in a corner of a room. The bars went from floor to ceiling on two sides and the door was open. The room beyond looked like a cross between an office and a laboratory. There was a desk with a lamp, pens, paper and a computer. A long workbench was against one wall, next to a row of glass cabinets filled with medical paraphernalia. Another counter was bedecked with technical apparatus and on the wall there was a flat-screen monitor that was switched off. The aspect of the situation that struck him most was that his was the only bed.

Behind the desk was a window with a clear view outside. There were skyscrapers, the central one of which was familiar: the Empire State building. He was looking at the top half from a similar height which meant he was in another Manhattan skyscraper. The mission was over. He had failed. After surviving the ferry he'd been transported to a surface hospital in New York. But then who was this woman and why was he not with his own people? The feeling that he should stay on his guard intensified.

'Where am I?' Stratton asked.

'You were going to tell me your name,' the woman said. The chill in her voice did not alter.

He wondered why she was asking for his name. Surely she knew who he was. If she didn't then who the hell was she? He decided to give her something. Until he was sure that the op was at an end he would continue to play the game. 'Nathan . . . Nathan Charon.'

He caught her expression just before she turned away and he had the feeling that she was disappointed. Or perhaps it was irritation. He looked out of the window as a bird flew close to the ledge before veering away. 'How long have I been here?' he asked.

'Two days,' she said, walking out of the cage without closing the door and leaning against the steel work surface of the counter from where she could study him.

He did the same, noting her sneakers, her strong, shapely legs, her square shoulders. This girl was in shape and was also very pleasing to the eye.

'Do you remember what happened?' she asked.

'I remember the ferry flooding,' he said, looking at a row of bottles containing different-coloured liquids on top of the medical cabinets behind her. It was certainly an odd-looking hospital room.

'Where are you from, Nathan?'

The question highlighted an aspect of this charade that Stratton had been most uncomfortable with. Charon was from Vermont but a cover story of years in the UK was intended to explain Stratton's English accent. The background details had been placed in Charon's file but Stratton's problem was not so much the alleged period during which he'd lived in the UK, it was the rest of his life, supposedly spent in Vermont. He'd read a brief prepared by the analysts but it would never be enough to get him off the hook if he was questioned. If the woman pushed the issue he would go to the emergency plan for that eventuality which was to go on the offensive and demand to see his lawyer if they were going to interrogate him. 'Vermont, originally. But I moved around a lot.'

'England, I suppose.'

'I spent a lot of years there.'

She took her time with her questions as if weighing each answer carefully.

'What happened on the ferry?'

She was cutting right to the chase. 'It began to flood. One of the guards released our chains.'

'Go on.'

The girl was acting more like an investigator or interrogator. He wondered about revealing Gann's part in the incident but decided it was in his best interests to appear to remember nothing. Once he became an integral part of the investigation it would detract from his purpose – if he had any purpose left, that was. 'I can remember hardly anything. I don't seem to remember getting on board, even. Certainly nothing after we climbed out of the escape hatch.'

'We?'

'I was with one other prisoner.'

She looked down at her feet. Stratton decided she was not a professional interrogator. She gave too much away with her eyes and body language. Something wasn't right about her. Whatever her job was it was privileged or she would not be here. She had rank. He would have expected the first person to question him to be highly qualified. She looked as if she was in her late twenties or early thirties. Subtract the years spent in college getting the degrees a person in her position would need and she could not have been in her job very long. She was acting professional but it was just that: an act. She had little real experience of what she was doing. That was obvious to someone like him, at least. It made his circumstances even more curious.

'Where is he?' Stratton asked.

'You and one of the guards were the only survivors.'

Stratton saw an image of Dan leaving the hatch just before him. He felt sorry for the man.

The bird returned to the window ledge before veering away again. Stratton realised there were no bars on the window. That didn't make sense. He was in a detention centre of sorts but one without bars on the windows. There would have to be some kind of exit control no matter how high up from the street the room was. The door into the room was made of frosted glass. The bird returned to the window but this time he realised there was something odd about it. The bird was performing exactly the same action every time.

'What am I doing in New York?' he asked.

The girl looked at the window and rolled her eyes, walked behind the desk, reached for the side of the frame and flicked a switch. The image disappeared. 'Doctor Mani thinks it's healthy to at least maintain a sense of natural surroundings down here.'

'I'm in Styx?' Stratton asked.

'Sorry if it confused you,' she said, without sounding sorry at all.

Stratton felt a sudden partial relief. But a residual fear remained. He was still on the mission, as far as he could tell, but it was all going wrong. Six men were dead, the cause of their deaths was sinister and he had only barely survived. The need to proceed with extreme caution was paramount. 'You a doctor?' he asked.

'No. I'm a prison inspector. I work for the Federal Bureau of Prisons, the programme-review division.'

She spoke as if it was a declaration, a statement of fact, defining her position clearly to him. Her attitude towards him was still hard to pin down. She was cold and authoritative, confident and aggressive. But she was not talking down to him.

She looked as if she was struggling with a thought. 'You have a problem,' she decided to reveal.

He couldn't begin even to guess what she meant.

The girl leaned on the desk and tapped the keypad on a laptop. The screen came to life and she turned it to face him. It was a copy of Nathan Charon's prison file.

'You've put me in a difficult position.'

'I don't understand.'

'You're not Nathan Charon.'

Stratton forced a smirk while at the same time trying to deal with this most dangerous development. Everything seemed to be unravelling before he could even get his foot in the bloody door of the place. 'Do I have brain damage?'

It was a pathetic effort which she was not even going to waste a second on. 'Who do you work for?' she insisted.

'I don't know what you mean.'

'Prior to your arrival at Styx your personal file was wired here from the Vermont Department of Corrections. The files of the other inmates were likewise wired from their respective state corrections departments. You also arrived with hard copies, which were recovered from the ferry. The files from the Vermont Department of Corrections and your hard copies match. The problem is that neither of your files match the one I have. I received mine from the Federal Bureau of Prisons Atlantic regional office. Whoever set you up as Nathan Charon was powerful enough to change your state file but not influential enough to alter your *federal* records – either that or they overlooked them. Your photograph is close, but it's not you. Most damning are your fingerprints. I did a comparison and they don't match. More interesting is that they don't match anyone's records. Not even the FBI's. I checked. Either you never had a US driving licence or you're a foreigner who skipped Immigration on his way into the US. You don't work for the CIA because there are enough of them down here already. But you *do* work for someone in the US government otherwise you couldn't have got in here.'

Stratton could only look at the girl blankly. He was well and truly busted. But there was something curious about the way she was presenting her findings. She seemed to be acting independently, for one thing. Another oddity was that there was no locked door between them, as if the fact that he was not a threat was a given. He thought about revealing his cover story about being an independent security surveyor. But his instincts warned him to keep that to himself for the moment. It was his get-out-of-jail card and he wasn't ready to get out yet. Perhaps there was mileage to be gained from her thinking that he was a US-government-sponsored implant, which technically he was. That put them on the same side, as long as she was who she said she was. 'What now?' he asked.

She went to her laptop, closed it and put it in a small briefcase which she zipped up. 'Do you know why they sabotaged the ferry?'

He did not but neither did he want to admit that he knew it had been sabotaged – not yet, at any rate. She was probably guessing anyway.

The young woman seemed to read his mind. 'You weren't the only undercover prisoner on the ferry. They either knew about you or about him.' She stared at him, waiting for something back. He just looked at her. 'Christ, you're some kind of asshole. I'm sticking my neck out here and you're giving me nothing.'

It did indeed appear that she had gone over the top to help him. By admitting she knew there was a fed on board and the reason for the sabotage she was also coming clean about her true affiliations. It was doubtful that she was one of the bad guys looking for a confession because she wouldn't need any more than she already had on him. 'What do you want from me?' Stratton asked.

'Something that tells me I haven't risked making myself vulnerable for nothing.'

They locked stares. She could sense he was no longer suspicious of her and, although she had initially been concerned over giving away too much about herself, it did calm her fears. She had not wanted to give him anything at first but her conscience would not allow her to ignore the danger he was in. He was clearly a US government employee and had almost died trying to do his job. It was a miracle he had survived. But he was still in serious danger and she could not turn her back on that. On the flip side, she could not do much to help him, either. It was all down to what kind of a man he was.

'Does anyone else know?' Stratton asked.

She shook her head. 'You want my advice, whatever panic button you have that gets you out of here, I'd push it now.'

It was sound advice, but he was not ready to act on it quite yet. 'I appreciate what you've done,' he said sincerely. 'Trust me, I do . . . I'm going to stay.'

His appreciation seemed genuine and that was good enough for her. He had come clean. She had never expected him to tell her which department he worked for or the details of his task although it was obvious enough. Everyone but the CIA wanted the facility closed down. His intention to stay on track with his task, considering what had happened to him and the dangers that remained, revealed a quality that impressed her. She could sense that she was in the company of no ordinary man.

There was a hiss from the next room that alerted them to someone arriving.

The girl quickly closed Stratton's cage door, picked up her bag and walked to the entrance. 'We probably won't meet again,' she said, reaching for the door. 'Good luck.'

'You too,' he said.

She paused for a second before opening the door and Stratton thought he saw her expression soften. She closed the door behind her.

He could hear her talking with a man for a few seconds then there was another loud hiss and a clunk. A moment later the frosted-glass door opened and a portly Indian man wearing the classic uniform of a doctor – a white coat and a stethoscope poking out of his breast pocket – walked in. He looked over his glasses at Stratton. 'Ah. Lazarus rises. And if you're not a Christian I don't mean to offend. How are you feeling?' he said cheerily, his Indian accent only barely perceptible behind some North American overtone whose identity Stratton could not begin to guess.

'Fine,' Stratton replied.

The doctor looked across the room at the false window and made a beeline for it. 'My name's Doctor Mani. I expect you're thirsty,' he said as he toggled the switch on the side of the frame until the New York skyline returned. The bird immediately attempted to land on the ledge. 'There. Can't stand the feeling I'm under the water all the time. I understand they're considering providing something like this for the inmates' cells. Or is it the galley? Yes, I think it's the galley. A bit of atmosphere during mealtimes. They come in practically any landscape. I think they even have one of Mars, though God only knows who would want to feel they were on another planet. As if this place wasn't enough,' he added as he adjusted the brightness and then stood back to admire it. 'Now then, soon as we have a drink I'll run a series of tests, see how you're coming along, and then let's see if we can get you back into the mainstream as soon as possible.'

Stratton remained seated on the edge of the bed, wondering what this man had done to deserve his job.

'Cat got your tongue?'

Stratton looked up at the doctor. He was still feeling unwell and was content to make it appear he was worse than he was.

'Can you hear me? Can you talk?' Dr Mani asked, putting on a professional smile.

'I can hear you OK.'

'Good . . . Now,' the doctor said, reaching for a small plastic container, 'first thing I need is a urine sample. Can you manage that for me?' he asked, handing the container to Stratton.

Stratton took it and forced a smile.

'I'll leave you alone for a moment,' the doctor said, leaving the room.

Stratton held the container and sighed. He decided now that he was in Styx he had officially begun his mission. He thought if he looked at it that way he could put behind him all the mishaps so far and start afresh. He was not surprised that this perception had not made him feel the slightest bit better.

Christine walked along a broad central corridor, the rock walls and ceiling dripping water onto a suspended shroud, intended to protect pedestrians, and on the outer edges of the metal walkway. A couple of prisoners wearing face masks and canisters on their backs were spraying the mildew and weeds that gathered in the crevices. A guard stood idly by. 'Mornin', mam,' he said as she passed, eyeing her bottom. The prisoners paused to do the same.

Christine ignored them and headed along the corridor, the sound of her footsteps mingling with the noises of running water moving along channels beneath her feet and hissing air ducts above. An indistinct voice came over a loudspeaker further down the tunnel, followed by what sounded like a gong. The prison provided a kind of talking clock accompanied by various sounds but as far as she could tell it was grossly inaccurate. Like so many aspects of the prison, the seeds of good intention were visible but the execution was abysmal.

She headed up a spiral staircase inside a vertical rock tunnel that opened into a spacious cavern. It was constructed of a combination of steel girders, concrete and rock. One wall had a line of large round portholes, the six-inch-thick glass yellow with reflections from outside lights that illuminated any creatures that passed by. There was a single large white airlock door in the cavern that was more ornate than the others, suggesting it was an 'exclusive' entrance. She pushed a button on the side of the door and looked at a camera in front of her.

'Give me one minute, would you, please,' a metallic voice asked.

Christine turned her back on the camera. She knew she looked as distracted as she felt and made an effort to calm herself. She crossed her arms and then quickly unfolded them, dangling them at her sides until her laptop case almost fell off her shoulder. It wasn't just the Nathan Charon situation that was unnerving her. The mysterious agent was an issue but was the least of her concerns at that moment. Time was her problem and compounding the pressure on her. It was running out and she had not yet devised a plan to complete her mission.

The door hissed and clunked behind her and she turned to watch it move back into its frame before it rolled out to one side.

Christine walked into Mandrick's office as the door hissed again and closed behind her.

Mandrick was seated at his desk facing her but he was looking at a computer monitor while he tapped at a keyboard. When he finished he unplugged a minicomputer from a cable attached to the mainframe and got to his feet. She watched as he clipped it onto his belt, averting her eyes as he looked at her.

'Christine,' he said, beaming as he walked from behind his desk, a hand outstretched to greet her. 'You always bring a smile to my heart whenever I see you.' He took her hand and kissed her on the cheek, clearly savouring the contact.

She smiled, struggling to make it look as natural as possible.

He held her gaze beyond cordiality before she broke it off, appearing to be a touch embarrassed.

'I can't help being forward with you,' he said. 'I have such little time left to impress you.'

'You impress me, Pieter. No need to worry about that.'

'Oh? How?'

'You run the most dangerous prison in the world for the most powerful country in the world. That's impressive.'

'And that's all that impresses you about me . . . my job?'

'No. But that's all we're going to talk about right now . . . What does a girl have to do to get a cup of coffee around here?'

Mandrick reluctantly broke away from her and walked over to an ornate wooden dresser with a couple of thermos flasks on a tray alongside some cups. 'When do you leave?' he asked as he filled two cups with the black liquid.

'I have a couple more inmates to interview, a guard or two. That's me pretty much finished.'

'Which prisoners would you like to interview?' he asked as he passed her a cup.

'You choose,' she said and shrugged, taking a sip. 'I'm just playing the numbers game.'

'You haven't asked to see any of our political prisoners.' He gave her a sideways glance.

'I told you the day I arrived. This inspection is apolitical. I'm here to review health and living conditions for staff and inmates . . . To tell you the truth, those Taliban guys scare the hell out of me.'

Mandrick stared at Christine for a moment, his smile growing thin. 'I don't believe you,' he said, his expression serious.

'What don't you believe?' she asked, her smile hanging in there.

'I don't believe you scare that easily. I know potency when I see it. Particularly in a woman.'

'I'm sure you're very experienced. But you're wrong this time,' she said. 'I'm a pussycat.'

His eyes flicked to her body, unable to resist looking at it. 'And how is our Mr Charon?' he asked. 'You've spent quite a lot of time with him since he arrived.'

Christine shrugged. 'I was waiting for him to regain consciousness. I'm going to be asked questions about the ferry incident.'

'There'll be an official enquiry.'

'Yes, but I was here when it happened. I'll have to refer to it in my report. I'll probably get roped into the inquiry.'

'Good. So we will see more of you.'

'Not down here, I hope.'

'My sentiments exactly.'

Mandrick was giving her the creeps and she hoped it didn't show.

'What did Charon have to say?'

'Aren't you going to talk to him yourself?'

'Of course. But you hogged his initial reaction.'

Christine made a show of rolling her eyes at the word 'hogged'. The subtle implication that she had a special interest in seeing Charon first was not lost on her. Mandrick often made little digs that suggested she was doing more than merely inspecting the prison. Sometimes she wondered if he really did know what she was doing and was just playing her along because he fancied his chances of getting her into bed. 'He can't remember much about it,' she said. 'All he recalls is the ferry flooding, the guard freeing them and him getting out of the hatch. I think he's just thankful to be alive.'

Mandrick considered her answer as he sipped his coffee, his eyes lowering to admire her body again. When he looked back at her face she forced another smile.

'Let's get down to more important matters,' he said. 'When you've finished your task I'm going to escort you back to Houston and take you to dinner. And until you promise me that you will accompany me I can't guarantee that any of the ferries will be working.'

'How can I refuse such charming blackmail?' she said.

'It wasn't an idle threat.'

'I didn't think it was,' she said, looking away.

'Why do I get the feeling that deep down you really don't like me? Or am I being too sensitive?'

'No. You're not . . . I despise you. But you've discovered one of my darkest secrets,' Christine said, putting down her cup and stepping closer to him. 'There's always been something sinister about the men I'm most attracted to. It's a good sign if I start off by loathing you.' Her face was inches from his.

'Not the characteristics of a pussycat,' he said. Mandrick enjoyed the closeness but despite her forwardness he could feel the wall between them as if it was made of granite. He trusted no one at the best of times but Christine was an uninvited and unwanted guest over whom he had limited control. He would be a fool to believe she was a mere inspector. He would doubt her as a matter of course but something about her made that doubt more emphatic. Even so, he would still scheme to bed her even if she turned out to be an undercover Supreme Court judge. Every time he saw her all he could think about was how she would look naked. He wondered if she deliberately wore tight jeans just to taunt him. He would have taken her to his bed while she was in the prison if she had allowed him to. But she was proving difficult to ensnare.

It was all a part of that wall between them. They ate dinner together every evening, along with the doctor and any visiting engineers as was normal when there were guests. But when the others were ready to leave Christine departed with them. He wondered if she would evade their dinner date in Houston. Without a doubt, there was something phoney about her. But her body was real and desirable enough and he wanted her despite his doubts.

The phone on his desk rang. 'Excuse me,' Mandrick said as he walked over and picked it up. He talked in a low voice, the background hum that seemed to permeate every corner of the prison helping to mask his words. He removed his minicomputer, opened the cover, selected one of a dozen micro data-storage cards and inserted it into the side of the device. After pushing several command icons he gave the caller some information.

Christine stared at the device. It had become the holy grail of her mission, the final phase before she could get out of the damned place. She had been sent to reconnoitre the prison and look for information. Her brief was not actually to acquire that information but to pinpoint its location. Any more would have been asking too much of her. Further ops would be devised to obtain it.

But Christine wanted to complete the mission in one go. She promised herself not to take unnecessary risks but the drive to get the computer was strong in her. Technical attacks against the prison and corporation data files had failed to produce anything of value. From the moment she first saw the minicomputer she knew it contained everything Mandrick reckoned was secret. If she could get hold of it, or the memory cards, she would have achieved far more than she had come for. If she left the prison that minute and reported her find her mission would have been a success. But she was impetuous and hungry for success. She knew it was recklessness encouraged by her ego. Still, the closer she got to Mandrick, or the closer she allowed him to get to her, the more she believed she could succeed. If she attempted it while she was in the prison it would be a two-phase operation: first to get her hands on the material, second to get it and herself to the surface. It didn't matter if Mandrick knew she had it once she was clear of Styx.

But that was the difficult part. If he found out before she reached the surface Christine would be in serious danger. The other option was to meet him in Houston and do the whole dinner thing. The risk with that would be if it was his habit to leave such a precious item in the safety of the prison.

Mandrick put down the phone and came back to her. 'Where were we?' he asked. 'Oh, yes. You were telling me how you loathed me enough to have dinner with me in Houston.'

A buzzer interrupted them. Mandrick looked up at the bank of monitors that displayed practically every part of the prison. One of them showed a man in slacks and a jacket standing in the cavern outside his office. 'There's my luck again. I know you were about to give yourself to me. But duty calls.' He produced his remote control and hit a button on it. There was a clunk as the door hissed and opened.

The man strode into the room, his manner authoritative. He was grim-faced and large, like a former lineman, still naturally tough but aged and out of condition. He seemed anxious to say something but held back as soon as he saw Christine.

'Hank. How was your trip?' Mandrick asked.

'Fine,' Hank replied dryly.

'This is Christine Wineker from the Federal Bureau of Prisons.'

'Yeah, I heard.' Hank could not make his reluctance to meet her more obvious.

'Pleased to meet you too,' Christine said. She knew he was CIA, probably one of the senior guys if not *the* senior, and that he suspected her and loathed her.

'Hank's one of our VPs,' Mandrick explained. 'I don't know what the hell he does, though. Just turns up here once in a while to get in the way.'

'We need to talk,' Hank said, ignoring the charade.

'I was on my way out,' Christine said, shouldering her laptop and heading for the door.

'Thanks for stopping by,' Mandrick said.

Christine did not look back. Mandrick closed the door behind her.

'What the fuck is going on?' Hank blurted out as soon as the door had sealed shut.

'You sound in a bad mood,' Mandrick said, walking over to his desk.

'I'm gone three goddamned days and the goddamned wheels start falling off the place. You gonna tell me that ferry disaster was an accident? I could tell it was a goddamned massacre all the way from Florida.'

'Why are you acting so surprised?' Mandrick's question was sincere.

'Are you fuckin' kidding me?!'

'Hank. The order came from your own people.'

'Bullshit!'

'OK. The order came from Forbes. Now, if you suddenly believe he'd make a decision like that on his own then you are crazy.'

Hank was stunned. His voice became quieter. 'You're serious?'

'He told me it was a direct request from your outfit.'

'Why?'

'The feds were trying to slip one of their people inside as an inmate. We had no ID so . . . everyone had to buy it . . . You clearly didn't get the memo?'

'They're out of their friggin' minds.'

'But we know they're not. They thought it through and decided it was a good idea.'

'It could close this place down.'

'They have to prove it wasn't an accident.'

'That's the first really dumb thing I've heard you say. I don't care how you did it – there'll be a clue and someone'll find it.'

'Hank. You've misread me. I couldn't agree more.'

'Then why the hell did you do it?'

'I didn't realise the Agency had given me veto power.'

'You should've called me.'

'Now you're starting to sound pretty dumb yourself.'

Hank had to agree. He just couldn't believe it. 'There were smarter ways of handling this.'

'There's one clue lying in the hospital.'

Hank looked at him. 'Styx hospital?'

Mandrick nodded. 'The lone survivor – from the prisoners, that is. The other one was Gann.'

Hank shut his eyes and squeezed his temples tightly. 'Shit. I should've guessed that moron was involved.'

'You thought I would get my own hands that dirty?'

Hank pondered the situation for a moment. 'How do we know he's not the fed?' he eventually asked.

'We don't.'

Hank went silent again.

'Interesting, isn't it? We don't kill him we could be damned, but if we do and he's the fed . . .'

'It doesn't seem to bother you,' Hank said accusingly.

'I take life as it comes.'

'You can afford to.'

'I'm not in control. I'm just a hired hand.'

'And getting well paid, too. How is that offshore bank account? Don't forget that's the reason this place came about in the first place.'

'This place was built by your people to interrogate political prisoners.'

'Maybe. But the mine's drying up, isn't it? I know that. You people want out now, don't you? And while we're on the subject of money, my bank account hasn't seen any zeros added to it for a couple months now. That looks to me like someone's planning on leaving without paying the rent that's due.'

'Why're you bitching at me? I'm on the same level as you when it comes to distribution.'

'Sure you are. How 'bout we take a look in your safe? I'll give odds there's a bag of gems sitting in there right now.'

Mandrick sighed, tired of the line the conversation was taking. 'When I first met you at the start of this project you gave me a long and patriotic speech about the purpose of this prison. You cited national security, revenge for nine-eleven, protection of fossil fuels and the lifeline of this great country's economy. You never mentioned money. I'm not pointing the finger, Hank. In the end it all comes down to money. And you're due your share.'

Hank looked away as if Mandrick had wounded him – which, in fact, he had. Hank was a patriot who had lost his way.

Mandrick saw the effect of his dig but he knew he could not afford to make an enemy out of Hank. 'You're wrong, anyway. We're not planning on leaving any time soon. I would know . . . No one's ripping you off, either. Pay's been slow the last couple of months because of the market. It's not the first time. It'll pick up . . . You're wrong about the mine, too. It's doing just fine.'

Hank regretted his own outburst. He didn't like to hear himself talking about money. There was a time when he would not have given it a second thought. But he was older now and the disillusionment of the job had been wearing him down over the years. He was still a patriot but he also wanted his share of the spoils since everyone else around him seemed to be getting theirs. There was no end to the stories about people he had either worked with or for who had made fortunes along the way.

He had begun to weaken around the time he started calculating the pension he could look forward to when he retired, realising how paltry it was considering all he had done for his country. Normally he didn't lose control the way he just had but the ferry disaster had set him off. It had been a crazy stunt but Mandrick was right. He needed to examine all the implications and possible Agency motives before he did or said anything else. The first thing he wanted to know was why the hell he hadn't been informed.

'When's that bitch outta here?' Hank asked, wanting to change the subject. 'I came back for a specific interrogation and I don't feel comfortable while she's snooping around.'

'I think she'll be gone tomorrow. I'm doing everything I can to facilitate her.' Mandrick privately enjoyed the double meaning. 'Anything I can do in the meantime?'

Hank walked over to Mandrick's drinks cabinet and poured himself a whisky. 'I need a pre-interrogation.'

Mandrick picked a pen up off his desk. 'Who?'

'Durrani. Four seven four five.'

'Duration?'

'I need him ready by tomorrow midday. You need to start right away.'

'He's not been through pre-int before. That makes it easier.'

Hank finished his drink and put the glass down. 'You tell your boss to make sure I get my money. Unless he gets a cave alongside Bin Laden there's nowhere on this planet he can hide from me.'

Mandrick hit a button and the door hissed as the seal deflated. Hank walked out of the room, leaving Mandrick with his thoughts. He set them aside, picked up the phone and punched in a number while at the same time opening a computer file. The senior operations controller answered the phone.

'I've got a pre-int for Durrani, number four seven four five,' Mandrick said, consulting his monitor. 'Cell number three eight eight . . . and get the right cell this time . . . Yeah, yeah, yeah. Just make sure. It's important.'

He put down the phone and sat back to resume thinking.

Chapter 10

Stratton, handcuffs securing his wrists, a clean laundry bag over one shoulder containing his bedsheets, towel and spare underclothes, walked along a dripping, dingy corridor that had been cut through the rock and smelled of strong disinfectant. The roughly hewn ceiling was arched and no more than a couple of feet above his head at the highest points. Water leaked through cracks and ran down the walls, providing moisture for the slimy kelp-like vegetation that clung to the rock in green and grey sheets. A gum-chewing guard wielding a baton which he spun on the end of its leather strap sauntered alongside Stratton. One of the low-voltage fluorescent lights flickered and dimmed up ahead as if it was about to die. The guard gave it a tap with his baton as they passed but the blow had no effect.

They were on level three which was where all Western prisoners were accommodated. Level one was operations, level two was given over to the kitchen, laundry and galley while level four housed the foreign Muslim prisoners. The layers below that housed the pumps, storerooms and various pieces of life-support systems machinery and were the main source of the constant humming that filled the prison. Then there were the various split levels and sections that contained the hospital, the ferry dock, Mandrick's office and what was commonly known as the spook wing where the Agency had its various quarters.

Stratton and the guard walked along a row of identical heavy steel doors spaced at regular intervals a few metres apart. All were painted in a dull green and displayed brown streaks that radiated from suppurating rust sores. Each had the same characteristic bulging rubber seal around the edges, indicating that they were pressure doors.

'Here we go,' the guard said, stopping outside one of the doors. 'Two, one, two.' He checked a pressure valve on the wall and pushed a button on the side of a small flat-screen monitor inside a clear protective plastic box. A fish-eye image crackled to life, showing a small room with a bed either side of it and a man in prison uniform seated at a small desk. A curtain drawn across one of the corners partially hid a toilet bowl.

The guard pushed several buttons on a keypad beside the monitor. 'Pete to OCR,' he said into a mike clipped to his jacket lapel. 'Prisoner Charon at cell two one two requires entry.'

'Copy Charon entering two one two,' a voice echoed and a second later there was a loud hiss, followed by a heavy clunk. As the seals shrunk the door was free to move inwards.

'Comin' in, Tusker,' the guard called out as he pushed open the door and remained in the opening. The man at the desk was typing on a laptop and acted as if he was not aware of the intrusion. 'I got some bad news for you, Tusker.'

The man continued to ignore the guard who grinned as if he was about to enjoy what he had to say next. 'We got you a roommate.' He chewed his gum noisily as his grin broadened.

The man stopped typing and slowly looked around at the guard. Then he shifted his gaze to Stratton. Tusker was in his sixties and nothing like what one might expect a special-category prisoner to look like.

'We got no space, for a few days at least,' the guard explained. 'Charlie section's got a serious mildew problem. We had to shut it down for the prison inspector. Soon as the inspector babe's gone we'll open it back up and you'll have your room back to yourself. That sound OK?'

The older man frowned and went back to his typing.

'Step inside,' the guard said to Stratton, who obeyed. 'Turn your back to me. Release the bag.'

Stratton let go of the end of the bag and it hit the floor. The guard unshackled him, pushed him into the cell and stood back as Stratton felt his wrists. 'You two get along, now. And don't be teaching him any of your bad habits, Tusker, ya hear?' He chuckled as he put his mike to his mouth. 'Close down two one two,' he said as he pulled the door shut with a clang. A second later there was a loud hiss as the seals inflated. Stratton felt the pressure-change in his ears. It was severe enough for him to have to hold his nose and blow, equalising his tubes.

Tusker winced as his hands shot to cover his ears. He was clearly in pain. 'Assholes,' he growled. 'Sons of bitches always slam it up – they know my ears can't adjust that quickly.'

Stratton looked around at the windowless damp walls, the beds and the toilet behind the curtain. He picked up his bag and paused, unsure which bed he was to use. Both were made up although one had several items of clothing neatly folded on it.

Tusker read Stratton's quandary, got to his feet, walked over to the bed that was covered in clothing, removed the items and placed them on the edge of the desk.

Stratton put his bundle down on the bed as Tusker went back to his desk. The pasty walls covered in mildew patches had been recently scrubbed and Stratton wondered how people could spend years of their lives in such confinement without going crazy.

He wondered what the older man was in this hole for. It must have been a serious crime for someone his age to wind up in Styx.

'Hi,' Stratton said, deciding to break the ice. 'Name's Nathan.'

'One second,' Tusker said, as if he needed to finish a train of thought.

Stratton sat on the edge of the bed and wondered what these

people did to pass the time. There was no TV, no entertainment that he could see other than books and the laptop. Perhaps the old guy was writing a book himself. The ones stacked on the desk appeared to be on the subject of engineering, except the one on the end. That was a copy of Jules Verne's *Twenty Thousand Leagues Under the Sea*. Apt, Stratton thought.

A vent in the ceiling came to life as a blast of air blew into the room. It lasted about ten seconds and ended in a low growling noise.

Tusker appeared to finish what he was doing and sat back for a moment as if it had been somewhat tiring. He closed the top of his computer and turned in his seat to look at Stratton. After studying him for a few seconds he held out a hand. 'Tusker Hamlin,' he said in a cordial if neutral tone.

Stratton knew the name immediately. He was in the presence of America's most infamous domestic terrorist. This guy was into everything from deadly toxins and chemical agents to home-made explosives. It must have been ten years ago that the media had been filled with the news of his capture. Stratton remembered the footage of a solitary dilapidated caravan in the midst of some vast forest miles from anywhere in one of the northern US states. He took Hamlin's hand and they shook. The older man's grip was firm and his palm calloused as if he'd been doing hard labour.

'You're lucky to be alive,' Hamlin said, sitting back in his chair.

Stratton could not disagree.

'Zack said if you hadn't floated out of the milk when you did he wouldn't have seen you.'

'Zack?'

'Diver who pulled you out and got your ticker goin' again.'

Stratton had wondered who he had to thank for saving his life.

'You believe in God?' Hamlin asked.

'More than I did last week.'

'Where you from?'

'Vermont. I spent a long time in the UK if you're wondering about the accent.'

'Never been there,' Hamlin said in a way that suggested he didn't care either. 'What you in for?

Stratton shrugged. 'Can't keep outta jail. I guess they think this place'll change my mind.'

'Let 'em think what they damn well want to,' Hamlin said, his mind suddenly elsewhere.

'Aren't you a bit old to be down here?' Stratton asked, genuinely curious. 'I didn't mean that to sound rude,' he added, intent on being respectful. This was the kind of place where a person needed to make friends, especially when he had enough enemies already.

Hamlin took a packet of tobacco from a pocket and proceeded to make a roll-up. 'They think they've finally found a prison that'll hold me . . . I've escaped from three so far.'

'I remember you. You made a lot of news . . . I guess they think you're still dangerous?'

'Assholes,' Hamlin muttered, licking the paper and completing the roll-up. 'I've always been fascinated by what I could make in my garage that would scare the bejeezus out of anyone. Made my first atomic bomb when I was twenty. That was without the plutonium, of course. Science department got into more trouble'n I did,' he said, lighting up and blowing the smoke at the ceiling. He held the tobacco out to Stratton who shook his head.

'Didn't you make some anthrax?'

'That was the one that shot me to infamy. Easiest thing I ever made,' Hamlin said, amused at the memory. 'All I did was go to the old testing grounds in Oklahoma and pluck me up some samples right out of an open field that wasn't even fenced. I grew the stuff in culture dishes – had enough to fill a biscuit tin within months.'

Stratton was fascinated by home-made devices himself, particularly explosives. Hearing such details first-hand from a grandmaster was entertaining. 'I remember you mostly for your mail bombs. I saw a diagram of one of your circuits. Very innovative.'

'You technical?'

'I'm not in your league.'

'My mistake was in getting too political,' Hamlin sighed, taking a long drag and clearly enjoying it. 'I should say, in going for the wrong political targets . . . Up until then I was just some anti-abortion, animal-rights, pro-environment nut who on occasion plucked a member or two of the general public to make a point. There was just one detective lookin' for me in those days. Then I sent a coupla letter bombs to a selection of high-ranking Republicans and the entire FBI was set loose on my ass.' The reminiscing amused him.

Stratton couldn't decide what to make of Hamlin. He didn't appear to be crazy. Had he not known the man's history he would have guessed him to be a normal harmless old codger. 'How do you rate this place – compared to other prisons you've been in?'

'This place? I'm havin' a great time!' Hamlin said. 'It's gonna be a little harder than the others to get out of, though.' He held the last quarter-inch of the roll-up between tobacco-stained fingertips and took a final drag. 'I'm busier than I've ever been,' he said as the vent kicked in again and the cell was filled with a current of air that did not smell particularly fresh. 'I keep those suckers runnin', for one,' he said, pointing to the vent.

Stratton looked up at the small air duct, its orifice coated in black dust. 'You help maintain the scrubbers?'

'Help? Since they put me in engineering the engineers don't come down here so much. I kinda made myself a little niche. They love it, I love it. They get to spend more time topside. I get to spend less time in here. I should get a piece o' their pay cheque.'

Stratton suddenly thought about his task. It was as if it had been waiting in his head for some attention, had lost patience and jumped out at him. He didn't have a plan yet but before he could begin to devise one he was going to have to get his hands on some information. It was too early to get frustrated although it already felt as if he'd been on this mission for an age. He needed to see the lie of the land, experience the routine and gather details about his target.

Stratton got to his feet, walked to the end of the little cell and turned around.

'You pacin' the room already?' Hamlin asked. He took one of the books off his desk and held it out to Stratton. 'Here.'

Stratton took it and looked at the front cover. It was a history of deep-sea diving, stretching back to ancient Greece and Aristotle.

'Hey. You never know when it'll come in handy,' Hamlin said, winking.

Stratton saw the funny side, decided to shelve his problems for the moment and sat back on his bed. Exercising some patience was sound advice. He opened the book and read the introduction. It made him think of his emergency diving equipment sitting at the base of the Styx umbilical just beyond the prison walls. Stratton shuddered at the thought of being out there once again with only a lungful of air to fuel a one-way journey to an objective he could not see. But there were the standby diving sets in the dock that he could utilise if he could get to them. The problem with that was getting inside the dock itself. But then, before he could escape he had to get the tablet.

Stratton told himself once more to be patient and to put the mission to one side for the moment.

A klaxon sounded somewhere outside and Stratton looked over at Hamlin who had gone back to his laptop.

'The dinner bell,' the older man said. 'Highlight of the afternoon for most. In the early days they fed us in the cells. That got to be too much work for the guards and so they opened up a mess hall.'

The door hissed loudly and the seal around it shrank.

'You been to the mess hall yet?' Hamlin asked as he got to his feet.

'No.'

'Watch yourself. It's a place where things can go wrong.'

The door moved in on its hinges and Hamlin helped it open. There was no one outside and Stratton leaned out to take a look.

Hamlin put a hand out to stop him. 'Steady, son,' he said in a low voice. 'From here on you don't move without being told. There're some guards ain't as kindly as others – one in particular.'

Stratton could guess who he was referring to.

'STEP OUTSIDE YOUR CELL INTO THE CORRIDOR!' boomed a voice from tinny speakers.

Hamlin obeyed and Stratton followed.

All the other doors along the corridor were open. A prisoner walked out of each one.

'TURN TO YOUR LEFT AND FACE THE RED LIGHT,' the voice demanded.

A red light shone above a door at the end of the corridor. Every prisoner obeyed lethargically. There was a loud hiss and a clunk and the door below the red light opened. Stratton could feel the pressure change and looked up at a CCTV camera that was pointing directly at him.

'KEEP THE SAME DISTANCE FROM THE MAN IN FRONT OF YOU. HE STOPS, YOU STOP. DO NOT BUNCH . . . FORWARD MARCH!'

Stratton trooped off behind Hamlin.

Gann stood in the operations control room looking at the monitors, in particular the one that showed Stratton heading through a door. He switched to another monitor showing Stratton stepping through the other side and followed his progress along a rocky, brightly lit corridor. When Stratton went out of sight

Gann ignored the other monitors and concentrated on his thoughts.

Stratton, in a line of prisoners, shuffled forward behind Hamlin towards an open airlock door. Before he reached it he got a once-over from a chemical scanner and a metal detector. None of the prisoners were wearing wrist or ankle shackles, which suggested a high level of confidence among the guards that there would be no disorder. On the other hand, since leaving his cell Stratton had not seen a guard other than behind a heavy glass porthole. The inmates' movements between their cells and the galley were controlled by airlock doors and loudspeakers. Stratton wondered what riot-control methods the facility employed in the event of a serious disturbance.

'NEXT,' a metallic voice boomed and Stratton stepped through the doorway. He glanced back at the faces lining up behind him, estimating the number of inmates at around two dozen. None of them appeared to be Afghan or Middle Eastern. 'MOVE ON,' the voice commanded and he continued along a short corridor to a door that led into the mess hall.

The room was large enough to comfortably seat fifty inmates. It was two storeys high, with a narrow balcony running around the four walls midway up. A handful of guards stood around the balcony at intervals, looking down on the prisoners as they filed inside. At each corner was a narrow airlock door with a thick glass porthole at head height. A dozen tables were arranged around the clean stone galley floor, with plastic chairs tucked underneath them. The line of inmates snaked from the entrance along one of the walls to a long countertop that began with a pile of plastic food trays and cutlery. There were no servers. The pre-heated meals, similar to military rations, were in sealed plastic bags and were arranged in labelled trays. A selection of biscuits and plastic drink cartons were stacked at the end. Stratton chose a couple of food sachets without taking much notice of the contents. He was more interested in his surroundings.

He followed Hamlin to a table where they set their trays down opposite each other. Two thuggish-looking inmates joined them. One of them appeared to have more than a mild interest in Stratton. Stratton ignored him and opened one of his food sachets. It contained a meaty sludge of some kind and he checked the sachet's label that described the contents as beef and vegetables in gravy. He was used to military field-ration packs and expected it to taste better than it looked, which was usually the case. He dipped a flimsy plastic fork into the dark brown pool, scooped up a chunk and put it in his mouth. It was as expected and, suddenly feeling hungry, he opened a packet of hard-tack biscuits to dip into the gravy.

One of the thugs at the end of the table was trying, with difficulty it seemed, to read the contents label on a packet. He emptied the sachet onto his tray and frowned at the sight of peaches in syrup. He opened another packet and poured what appeared to be a risotto of some kind into the indentation beside the peaches. He then emptied the contents of a third, which, like Stratton's main course, was beef and vegetables in gravy, into the space between the others where it trickled into both. Unperturbed, he dipped a fork into the mess and began to eat it. His stare wandered back to Stratton as he chomped noisily. Stratton glanced at him. The cold malice in the man's unintelligent eyes was raw. Stratton looked away, fully expecting to see more of that Neanderthal machismo in a place like this.

An airlock door on the balcony opened and Gann stepped out. He leaned on the rail as he looked down at the tables and found Stratton. His gaze moved to the thugs at the same table. One of them surreptitiously nudged his colleague and indicated Gann with an upward movement of his eyes. The second thug glanced up at Gann, looked over at Stratton and then back down at his food. An airlock door on the other side of the galley floor opened.

Hamlin heard the hiss above the general din and looked in that direction, stopping the movement of a forkful of food heading towards his open mouth. 'Now that ain't usual,' he said, putting the fork down.

Stratton followed Hamlin's gaze across the room. Afghan prisoners, all wearing Muslim skullcaps and sporting untrimmed beards, were filing into the room.

'The Talibuttfucks don't normally eat the same time as us,' Hamlin said, looking around the room for reactions from the other tables. 'This ain't good.'

The sounds of chewing and talking died down as practically every Westerner stopped eating to look at the late arrivals. Angry expressions formed on faces, low, conspiratorial comments were exchanged and the tension in the mess hall rose perceptibly.

'What the fuck are these assholes doin' in here?' the thug across from Stratton said, loud enough for those at the tables around him to hear.

Stratton looked up at the guards around the balcony who were watching with the curiosity of those conducting a potentially entertaining experiment. He saw Gann, who'd been looking at the Afghans, shift his gaze to the thugs at Stratton's table. Stratton watched the thug exchange glances with Gann and look directly at him. A warning bell went off in his head. Something was about to happen and it would appear that Stratton had a part to play in it.

The Afghans picked up their trays and eating utensils and for the most part kept their dark eyes fixed ahead, though one or two glanced uncomfortably at the Westerners.

Stratton had lost interest in the thugs for the moment as he searched for the focus of his mission. He had studied photographs of Durrani, courtesy of the CIA after the British SIS had requested copies, but he knew from long experience how difficult it was to identify a person from a photograph. The good news in this instance was that the photo was a recent one. Durrani's hair was bushy, his beard uncropped. The problem was that nearly all the Afghans were sporting similar styles.

Stratton scanned each man down the line, stopping at the second-to-last one coming through the door. Stratton was positive that it was Durrani. Because of the prison uniform the man was wearing he could not see any of the listed VDMs (Visual Distinguishing Marks) since they were all on Durrani's torso. The small incision in his lower abdomen would be the ultimate proof. Stratton went back along the line of faces just to make sure and by the time he reached the end he was certain his original man was Durrani.

There was something exhilarating, even exciting about being so close to his quarry. This was the first stage in the target-information gathering phase. Durrani was alive and well and in the prison.

A packet of food flew from somewhere and landed on the wall above the line of Afghans.

'Shit!' Hamlin cursed. 'I know how *this* is gonna end up.'

'We should move back and stay out of it,' Stratton said, taking hold of the older man's arm.

'There's nowhere you can escape what they're gonna do to us now.'

Stratton had no idea what the old man meant as they got to their feet.

A chair sailed across the room towards the Afghans.

The two thugs at Stratton's table stood up. Both men appeared to be more interested in Stratton than they were in the Afghans.

Stratton and Hamlin headed for a far wall as the shouting and missile-throwing intensified. The Afghans closed ranks and retaliated by launching anything to hand at the front line of aggressors. One of them chucked a tray like a frisbee, striking an inmate in the face and giving him a bloody injury. It was the starting signal that set the Western prisoners going and a group of them hurled themselves at the Afghans. The clash was brutal and fists and feet swung violently.

The two thugs did not join the mêlée, taking advantage of the disturbance to close in on Stratton. He moved away from Hamlin, looking around for a weapon to replace the plastic fork in his hand.

Hamlin moved into a corner and slid down it until he was sitting on his heels. He put his hands over his head as if the building was about to fall on him and waited for what he believed to be inevitable.

The thugs split up to come at Stratton from different angles. Having failed to find a weapon he raised his fists in a boxer's stance, shuffling back. His right hand was cocked close to his chest with the thumb towards his opponents, concealing the end of the plastic fork protruding from the back of his fist. Working on the principle that it was generally a good idea to take out the biggest danger first he manoeuvred himself closer to the larger thug. The other thug then showed signs of wanting to engage first when he picked up a plastic chair.

As the men closed in the thug with the chair launched it. Stratton did not duck low enough and a leg struck the side of his head. The larger thug took advantage of the distraction and made his move.

Stratton was nothing if not decisive when it came time to attacking and he did not hesitate. The thug came in quickly and swung at him with a powerful haymaker. Stratton ducked nimbly underneath it, stepped to one side of the big man and released his cocked fist. But instead of punching straight he swung it in a tight arc and plunged the end of the fork into the man's eye – which exploded in a spurt of retinal fluid, followed by a geyser of blood.

The thug let out a scream as his knees buckled. The second thug was already on top of Stratton and grabbed his collar as his other hand followed up with a blow. Stratton threw his arm over the top of the extended arm of the thug who had a hold of him, bringing it down the other side and up again in between them. The action straightened the thug's arm by applying pressure to his elbow. Stratton continued the move, standing on tiptoe, and his momentum snapped the joint. The second thug's howl rose above the general cacophony. At the same time Stratton swung his other hand with the plastic fork in it high and then down onto the corner of the man's neck, driving the prongs of the fork deep into the flesh. The broken elbow had done the job but the follow-up certainly added to the thug's agony. He dropped to the floor, screaming.

Stratton looked up to see the guards on the balcony stepping through the airlock doors that closed behind them. Hamlin was still sitting on the floor with his head in his hands.

The battle was in full swing. Some of the Afghans tried to stay together while others who had been dragged away from their colleagues were receiving a hiding.

The balcony was now void of guards and Stratton had the distinct feeling something ominous was about to happen. But at the same time it was a great opportunity to get closer to his target.

He saw Durrani and another Afghan scurry behind the counter. He headed towards them, pushing his way through the mêlée while fending off blows. He leaped over the counter, dropped to his knees on the other side and found himself facing Durrani an arm's length away. There was not a trace of fear in the man's eyes. Durrani's colleague was busy fighting behind him, clutching at the throat of a man who was doing the same to him. Durrani stared at Stratton, years of battle experience etched into his brain.

He lunged at Stratton who moved deftly aside while at the

same time slamming his forearm against the Afghan's throat and forcing him against the side of the counter and down. Durrani was trapped and grabbed Stratton's arm in an effort to release the choke hold. Stratton replaced his arm with his knee, pinning the Afghan even more firmly. He took advantage of the moment, not to strike another blow but to confirm what he most needed to know. He raised Durrani's shirt and pulled down his trousers to expose the scar. It was still pink, the cut itself ugly due to it healing without stitches.

Durrani was momentarily confused.

Stratton looked into his eyes and for a second they weighed each other up. 'Durrani?' he asked.

Durrani was suddenly horrified. This man was not here to beat him. He wanted his treasure. More alarming was that he knew exactly where to look for it. With a combination of rage and desperation Durrani mustered every ounce of strength he possessed and threw Stratton off him. Stratton fell onto his back and the Afghan was on him like a wolf. He grappled for Stratton's throat, driven not just to defend himself but to destroy this man who knew his precious secret.

Stratton was momentarily overpowered by the force of Durrani's attack and struggled to twist out of his grip.

As Durrani fought to cut off Stratton's air he was suddenly overwhelmed by a feeling of giddiness. The face of the man around whose neck his hands were tightening started to blur. Stratton punched up an arm and pushed his fingers into Durrani's larynx but as he did so he too felt horribly dizzy. His eyes went in and out of focus and he struggled to breathe.

They were not the only two experiencing such difficulties. The riot had suddenly ceased with everyone in the room down on the floor and fighting to breathe. A man screamed as another lurched to his feet, staggered across the room as if blind and fell down hard onto his face.

Stratton fought to hold on to consciousness but his brain felt as though it was being squeezed like a sponge. All he could do was lie still and concentrate on breathing. A few seconds later his mind drifted into unconsciousness.

Chapter 11

Mandrick was at his desk going through a list of emails while Hank Palmerston sat on the other side of the room nursing a cup of coffee and scowling to himself. His head jerked up at the sound of a buzzer. Mandrick glanced at the monitor on his desk and pushed a button on his remote. The door to the office hissed and clunked as it swung inwards and Gann stepped into the room.

Hank's eyes narrowed as he stared at the senior guard whom he disliked intensely.

'You wanted to see me,' Gann said, looking confident despite knowing why he had been summoned.

'You're either a total dumb-fuck,' Hank said, putting down his coffee, 'or . . . nah. There ain't any other explanation. You *are* a dumb-fuck.'

Gann's barely visible reaction was a subtle tightening of his jaw. Having always been employed by aggressive hard-ass men physically inferior to him, controlling himself was something he'd had plenty of opportunity to practise. Gann knew his place in the pecking order and calmed his intense desire to attack the man. Maybe one day, when this was all over and if by chance he happened to bump into Hank somewhere, he'd tear him apart. But for the time being he could not. Hank was a senior CIA field operative and that was reason enough to allow the prick to walk all over him.

'Anyone wanna hear my reasonin'?' Gann asked.

Hank's face broke into a smirk of stupefied disbelief. 'It's got reasoning,' he said to Mandrick. 'Go on. Please do go on. I've got to hear why one of my Talibutts is dead with a broken neck, two of 'em are blinded, one has a broken back and may never walk again and three of 'em have been so badly beaten in the head that I might as well send 'em back home for all the good they are to me now. And all while a federal prison inspector is crawling around the goddamn place. Do tell.'

Gann's expression suggested he conceded that the number of casualties was excessive. Otherwise, he remained confident of his actions. 'I think that Charon guy is a federal agent.'

Hank looked at Mandrick for an explanation. Mandrick raised his eyebrows in denial.

'I ain't as stupid as you think I am,' Gann said. 'I figured out there was a fed agent on the ferry myself. Why else would we have to kill everyone? But now I think the only guy to escape the ferry was the only one who shoulda died.'

Hank's jaw clenched. 'You mixed my Talibutts with the regular prisoners knowing it would cause a riot because you think there's a fed in the building? You know something . . .' he said, pausing to control himself. 'You're so fuckin' dumb I'm irritated just by the sight of you.'

Gann wondered just how problematic it really would be to kill a CIA agent. 'I didn't suspect it so much before the riot.'

Hank's brow furrowed.

'I always suspected there was something strange about the guy,' Gann went on. 'Right from when I first met 'im. Even before the accident. There was somethin' about him, the way he was always lookin' at people and things, but not in a normal way.'

Hank squared up to Gann who was a head taller and much broader. 'I don't give a damn if J. Edgar fuckin' Hoover himself turned up for lunch . . . Federal agent my ass. You must think I'm as stupid as you are. I know why you want to kill Charon. He's the only person who can finger you for the ferry sabotage.'

Gann smirked. Hank was completely right, up until the fight in the galley. 'So I guess you're not interested to know if one of my inmates is interested in one of yours?' Gann looked smug.

Hank squinted at the oversized guard. 'What're you talking about?'

'Like I said. Charon is a mother fuckin' spy. He ain't here to do time. He's here for one of your Talibutts. I got proof, too,' he said, producing a mini-CD from his breast pocket. 'Take a look at it. It's from one of the cameras in the galley.'

Hank took the CD, eyeing Gann suspiciously, placed it in a slot on the panel and hit the play button. Mandrick got up from his seat and walked around the desk to get a closer look.

An image of the galley looking down from above flickered onto one of the monitors.

'This is just before it went off,' Gann said, moving to the monitor to point things out. 'While everyone else is movin' towards the Talibutts, Charon and his cellmate Hamlin move back. They don't want any of the action. Now, my boys move in . . .'

'Your boys?' Hank interrupted.

'My job – orders from your boss, as I understand it – was to take out the people in that ferry and it ain't done until Charon is history.'

Hank's expression tightened. He glanced at Mandrick, wondering if he was in on this. Mandrick remained poker-faced.

'Now look at this. Charon here wastes my guys in just two moves. He didn't learn that in the joint . . . Then he starts to move back to safety. Remember, he don't want any part of this fight. But then he sees somethin' and in a second he's the other side of the room and on top of one of the Talibutts. But take a look at this. He ain't there for the fightin'. He even says somethin' to the guy. Whatever it is, the guy gets mad and then the depressurisation got to 'em.'

Hank was not entirely convinced and replayed the last segment of the recording.

'I don't know what he's doin',' Gann said. 'But I know when something stinks – and that guy stinks.'

Hank freeze-framed on a close-up of the Afghan.

'The Talibutt's name is Durrani,' Gann offered. He could see that he had scored with the video.

Mandrick remembered the name as the one Hank had given to him earlier when he'd asked him to carry out a pre-interrogation softening-up. He stared at the side of Hank's head, wondering what was going on inside it.

Hank knew it was Durrani the moment he saw him on the monitor. The Afghan was the reason for his present visit. He pondered the various permutations of the situation, unable to make anything out of it at that moment. But the observations, if accurate, certainly gave food for thought. Cogwheels of possibility began to turn and click as an intelligence with twenty-two years of experience in the business filed the information in readiness for any future connections.

Hank had spent the last ten years specialising in interrogation and information-extrapolation techniques with Asian and Middle Eastern Muslim subjects. He began his Agency career in Pakistan near the end of the Russian occupation of Afghanistan, spending much of those early days operating out of an office in the US embassy in Islamabad. For most of that period he liaised with the Saudi Arabian and Pakistani intelligence services in their combined efforts to finance, supply and train the Afghan mujahedeen in order to oust the Russians. Then, when the communist grip on Russia finally collapsed along with the Berlin Wall, Hank was already taking seriously the new danger shaping up to take its place in the form of Islamic fundamentalism. He was in Langley when Mir Aimal Kasi gunned down five CIA staff as they waited at the checkpoint to drive into the CIA headquarters. A month later in New York Ramzi Yousef parked a vehicle on level B-2 of the World Trade Center and detonated a bomb that killed six people in a cafeteria above. The two young men, both of Pakistani origin, neither of whom knew that the other existed, casually left the country on flights to Pakistan hours after their attack.

Hank moved to Afghanistan to begin the overseas hunt for them. He also got involved in several operations intended to kill or kidnap a dangerous upstart called Osama bin Laden. He lived through the formative days of the great jihad against America that eventually led to the successful destruction of the Twin Towers. He remained in Afghanistan to welcome the first American troops and followed them into Kabul to set up the Agency's new offices. Hank played his part in the defeat of the Taliban only to then suffer the indignity of their subsequent reorganisation with the help of many of his 'old friends' in the Saudi Arabian and Pakistan intelligence services who had their own agendas that were far removed from his.

With the rise of the Iraqi insurgency after the US-led invasion of that country Hank was assigned to aid in the setting-up of information-gathering cells around the world. But following the constant media attacks against Guantánamo Bay and the subsequent witch-hunt by many countries against CIA interrogation centres within their borders, he was grateful for a chance to take a key development role in what could only be described as a bizarre and audacious undertaking. Not only did Styx eventually open for business but it ended up yielding high-quality information while attracting the minimum possible outside scrutiny. When it came to security, media curiosity, eavesdropping and covert investigations, a prison beneath the surface of the ocean was like having one on the Moon. It was almost perfect . . . almost, but not quite.

Hank had never been under any illusion that Styx would last for ever. But he thought it would at least survive for a decade or two and, with luck, perhaps even see the Agency through to the end of the jihad. Now, after only two years, organisational cracks were starting to form in the administrative structure of the little oceanic citadel that he'd had such high hopes for. The FBI was trying to investigate the CIA interrogations as well as the so-called mining infractions by the host corporation. The media had become equally keen to report on anything to do with the prison. The White House was afraid of what the FBI and the media might find. And the only thing holding it all together outside the Agency was the greed of a handful of civilians who ran the place. The key, with them at least, was to ensure that their greed was not completely sated. Rumours that the mine was drying up did not help matters at all. Quite the reverse, in fact. He was in danger of losing the only glue holding it all together.

But it wasn't over yet. Not by a long shot. Not if Hank could help it. 'I want you to listen to me carefully,' he said to Gann. 'Nothing else happens to anyone in this prison unless I say so. Is that clear?'

'What about Charon?' Gann asked.

'If he dies after surviving one dubious disaster already it'll only bring a hundred of his buddies crawling all over this place. He isn't going anywhere and he has no one to talk to but us – so relax.'

Mandrick thought about mentioning that Christine had met with Charon when he first became conscious. But that might upset more than one apple-cart. If Gann knew as much he might just be stupid enough to try and kill her too. Hank would be none too pleased either, especially with this new implication. Mandrick had a lot of plans in various stages of development, all of them based around his own interests. One of them was Christine and if he smeared her with more suspicion than she had already attracted he might as well forget about her. But he didn't want to, not just yet. He would hold on to his information for the time being.

'I want you to hoist in one last thing,' Hank said to Gann. 'One important piece of information that you should never forget . . . You listening?'

Gann nodded, a feeling of superiority stealing over him. He felt he was a little more equal to the agent than when he'd walked into the room minutes earlier.

'You're a moron,' Hank said with utter conviction. 'You've always been a moron and nothing will change that.'

Gann felt his temples throb as he stared into the eyes of the chubby man within a haymaker's reach of him.

'Morons don't think for themselves,' Hank went on. 'You got that?'

Mandrick knew Gann a lot better than Hank did but it would appear that the CIA agent was a far better judge of character. Mandrick was waiting for Gann to slap Hank in the chops, almost tensing in expectation of the blow, and wondering what his reaction should be. He was impressed with both men, and somewhat relieved, when the punch did not come.

Mandrick had to agree with Hank's basic sentiments, though. Gann was not the brightest lamp in the street. But then, neither was he a complete idiot. He had managed to carry out what had to be acknowledged as a complicated sabotage of a Styx ferry that, with a little help from Mandrick, would be difficult to prove had been foul play. Admittedly, there was the Charon factor, of course, but that aside it had been a good effort. And the fact that he had refrained from dropping Hank was a further indication of Gann's basic good sense. However, he doubted that Gann would forget the insult soon – or ever, for that matter. Mandrick might have misjudged Gann's ability to hold back his violent impulses in the short term but he was confident that at that very moment the man was plotting Hank's demise for some day in the future.

'You people are falling apart,' Hank said, redirecting his ire at Mandrick. 'You don't have the balls to hold this place together.'

Mandrick sighed. 'We're tougher than you think. A lot's happened but we can get away with a lot more.'

'You always tell people what they want to hear, don't you, Mandrick? You want me to think you believe we'll come after you when you jump. But the truth is, guys like you never really do believe it until it's too late.' Hank stared into Mandrick's eyes. 'I've been buying and selling truth and lies for a long time and from people far better equipped to play the game than you. You're lying to me, Mandrick. It's clear as a mountain stream to these old eyes. You know what's better than getting even with someone who screws with you?'

Mandrick didn't bother to try and guess. He was busy assessing Hank's sincerity and to his alarm he found him convincing.

'Getting even with him *before* he screws you,' Hank said. 'That's the smart play. Open the door.'

Mandrick did not react to the threat although more than a tingle of discomfort rippled through him. He opened the door and watched Hank walk out of the room.

There was always going to be an endgame to this whole scenario and Mandrick often felt concern at his apparent powerlessness to influence it one way or another. But perhaps that was not the case any more. It would appear that the ticking clock was going faster than he'd thought a few hours earlier. Hank had shone a narrow beam of light onto the pitfalls that faced all the players in this complicated game. The Agency controlled almost everything, but not quite. Every player had a destructive force that they could unleash and in such a game the advantage went to he who struck first. Mandrick and the Felix Corp were in it for the money but receiving it wasn't enough. The real issue was holding onto the freedom to spend it when the top eventually did blow off.

'He thinks he's in charge around here but he ain't,' chirped Gann.

Mandrick glanced at Gann, wondering why Forbes had inflicted such an uncontrollable beast on him.

'Mr Forbes is in charge of this place. And until he tells me to lay off Charon I'll do what I think is best for this place. The CI friggin' A can go screw themselves.'

Gann headed for the door. Mandrick considered trying to convince him not to go against Hank but decided not to bother. The seams were cracking all over the place and Mandrick felt it was now beyond his ability to hold them together. Gann was, understandably, concerned about being accused of sabotaging the ferry and therefore had every right to protect himself. There was no way that Gann was going to let Charon get out of the prison alive and so he might as well get on with it.

Gann left the room and Mandrick went back to his desk and slumped into his chair. He suddenly felt more vulnerable than he had ever been and there was only one solution. He needed more control of his destiny. To get that he needed to act first. In short, he needed to escape. But it wasn't *getting* free of Styx that was a problem. He could leave that afternoon. He was the warden. The problem was *staying* free. Hank had underlined that fact most clearly. The only way Mandrick could keep the CIA off his back was to have a value to them. It was that lack of value that was frustrating him.

The phone on his desk chirped, taking him out of the depths of his thoughts, and he plucked the receiver out of its cradle. 'Mandrick.'

'Hi,' a woman's voice said.

It was Christine and the image of her body immediately acted like a tonic. 'Hi yourself.'

'I'd like to see you.'

He never believed her when she was so forward. If she wanted to see him it was nothing to do with romance. 'See me or interrogate me about the mess hall incident?'

'What mess hall incident?'

'That's very good, Christine. You'll become more memorable with comments like that.'

She laughed. 'I was told one of the guards got his timings mixed up.'

'It's inexcusable. We're taking it very seriously, of course.'

'I wanted to tell you I'm pretty much finished.'

'I'm sorry to hear that. You're the only breath of fresh air in this place. You'll be at dinner tonight?'

'Of course.'

'I'll see you then . . . Perhaps we can talk afterwards.'

'That would be nice ... Can I book a ferry for later this evening?'

'You want to leave straight after dinner?'

'After our little talk,' she said coquettishly.

'I see,' Mandrick said, the excitement rising in him despite his better judgement. The thought then struck him that he might leave with her. Perhaps they could both depart after dinner and enjoy the following day together in Houston, relaxing at his apartment after the decompression. It was worth considering. 'I'll make the arrangements.'

'See you later.'

'Bye,' he said, replacing the phone.

That was pleasantly unexpected, he thought. Christine was suddenly within his grasp and it made him feel far more excited and attracted to her, a very welcome distraction from everything else. Mandrick's natural suspicion brought up the question of why she had changed from challenging to amenable so suddenly. He decided that perhaps it was not so sudden. He had been working his charm on her from the moment they'd first met. And time was running out for them to get it together which could have helped to encourage her. Or perhaps it was simply one of the mysterious complexities of the female gender.

On the other hand, this was probably a bad time to be leaving the prison. Things could get ugly over the next few days and being topside would lose him any control he might have. Perhaps it was time to put together his endgame plan. It was based on the premise that, when this house of cards toppled, if he could not be of value to the CIA alive he would have to let them think he was dead. Its magnitude was unnerving and challenging, not the most perfect solution but a good one and, more important, the only one he had.

Christine was highly desirable but he couldn't allow the craving for a beautiful woman to cloud his common sense. That would be fatal.

Christine put down the receiver and stared thoughtfully at the colourful eiderdown covering her small bed that took up almost half of the otherwise drab white-painted concrete room. She sat down at a simple dresser, the only other piece of furniture in the room, and brought up an internet mailing page on her laptop screen. The vent in the ceiling clicked on to adjust the air. She paused to clear her ears before typing a short message that explained to the recipient that she was preparing to finalise her plans for departure.

She had set her own clock ticking. She could quit there and then, throw in the towel, tell Mandrick that she needed to get out of Styx immediately and turn her back on the rest of her plans. But that was not about to happen. Not without reasons better than those she had. She had waited her entire life for this moment, not that she ever knew what it would entail. But it had all the ingredients she had dreamed of as far back as her teens: an operation concerning national security; dangerous and, most significant, operating alone and under cover. She was a woman doing a man's job in a man's world and in the highly competitive arena she had chosen to work in that was no small achievement.

It had been a relatively short and hazard-free journey to the rare, enviable and highly classified position of Secret Service Special Operative to the Oval Office. The post achieved the highest level of secrecy by circumventing the channels used by all other mainstream and military intelligence-agency recruitment procedures. But Christine was nobody's fool and was aware that getting the important job had been due more to luck than to ability. On the other hand, as her grandmother had always told her, 'The harder you work, the luckier you'll be.' The words were true enough. Her appointment had had a lot to do with being in the right place at the right time. But she had certainly worked tirelessly towards the job throughout her life.

Right from childhood Christine had refused to conform to the generally accepted standards of her gender – by refusing to wear dresses, for instance. She would only ever agree to put on traditional female trappings after heavy negotiations with her parents, always bartering an occasional act of conformity for things considered too masculine for a young lady. At ten she wanted boxing lessons, at eleven she accepted bridesmaid duties only if she could join a boys' soccer club since there was no local girls' team. Other demands over the years included baseball, fencing, rock climbing, karate and clay-pigeon shooting, not all of which she persisted with. But her hunger to pursue such energetic pastimes never seemed to diminish.

Christine's parents regarded her macho aspirations as delusional, superficial and immature until the day she returned home for dinner after a game of 'Smear the Queen', a full-contact American football game without pads or helmet. She was clearly in pain as she sat down for the meal but stoically refused any attention. It later transpired that her collarbone had been broken in two places and she had several cracked ribs, a fractured wrist and a broken thumb. What was more, Christine had received the injuries at various points throughout the game but had refused to leave the field until the end.

By the time Christine attended college she had not only grown into a very beautiful girl but her femininity had blossomed along with it. Her interest in boys was growing beyond them as mere objects to compete against physically but although there was never a shortage of admirers she found it impossible to attract one who matched her strength of mind and spirit.

Christine attended the University of Virginia to begin an MBA course but soon after arriving she was invited to take a Juris doctorate. Her parents were keen on her becoming a lawyer and so Christine accepted the challenge but only if she could take up barrel racing. They agreed.

In her final year at university she placed second in the Quarter Horse World Championships and graduated *summa cum laude*, finishing third in her class. The prospect of becoming a lawyer failed to inspire her but she had put the work in, achieved the grades and had to face the simple fact that dreams were dreams and reality was reality. And so it was with a sense of fatalism and little enthusiasm that she prepared to apply for an internship.

But things were never to develop in that direction and fate played its hand. The law school held a job fair the week of her graduation which Christine decided to visit out of curiosity. To her surprise she happened upon a recruiting booth for the Federal Bureau of Investigation. The agent who ran the booth did not make it sound as attractive as she had expected although she reckoned it was still more inspiring than becoming a lawyer. But any desire to sign up was squashed when he explained the qualifications required. Christine would need at least a college degree, an MBA and three years' work experience or be fluent in a foreign language. She had the degree but not enough work experience and no foreign language.

Christine left the booth and as she headed for the exit she was consumed by a feeling of loss and disappointment. She stopped to look back in the direction of the FBI booth, wondering if there was any other way she might be able to join when she saw a booth inviting applications for the United States Secret Service.

The Secret Service did not interest Christine as much as the FBI did but for reasons she could not explain she felt compelled to talk to the agent. After telling him about her qualifications he offered her a position on the next recruit intake. He was much older and wiser than the FBI agent and, although her academic certificates were more than enough, what impressed him more were her other accomplishments. He noted that her riding showed dedication, her captaincy of the college hockey team and her position as pitcher for the local baseball team displayed leadership and toughness, and her experience as a hockey referee indicated an ability to make quick decisions and to stick with them. A month later she was on her way to the Secret Service Training Center in Beltsville, Maryland.

The course began with a two-week initiation phase designed to assess the candidates' general fitncss and their skills with small-arms weaponry. On completion, the recruits travelled to the Federal Law Enforcement Training Center in Glynco, Georgia where they spent ten weeks learning small-arms skills, hand-to-hand combat and basic law concerning arrest, search and seizure. The final phase took place back at the Secret Service School in Maryland, specifically at the famed James J. Rowley Training Center where the remaining students faced gruelling physical tests while at the same time learning personnel-protection procedures and investigation skills. Christine graduated top of her class in all disciplines, including fitness, outdoing all the men. But at the end of it she suddenly doubted that her new career would give her the adventures she had always yearned for.

After graduation the new agents were asked to list their job preferences and, unsure of what she now wanted to do, Christine selected the Presidential Protection Division, a competitive posting with a long waiting list. It was beginning to look as if her destiny was to be little more than a glorified bodyguard. But fate was not yet done with her.

The First Lady wanted a female agent as her personal minder but her son, a keen sportsman in his early teens, baulked at the idea. The President's wife also doubted whether the service had a woman who would be able to keep up with him but she asked to see a list of candidates anyway. When she read Christine's resumé she demanded that the agent should be fast-tracked to the residence immediately.

When Christine learned that she was to be a babysitter it gave her even more pause for thought. But with little choice in the matter she took on the job, albeit with forced enthusiasm. The boy was soon impressed with Christine's knowledge and experience in so many sports disciplines, none of which he could best her in. He was a polite, disciplined and pleasant boy whose company Christine eventually began to enjoy though it did little to erode the lingering doubt that she was wasting her time.

A few months into the job Christine accompanied the First Lady and her son on a short politically motivated holiday to Cape Town. During an early dinner at a popular restaurant three local robbers, one of them armed with a revolver, chose the location to practise their profession. They were unaware that the wife of the President of the United States was dining inside at the time and apparently did not notice the collection of immaculate black-tinted suburbans and limousines outside the front, each with a smartly dressed driver at the wheel.

The robbers, posing as staff, made their way through the kitchen and into the dining room without attracting the attention of the Secret Service agents having dinner at a table in a corner away from the VIPs. Christine was eating with the First Lady, her son and a South African dignitary when the dastardly intruders revealed their purpose with a shout, the one with the revolver coincidentally holding it up near the First Lady's head.

The robbers ordered everyone to lie face down on the floor and contribute their watches, cellphones, jewellery and the contents of their wallets. Every agent had a concealed semi-automatic pistol but the robber with the weapon was behind the First Lady, thus presenting a difficult situation for them. They could never allow any harm to come to their charges which meant they could do nothing to escalate the situation.

Christine's pistol was in her tailor-made bumbag around her waist but she was directly under the gaze of the robber with the gun. The First Lady showed her grit when she looked at Christine with an expression of stone-cold malevolence. The robber was swinging his gun around as he shouted, the barrel sometimes moving to aim at the President's son who was looking extremely nervous, his eyes darting between Christine and the other agents as if he was about to run to them. Christine gestured to him to stay calm, worried that he might do something to increase the nervousness of the robbers.

The handful of people at the surrounding tables began lowering themselves to the floor when the First Lady got up from her chair and looked contemptuously at the armed robber. 'Why don't you lower your gun? Then perhaps I'll do what you say,' she said.

Christine initially feared that her boss was simply flirting with the danger and then a second later realised she was deliberately trying to distract the man. She was later overheard saying she knew Christine would take the opening.

As Christine lowered herself to the floor she paused in a position not unlike that of a hundred-metre sprinter waiting for the starter pistol.

'Shut up!' the robber shouted, pointing the revolver directly at the President's wife. 'Get down on the floor or I'll shoot you.'

When Christine made the lunge she put all her power behind it. On making contact with the robber, her outstretched hand pushed the barrel of the weapon towards the ceiling and she practically knocked the man out as her shoulder struck him in the side of his ribcage. The blow launched him across the room and over a table where his head hit a wall, finishing off the job.

The other agents did not lose a second in tearing into the other two crooks, throwing them to the floor where, seconds later, they were bound tightly in plastic cuffs, napkins secured over their eyes. Christine quickly ushered the First Lady, her son and the dignitary out of the restaurant and into the limo which sped away, followed by a couple of the heavy suburbans.

The incident hit the media, although the identity of the agent who saved the day was kept secret, except around the Washington corridors of power. The President heard the details first-hand: his son gave him glowing accounts of Christine's lightning reactions and decisiveness.

A couple of weeks later a vacancy for a Special Secret Service Operative to the Oval Office occurred and Christine's name was placed on the list. But despite her recent heroics it was reckoned that she was unlikely to get a position that in the past had always been filled by men. Another argument against her was her lack of experience.

The First Lady, however, was determined to reward Christine for her valour in the Cape, intuitively aware that the young woman would much rather be doing something more adventurous than working as a bodyguard and sports instructor. Despite stiff opposition from several senior staff members the First Lady demonstrated her influence over the President and within a month Christine was swearing her allegiance to the country's leader in a private ceremony before heading off to Fort Bragg to begin a three-month training course. It was the first of five different locations in the USA and two in Europe where she would learn a variety of skills that included the use of sophisticated communications systems, imaging, the handling of explosives and a variety of weapons, unarmed combat, aggression training and, finally, a couple of weeks learning a special operative's general knowledge base of skills and techniques.

When Christine graduated she was provided with an apartment in Alexander and received instructions to no longer associate freely with her former Secret Service colleagues. Those agents also understood that if they were ever to see her outside the confines of the White House they were not to acknowledge her. That included an agent with whom she was having an affair, which was a blessing since he was madly in love with her but she could not reciprocate to the same extent. It was not a major concern to her that she seemed unable to find a man who was even remotely right for her but she was beginning to wonder if the problem lay with her own personality. But this was the wrong time in her life to cultivate any kind of relationship anyway and so it wasn't even worth thinking about. She could only hope she was kept busy enough so that she did not have time to dwell on such issues. She was not to be disappointed.

She got her first assignment a few days after she'd settled into her apartment, although it was no more than a simple courier task to an embassy contact in Warsaw. Her next dozen jobs were similarly low-level adventures and even though she suspected that she was still being assessed she did begin to wonder if there was ever going to be anything more interesting for an Oval Office operative. And had the world remained on the same even keel the chances were that she might not have seen a great deal more excitement. But if history really is 'philosophy by example' the world will always be a roller coaster swooping up and down between war and peace.

Christine had been an operative for only nine months when New York's Twin Towers were brought down by Muslim extremists, after which her life – like those of so many others – was never to be the same again. The tasks she was assigned suddenly became more intense, secretive and dangerous as America's Cold

War infrastructure was ripped out by its roots and the machinery to wage a world war against Islamic terrorists was hastily assembled. There was an immediate shortage of experienced operatives and Christine found herself busier than she could ever have imagined. In between jobs she was sent on crash courses to learn Arabic and Farsi where she was taught to converse, read and write in those languages at a basic but workable level.

There is nothing like a war to sort the true men and women from the boys and girls and within two years it was hinted to Christine by a senior member of the White House staff that she was near the top of the most-favoured-operatives list. A year later, when she was called to a briefing and given her task at Styx prison, she knew she had finally arrived at the place she had dreamed of since her youth.

But the more difficult and dangerous a task, the greater the risk of failure: the higher one climbed the further one could fall. As she listened to the details of the mission it became clear that it could be a matter of physical survival, not just of boosting her reputation.

Christine closed her laptop, got to her feet, sat on her bed and lay back on the pillow. It was time once more to go through thoroughly the various steps she needed to take in this final phase, to examine the many things that could go wrong and, as far as possible, to determine what her reactions to them might be.

Chapter 12

Stratton woke up to the sound of his cell door depressurising and the feeling of his ears popping. He struggled to open his eyelids – they'd been sealed shut by the dried eye discharge that everyone in Styx appeared to suffer from while they slept. He felt for a bottle of water on the floor by his bed, dabbed some on his eyes and pulled the lids apart as someone came in.

Hamlin walked unsteadily into the room and the door closed as he sat down heavily on his bed. The drastic depressurisation of the mess hall during the riot had clearly taken its toll on the older man. Stratton had recovered minutes after the pressure levels had returned to normal but several of the inmates, particularly the injured, had required medical attention. Hamlin was one of those who'd been taken away on a gurney. Some people were more susceptible than others to variations in the pressures of the gases that make up air, notably in the oxygen level. Hamlin was one of those who did not fare well under such conditions and judging by his startled reaction immediately before the 'attack' he had obviously experienced something like it before and had known he was about to suffer.

'You OK?' Stratton asked sympathetically.

Hamlin did not acknowledge him and seemed to be focusing all his mental resources on simply keeping breathing. He eventually raised his head and opened his red-rimmed eyes to look at his cellmate. 'I don't have the constitution for this place,' he said, sounding strained. 'I can't survive here much longer.'

Stratton could not help wanting to give Hamlin some kind of psychological support. The man was a jailbird and would remain so for the rest of his natural life but Stratton had seen his 'normal' side and had to admit to liking that aspect of him. Perhaps it went deeper than that. Stratton was, after all, stuck inside a maximum-security prison in a grotty cell surrounded by a host of dangers, most of them unknown. It was only natural under such circumstances to seek out friends and allies, particularly when you had none to start with. 'I don't suppose there's anything I can do?' he asked.

Hamlin looked slightly amused by a thought that came to him. 'After my conviction, the FBI showed me a letter they found in my files that I wrote some years before. It was to the President of the United States, letting him know how I felt about some of his foreign and domestic policies. I suggested he should quit or go the way of JFK. I never sent it but the feds decided it was a serious threat because it came from me. I never meant it as a direct threat. It was just a suggestion, you know? . . . They told me I'd never make parole. The only way I was leaving jail was in a body bag.' His expression changed to one of determination. 'I'm gonna prove those sons of bitches wrong,' he said, glancing at Stratton for any reaction to his comment.

Stratton took it as bravado.

'You're an odd fish, fellah, ain't yer?' Hamlin enquired.

Stratton wasn't sure how he was intended to take this comment.

'Somethin' about you. Can't point to it but . . . I don't know. Somethin'.'

'I don't mean to make you feel uncomfortable.'

'Ain't nothin' like that. More like the opposite . . . Maximum-security cons have one thing in common. They ain't ever goin' anywhere, other than another prison. They don't kid themselves about it, either . . . least, not deep in their souls they don't . . . We're all partly dead because of it. You can see it in the way we move, walk, talk. Part-dead people can't hide it . . . You ain't part-dead.'

Hamlin continued to search Stratton's eyes in case he was wrong. 'Maybe it's because you just don't *know* you're part-dead,' he eventually decided, looking away.

He remembered something else he wanted to say to Stratton and, putting a finger to his lips, reached across to his desk and switched on a tape recording of some classical music. He increased the volume and leaned towards Stratton in a conspiratorial manner. 'You know Gann's got a problem with you, don't yer?' he said in a gruff whisper.

Stratton shrugged, going along with the intrigue. 'Why?'

'There ain't a lotta secrets in a prison. If the guards know somethin' the cons'll soon learn about it . . . I don't know why he wants you, though. That never came down the vine . . . Gann don't need a reason to hate someone, anyhow. He's just a mean son of a bitch.'

'I don't suppose there's much I can do about that.'

'I guess not,' Hamlin agreed.

'Unless I got to him first.'

'Fat chance of that.'

Stratton studied Hamlin, weighing him up, trying to decide if he could use him in a plan he had been hatching. The trick would be to make it of benefit to the older man too. It was something Hamlin had said that had triggered the idea. He had expressed a desire to get out of Styx – not that any such yearning was exactly surprising. But it had been more than a simple wish. Hamlin had implied that he really could escape and Stratton had to take this seriously, no matter how much of a long shot it was. Escaping from Styx would take some brilliant planning and knowledge of the prison if it was to be done without help from the outside. Hamlin had the credentials and, in his role as prison engineer, had perhaps also had the opportunity to come up with something. The more obstacles Stratton could break down the better chance he had of finding a way to Durrani.

Nothing was impossible and Stratton felt confident that if he had the time he could at least devise a plan. Successfully carrying it out would be another matter, of course. The point was that escape wasn't impossible. You just had to be smart enough to work it out. There was a risk in involving Hamlin but since Stratton had nothing else to go on but the few hours he had spent in the man's company he decided to rely on his instincts.

Stratton turned his attention to the heavy steel door with its thick rubber seam surrounding it. 'You know these doors are sensitive to external pressure?' he asked.

Hamlin looked at him oddly. 'I know just about everything there is to know about this place, including these doors. I service the machinery that maintains the pressure tanks, remember?'

Stratton looked at him soberly. 'So I'm right.'

'It don't take a genius to figure that out, considering there ain't any locks. Day one I calculated the difference between the inside and outside pressure and at its lowest there's over eight tons keeping that door closed. It would take you, me and a herd of percherons to shift it, and only if there was a handle strong enough to tie them to which there ain't.'

'Unless the pressure was equalised.'

Hamlin smirked. 'That's what everyone spends day two trying to figure out. The pressure in every corner of this entire rabbit warren is controlled from the OCR and even the operators couldn't override the system without tripping a whole bunch of safety devices, procedures, air-locks, alarms and what-you-gots.'

Stratton didn't seem perturbed by Hamlin's negativity. 'Way I understand it is there are a pair of sensors that monitor the different pressures either side. Those sensors are inside the actual door.'

Hamlin scrutinised Stratton more closely. 'It took me till near the end of day three to figure that out.'

'If the sensors detect the pressure on one side equalising with that on the inside they'll automatically compensate,' Stratton continued.

'Unless they're overridden by the OCR which is what happens every time the door is opened . . . I know what you're thinking. Same thing everyone else does eventually. How to manipulate the sensors? There's only one problem, though—'

'And that's the reason you've never been able to figure out how to do it,' Stratton interrupted. 'You don't know precisely where the sensors are.'

Hamlin was growing fascinated with Stratton's line of speculation and he moved closer, his gravelly voice low. 'That's right,' he said, staring into Stratton's eyes. 'If you did, and if you had the right tools, you might be able to isolate the "inside" sensor and make the "outside" one think the pressure inside was higher than what it actually is.'

'And if that could be achieved the system would compensate by decreasing the inside pressure.'

'And when it drops below that of the outside, the door'll pop open . . . Nice theory, ain't it? . . . So far that brings you up to date with me.'

'Unless I knew precisely where the sensor was,' Stratton said.

Hamlin leaned back to look at Stratton from a broader perspective, his expression a mixture of surprise and suspicion.

'You got a pen?' Stratton asked. 'Better still, the tip of a small blade?'

Hamlin continued to study Stratton, trying to make up his mind about him. The guy was either full of shit or he had something very interesting to offer. There was only one way to find out.

Hamlin got to his feet, went to his desk, felt the back of one of the legs and opened a compartment that had been cleverly carved into it. He pulled out a thin strip of metal that had been fashioned into a blade the length of a pen, with string wrapped around one end to form a haft. He handed it to Stratton who got to his feet, faced the door and rubbed the pads of his fingers gently along the seal. Hamlin moved to his side, studying the seal as if he might have missed something the hundred or more times he had meticulously examined it in the past.

'You've noticed these small flaps in the seal?' Stratton said, poking the tip of the blade into one of the creases and prising it open. 'They go all the way around.'

'Sure. They're breathers. Otherwise the seals could blow up like balloons if there was a pressure spike. It's where the hiss comes from when the door opens.'

'And you know there's another seal inside this one.'

'The operating seals, one either side. I've seen these doors stripped down.'

'Did you notice that the operating seals don't have any of these breathers?'

'That's because the sensors are inside them. That's obvious. But it wouldn't have to be no bigger than a pinhead. And if you didn't know exactly where it was you'd never be able to isolate it without ripping out the entire seal – by which time it would no longer operate and you'd be stuck until a team of engineers came down to get you out.'

'The engineers know where the sensors are because they have to service them on occasion.'

'Sure. They just never let me in on that secret,' Hamlin said, starting to get irritated.

'What if I said I knew exactly where the inside sensor was?'

'How the hell would you know that?'

'I got friends,' Stratton said, keeping his voice low. 'I used to be into sat diving. When certain old buddies learned I was heading for Styx they made sure I got a few details they happened to have on this place in case I could use them. I don't know how much use it is,' he added, stepping back to look at the door and then at Hamlin. 'What would you do if you could get the other side of this door?' he asked, tossing out a little bait.

Hamlin remained very much unsure of his new cellmate. 'I want nothin' to do with puttin' the hits on Gann.'

'So you're saying that even if we could open this door without anyone knowing, it wouldn't be of interest to you?'

Hamlin sniffed the bait and found his mouth watering a little.

Stratton read Hamlin's silence to suggest he would be very interested.

'The inside or high-pressure sensor is dead centre on the door-hinge side,' Stratton said, rubbing the spot. 'If we could cut the outer seal just here, then cut into the operating seal, isolate the sensor with a cup of some kind, increase the pressure inside the cup . . . bingo!'

Hamlin was with him every step of the way. 'We could do that easily with a small electric pump.'

'You can get a pump?'

'We're at the bottom of the ocean. Pumps we got.' But Hamlin was still very unsure about a lot of other things. He leaned forward to whisper over the music. 'You open this door, you just got more doors. You got cameras too. Anyone in OCR, the warden's office or the guardroom sees you and that's it. They'll seal you off wherever you are and do what they did in the galley.'

'Then I suppose I'd need to know where Gann was when I opened the door.'

As the notion took root Hamlin's thoughts turned to his own purposes rather than Stratton's. He was hooked on the idea but tried not to show it. If he could get through the door he didn't give a damn what Stratton wanted to do. He knew exactly where *he* would head for.

Stratton sighed dramatically as part of his charade. 'I guess the theory is fine but the practical side would be pretty impossible,' he said, backing off and sitting on his bed.

Hamlin sat down opposite, watching his room-mate and still trying to figure him out. 'But if you could? You beat Gann to death and then walk back into your cell? You ain't gettin' any further.'

'Maybe you're not the only one with an escape plan.'

'Who said I had a plan?'

'You did.'

'I said I'd like to prove 'em wrong. That could mean a lotta different things.'

Stratton looked away as if he'd grown tired of Hamlin's games.

'So you've been here five minutes and you've got an escape plan,' Hamlin scoffed.

'Like I said . . .'

'Yeah, you got friends.'

'Let's just forget it.'

Hamlin didn't want to. He enjoyed nothing more than talking through new technical matters. But this one was of much greater personal interest to him. 'Supposin' we could get through that door. I'm into the whole mutual support thing but only so far. I'd wanna do my own thing. I wouldn't want anything to do with your problems – or your plans.'

'I would neither expect nor want you to. No disrespect but you're no spring chicken any more.'

Hamlin rested back against the wall, still eyeing Stratton suspiciously. 'I don't know about you, my friend . . . It's still the missing part-death side of you that bugs me.'

'Maybe you haven't been around a true optimist for a while.'

Hamlin was not sure why, but he was beginning to trust Stratton.

'Tusker?' a voice boomed over a speaker in a grille beside the air duct.

Hamlin got to his feet and turned down the tape player. 'Yes, sir.'

'How you feelin', Tusker?'

'Not too bad. I'm still gonna sue, though.'

'You know I'd be a witness for yer if I could, Tusker.'

'Generous of you to consider it, anyhow.'

'You feel up to doing some work? We got a torn filter on number two scrubber.'

'I warned you about that one a week ago.'

'Yeah, well, now it's torn. You wanna take a look at it?'

'Where's the engineer?'

'He's not feeling too good.'

'And if I don't?' Hamlin said, winking at Stratton. A short silence followed. 'He'd have to get his drunken ass off his mattress, wouldn't he?'

'You gonna do it or not, Tusker?'

'I'll do it for a cup o' one of them fine clarets the warden always has for dinner.'

'I'll try.'

'Come on, Busby. You can do better'n that.'

'OK,' the operations officer agreed. 'I'll send someone down to escort you in five minutes.'

Hamlin looked at Stratton as a thought struck him. 'Hey? Busby? Those scrubbers are a bitch to pull and, well, I ain't feelin' all that good. How 'bout my cellmate here givin' me a hand?'

'Not a problem. Maybe you can teach him a thing or two for when you're too goddamned old to do it any more.'

'That's thoughtful,' Hamlin said, making a lewd gesture. He slumped back tiredly and looked at the door again, studying the frame around it. He got to his feet and felt the area where Stratton indicated the sensor lay beneath the rubber. 'We're gonna get ourselves a pump and open us a door,' he said in a low voice. 'But not this one.' He looked at Stratton. 'I've got me a door that, I admit, suits me very well, but I think you'll find it'll also suit you better'n this one.' Hamlin went back to the door and his own selfish motives. 'Then I'm gonna show those motherfuckers that Tusker Hamlin still has a few tricks up his old sleeve.'

Stratton watched as the man's faced cracked into a strange smile and asked himself who was manipulating who.

Durrani was kneeling on the bare floor of his cell, sitting back on his heels, his palms flat on his thighs, his back to the door while he prayed towards the far left corner of the concrete room. He had been told by fellow Muslims when he'd first arrived that the apex of the angle of the corner pointed in the direction of Mecca. With no way of ascertaining the accuracy of the claim he took it as fact. He was not permitted a prayer mat and his copy of the Koran had been confiscated for reasons unknown to him the day before so he uttered what chants he could remember, praising Allah and leaning forward to kiss the floor at intervals.

Durrani had never been particularly religious but since his incarceration in Styx, with encouragement from his colleagues, he had found the incentive to at least go through the motions of daily prayer. This kind of prison, without sunlight, a view of his beloved landscape or even the smell of it, was like a living death. He found it ironic that having never seen the sea until the boat ride to the surface ferry platform and coming from a country that was landlocked he now lived deep inside an ocean. Even if he could escape the walls he would be unable to swim.

But despite his past and present circumstances Durrani was not entirely convinced of the rewards that the Koran promised its followers on the other side of the grave. Praying did, however, break up the day: it gave him something to do and if God did turn out to be all he was cracked up to be then at least Durrani was hedging his bets. On completion of each prayer session he mentioned to Allah that he would forgo the promised paradise if he could see his homeland one last time. It was all about maintaining a level of optimism. But deep down Durrani feared his lifelong trend of general misfortune would persist until the end.

One of the difficulties with praying, however, was working out the timings of the five different prayer sessions each day since he was not permitted a timepiece and there was no rising or setting of the sun. Trying to divide the day into five equal portions did, however, confirm his suspicions that the guards were messing with his head beyond what one might expect from the normal rigours of prison life. He received three meals a day, occasionally in the mess hall although most often a tray was brought to his cell. But the periods between meals varied between what seemed to be a couple of hours to five or six or more. The cell lighting worked hand in hand with the feeding. The lighting programme was supposed to simulate sixteen hours of daytime and eight hours of night but Durrani was convinced that some cycles were at least twice as long as they were supposed to be while others were only half the 'official' duration.

There was never a period when he felt completely well, either, although he was not the only one. He was always getting coughs and throat and lung irritations and, like most prisoners in Styx, had developed horrible sores and rashes all over his body. But then, living under constant pressure, far greater than anywhere on the surface of the planet, was not normal and it undoubtedly did strange things to the body as well as to the mind. The temperature also varied greatly but on average it was far too warm and the ambient atmosphere was always humid. Mould and fungus built up quickly in his cell and the guards often failed to provide enough disinfectant to kill the bacteria that thrived in such conditions.

Another source of suffering was the poor air quality. Durrani would sometimes wake from a deep sleep unable to breathe properly, as if there was not enough oxygen in the air. At other times he would feel intoxicated and experience blackouts, unable to remember what he had done only hours before. According to colleagues these were the symptoms of oxygen poisoning and, again, he reckoned it was due to deliberate manipulation by the guards.

The combinations of these physical and mental assaults were gradually wearing him down but the most significant change in his state of mind, and one that probably went unnoticed by his jailers, was his attitude towards his fellow Afghans. Having spent all of his life deliberately avoiding close human contact, with a couple of notable exceptions concerning the fairer sex, he now cherished the rare occasions when he was allowed to mingle with his colleagues. He was still aloof and distant, never discussing his personal history and certainly not his lineage. But he looked forward to the gatherings with anticipation. It was not so much the physical closeness that he sought, nor his compatriots' advice or encouragement. It was simply the direct experience of seeing them there. Durrani sometimes woke up in the darkness with the fear that he was the only prisoner left in Styx.

He suddenly stopped in mid-prayer, his senses, which had become highly tuned, warning him of a sudden drop in pressure. He felt a burning sensation in his lungs and his face reddened as his heart rate increased significantly. This was the third attack since he'd been returned to his cell after the mess-hall incident. He dropped to the floor and lay on his back, complete lack of movement his only defence against the drastic reduction in the amount of oxygen he was able to extract from the air.

The small light bulb on the wall above his bed suddenly went out and his cell was plunged into total darkness. Durrani concentrated on remaining conscious, calculating by estimating the duration of his prayer sessions how long the day had been. He heard the door seals hiss and knew why the air had been thinned and what was coming now. It was barely hours since they'd last come for him. He had hoped they had finished with him. How foolish of him. It would never end.

The door opened with a loud creaking sound and the beam of a sharp blue halogen light searched the room until it rested on his face. 'Stay still!' a voice commanded in heavily accented Farsi as two figures moved inside. He was grabbed around the arms, raised to his feet and held as a sacking hood was placed over his head.

Durrani did not resist as he was manhandled out of the cell in his bare feet and along a slippery damp stone walkway. His guides were not particularly rough with him as long as he remained compliant. Resistance was futile, a lesson he had learned during his first visit to the Styx interrogation room. If he struggled his arms were twisted up his back. If he refused to walk he was released and seconds later a powerful electrode was thrust into his groin, racking his entire body with a pain so intense that it induced vomiting and rectal evacuation. After that he was not interested enough to find out what they would do to him if he resisted further.

Durrani was brought to a halt while a door hissed open in front of him. He was guided through it and up a flight of stairs. This was the usual route he remembered. It led to another corridor at the top of the metal stairs where he was steered left into a room and then into a chair. His hood would then be removed and he would find himself sitting at a table, with a white man sitting on the other side, aiming a microphone at him. A wire leading to a recording device was attached to the mike.

On the whole his interrogations had not been particularly harsh. The first series had been at a camp in Germany, his first stop after being flown out of Afghanistan. It had been run by soldiers and a handful of men in suits and had been all very unsophisticated and procedural. After confirming his identity, place of birth and the school he went to Durrani was asked about the operations he'd taken part in, the names of various commanders and the locations of meeting places, training camps, weapons caches and so on. He answered many of their questions in one of two alternative ways: the ones he felt were inconsequential he answered truthfully, those that he considered more important he lied about.

His interrogators did not appear to know anything about him such as the identity of his true father or the fact that he was part Hazara. 'Tell us now for we will always find out in the end and it will be worse for you,' they had threatened. He did not believe them.

As Durrani shuffled along the corridor between his guards their grip on him tightened perceptibly and he was alarmed by the feeling that they had passed the point where they usually turned off into the interrogation room. He wondered if he was confused about the route but when they took a sharp left-hand corner and passed through a narrow rocky corridor only wide enough for one person he knew this was a different place.

Durrani was guided through a narrow doorway and brought to an abrupt halt, turned around and pushed down into an uncomfortable metal chair. His arms were placed on the hand rests where spring-loaded clamps held them in place, something else that was new to him, and his feet were secured in the same manner to the chair legs. The guards had, without doubt, become more aggressive and the rate of Durrani's breathing increased in line with his nervousness as a horrible thought suddenly nagged at him. He recalled a story, told during a previous gathering of the Taliban prisoners in the food hall, about a special room in Styx with a metal chair in the centre of it and how those who visited it were usually not heard from for weeks after. Sometimes never again.

Durrani's hood was pulled off and he struggled to focus his eyes in the dim light. His shirt was pulled open to expose his bare chest, whereupon a man proceeded to stick small pads on the ends of wires to his flesh in various places. Several were taped to his chest in the area of his heart while others were attached to his neck and temples. Rings with wires coming off them were placed over a finger on each hand as well as on both of his big toes. The wires all came together at a box attached to the wall and after a brief check of the connections the man left the room followed by the guards.

The door closed behind them with a hiss and a clunk.

Durrani looked around him. The small concrete room was circular and otherwise empty. A light glowed on the wall directly in front of and slightly above him. Its source was a rectangular piece of glass, behind which a figure could be seen. The glass was foggy and several inches thick making it impossible to determine the person's features. Only when a voice filled the room through tinny speakers, a voice which Durrani presumed belonged to the person behind the glass, did it become plain that the blurred figure was that of a man.

'Why were you crossing the border the day you were captured by American soldiers?' the man asked in passable Farsi.

Durrani did not answer. In the silence he could hear the echo of dripping water. He looked at the floor, his eyes by now almost fully adjusted to the dim light. It was wet. A drip struck the top of his head and he looked up to see a circle in the vaulted ceiling directly above him. It was a robust metal hatch set within a thick concrete ring. Another drip struck him in the eye, the salt water stinging, made worse because he was unable to reach it with either of his clamped hands.

'Do you refuse to answer my question or are you considering your reply?'

Durrani looked at the ghostly figure and thought now that he could make out another in the background. He expected some form of punishment for not answering. After his earlier interrogations he had wondered to what extent his captors were prepared to torture him and how he would react. When sleep deprivation, loud noises, physical discomfort and shouting appeared to be the full extent of their techniques he had put their restraint down to the usual weakness of Western institutions and their fear of the media, human-rights groups and liberal politicians. But as he stared at the figure behind the glass and took in the characteristics of his confines it struck him that this time he might have made an error of judgement.

'I will ask you once more,' the voice boomed. 'Why were you crossing the border the day you were captured?'

Durrani looked down at the floor, a signal that the man behind the glass appeared to take as a refusal to answer. There was a loud clunk from somewhere in the room, followed by a whirling sound and the noise of the sucking-in of air. Durrani immediately felt the change in pressure in his ears and his face flushed as his entire body tightened. He shook uncontrollably and struggled to breathe. It was as if he'd been gripped by a giant hand that was squeezing him like a sponge. It lasted only a few seconds before he was released, only to swiftly experience the opposite effect. Now he felt as if he was being blown up like a balloon.

The resulting intense discomfort and confusion were unlike anything he had ever experienced before. Just as it seemed his body was going to blow apart, his rib joints straining to disconnect, another loud clunk signalled a reversal of the pumps and a return to normal pressure. When Durrani unclenched his hands he looked down at them to see the fingers had swollen to twice their normal size.

'You just went for a trip towards the surface,' the voice echoed. 'Another few feet and you would have started to stretch like a balloon . . . You see, there's gas in every inch of your body, dissolved into your flesh, blood, other fluids. Even your bones. Nitrogen mostly, the rest oxygen, carbon dioxide, inert gases . . . You ever open a bottle of fizzy drink? Of course you have. Remember how the bubbles suddenly appeared everywhere in the bottle as if by magic? And if you took the top off too quickly the froth would gush out of the bottle? Remember that? Well, that's exactly what happens to the human body if it's depressurised too quickly. Divers call it the bends . . . That's what I'm doing to you . . . Of course, it's not an exact science. I drop the pressure a little, you get a body full of bubbles – the more I drop the pressure, the bigger the bubbles get. Problem is it only takes one little bubble to block the wrong vein in your brain and that's it. Permanent brain damage. Even death. What I'm aiming to do is keep you alive. I'm getting pretty good at it now. Had a bit of practice . . . Made some mistakes, but that's life. Now, let's go back in time a little, to before you were captured. Only a few days before . . . You were in Kabul, is that right?'

Durrani's breathing remained laboured, the pains in his chest still severe, as if every joint in his ribcage had been pulled apart and then harshly pushed back together.

'You've got to give me something soon,' the interrogator said. 'Even if it's something small. Otherwise this is going to be a long and very painful day for you.'

Durrani stared at the floor ahead, trying to control the shaking that suddenly gripped his body. The heavy clunk came again and he jerked in fearful anticipation as the sound triggered the air pump and the drop in pressure. The pain was immediate and even more intense than it had been previously. Durrani let out a howl as the veins in his neck seemed to swell beyond their physically possible limits. He could feel his eyes bulging in their sockets and heard cracking sounds in his head as if the bone plates that made up his skull were pulling apart. Seconds later another clunk signalled another reverse of pressure and Durrani exhaled massively before breaking into a coughing fit. His nose began to run, but it was blood, not mucus dribbling into his mouth. Durrani could taste it and as the more intense pains subsided he let out a long moan.

'You came from Kabul,' the voice continued as Durrani's shoulders sagged with relief.

Durrani could not see the floor clearly any more – his eyes were out of focus, and he feared for the damage the torture was doing to his body.

'Talk to me, Durrani!'

Durrani looked up at the window, no longer able to see any figure behind it, and nodded as he muttered something inaudible.

'I can't hear you.'

'I . . . I will talk,' Durrani said louder.

'Good . . . you know it makes sense . . . Let's go back a little further, just for a moment. Not too far back. A day or so before you left Kabul for the last time there was an attack on a military helicopter, a British helicopter. It was brought down by a rocket. Everyone on board was killed. You know anything about that helicopter? You know anything about the rocket?'

Durrani's breathing increased in anticipation of the next assault on his body, the very thought of which filled him with horror. He wanted very much to say something, to answer the question, but somehow found the strength not to. When the clunk came he tensed so fiercely that he cut the skin against the clamps holding his arms to the chair. Then suddenly another clunk announced the mechanism moving quickly into reverse.

'You don't ever have to hear that sound again if you don't want to . . . You're going to tell me what I want to know in the end. Everyone who sits where you are right now always does. Why go through all that pain, all that damage to your body? Some people have never walked again after leaving this room . . . I'm told it has something to do with bubbles expanding in their lower spine. If that damage goes higher you may lose the use of your arms as well. Is it worth it? Really? Ask yourself if it's really worth it . . . Do you know about the helicopter that was shot down?'

Durrani lowered his head and nodded slightly.

'I didn't quite get that. Was that a yes?'

Durrani nodded again, this time more emphatically.

'Was it you who shot that helicopter down?'

Durrani nodded.

'And then you went to the wreckage, didn't you?'

Durrani did not move.

'What did you take from the wreckage?'

Durrani clenched his jaw. The interrogator knew something but not everything. If he did he would have already cut his abdomen open and found the little packet. Durrani had arrived at the point he could not go beyond without shaming himself, without failing.

'I know you took something from the wreckage. What was it, Durrani? What did you find that you were taking to Peshawar?'

Durrani breathed deeply and tried to prepare himself for the pain that was about to come. He hoped that it would bring death, for that was his only escape now.

The clunk came, followed by the whirling and sucking of air. The pressure dropped, one of his eardrums burst and his eyes pushed out against his eyelids that were squeezed tightly shut. He let out a high-pitched scream as if the life was being squeezed out of every inch of his body. Then something inside him snapped and what light there was went out.

Hank Palmerston sat behind the interrogator, both men squinting through the thick glass at Durrani slumped in his chair.

'You went too far, you assholes,' Hank muttered.

The technician who had stuck the sensors to Durrani was seated in a corner in front of several life-monitoring devices. 'He's not dead,' he said. 'He's just unconscious.'

'That machine tell you when he's gonna come out of it and in what condition?'

'He has normal brain and sensory nerve activity at all extremities,' the technician confirmed. 'We just took him beyond his pain threshold.'

Hank shook his head as he got to his feet. 'Two fuckin' years you've been doing this and you still can't get it right . . . Now you listen to me,' he said, leaning heavily over the back of the young Ivy League CIA interrogator who remained sitting in his chair and facing the glass. 'We know that helicopter was a British intelligence operation carrying a VIP passenger to Bagram. We know this guy shot it down. We know he found something in the wreckage. We know he took it to his boss in Kabul who then sent him into Pakistan with it . . . What we *don't* know is what he found in the wreckage, if it was the same thing he was carrying, who he was taking it to or why, or where the hell it is now! But maybe he could help us with a few of those questions, that man sat unconscious in the chair, the one who can't talk to us ANY FUCKING MORE!!! . . . And now it would seem that we're not the only people in this place interested in talking to him. When I heard the feds were sending an agent down here I assumed it was to spy on us and the pricks who run this place. If that's true, which I have every reason to believe it is, then who's this guy Charon and what's his interest in Durrani? Is he a fed? If not, who's he working for? Now you're probably asking yourself, why should we care anyway? Well, I'll tell you. This place, and places like it, produce the information that allows our citizens to sleep safely in their beds at night, to go about their normal daily lives, to fill up their gas tanks without worrying if they'll be able to fill them up next time they get low. But the only threat to places like this, information-providing institutions of national importance, comes not from our enemies but from ourselves. We're falling apart from the inside, like the Roman Empire. We're eating our own flesh, coming up with laws and rules we can't possibly live up to. They might be great and righteous rules, but they're a thousand years too early. And so it's up to us to keep this country safe any way we can. And if it means taking on our own people, then so be it. How we do it is to find ways of convincing the doubters to see things our way. Now I'm an intelligence officer. The only weapon I've ever used is information. But it's more powerful than any gun or any bomb. Whatever Durrani knows is worth something, a lot maybe. I want to know what it is – but

I can't get information from UNCONSCIOUS PEOPLE!!! . . . Have I made myself clear?!'

The interrogator remained motionless as Hank's voice echoed in the small stone and concrete room. He was intimidated by Hank, his overbearing boss, but arrogant enough to show no reaction to Hank bawling him out.

Hank left the room. When the door closed the technician looked over at the interrogator like a sixth-former after a scolding from a teacher. 'He'll be OK. His signs are rising.'

'Get him to the hospital,' the interrogator said. 'Then, soon as he's ready, get him back in here.'

The interrogator's voice crackled from a speaker as Mandrick sat listening in his chair behind his desk. He stared thoughtfully up at his vaulted stone ceiling with its damp rusty scars leading from the ends of massive central bolts down to the tops of the walls where they disappeared behind ornate façades erected to hide the unsightly concrete. The CIA were unaware that a listening device had been secreted in their interrogation room. Hank would have been very upset to discover that the tiny transmitter was linked to a receiver in the warden's office. Mandrick was surprised how easy the bug had been to fit: he'd ordered it online from a commercial spyware supplier in Los Angeles and had then taken an installation lesson from a private detective agency in Houston. It had been just as easy to keep it from being discovered since, as warden, he was informed whenever the Agency's electronic eavesdropping detection unit was due to arrive.

Mandrick's reason for planting the device was to help him collect personal insurance against any CIA backlash when the time came for him to pull out of Styx. His eventual departure was always going to be interesting, he realised. He knew far too much about the irregularities of their operation and being a civilian made controlling him complicated. On the other hand, it was the

CIA who had originally installed him in the position and that meant they'd also have an exit strategy for him.

There was no doubt in Mandrick's mind that the Agency had a plan in place for whenever he might leave. His fear, reality-based or otherwise, was that any such scheme would not be agreeable to him. He wanted to leave on his own terms, which could prove dangerous. He knew as well as the Agency did that if he happened to vanish one day it would go largely unnoticed. For those few who might wonder about where Mandrick might have gone his disappearance could be simply explained. Rumours of the corruption that went on in Styx could be leaked, specifically stories of tax evasion. Since Mandrick was at the helm of Felix Corp's undersea interests, any mysterious vanishing by him would not be a huge surprise to anyone.

But his most valuable insurance so far against such an event being engineered by the CIA was the evidence he had accumulated showing the Agency's use of decompression as a torture. It was a serious violation of the Geneva Convention, for one thing. Still, the Agency could probably get away with the explanation that it was some localised misconduct by Hank Palmerston done without Langley's knowledge. They would suffer but not long-term. There was a war on and it was not the time to start ripping into the nation's most important anti-terrorist information gatherers. Therefore it was not the quality of insurance Mandrick was looking for. He needed something big enough to barter for a long-lived amnesty, something he could either offer as exchange for his safe departure when the time came, or use as a deterrent that he could threaten to release if anything suspicious should befall him. It was a dangerous game – but then, that was the business he was in.

Mandrick unclipped his minicomputer from his belt and plugged it into the mainframe lead. He inserted a new storage card into the minicomputer's socket and downloaded the recent interrogation conversation onto it. After unplugging the minicomputer and clipping it back onto his belt he saved the original conversation to a file.

A gentle beep sounded and he looked at the control panel to see a small red light blinking. It was the secure landline and, knowing who it was, he picked up the receiver. 'My office is empty,' Mandrick said.

'So's mine,' a voice replied. It was Forbes. 'I don't think our problem has gone away.' Forbes sounded edgy. 'Frankly, I'm concerned . . . Can you hear me OK?'

Mandrick was tired of what he considered to be Forbes's ever-increasing spinelessness. 'I'm here.'

'We may have taken this train as far as it's going to go. I'm getting hints of building pressure within the House. Several Representatives have sent me enquiries. Felix executives have reported probes into their assets, which has to be the work of the FBI. It doesn't look good. This thing could explode any time. You may have to start making preparations.'

Mandrick sighed to himself. Wasn't the FBI undercover agent clue enough? 'I understand,' he said, allowing Forbes to maintain the illusion that he was in control of everything.

Mandrick found it bizarre how the man did not understand that when jumping from a sinking ship it was a case of every man for himself. Forbes always sounded as if the dissolution of Styx was going to be an orderly evacuation with some kind of convivial reunion afterwards where all the players met for drinks and canapés. He wanted to suggest to the congressman that he should not only be concentrating on his own escape but also how he was going to *stay* escaped. But if the man was unable to see the obvious dangers then no amount of advice Mandrick might offer would be of help. Not that Mandrick gave a damn about his boss anyway.

'Doesn't it bother you?' Forbes asked after Mandrick's long spell of silence. 'You don't sound concerned?'

'We knew it was going to end one day.'

'But not like this. Not now. Of course we considered it. I have my contingency plans. But we never really believed it would happen so soon – at least, I didn't. I don't think you did either, did you?'

'It's always wise to be prepared.'

'Then you're saying you're ready to go ahead?'

'Not entirely. I will be when the time comes.'

'I'm asking you if you're prepared to carry out the doomsday phase, God damn it – as we discussed?'

'Of course.' Mandrick wanted to add that it was a most essential phase of his own plan of escape but he refrained. It was evident the senator could not be trusted and was more than capable of offering Mandrick up to save himself. Come to think of it, that would make good sense on his part.

Mandrick suddenly felt uneasy as the notion took root. It was immediately followed by a tinge of panic as he feared he was falling behind and that Forbes was actually setting him up. He suddenly wondered if he should be making his move sooner than he'd thought.

'Minimum risk to crew and inmates. I think that's essential. It's the ramifications of our actions that will be our undoing.'

'Of course,' Mandrick said. Inwardly he was in complete disagreement, wondering if Forbes was just being smart.

'You must see that if we cover our tracks as best we can then there will be less interest in pursuing us.'

'I understand,' Mandrick said, deciding that if Forbes was not subtly trying to entrap him then the man was sounding like an idiot.

'As long as you do . . . Fine, then. I'll get back to you as soon as I hear anything else. Do nothing without my say-so. Is that understood?'

'Of course.' That was it, Mandrick decided. As far as his suspicions were concerned that last instruction gave Forbes's game plan away. Forbes was trying to control the final stage of the abandonment of Styx, the doomsday phase, which included both their escapes. Mandrick reasoned that if he was wrong and had misjudged Forbes it did not matter. He could not afford to take the risk and had to stay a step ahead of his boss.

'I'll speak to you later,' Forbes said and the phone went dead.

Mandrick replaced the receiver. The feeling of independence he had once enjoyed while in Styx had turned into one of isolation. The lines of control from the shore had stretched to breaking point as his ship headed towards the void. Mandrick had to scuttle it while he still could.

Since it was now unlikely that he would obtain any kind of insurance against the CIA he would have to fall back on his original plan – which was to devise a scenario that provided substantial evidence of his death without his body having to be found. That was not impossible. It would all depend on the execution of his plan.

As Mandrick got to his feet the door buzzer sounded and he looked at the monitor to see Christine standing outside. She appeared relaxed and confident as usual but as he studied her, zooming the camera in on her face, examining her extraordinary natural beauty, he thought he could detect a trace of tension in her body language.

He checked his watch. Dinner wasn't for a couple more hours. She was early. An enigma, he mused. His gut feeling told him that she was as much a prison inspector as the pope was. She'd been the first person to talk to Charon when he came around. Charon was a damned spy for someone. The place was probably crawling with spies. But he could care less now. It was time to pull the plug on the operation – an apt way of putting it, he reckoned.

Mandrick considered sending her away but decided that he couldn't. If she was a spy then the blossoming romance between them was an act on her part. She was planning on leaving that evening but he couldn't go with her now. Their 'affair' would end this night. She was here for something, to give or to take. Perhaps it was to give first and take later. Having his way with her for half an hour or so would not cripple his plan. The thought amused him. He had the weight of the world on his shoulders, desperate to finalise a strategy for his own survival and yet here he was pausing to consider a piece of ass. What a maverick he was. It gave him a feeling of masterfulness, of superiority. He was a true buccaneer, a mercenary to the core, a rebel and adventurer. What could be more heroic than to take a break at such a crucial juncture for a romantic interlude?

He hit the button beside the intercom and as the door hissed, clunked and opened he stepped from behind his desk and into the centre of the room.

Chapter 13

Hamlin, followed by Stratton and a guard, led the way down a narrow, sloping, dimly lit corridor. The mould and fungus common to Styx had taken a particularly firm grip of this section of the prison. Dripping lengths hung from rusting ceiling girders and intertwined between the conduit and cables that followed the contours of the walls. Hamlin slipped on a patch of slimy plankton and Stratton only just managed to grab him before he fell on his backside.

'Thanks,' Hamlin said, taking a moment to recover and catch his breath. 'This road is long overdue for a clean-up, Jed.'

'You know we don't have enough inmates to maintain the whole place,' the guard replied.

'I don't see why we can't use the Buttfucks,' Hamlin said, taking a grimy cloth from his pocket and wiping the sweat from his face and neck.

'I don't make the rules,' the guard said, loosening his jacket. Sweat stains were clearly visible on it around his chest and armpits.

'If you got rid of these damned plants you could reduce the humidity down here,' Hamlin argued.

'And then you guys'd complain about the disinfectant.'

'It ain't disinfectant, Jed, it's industrial-strength weedkiller,' Hamlin sighed, as if he had complained about it a hundred times. 'Like we ain't got enough health hazards down here we gotta soak up that shit.'

'Quit bitchin', Tusker, and get movin'.'

'Just give me a minute, will yer? My old lungs don't process the air as good as they should. I use the term "air" loosely, of course. Smells like raw sewage. We can only guess what we're taking into our lungs.'

The guard rolled his eyes.

A tinny computer-generated voice announced the time over the speakers.

Stratton wiped the sweat from his face with his sleeve as he waited for Hamlin to move on. He pondered on the humming sound that had grown louder with their descent. The sound of water was still the most noticeable noise; a green, frothy liquid ran down a gutter on one side of the concrete path. The wall on the same side was practically hidden by a variety of piping and conduits, some of it hanging loosely where the original fastenings had corroded or broken off.

Hamlin sighed heavily and moved on, ducking below a large metal brace that secured a cluster of enormous air ducts to the ceiling. The men weaved between clumps of dripping fungus as they headed steadily downhill.

The lights dimmed suddenly as the voltage dropped. The guard produced a flashlight as Hamlin slowed to a more careful pace. The sloping path became long steps as its angle steepened. Stratton reckoned that they were approaching the lowest depths of the prison. A broad tunnel appeared ahead, cutting across their path. As the lights returned to full brightness voices penetrated through the other noises, accompanied by the sound of heavy footsteps. Stratton realised the sound was coming from behind them.

'Step aside,' a voice called out and the three men moved against the pipe-covered wall.

A guard led half a dozen prisoners at a brisk pace down the long steps. The perspiring inmates were all wearing heavy-duty overalls, robust boots, mining helmets and harnesses from which various tools and pouches hung. They shuffled past, their hammers and chisels clanking, each man carrying an emergency breathing tank on his back with a full-face mask hanging from the valves by the head-straps.

'That's you in a couple of days, buddy,' Hamlin said to Stratton.

'They're still mining pretty actively,' Stratton observed. The report on the old mine had made only scant reference to current activity.

'Some prisons do licence plates and street signs. Our extra-curricular is workin' the face.'

As the tail-end guard went past them into the larger tunnel he called for a halt. 'Take a breather,' he said, his voice echoing. 'Last smoke before we go in.'

The guard looked at Stratton with sudden recognition and gave him a nod. 'How you feelin'?' he asked.

Stratton thought it was a strange question from a guard but he nodded anyway.

The guard joined Jed and his colleague and they all lit one up.

'You don't remember him, I s'pose,' Hamlin said.

Stratton shook his head. 'Should I?'

'That's Zack. He's the guy who saved your ass from drownin'.'

Stratton looked back at the guard. These were odd circumstances in which to show appreciation to someone for saving your life.

'Don't worry about it,' Hamlin said as if he could read Stratton's thoughts. 'He's just as likely to take it back if you step outta line. He's one of the fair ones . . . It's what this place was before they converted it,' Hamlin said.

Stratton looked at him, wondering what he was talking about.

'This place. It was a mining and agriculture experiment.'

Stratton acted as if he knew nothing about the facility's past. 'What are they mining?'

'Gems. When it was an experiment it cost the taxpayer a fortune to run and the yield didn't even begin to cover the expenses. When it got closed down they kept the water pumps running. Rumour is that an engineer working on the site in those days wasn't straight-up about the mine's true potential. As they were closing down he found a new strike – a big one. Next thing you know a bunch of private investors came up with the plan to reopen the project as a prison. Pretty obvious all they really wanted was access to the mine. Pretty smart to get Uncle Sam to pay for the reopening and running of the facility. Even smarter to have a work force that don't cost anything, ain't goin' anywhere and can't tell anyone what's goin' on down here. Some of the guys have kept a few rocks for themselves but they ain't goin' anywhere with 'em. The guards get a nice fat tax-free bonus each month in a brown envelope to keep 'em sweet. And the CIA turns a blind eye to it all and even plays safety for the corporation because they get what they want.'

'Pretty smart set-up all around,' Stratton agreed.

Hamlin looked at him, the trace of a scowl on his face. 'You think I'm as dumb as you, don't you?'

Stratton looked into his angry eyes and was reminded of how unhinged the man really was. 'We're the ones down here working for them,' Stratton said, pushing it, curious about the old man's mental state. Hamlin was probably a genius which, as the saying went, was often close to madness.

'Not for long, my friend. These pricks'll remember the day they locked Tusker Hamlin up in here. They said it would be the last anyone ever heard from me. Well, they're wrong, Mister Charon. They're wrong.'

Hamlin continued to stare at Stratton, his look turning to one of curiosity. 'Charon,' Hamlin said, this time pronouncing it 'Kar-on', a smirk forming on his lips. 'That's very amusing . . . Now I know who you are.'

Stratton held his gaze. Since the guards were within earshot he was prepared to defend himself against any accusation that Hamlin might make.

'You're the ferryman.'

Stratton had no clue what the man was talking about.

'The Styx ferryman,' Hamlin continued. 'Karon was sent by the gods to carry the dead souls of evil men down the Styx river and into hell.'

Stratton remembered the mythological story although he did not recall a ferryman. Hamlin had had him worried there for a moment.

'OK, you guys,' the guard called out. 'Let's get going. See yer later,' he said, waving to his colleagues.

Stratton and Hamlin watched the miners trudge into the mine entrance. 'What's it like in there?' Stratton asked.

'Dunno,' Hamlin said. 'Never wanted to find out. Another reason I made myself an indispensable engineer.'

The two men followed their guard further down the low-ceilinged tunnel for a short distance and stopped outside a large airlock door set in a broad reinforced concrete wall. The door had originally been painted blue but most of the coating had fallen off to reveal rusting metal below.

'Jed at the air room,' the guard said into his radio as he looked up at a black semi-sphere fixed to the ceiling above them. A second later there was a loud hiss, followed by a heavy clunk, and the door moved but only a couple of inches. The guard leaned his shoulder against it to help it open. 'Piece o'shit door,' he grunted as he put all his effort behind it. The door opened slowly and he stepped back, out of breath, to let Hamlin and Stratton lead the way inside.

Two things struck Stratton with some force as the door opened. One was the sudden increase in machinery noise, the other was an intense smell like rotten eggs.

'You'll get used to it,' the guard said, pushing him in.

Hamlin stepped through the door as if eager to get on with the job. 'I find it almost refreshing,' he said above the increased noise, sucking in the air as if it was nectar.

'You would, you strange motherfucker,' the guard said.

Hamlin pulled two pairs of ear defenders out of a box by the door and handed one set to Stratton. They afforded some relief from the high-pitched noise.

They were in a cavernous space, the largest single chamber in the facility. A thousand miles of ducts twisted in and out of several machines and up to the ceiling which they practically covered, finally disappearing through the walls in several places. In the spacious centre was a large wooden workbench covered in various machine parts and tools, with power jacks dangling from the ceiling. It was a dishevelled-looking place, untidy, rusty and disorganised, like the bowels of a neglected supertanker. Metal stairways led up to various service gantries and walkways surrounding the bigger machines.

'I'll leave you guys to get on with it,' shouted the guard.

'Don't hurry back,' Hamlin replied caustically.

The guard waved him off and stepped back through the door, which closed behind him and sealed shut.

When Stratton looked back at Hamlin the man was grinning at him. 'Welcome to my office,' Hamlin shouted.

Stratton walked into the cavern, turning around to take it all in. 'How much of the prison's air does this place scrub?' Stratton asked.

'These only run the mine and inmate levels now. You'd need twice the number of scrubbers, all working efficiently, plus a couple thousand litres of oxygen a day to cover the entire place. There's a mother of a surface barge takes care of the living quarters . . . The desalinators over there only provide part of the potable water. Those pumps're pretty essential, though,' he said, indicating four squat machines along one of the far walls, two of them running and responsible for much of the noise. 'They dump a lot of the water. If they fail you're lookin' at shuttin' down the entire lower sections, including the mine.'

'If this place is so important how come they let you down here on your own?'

'They got pretty lax with me over time. I do a good job, I'm twenty-four seven, and I'm free. I guess they think I'm harmless. There's nothin' serious I can do down here – or so they think. But they don't know Tusker Hamlin as well as they think they do.'

Stratton chose not to question the remark and walked over to dozens of large steel gas bottles stacked in frames along a wall. They were an argon-oxygen mix, all connected together through an array of high-pressure pipes.

'OCR emergency gas,' Hamlin said. 'It ain't essential, though. Just a back-up.'

Stratton reckoned that two men could barely lift one of the bottles, never mind carry it very far. He had no specific interest in them and was simply filing away anything that might be of value.

'Shall we get on with it, then?' Hamlin asked, standing behind him.

Stratton had not heard him draw close. He looked around at the man and saw that he was wearing a strange smirk.

'The door,' Hamlin said. 'Let's test your theory.'

'You mean open it?'

'Sure. What else?'

'It's not something you can test and put away for another day. They'll know in OCR as soon as it opens. We'll only get one hit.'

'Time's running out for the both of us, especially for you,' Hamlin said. 'Gann ain't the patient type. He's gonna make his move soon.'

Hamlin was attempting to manipulate him by playing up the Gann threat. But the older man did not know how right he was. Gann was coming after him because he was the only witness to the ferry sabotage. This was no longer just a mission to get the tablet from Durrani. It had also become largely about Stratton's survival.

He suddenly felt overwhelmed, his confidence about completing the mission in tatters. There was no way out for him, either. Even giving himself up and telling the truth about why he was in Styx was not going to save him. It would only make matters worse since his credibility as a witness would be too high. Stratton had bounced into the operation, all cocky and confident, not only about getting hold of the tablet but also making an historic escape. What an arrogant prick he was, he thought.

Stratton could feel his temples tighten as he realised the true level of his desperation. He was well and truly screwed. And now Hamlin wanted to open the door. But into what? Stratton had no idea where to go or what to do. Was everything down to waiting in ambush in some dark corner in the hope that Gann would amble past so that he could jump him? That was the best Stratton could come up with. It was pathetic. He felt like an amateur.

He looked at Hamlin who now represented the last vestige of hope he had to cling on to. His survival depended now on the plans of an old lunatic. Things could not get any worse. 'Where're you going if we get through that door?'

'Let me explain somethin' to you. I've spent two years, ever since the first day I walked into this joint, figuring out how to get out of here. One thing I hadn't been able to figure were the doors and you walked into my life with the answer. That's providence and I'm grabbing it with both hands. But I don't owe you anything.'

'Nothing for showing you how to open the door?'

'You need that as much as I do. Maybe more. At least I have time on my hands. Yours is running out.'

'You don't even know it'll work.'

'It'll work. You gave me the missing piece of the puzzle.'

'Why can't you take me with you to the ferry? That's the only way out.'

'Why don't you just concentrate on your own problems?'

'Getting out that door doesn't get me to Gann.'

'Oh, I dunno. A resourceful guy might stack things in his favour.'

'You're full of shit, Hamlin. You're just a crazy old man. I don't see why I should help you if you can't help me.'

Hamlin started to grin widely, displaying his stained and cracked teeth. 'Maybe I can.'

'I'm beginning to think you're just an old windbag.'

Hamlin was still smiling. 'I don't know why I like you, ferryman. But I do . . . I know this place better'n anyone, even the people who built it, because I know the changes that were made when the corporation moved in. The original experiment needed independence from a surface barge. A life-support system floating on the surface defeated the whole idea. Failure in that department was probably why it got cancelled. The current surface barge was put in for the prison. They depend on it. It's the key to helping the both of us. We need confusion. The barge provides air, water, power. We screw the barge up and we got ourselves a pretty neat diversion, just like a military operation.'

'How can you do that from down here?'

Hamlin gave him a knowing smile once again. 'This room houses all the distribution conduits for the prison since it was intended to be the main life-support factory. When they brought the barge in it made sense to utilise the distribution system that was already in place. That's what I figured, at least. So I searched around. I discovered I was wrong to a certain extent. They rebuilt the water- and air-distribution system, added water pumps to level three, shut down the sterilisers and desalinators, reduced the workload for the air scrubbers. But what they did end up utilising was some eighty per cent of the power-distribution conduits.'

Hamlin walked over to a metal staircase and climbed to the top. 'Come take a look,' he said.

Stratton followed.

Hamlin led him along a gantry, around a corner, behind the line of scrubbers to an ordinary door. He reached for a small rock in the stone wall, removed it, put his hand inside the hole and withdrew a key. 'One of the service engineers always used to leave the key in the door while he was working in here. I made a mould out of putty, took the key out of the lock one day and made an impression. Took me a while to make a copy of the key,' he said as he put the key into the lock. 'It ain't a perfect copy,' he said, concentrating while manipulating it, massaging it back and forth. The key finally raised the tumblers and turned. 'But it works in the end,' he said as he opened the door.

Inside were several large dust-covered electrical cabinets. 'These are just two of the transformers. But they're an important pair – if you wanna screw up the others, that is.'

Hamlin opened the cupboards and Stratton looked at the complex array of high-powered cables, switches and junctions. 'How do you know what feeds what?' he asked.

Hamlin was still wearing that know-it-all grin. He reached behind one of the cabinets and retrieved a long tube of paper, placed it on a table and unrolled it. It was an electrical blueprint, a complex diagram that was practically meaningless to Stratton. 'I took this off one of the engineers about a year ago. I know every damn circuit on here.'

'You can control the prison's circuitry from here?'

'No. Can't do that. But I can sure as hell screw it up. I can trip circuit-breakers all over that damned barge. The barge isn't manned twenty-four seven. Even if there was an engineer on board it'd take him a while to figure it out. And no engineer would reconnect a circuit before they knew why it broke in the first place.'

'You can cut the power to the prison?'

'Some of it.'

'But there's an auxiliary power system.'

'Sure. But it only runs essentials. In this place that's mostly life support. Security always comes second to safety. I'd say you'd have as much as eight hours before the system was back on line. That long enough for you?'

'Internal doors?'

'Level access will become emergency access, not security. They'll all go green.'

'The ferry dock?'

'Uh-uh. External access is safety so they'll stay secure. I don't know about cell doors and internal security such as that one,' Hamlin said, indicating the door to the scrubber room. 'That's why we have to open it manually before we blow the fuses, otherwise we'd have no power to do it after. You see what I'm tellin' you?'

Stratton did. His mind raced at the possibilities. He could get back up to the other levels. But he still wouldn't be able to get to Durrani unless he knew precisely where the Afghan was. His only chance was to get to Gann first. If he could then he might be able to resume his original plan, having neutralised the main threat to his life. It looked like that plan still amounted to nothing more than lying in wait. But if the entire facility was in turmoil there was a good chance Gann would turn up and an equally good chance Stratton could find a dark, unobserved place from which to jump out at him. The overall plan was sketchy at best but it opened up possibilities. Suddenly he reckoned that once he was through the door he didn't need Hamlin after all. That was a relief in itself. 'OK,' he said.

'You go right. I turn left,' Hamlin said, wanting assurance.

Stratton could not imagine why Hamlin would want to head deeper into the complex. Left was essentially down. As far as he could remember there was nothing in that direction but the mine and some more caverns. 'You go where you want. I'm heading up.'

'Good.' Hamlin grinned. 'To make the most of it we should open the door at the same time the circuit-breakers snap. That way, when the alarm triggers in OCR they'll think it's part of the electrical fault. They'll have too much else to worry about than a door opening down at this level anyway.'

Stratton began to prepare himself mentally for the push. Like a runner approaching the starting line, he was thinking ahead to the first curve in the track. Charging up the corridor would be no different from crashing into a house and not knowing where the enemy was.

'Let's do it,' Hamlin said as he left the room and headed along the gantry and down the steps. 'A drill saw and something to isolate the sensor,' he called out as he hurried down the steps.

Doctor Mani stood over Durrani who was lying on the operating table in a near-unconscious state. As usual, the medic was not expecting to find much in the way of outward signs of injury after an over-zealous pressure interrogation but he did a cursory check as always. Durrani moaned as Mani pushed open his eyelids to inspect his pupils with a light, looking for any sign of brain damage.

The door opened and Gann walked in. 'How is he?' he asked, towering over Mani.

'They might've gone too far with this one. How many times have I warned those idiots?' Mani said, pulling open Durrani's shirt. He plugged the two earpieces of his stethoscope into his ears and moved the other end from one place to another around the Afghan's chest while listening to the man's erratic breathing. 'God knows how many of his bronchial sacs are ruptured.' Mani felt along the sides of Durrani's ribcage. 'I think he's dislocated several ribs.'

'Is he gonna live?' Gann asked, not particularly interested from any humane point of view. He collected knowledge of the human body's endurance to violence like a stunt-car racer took an interest in car wrecks.

'He'll live. Question is how comfortably. Unless he's suffered brain damage in which case it won't matter, I suppose.'

'I heard the tech say they took him equal to almost halfway to the surface. His lungs must've been tryin' to push outta his backside.' Gann grinned at his description.

'Charming,' Mani said dryly as he wheeled a scanner over to the table and positioned it above Durrani's throat. 'Would you move aside, please?' he said to Gann who was blocking the doctor's view of a monitor on a nearby counter.

Gann obliged just enough, craning to look down at Durrani. 'He's gotta bit of red froth comin' out the side of his mouth.'

'Thank you. Now, please, give me room.' Mani slowly moved the scanner down Durrani's torso, his eyes glued to the monitor that showed the Afghan's chest cavity in a variety of colours indicating bone, air spaces, flesh and fluids. 'This man cannot go back into that chamber – ever. He won't survive another massive decompression.'

'They've got other methods,' Gann said matter-of-factly.

Mani glanced sideways at Gann who was now concentrating on the monitor. He had known the man since arriving at the prison a year and a half ago to relieve the original doctor and had never ceased to be amazed at the depths of human depravity Gann was capable of reaching. Mani had never come across such an animal before. He more or less understood the need for such types in a high-security guard system of this nature and accepted it was a small community and that contact was unavoidable. But he wished he did not have to communicate face to face with him and his kind quite so much as he did. Preferably he wouldn't have had anything at all to do with them. What irritated Mani most was how Gann treated him as some kind of colleague or, worse, accomplice. Mani accepted that he was a part of the Styx corruption but he never saw himself as anywhere near Gann's sordid level.

'You can speak their language, can't you?' Gann asked.

'A little. I'm not fluent.'

'When he comes around I want you to ask him some questions.'

'Fine. Come back next week sometime.'

Gann looked at the side of Mani's head as he suppressed an urge to punch it. He regarded the doctor as a subordinate and was not used to being talked to by him in that way. He wondered if it was perhaps time to remind the man of his position in the prison hierarchy. 'I wanna know what Charon was doing with him in the galley,' he said.

Mani sensed the irritation in Gann's voice and realised his last comment had not gone down very well. 'Sure. I'll ask him . . . Anything else?'

Gann sensed the new patronising tone. 'Maybe I'll just wait until he comes around.'

Mani was always careful not to upset Gann, having experienced his venom on his first day on the job. Styx's original doctor had also been an Asian – a coincidence, although that fellow was a Sikh. He had arrived wearing his turban, which did not go down very well among the guards, particularly with Gann. It was too similar to the traditional black headdress of the Taliban and as far as Gann was concerned the doctor had to be more or less the same as them. Mani never met the man and did not know how he had come to be employed as the prison doctor but when he'd refused to remove his turban he'd had to go.

When Gann found out that Mani was Hindu he confronted him right away, telling him he didn't trust anyone who was religious, especially on this job, and a religious Asian was off the chart. Gann didn't think there was any difference between Hinduism and Islam and therefore Mani was considered to be doubly untrustworthy. It took a long and patient conversation to persuade Gann that Hinduism was not a religion but a way of life, a philosophy. It was far older than Christianity, which in turn was hundreds of years older than Islam. Mani did not worship a god or single out any prophet and he had no set rituals or performances – like praying on a mat, for instance.

Gann only began to accept Mani when the Indian assured him that he had no time for Muslims. Hinduism, he explained, did not get in the way of making money even by dubious means as long as there was a sound philosophy behind it. Mani pitched himself as simply a healer. The philosophy was flawed but not sufficiently so to keep Mani from turning up to work. Besides, there was also the small matter of him being unable to practise his profession anywhere else in America.

Mani had been struck off the medical register after a patient he was treating had died. He was running a detoxification clinic at the time and was accused of serious malpractice after giving a heroin addict an experimental cocktail of opiate antagonists that led to a fatal seizure.

Mani might have avoided the subsequent litigation had it not come to light that he also happened to be a director of a company that was concentrating on commercialising an ultra-rapid detoxification treatment that had not been officially approved. In addition, he recruited heroin addicts as guinea pigs for experiments without informing them of the extreme risks. Mani was lucky not to have been incarcerated when it also transpired that the dead patient was not his first failure. No others had died but many were found to be suffering from a variety of debilitating physical and mental conditions. Fortunately for him the evidence that his treatment had been directly responsible was inconclusive. But the court case cost Mani every penny he had and, unable to practise, he found himself in a desperate situation.

Mani was an Indian immigrant who had moved to America with his parents when he was five years old and, much as he loathed the thought, he considered moving back to Calcutta where he'd been born to continue making a living the only way he knew how. He sold his car, the last remaining possession of value he had, in order to buy the air ticket. But two days before he was due to leave America he was approached by a man who said he represented the Felix Corporation in Houston and that they had a job they would like him to consider.

When Mani started to explain he was no longer able to practise the man said he knew everything about Mani's past and that the Indian had all the right qualifications for the job. By that he meant Mani was not only a doctor but was also corrupt. And there was no need to be concerned about the legalities since the job was not on the American mainland. When Mani learned the whereabouts of his new practice he brought up the obvious point that the prison was still in sovereign waters. It was explained to him that certain legal technicalities allowed him to work offshore as a medical-supplies officer as long as he didn't call himself a doctor.

As a medical-supplies officer Mani was permitted to give demonstrations to the guards of how to use the most basic of equipment, which he was required to do whenever there was an illness or injury. It was one of the reasons why Gann felt free to come and go as he pleased – not that the man needed a reason. Gann enjoyed watching Mani ply his trade, the more serious the medical problem the better.

Mani loosened Durrani's trousers and pulled them down to expose his abdomen. He felt around the area, firmly pressing the flesh in places in search of any muscle tightening that might indicate an internal injury. Finding no obvious signs of damage he realigned the scanner and slowly moved it from Durrani's ribcage onto his abdomen. As it moved down to Durrani's hips a small black object just above his groin area appeared on the monitor.

Mani's brow furrowed as he tuned the scanner's focus. The object became clearer.

'What's that?' Gann asked.

'I have no idea.'

'He swallow something?'

'It's not in the gut,' Mani said as he examined the flesh to find the small pink scar.

'Maybe it's a piece of shrapnel,' Gann suggested. 'These guys've been in all kinds of shit.'

'Maybe,' Mani muttered as he took a closer look at the object on the monitor. 'It doesn't look like a random splinter or a bullet. That bit there.'

Gann drew closer to the monitor, squinting as he examined the dark patch. 'No shit. That ain't no shrapnel.'

Mani went back to Durrani's abdomen and felt around the scar, prodding his fingers into the flesh.

'Cut it out,' Gann suggested enthusiastically.

'You think I should?' Mani was unsure.

'Sure as shit you cut it out.'

'I should call Mandrick.'

'Look, pal. I'm tellin' you to cut that out. He's got somethin' in there. He's smuggled it in. He could come to at any time and . . . I dunno, maybe activate it or somethin'.'

'I don't think it's a bomb,' Mani said sardonically.

'Maybe it's some kinda suicide device. If he wakes up he might kill himself.'

'I didn't think the Taliban were that sophisticated.'

'Maybe he ain't a Talibuttfuck. Maybe he works for the Russians.'

Mani thought that sounded just as ludicrous. 'I think we should go and see Mandrick.'

'OK. I'll stay here. But if he starts comin' to I'll cut it out myself.'

Mani believed Gann would do it too, and probably with his penknife. He ran his fingers through his thick short black hair, frustrated by his indecision. 'OK,' he said finally. 'I'll open him up and take a look.'

'It ain't gonna do him no harm anyhow.'

'I'll do it, OK?' Mani whined, taking a paper bag off a nearby silver trolley and opening it. Inside was a plastic bowl with a collection of surgical instruments each in its own sterile bag, an assortment of absorbent gauzes and a pair of plastic gloves. He took a syringe and a small bottle from a drawer under the counter top, removed the sterile cover from the syringe, pushed the needle through the top of a bottle and drew out some of the liquid.

'He don't need anaesthetic.'

'The pain might wake him up and that would not be a good idea if I've got my hand inside him at the time.'

'I'll take care of him if he wakes up, don't you worry about that.'

Mani shook his head, containing his impatience and anger. He wanted to tell Gann he was the biggest idiot he had ever met but the satisfaction might come at an unacceptable price. 'Would you mind just staying back and allowing me to do my job, please?'

Gann frowned as he took a step back and leaned against the counter.

Mani injected Durrani's skin in several places around the small scar, placed the syringe on the trolley and pulled on the gloves. He inspected the scar closely again, pulling at the skin lightly to test its elasticity. He pulled the sterile wrapping from a scalpel and positioned it over the skin. Gann leaned forward to get a closer look.

Mani cut into the flesh, keeping the incision to the length of the scar. Blood immediately dribbled down the side of Durrani's abdomen. Mani wiped it and dabbed the cut. The bleeding was minimal. Mani stuck a finger into the opening and moved it around. He couldn't feel anything solid and pushed a couple of fingers in up to his knuckles. He shook his head in frustration as he took out his bloody fingers. 'I can't find it. I'll use the scanner – would you mind?' he said, indicating the scanner above Durrani's chest and his bloody hand that he could not use to take a hold of it.

Gann was eager to be of help in this kind of surgical situation and he moved the scanner down Durrani's body, watching the monitor until the black object appeared. Mani took a pair of forceps from its bag and slipped the end into the cut while looking at the monitor. He opened the forceps and soon had the ends placed either side of the object. He carefully closed the ends around the item. He withdrew the forceps, the small device in its little bag sliding out of the bloody hole.

Mani placed it in the bowl and, with Gann literally breathing down his neck, he wiped the bag clean of blood.

'Take it outta the bag. Let's have a look at it.'

Mani took a pair of scissors from the tray and snipped one end of the bag. The small memory card fell out of the bag onto a piece of gauze and both men stared at it.

'What do you make of it?' Mani asked.

'No idea,' Gann said.

Mani used the scissors to turn it on its side. He took a magnifying glass off the counter and examined the object more closely. 'Whatever it is, it's very sophisticated.' He held it with the forceps and used the scalpel to gently pick at what looked like a join. The gap widened slightly and he applied a little more pressure. The piece slid fully open to reveal a finely patterned gold strip similar to that on the face of a SIM card. 'It looks like some kind of memory chip.'

Gann took the magnifying glass and had a look for himself. 'Yeah. Like you get in digital cameras,' he muttered. Tumblers started moving inside his head. 'That's why that Charon guy was talking to him. And that's why he pulled his shirt up. He was looking for this. He ain't workin' for our side otherwise he wouldn't need to be sneakin' around as a prisoner. Charon's a friggin' spy.'

Mani wasn't entirely sure what Gann was going on about and

didn't particularly care. He took a small zip-lock bag from a drawer, placed the card inside it, sealed it and removed his gloves. 'I'm taking this to Mandrick,' he said.

'Fine,' Gann said, uninterested in the device. 'And I think I'll have that little meetin' with Charon that I was plannin'.'

Mani placed a piece of gauze over Durrani's wound as Gann walked purposefully out of the room. The doctor left shortly after and closed the door behind him.

Durrani's eyelids flickered and slowly opened.

Chapter 14

When Christine walked into Mandrick's office he immediately noticed something about her that he had been unable to see on the monitor. She had groomed herself, only a little, but more than she had in the past. There was also a hint of eyeliner. That was a significant effort for her.

Christine saw the lecherous glint in his eye as she entered the room. Mandrick was standing there with a superior demeanour as if he was all-knowing. Once again she suddenly wondered if he knew who she really was, or at least that she wasn't what she claimed to be. It was not just with Mandrick either. She never completely trusted her cover, always feeling most unlike prison-inspector material. Every time someone looked her directly in the eye she would stare back at them searching for traces of suspicion. There were so many reasons to get the job finished and be out of the damned place.

She forced a smile. 'Have I caught you at a bad time?'

'No. I was about to do my rounds of the prison but I'm happy to put it off.'

'I can come back later if you'd prefer,' Christine said, stepping closer to him while at the same time wondering if her discomfort at being so close to him was obvious.

Despite being certain of her duplicity Mandrick was struck once again by her attractive qualities. As well as her beauty and intelligence she had an aura about her, an undeniable strength beyond her physical athleticism. She was a superior creature. There were times when he felt strangely inadequate beside her. The feeling was bizarre and on certain levels it irritated him. Which was why he became far more of a predator in her company than he would normally be with women.

He moved towards her. Inwardly she braced herself, expecting him to take hold of her. But he brushed past like a matador.

'Can I get you a drink?' Mandrick asked, going to an antique bureau and a collection of fine crystal decanters and tumblers.

'I shouldn't really.'

'Is that for medical or professional reasons?'

Christine grinned. 'How does it affect you at this depth?'

'You do get more of a buzz for your dollar . . . But don't let me pressure you.'

'Very funny.'

'Bourbon do?'

'Sure.'

Mandrick poured two glasses, opened a small fridge beside the bureau, took out a bowl of ice, plopped a couple of cubes in each glass and brought them over to her.

Christine took the drink and held it to her mouth as she watched him take a sip of his. She let the glass touch her lips and poured a little of the burnt-gold fluid between them. It tasted bitter to her. She didn't like hard liquor but on this occasion it reminded her of younger days in college after a game of touch football or baseball, joining the guys for a drink. They'd been purely bonding moments for her but fun nonetheless. Now those days seemed like ancient history. From college girl to secret undercover agent standing in the warden's office of a damp, humid prison far beneath the Gulf of Mexico.

As she watched Mandrick eyeing her with the confidence of a great cat, she was less sure of her strategy than ever. Her scheme was nothing more complex than to separate him from his minicomputer, remove the memory-storage cards without him knowing and then head for his personal escape pod. There were some glaring flaws in the plan. The first was the difficulty of getting the keypad entry code to gain access to the pod. She didn't know it. The only way around that was to somehow get Mandrick to show her the inside of the pod and then make her move to get inside it and eject. The other flaw was that as she arrived on the surface he could have her picked up by his own people. She would be stuck inside the pod for hours anyway, waiting to decompress. He would also have plenty of time to cancel some of the information on the storage cards; PIN codes and passwords, for instance.

It was not the best of plans by a long stretch but Christine was out of other ideas. She almost scratched the whole notion several times but the only reason she continued to pursue it was that she was not entirely desperate to pull it off. Taking the storage cards was surplus to the mission objective, anyway. It was all about personal ambition. If the ideal opportunity failed to materialise she would cancel it and surface just with her report.

At that moment the scheme was certainly looking doubtful. Mandrick was being more forward with her than he'd been at any other time. He had a hunger in his eyes. She reckoned she had been too overtly sexual in setting him up and he was clearly expecting more than she was prepared to give. 'Why don't you take me on a tour?' she suggested. 'I can come on your rounds with you.'

He put his glass down, moved closer and stopped in front of her, his eyes boring into hers. 'What are you doing here, Christine?' he asked in a cold voice.

'You mean in this room, now?' she replied, holding on to her composure.

'That, yes. But first the prison. What are you doing here?'

'You know what I'm doing here.'

'I know what you *said* you're doing here. But we all know that's a load of crap.'

Christine could never tell Mandrick the truth. Her career would be over. Perhaps even her life. He'd been prepared to kill an FBI agent. Why not an Oval Office agent? There was no real difference at the end of the day. He had no proof that she was not a prison inspector. He couldn't have. He was guessing. She had no choice but to maintain her claim. 'Where has this come from? I don't understand you,' she said.

'OK. So if you won't answer that question, why are you in this room putting on this pathetic display, attempting to seduce me when it's the furthest thing from your thoughts?'

Christine tried to laugh it off. She put her drink down. 'Well. This is interesting. I thought we . . . I'm sorry. I obviously have it all wrong. Perhaps I should go.'

As she moved past Mandrick he grabbed her hand and pulled her close to him.

'Let go of me,' she demanded.

He wrapped his other arm around her before she could pull away. 'How 'bout we make a deal?' he said, holding her tightly, his nose almost touching hers. 'You give me what I want and we'll talk about your side of the deal. I might surprise you.' He moved a hand down her back and over her bottom, sliding it between the cheeks.

A combination of rage and utter disgust engulfed Christine and she slammed her forehead into his nose, breaking it and immediately following through by crashing a heel down onto the top of one of his feet. To his credit he managed to keep hold of her but she punished him further by bringing a knee up into his groin. It was this blow that finally forced him to release her.

She went to the control panel and hit a button. As the door hissed open she made her way past him towards it. But before she could reach it another hiss signalled a reverse of the pneumatic valves and the door remained closed.

Christine turned to face Mandrick. He was straightening himself up, trying to ignore the pain in his groin while dabbing at his bloody nose with the sleeve of his jacket.

'That smart,' he said, blinking away the water in his eyes. 'Never experienced that combination before . . . You make that up or did they teach you that in prison-inspection school?'

'Let me out of here,' she said coldly.

Mandrick exhaled loudly and relaxed his shoulders to help ease the tension. 'Funny how quickly you can go off someone.'

'Open the door,' she said in a deliberate tone.

He held up the remote. 'Why don't you try and take it?'

Christine was experiencing a whole load of feelings, a growing concern predominant among them. But she no longer felt unsure. The job had come down to a physical conflict between the pair of them. She didn't have to pretend to seduce him for a second longer. That was some relief in itself. If she could take him down she might even achieve the result she wanted. But she would have to flatten him, knock him out, tie him up, restrain him for several hours. She knew nothing about Mandrick's past: his dossier was surprisingly slender for a file that was the result of a White House background check. There was a toughness about him which she put down to character rather than physique.

However, he seemed to have dealt with the blows she'd given him quite quickly. He could take pain. If he did possess some level of fighting skill, which she doubted, she was confident she could take him. She had quite a few tricks designed for the weaker sex up her sleeve, not that she was much weaker than him. They were techniques rather than skills, such as knowing how best to strike at weak points. She was also confident that she was fitter than him.

Had Christine known Mandrick's pedigree, the numerous African battlefields that he had fought on, conflicts she could hardly imagine, she would probably never have entered the room. There was a world of a difference between skills learned in a dojo and those acquired in battle while fighting for one's life. More importantly, Mandrick knew what it was like to kill and, worse still for her, he had never lost the taste for it.

She decided to strike first, which suited Mandrick as he was more adept at countermoves. She lunged at him with a dummy kick intended to bring his hands low so that she could punch him in the throat. But he stepped aside and parried her fist with a calm ease that took her by surprise. She went for a straight kick to his shin. He avoided it and lunged at her but she caught his hand and tried to turn the wrist in. He took her feet away from under her with a side-sweep and she almost fell on her back. But as he came in to take advantage of her lost balance and grab her hand she elbowed him in the face with her other arm. Mandrick went back, reeling a little from the blow and looking at her with malice. Christine was confident that if she could keep this up she just might take him. But Mandrick had home-field advantage.

He lured her forward as he stepped backwards, feigning fear and weakness, dodging attack after attack, blocking where he could as if he was retreating. On the wall behind him was a large air pipe with an opening at chest height that had a mesh grille across it. The warden's office was the only room in the facility apart from the OCR that had a manual air-pressure control. It was an emergency feature, an override that allowed the operator to rapidly increase or decrease the pressure in the room either to open the door or prevent it from being opened.

Mandrick put his back to the pipe so that he knew exactly where he was. As Christine came in for another blow he took a step forward, trapped her arm, pulled her around, slammed her back against the pipe and threw a lever on the side of the vent. There was a sudden rush of air that reached an immediate and painful pitch. Before Christine realised what was happening her back was sucked against the mesh. She twisted violently in an effort to free herself but was stuck like a fly to sticky paper.

Mandrick stepped back, feeling his bruised face and taking his time about it. 'Now it's my turn.'

As Christine struggled to reach behind her back for the valve handle Mandrick punched her on the side of her face as hard as he could. The blow knocked her almost unconscious. Her knees nearly gave way and she could only watch as he drew his fist back for another punch. This time he changed its direction and struck her in the gut. It struck so hard and low that she almost threw up. He followed through with a knee to her groin, then grabbed her by her throat and held her windpipe tightly, squeezing it until she began to choke.

'I'm not interested in who you work for,' Mandrick hissed between clenched teeth. 'That should worry you.' He slammed his elbow into the side of her face and she went limp. Unable to focus properly she fought to stay conscious.

'It would be churlish of me not to take full advantage of the situation, don't you think?' he said, ripping open her shirt to reveal her bra. He squeezed her breasts. 'Very firm . . . Fortunately for you I'm not into necrophilia.'

A buzzer sounded above the hissing of air.

'For Christ's sake,' he muttered.

The buzzer went again soon after and he looked at the monitor to see that it was Doctor Mani. He hit the intercom on his desk. 'What is it?' he asked, still slightly out of breath.

'Mr Mandrick? I have something very important to show you.'

'Can it wait? I have my hands full.'

'I think you would be very angry with me if I said yes. This is most important or I would never dream of insisting.'

Mandrick sighed and straightened his clothes. 'I guess it just wasn't meant to be,' he said, turning the vent lever back into the neutral position. The air stopped hissing, releasing Christine who hit the floor like a sack of vegetables. Mandrick pressed the entry button on the desk and the door opened.

Mani hurried inside.

'What do you want?' Mandrick said, feeling his nose.

Mani paused on seeing Mandrick's somewhat dishevelled appearance but quickly put any disquiet aside and focused on the urgency of his visit. 'Sir,' he began but stopped in his tracks as he saw Christine lying on the floor. 'Dear God,' he exclaimed, hurrying over to her. 'What happened?'

Mandrick was more concerned about his swollen nose and its blocked airways. 'We had a disagreement,' he said nasally.

The doctor looked confusedly between Mandrick and Christine, noticing now that her shirt had been torn open.

'She's a spy – FBI, probably – trying to steal something, I expect. She's one tough bitch, I'll say that for her,' Mandrick added, feeling his cheekbones again.

'What did you do to her?' the doctor asked, his tacit disapproval obvious as he inspected Christine's bruised face and checked to see if she was breathing.

'Christ's sake, Mani, she attacked me. Just because she came off worse doesn't mean I'm the bad guy.'

The doctor shook his head. The girl appeared to be OK apart from a possible concussion. 'I'll have to get her to the hospital.'

'Do what the hell you want with her . . . What was so important?'

The doctor had almost forgotten. Quickly, he got to his feet and reached into a pocket. 'This was inside that Afghan they brought in,' he said, taking out the plastic bag with the card inside.

Mandrick took the bag and inspected it. 'Durrani?'

'That's right. It was in his abdomen. It had been placed there surgically.'

'Any idea what it is?' Mandrick asked, in case the doctor had an opinion different from his own.

'We thought it was a memory card of some kind.'

'We?'

'Gann was with me when I found it.'

Mandrick took the device out of the bag and examined the embossed gold circuitry, agreeing with the assessment. 'Anyone else know about this? Hank, for instance?'

'I came right here.'

'And Gann?'

'He was going on about that prisoner, Charon – the one who survived the ferry accident. I think he went to talk to him.'

'Talk, eh?' Mandrick muttered to himself. 'Yeah, I bet.' He checked his watch. Things were stacking up rapidly to push him in one direction: a dead FBI agent, a panicking Forbes, a threatening Hank, an unconscious prison inspector, and now this memory card or whatever it was. It was clearly important and unknown to the CIA. Perhaps it was the insurance he was looking for. Hank was interested in Durrani for a reason, and so was Charon who, just to add to matters, was probably about to die at the hands of Gann if for no other reason than that he'd witnessed the ferry sabotage. Mandrick could not risk Hank finding out about the chip, whatever it was, and Gann could not be relied upon to keep his mouth shut. It was time to go.

'I'll be honest with you, Mandrick. I'm beginning to feel very uncomfortable with this whole set-up down here . . . It's beginning to feel like a powder keg about to blow.'

'You're a very perceptive man,' Mandrick said.

'The company would warn us if things were going to go wrong, wouldn't they?'

'I think the signs would be there for all to see.'

'I'll take my lead from you, then.'

'You see me jump, you go right ahead and jump too,' Mandrick said, with a sarcastic smile.

Mani nodded. 'What about that?' he asked, indicating the memory card.

'You think I should take it to the FBI?'

'Why not? Insurance. We need to start thinking about protecting ourselves.'

'Quite right.'

Christine moaned.

'I'd better get her to the hospital,' Mani said, crouching beside her. 'Come on. Up you get. You'll be fine. Help me get you to the hospital.'

Christine appeared to understand enough to help him get her to her feet although everything else was a blur. Mandrick's image kept flashing across her mind, a memory only, disconnected to time and her current location despite her efforts to marshal her thoughts. She heard the doctor's gentle voice that she remembered and trusted urging her to take a step. She obeyed.

Mandrick watched Mani help Christine through the door. He hit the close button and removed his minicomputer from his belt, opened the leather cover, placed the card inside one of the small pockets and returned it to his belt.

He opened a cupboard beside his desk to reveal a safe with a keypad on its face and punched in several numbers. A beep indicated that it had unlocked. He pulled open the door, removed a CD box on top of a pile of US banknotes, opened it, selected a red CD at the back of the box and carried it over to the main operations panel with a degree of care.

Mandrick hit several commands on a keyboard, following a series of paths offered on the monitor, and pushed the CD into a slot on the panel. A few seconds later an alert flashed on the monitor, warning that the disk was unauthorised and could contain potentially lethal viruses. Permission to continue was authorised for password holders only and Mandrick typed in a code. Seconds later the monitor indicated that the CD had been accepted.

The image changed to a graph of the prison's gas systems, showing the different pressures throughout. As the information reeled off the CD a warning flashed onto the screen that deleting certain files could have disastrous effects.

Mandrick left the program to run as he picked up a waterproof bag, put it on his desk, removed the money from the safe and placed it in the bag along with the other CDs, some paperwork and a pistol. The last item he removed from the safe was a leather pouch whose opening was secured with a drawstring, which he untied. Inside were a substantial number of gems of various colours and sizes. He refastened the drawstring, placed the pouch inside the waterproof bag and looked around to see if he had forgotten anything. His hand went to his belt and his mini-computer which he unhooked, placed in the bag and pulled an airtight zip tightly across. That was everything.

He went back to the monitor to check on the progress of the virus. The warnings continued as one section after another began to flash red.

Mandrick picked up the phone on his desk and punched in a number. 'Mandrick here. Are the ferries ready for that scheduled stores run? . . . Good. I want you to send them. I want all those stores cleared off the platform and brought down here . . . Yes, do it now. I know there's a ferry booked for the inspector this evening but she's not leaving until tomorrow . . . Just do what I goddamn say, OK?' He put the phone down, checked his watch and went back to the computer monitor that showed how the virus was spreading.

In the OCR a light flickered on the main panel, accompanied by a beep. The controller and his assistant were seated at a table, eating sandwiches and drinking coffee.

The assistant took a large bite out of his sandwich, got to his feet, walked over to the panel and eyed the read-out curiously as he brushed his hands on his chest. 'Pressure spike in C cell,' he said, his mouth full of food.

'The interrogation chamber?' the senior controller asked as he flicked through the pages of a girlie magazine.

'Yep.'

'They've got nothing booked for right now.'

'Nope,' the assistant agreed, checking a calendar on the side of the panel.

'Give 'em a call. Tell 'em we'd appreciate it if they let us know before they start playing their little games.'

'You want me to ask it exactly like that?'

The senior controller frowned without looking at his colleague. 'Just ask 'em what they're doing.'

The assistant picked up a phone and punched in a number.

The CIA interrogation-room technician was in the pressure chamber, checking the wiring to the central chair, when the phone on the wall buzzed. As he stood up to reach for it he felt suddenly flushed and paused to loosen the clothing around his neck.

Two interrogation officers were in the elevated room, going over several files and making notes. 'You getting hot?' one of them asked.

'Yeah,' his colleague replied, loosening his collar as he looked through the thick glass at the tech reaching for the phone.

The tech picked up the receiver. 'C cell.'

'You guys working that room today?' the assistant controller asked.

'Just some routine wiring. No one's touching the pressure.'

'Well, *someone*'s screwing around with it.'

'I can feel it. The air's getting pretty thick in here.'

The assistant controller scrutinised the gauges. 'Holy cow! You're down more'n a hundred feet below ambient.'

The interrogation room was filled with a loud crunching sound from above. The technician looked up as dust sprinkled down onto him. 'There's something happening with the ceiling,' he said, his expression deepening with concern.

'Harry, we got a problem,' the assistant controller said to his boss as he pushed a couple of switches to check several other read-outs. 'You'd better get outta there,' he said into the phone. 'The pressure's dropping and the oxygen level isn't compensating.'

The technician was overcome by dizziness as his face reddened. Another loud crunching sound and this time a large crack was visible around the ceiling hatch. The technician dropped the phone and headed for the pressure door that was closed.

The agent in the booth watched the technician stagger to the door and pull on the handle. 'What's up with Marty?' he said, getting to his feet.

The pressure door would not respond to the open button and the technician dropped to his knees as he fought to breathe. A third loud crunch was accompanied by high-pressure water shooting through the cracks. A second later the ceiling collapsed ahead of a wall of water and the technician disappeared under the tremendous force of it all.

The agents in the booth stepped back from the glass as the room beyond it filled with water. The technician's severed head rolled across the glass and both men went for the door. It did not respond to the control lever and they pulled on the handle with all their might. Cracks suddenly streaked across the thick glass and as the two men fought the door the centre of the window gave way and the water burst into the room.

'Hello,' the assistant controller shouted into the phone. All he could hear was static and he looked over at his boss. 'I think we've got a problem.'

Hamlin finished cutting a hole in the thick rubber door seal large enough to poke a couple of fingers into, withdrew the saw bit and inspected his work, using a small flashlight. 'Does that look like it to you?' he said, stepping back so that Stratton could take a look.

Stratton scrutinised inside the hole. 'That's it,' he agreed.

He handed Hamlin a small bottle cap with a heavily greased rim. Hamlin pushed it in through the hole and positioned it over the sensor.

'It's in place,' Hamlin said as he felt around inside the hole, making sure he was right.

Stratton handed him a flat piece of rubber with a sealing-compound coating one side. Hamlin placed it over the hole he had cut, ensuring it made a tight seal. 'Perfect . . . I got a good feelin' about you, ferryman. I think you're lucky.'

Stratton was bemused by Hamlin's upbeat attitude and was burning to know what was fuelling his confidence.

'Let's help things along a ways, why don't we?' Hamlin said as he walked over to the rack of emergency air bottles and, using a wrench, tried to unscrew one of the ends. 'Gimme a hand here,' he asked as he strained.

Stratton joined him and, with their combined strength applied to the nut, it began to loosen. Hamlin repositioned the wrench and they pushed again. As the thread unscrewed gas began to hiss from the joint until it became almost deafening.

'That should do it,' Hamlin shouted. 'You ready?'

Stratton gave him a thumbs-up.

Hamlin made his way up the steps and into the transformer room. He collected several prepared cables with crocodile clips on the ends and began connecting them to an assortment of cable hubs, leaving the final couple of clips disconnected. He pulled on a pair of rubber gloves and, using a large pair of pliers with rubber tubing over the handles, gripped one of the remaining crocodile clips and connected it to a terminal. A couple of sparks flew and he picked up the last clip with the pliers, leaned out of the doorway and looked down at Stratton. 'How's it lookin'?' he shouted.

Stratton was checking the seals. He looked up at Hamlin and shook his head. 'Can't see a change yet!'

'Give it a minute!' Hamlin remained confident as he stared up at a large square air duct hanging down from the centre of the rock-and-girder ceiling. The fins that ran across its face opened wider, indicating a sudden flow of air coming out of it. 'Here she comes!' Hamlin shouted.

Stratton followed his gaze to see evidence that the pressure compensator had tripped.

The door seals began to flatten slowly and the door itself moved perceptibly. Stratton gripped the handle and pulled with all his might. The door moved more freely and as it opened he grabbed the inner edge.

When the gap was wide enough he moved his head to look through into the corridor. A large fist slammed into his face and sent him flying back into the room and onto the floor.

Stratton lay on his back, reeling from the punch and with blood trickling from his nose. Through watering eyes he watched Gann step into the room.

Gann picked up a heavy wrench, tested its weight and held it like a baseball bat. 'Not as smart as you think you are, Mister Charon or whoever you are.'

Stratton wriggled backwards, quickly wiping his eyes and searching for anything he could use as a weapon. There was nothing close to hand.

'Just left a friend of yours in the hospital. Your Afghan pal – didn't think I knew about him, did you? And it was me who found you out, not the CIA or the big guys who run this place. And guess what else? We found something inside his gut.'

Stratton was appalled by what Gann was saying but he had more important matters to deal with right at that moment.

Gann moved over him, the wrench held high. 'Your next stop is the morgue.' He grimaced as he made ready to bring the heavy tool back down. At that precise moment Hamlin connected the remaining crocodile clip, causing a massive short circuit that sparked wildly. All the lights immediately went out, plunging the room into total darkness.

Gann brought the wrench down with all his might and the end slammed home.

The emergency lights flickered on as the auxiliary power kicked in, dimmer than before but enough for Gann to see the end of his wrench sitting in a chipped indentation that it had made in the concrete. At first he could see no sign of Stratton. Then he looked up to see him getting to his feet from where he had rolled when the lights had gone out.

Stratton found an iron bar and held it up, ready to do combat. Gann straightened himself as he adjusted the wrench in his hands and smiled thinly. 'This could be more fun than I'd expected,' he growled. He took a step towards Stratton who backed up to the metal stairs between the scrubbers.

Gann came at him, swinging the wrench in a wide are. Stratton held up his bar to block the blow. Gann smashed it out of his hand and it went clattering across the floor.

As Gann came in for a speedy follow-up Stratton's heels struck the bottom step and he stumbled backwards. Gann brought the wrench down with all his might, Stratton only barely managing to roll aside again as the end of the tool dented the metal step with a thunderous clang. Stratton instantly threw out a kick that connected with Gann's groin. The big man was halted in his tracks and he gave out a moan as the pain shot through his crotch.

Stratton scurried backwards up the stairs, not prepared to tackle Gann man-to-man just yet. The brute had twice his strength and, like a bull in the ring, needed weakening considerably before the power gap between them could be closed.

Gann brought his pain under control, held the wrench ready to resume the conflict and made his way up the steps, his expression a twisted grimace of malicious determination. The only thing in Stratton's reach was a wooden board which he picked up, holding it like a shield in front of himself. Gann reached the gantry and launched a side blow. Stratton brought the shield across to block it but the force knocked him off the gantry and several feet down onto the top of one of the scrubbing machines, which he landed on back first. Gann jumped over the rail and down onto the machine into the cloud of dust that Stratton's impact had kicked up. He loomed above his winded prey, savouring the moment.

Stratton had nowhere to go in the narrow space. There was a long drop either side to the floor. Gann raised the wrench for a deadly blow but a chunk of metal, a machine part of some kind, flew through the air and struck him on the side of his head, knocking him off balance. Stratton took immediate advantage and kicked the side of Gann's knee, causing it to bend, and followed that up with a thrust from his other leg. Gann lost his balance and struggled to grab the gantry rail, missing it and falling off the machine onto an exhaust pipe several feet below before rolling off that and hitting the floor.

Stratton got to his feet and looked down to see Gann lying with his face against the concrete. He was stirring slowly, the wind knocked out of him.

Hamlin hurried along the gantry towards Stratton.

'Get out of here,' Stratton shouted.

Hamlin needed no further encouragement and headed down the stairs. Stratton jumped over the gantry rail and followed hard on his heels.

Hamlin reached the bottom step, lost his footing and fell sprawling on the floor. Stratton hurried to pick him up and as the older man staggered to his feet a dart struck Stratton in the side of his neck. He let out a scream as two hundred kilovolts shot through his body from a taser in Gann's hand. Stratton dropped to the floor, his limbs shaking as Hamlin ran for the door. Gann dropped the taser and threw his wrench at Hamlin, catching him around the legs. Hamlin went sprawling once again.

For the moment Gann ignored Stratton who lay on the floor twitching like an epileptic. He went for Hamlin instead. He picked the older man up by his neck, grabbed his head as if he was going to rip it off and jerked it around into an unnatural position to face him. 'Looks like it's time for you to say goodbye too,' Gann snarled as he slammed Hamlin's head into the metal door, spun him around and used him like a punching bag, pounding his hammer fists into the other man's ribs, smashing them one by one. Hamlin went limp and Gann looked around to see Stratton roll onto his knees, the taser dart out of his neck.

Gann let Hamlin drop to the floor and marched over to Stratton.

Stratton fought to focus his eyes, saw a shackle on the floor within arm's reach and reached for it. Gann grabbed him mercilessly by the back of the neck, picked him up like a rag doll, and spun him round as he raised a fist, his face twisted in effort. But as his knuckles ploughed through the air towards Stratton's head the shackle struck Gann in the jaw, shattering several of his teeth.

Gann staggered back, releasing Stratton who came in quickly for another blow. But Gann was not finished by a long shot and blocked the attack, following it up with a vicious punch to Stratton's sternum that sent him flying back.

Gann stood upright, taking a moment to gather himself and spit out his broken teeth. He felt his jaw as he stared at Stratton, blood trickling from his mouth. The brute was utterly incensed. 'I am going to tear you apart,' he shouted, his voice rising to a crescendo as he lunged forward.

Stratton ducked a haymaker and countered with a blow to Gann's body that seemed to have no effect. Gann swung again as he ploughed on, Stratton managing to dodge blow after blow although it did not look as if he would remain lucky for long. He didn't. A blow connected with the side of his head, sending him reeling back into one of the scrubbers. The machine was running noisily, a powerful electric motor turning a large shaft that was exposed for a metre where it went into the housing, a large knuckle joint in its centre. Gann grabbed Stratton by the neck and hauled him towards the fiercely spinning shaft. Stratton splayed out his hands, grabbing the sides of the machine, desperation taking hold of him as he felt helpless in Gann's powerful grip.

Gann gritted his teeth as he pushed Stratton's head ever closer to the spinning knuckle joint. Blood and sweat poured from Stratton's grimy face as he fought back with every vestige of his remaining strength. But he could not match Gann's power. He blinked at the joint spinning inches from his face, knowing that Gann was intent on seeing his features sheared away. He suddenly saw two large buttons, one red, the other green, just beyond the shaft. He had no idea what they operated but he was out of options. He released his weakening grip on the edge of the machine, twisted his body round, his face passing millimetres from the joint, reached out and hit the red button. The machine immediately slowed to a stop as Stratton fell onto the smooth section of the shaft just beside the joint.

Gann twisted Stratton back over and held him down onto the shaft. 'You wriggle like a worm,' he snarled as he brought his fist down onto the side of Stratton's face.

Stratton was trapped under Gann's weight and strength and one more blow like the last would finish him. Gann raised his fist again, gritting his teeth, his aim clearly to bury it deep into Stratton's bloody face and end the fight. Stratton made a supreme effort and twisted his head to one side just enough to avoid the main impact of the blow that glanced off his cheek. Gann's weight followed him through and his hand slammed down into the knuckle joint. Stratton did not waste a second – he reached out and struck the green button. Before Gann could pull his hand free the shaft turned. He let out a howl that could have been heard throughout the prison as the knuckle joint turned, trapping his hand. As his arm wrapped around the turning joint the bones in the entire limb broke all the way up to his shoulder as they were twisted around it. The machine jammed and Stratton pushed himself out from under Gann's bulk.

Gann screamed like a banshee, sparks flying from the machine as the motor short-circuited. Flames shot from the housing and ignited Gann's uniform as he fought like a wild man to extract his mangled arm. But his efforts were in vain – the arm was jammed fast. The pain was too much for him and he went limp as the fire engulfed his head. His legs gave way beneath him.

Stratton stepped back towards the door, turning to look for Hamlin. But there was no sign of the older man. He hurried outside into the corridor but Hamlin had gone.

Doctor Mani helped Christine through the door into the hospital and sat her down on the edge of the operating table. She was aware of her surroundings and focused all her efforts on pulling herself back together.

'He did you over pretty good,' Mani said, holding a swab and a bottle of antiseptic liquid. 'Let me have a look.' He gently lifted up her chin. The blood had dried around her swollen nose and lips and there was a large bruise on the side of her jaw. She winced as the doctor dabbed a cut. 'Can you clench your jaw?'

Christine clamped her teeth together and moved her jaw from side to side.

'Any loose teeth?' he asked as he felt her cheekbones and nose.

'I'm fine,' she said moving his hands away.

'What about the rest of you? Any broken bones, you think? I should check.'

'I'm OK,' she insisted as she slid off the edge of the table to stand, a little wobbly at first.

Mani looked down at the table, suddenly remembering that there had been someone on it when he had left earlier.

At the same instant Christine looked past him and froze.

'Where's the Afghan prisoner . . . ?'

'Behind you,' she said softly.

Mani turned to see the Afghan standing on the other side of the room, holding his gut with one hand, a long, slender surgical blade in the other. 'Oh, dear,' Mani muttered.

Durrani took a couple of steps towards them, holding himself erect with some difficulty.

'Why don't you let me fix you up?' Mani said nervously, his gaze flicking between the silver blade in the Afghan's hand and his dark eyes focused on him.

Durrani tottered slightly, fighting to control his limbs. His head throbbed and his lungs ached with every breath. He could barely see – everything was a blur – but he could distinguish the human forms in front of him. He stopped in front of Mani.

'Please put the knife down,' Mani's voice quivered.

Durrani did not understand a word the doctor was saying. He had met him twice since his arrival, both for cursory medical examinations, and knew he could speak some Farsi. Durrani muttered a few words, his voice weak.

Mani was not sure what the Afghan had said at first and then realised he was asking for something to be given back to him.

'I don't have it,' Mani replied in English, suddenly unsure how to say it in Farsi. 'It's not here. I promise you.'

Durrani assumed the man had not understood him. He also knew it was a waste of time and that he would never see the implanted object he had been entrusted with again. It had belonged to the enemy and they now had it back in their hands.

Durrani removed his hand from his wound, exposing it.

Mani glanced down at the open cut, then back to Durrani's eyes that were filled with menace. Beads of sweat formed at the doctor's temples. 'I don't have it, I tell you,' he stammered in Farsi. 'I can stitch up your wound. Shall I do that?' Mani's voice quivered as he gestured towards his instrument trolley.

Durrani held a hand out to stop him. He had come to terms with his failure. He had never had any illusions about escaping but there had always been the possibility of release one day. Now that his secret had been discovered hoping for anything else was pointless. They would soon take him back into that room and interrogate him further. Durrani would rather die. This was the only opportunity he would ever have to control his destiny and he was going to take it. And like a good soldier he would take as many of the enemy with him as he could.

Durrani shoved the blade deep into Mani's gut just below the sternum. Mani tensed as the cold blade entered him and his eyes widened in horror as he grabbed Durrani's hand. Durrani clenched his jaw with the strain as he pushed the blade to one side. Mani's knees started to give.

Unable to hold Mani's weight, Durrani pulled out the knife and let the doctor drop to the floor. The effort caused a bolt of pain to shoot through his body and he thought he might lose his balance. But he summoned all his will to remain strong and upright, long enough to focus on the next face in front of him and kill whoever it belonged to. The person did not move and Durrani steeled himself to take one step closer to repeat the deadly thrust.

Christine stared at the half-naked man and the bloody blade in his hand. She might be weak and dazed but faced with the threat of death she would muster every ounce of strength to defend herself. She considered making the first move. The man was exhausted and in pain like her. But the knife gave him a serious advantage. Her heart pounded in her chest. Mani was moving at her feet, making gurgling moans, but she put him out of her mind at that moment. Adrenalin coursed through her veins.

'Why are you doing this?' she stammered, trying to distract him. 'I can help you,' she said, even though she suspected he could not understand her. She kept her voice soft and tender, trying to sound compassionate and unafraid. 'Please let me help you.' She stared into his eyes, waiting for the change in them that would signal his thrust. She would try and block it, move aside and counter. Her instincts would take over and unleash all the power she had until he was beaten.

But instead of tensing for the thrust Durrani remained still.

Christine could sense his sudden hesitation and wondered if he had understood her.

Durrani had indeed paused. He had fully intended to close the gap between them and thrust the knife deep into the blurred outline. But the voice stopped him, the voice of a woman, the first he had heard in a long time. He could not understand the words but he could hear the soft, pleading tones. Indelible memories returned. Since his incarceration with nothing to do but think he had experienced countless recollections of his mother, many of them tormenting. He had also been haunted by memories of the girl in the street when he'd been a boy, and in particular of the one he'd shot in Yakaolang while she pleaded for her brother's life. Although they had been separate incidents, over the years those women had become one in his mind. And now she was standing in front of him, talking to him, pleading for him to recognise her.

Christine could only guess at the sudden change that had come over the Afghan. She had not expected her words to alter his murderous intent. But, bizarrely, that was exactly what had apparently happened. 'It's OK,' she went on, maintaining the same soothing tone. 'I know how you feel. I understand . . . I do.'

The room suddenly reverberated with the shriek of klaxons. Durrani snapped out of his trance. His grip on the knife tightened, his jaw clenched, his eyes narrowed. He came out of the fog and back into reality and stepped forward to make his thrust.

The lights went out.

Chapter 15

The auxiliary lights came on in the OCR room, triggering a cacophony of alarms, beeps and flashing warning lights as the controller and his assistant frantically moved between computer consoles, operating panels and monitors trying to figure out what precisely was happening.

'This is crazy!' the senior controller shouted, his stress level rising perceptibly. 'I've got pressure differentials spiking all over the goddamned place.'

'There's no power from the surface barge!' the assistant called out.

'What in God's name is going on?'

The controller flicked through CCTV cameras all over the prison. Many did not function, some showed quiet, empty corridors while others revealed water rushing in through doors and along passageways.

'Where's the breach?' the controller demanded.

'There's more'n one, that's for sure.'

'Galley's showing four bars below normal. If it continues to drop the walls'll give.'

'Holy cow! We got a serious drop in pressure on level four. I can't stabilise it.'

'There's no compensation control. Do we have comms with the terminal?'

The assistant grabbed up a radio handset and pushed a pre-set frequency button. 'Mother one, this is Styx, copy!'

The speakers remained silent.

'Mother one, this is Styx!' the assistant repeated. 'We have an emergency situation, do you copy?'

'Styx,' a voice crackled over the speakers. 'This is mother one, come in.'

The senior controller grabbed the handset from his assistant. 'Be advised we have a serious emergency down here. I'm talking very serious. Remain on standby, OK?'

'Can you describe the nature of the emergency?'

'We're flooding on just about every level as far as we can tell! Stand by.'

The controller hit a speaker button on the phone and punched in a couple of numbers.

Mandrick looked around at the flashing red light on his desk phone, took another glance at the computer monitor to see how the virus was spreading, walked over and picked up the phone. 'Mandrick.'

'Warden. We have a crisis situation.'

'I'm listening.'

'The pressure's out of control. We're flooding. The perimeter's been breached in several places. We could be heading for total perimeter failure. We're not sure how or where it started. Maybe C cell. The equalisers aren't compensating. We've got a negative pressure migration to levels three and five which we are currently unable to control.'

'What about the access doors on those levels?' Mandrick asked casually, his voice booming over the speakers in the operations control room.

'When the pressure equalised most of the doors popped before I could set all the manual overrides. We need people to physically close them,' the controller said, looking at a monitor that showed a torrent of water gushing along a corridor. 'Right now I don't see how that's possible.'

'Your prognosis?' Mandrick asked as he reached for his waterproof bag.

'Well . . . the mains-power outage isn't good. It's like the barge has shut down.' The controller looked at a computer monitor that mirrored the one in Mandrick's office. 'The auto system has failed or is about to. It looks to me as if the program's erasing itself. I don't understand how we can have so many unrelated failures all happening at the same time.'

Mandrick was also curious since his virus program was only designed to affect the pressure compensators. 'Did you say that the surface power's been cut?' he asked, certain his virus was not supposed to cause anything like that to happen.

'Yes, sir. We're running on UPS auxiliary, emergency systems only.'

'Can we consolidate?' Mandrick wanted to know.

The controller looked around the room at the orchestra of complaining systems monitors and at his assistant who gave him a dour look before shaking his head. 'I'd have to say that's a negative, sir,' the controller finally said. Despite the seriousness of the emergency he was well aware of the implications of making such a firm decision. He could already see himself facing the judicial enquiry and being grilled for the reasons behind such a catastrophic assessment. 'If we move now we might be able to get everyone to the barges.'

'I understand,' Mandrick said, pouring himself a Scotch, taking a sip and then knocking it back, wincing as the fiery liquor coursed down his throat. 'Give the order to abandon the facility.'

The controller looked at his assistant just in case there was anything to suggest that the order was premature. Nothing was forthcoming.

'Did you hear me, controller?' Mandrick asked, his voice echoing in the OCR.

'Will do, sir . . . and sir?'

'Yes?'

'Good luck.'

'You too,' Mandrick said, replacing the receiver and picking up his bag. He paused to take a last look around, imagining the room flooded and wondering how long it would be, if ever, before anyone set a foot – or a fin – inside it again.

He headed across the room, operated the door which needed his help to open and stepped out into the corridor. Water several inches deep flowed past him from the steps above.

The alarms dimmed as a voice broke through them. 'ABANDON THE FACILITY!' it called out in a relatively calm voice. 'ALL PERSONNEL TO THE ESCAPE BARGES ON LEVEL TWO!'

Mandrick exhaled philosophically. He had done it. It was something he had, bizarrely perhaps, looked forward to for a long time. This was what he called power. He had single-handedly brought Styx to an end, the implications of which would spread around the globe. Some would rejoice, some would despair, while others would be horrified or even amused.

He looked down at the dirty, frothy water swirling around his feet, feeling the chill of it soaking into his socks. He smiled and headed up the stairs.

Several prison guards ran along a cell-block corridor that was ankle deep in water, flinging open cell doors and yelling for the inmates to get out. The Afghans needed no interpretation to understand the events taking place. Panic was the overriding emotion as prisoners and guards hurried together in the direction indicated by illuminated emergency arrows. A handful of prisoners following a guard turned a corner only to be struck by a torrent of water that washed them back. All save one, a man who was struck unconscious when his head hit the wall, managed to regain a footing and cling to the walls. They pulled themselves and their unconscious comrade along the corridor to a metal stairway that led out of the water and to the next level.

Stratton was running up the broad tunnel from the scrubber room when the klaxons first sounded. He paused at the entrance to the steeper, narrower tunnel that led to the upper level, noting the significant increase in the volume of water running down the guttering. As he headed up it he could only wonder what the hell Hamlin had done.

Stratton arrived at the access-level door that had a huge '5' painted on it to find it firmly shut. He pulled on the handle but it was like trying to move a mountain. Hamlin had got it wrong. The seals had collapsed, showing an equalising of pressure, but the door was firmly shut. Water was seeping in through a small gap in the seal at the bottom. He remembered the emergency manual overrides fitted to all level-access doors in the event of a pressure failure and found the small slot behind some fungus on the wall high and to the right of the door frame. He felt for the recessed hexagonal nut but without a key he would never be able to turn it.

Sounds came from behind him, penetrating the rhythmic toll of the alarms, and Stratton jerked around to see several figures approaching. It was the group of miners, led by the guard who had saved his life.

The guard went straight for the door and yanked on the handle. Unable to budge it he pulled his radio handset off the clip on his lapel and held it to his mouth. 'OCR! This is Zack on mine access to level five,' he shouted. 'I need the access door opened!'

There was no reply.

'Come on,' the guard said agitatedly. 'OCR. Open mine access level five. Come on, guys. Hear me!'

In the OCR room the senior controller was preparing to abandon his post when he heard the call. His self-preservation urge was to get going but his conscience would not allow him to and he stepped back into the communications console, picked up the mike and hit a button on the control monitor. 'Zack. As far as I can tell all emergency manual overrides have been activated. Do you have your key?'

'Yes,' Zack shouted, feeling around the back of his waist belt and finding the heavy handle.

'When you get through head for the barges. I'll see you there.'

'Secure yourselves!' Zack shouted as he unhooked the handle from the back of his belt. 'Get away from the door! There could be a lotta water on the other side.'

Stratton noted the way the water was gushing fiercely from under the bottom of the door and pushed one hand behind several pipes up to his elbow, grabbing it tightly with the other. Prisoners scurried to find secure points.

Zack inserted the end of the key, which was like an old crank-starter, into the slot and positioned it over the hexagonal nut. He put all his weight against the handle, which took several jerks to get moving. When it eventually did it turned easily.

There was a grinding sound inside the door as the guard furiously wound the handle that operated a system of low-ratio gears. For every spin the lock moved barely a millimetre inside the door. It was taking an age. Every man strengthened his grip on his strongpoint in anticipation of the deluge to come. Just when it seemed as if the mechanism had failed and the guard's efforts were in vain the door burst open in front of a massive wall of water. The door slammed into the wall, almost coming off its hinges, and the sea crashed into the narrow corridor as if a dam had burst.

Two of the prisoners and the other guard, who'd been at the rear of the column, immediately lost their hold and were swept away down the corridor, their cries quickly muffled as the water slammed them into the walls before engulfing them.

Zack was struck on his side by the initial impact and although he managed to cling to a pipe for a few seconds he soon lost his handhold. Stratton automatically stretched a hand out to him and caught hold of his harness strap. Stratton's arm around the pipe felt like it was going to rip out of his shoulder as the guard thrashed around in a desperate effort to grab anything that was fixed to the wall. The most powerful initial thrust of the water was quickly spent and as Zack gripped a bracket Stratton released him. The panting guard looked Stratton in the eye and gave him a nod.

Without wasting another second Zack got to his feet. 'Get going!' he shouted to everyone in front of and behind him. 'Move! Move!'

The prisoners needed no encouragement as they scrambled through the door.

Stratton joined the group, hurrying up the inclined corridor where it met a main-line tunnel running across its path, water splashing along it. Cardboard cartons and various wrappings covered the surface as if the intruding ocean had emptied out a storeroom of some kind.

Zack stopped at the junction to guide his men in the direction of the flashing emergency arrows. 'That way, that way. Go! Go!'

The men scurried around the corner looking like half-drowned cats, exhausted but with plenty of energy left to save their own lives.

As Stratton reached the junction he saw a sign below one of the emergency lights that indicated the hospital was in the opposite direction to the escape barges. He took a moment to consider his options. They were basically to forget the mission and save himself without further ado. Or risk a couple more minutes to try and find his target. Gann had said that Durrani was in the hospital – where he might still be. Or the Afghan might already be on his way to the escape barges. Gann had implied that the tablet had been found. But no one had expected this level of mayhem. Anything could have happened. Stratton was suddenly feeling lucky. Perhaps Hamlin's diversion might work well in his favour. He might still be able to complete his mission after all.

Stratton moved off in the direction of the hospital.

'Hey!' the guard shouted.

Stratton paused to look back, wondering if Zack was coming after him. But the guard had not moved and was simply looking at him curiously. 'The barges are this way,' he said.

'I know.'

Zack looked bemused as Stratton continued on his way. He shook his head and turned to follow his men.

'Hey, Zack,' Stratton shouted.

The guard looked back at him.

Stratton was standing in the near-darkness in knee-deep water with trash floating all around him. 'Thanks,' he said.

Zack remained confused by Stratton's choice of direction but acknowledged the prisoner's gratitude with a wave of his hand.

Stratton disappeared and Zack caught up with his men. They climbed several ladders and stairways, scurried along a corridor through an open pressure door, and met up with several more prisoners and guards coming from another direction. Together they surged through a doorway leading into what a sign above described as the escape room.

It was a large cavern containing two open airlock doors. A couple of guards stood outside each, ushering men through. The airlocks were short passageways into two escape barges. These were rudimentary vessels made of riveted plates of steel, their interiors lined with simple benches and dozens of large gas cylinders fixed into brackets against the walls. The floor was covered in rough wooden decking below which the bilges were visible. There were no portholes.

'Find a seat and strap yourselves in,' a guard ordered.

Anxious Afghan and Western prisoners, all dripping wet, some bruised and injured, sat side by side, fastening seat belts around their waists. A guard vomited up part of his fear. Several dripping-wet CIA men ran in and joined their enemies as the klaxons continued to wail, adding to the urgency of the collective desperation.

The operations controller emerged from one of the barges and walked towards Zack who was standing outside the entrance to the other vessel. 'Are you full?' he asked.

'Almost,' Zack said. 'How many do you think we're down?'

'Rough count I'd say we were down eighteen prisoners, five guards, two service staff. Anyone seen the doc?'

There was no reply.

Hank Palmerston squelched into the hall ahead of a handful of prisoners and a guard, all of whom looked exhausted and bedraggled. 'I got two people trapped in C Cell,' Hank said angrily. 'Your fuckin' door won't open.'

'I didn't build the goddamn place,' the controller shouted back. He walked over to a wall between the two airlocks where a systems panel displayed various valves and gauges.

'We gotta get that door open,' Hank persisted, following him.

'You had the brief when you got here. When the power failed their door should've gone to manual override. They have a key in the room.'

'Well, something ain't working.'

The controller ignored Hank as he checked various gauges.

'You're just gonna leave 'em there?' Hank growled.

'They're probably already dead.'

'That ain't good enough.'

The controller left the panel and walked past him. 'Zack. Your barge leaves now. I'll wait as long as I can before I push off.'

Zack ushered his guards into his barge and prepared to close the airtight door.

'Are you gonna help my guys or not?' Hank asked angrily.

The controller walked over to a guard, pulled a crank key off his belt and held it out to Hank. 'I've got a job to do. *You* go save 'em.'

Hank took the handle and looked back at the entrance to the room. The water was flooding in.

'C Cell's on level one but as you know you've got to pass through level three to get to it from here,' the controller said, trying to maintain his calm. 'Before you go you might want to consider the chances that you'll make it back here.'

'You ain't gonna wait?'

'I'll wait as long as I can!' the controller shouted at the top of his voice. 'That means when I think the remaining escape barge is at risk by staying here we're cutting loose! With or without you. Is that clear?' he shouted, his face red.

Hank looked at the other guards, realised that he was being unreasonable and lost some of his steam. 'Do you know where Mandrick is?' he asked in a more subdued voice.

'At his own presidential escape pod if he has any sense. It's easier to get to him from C Cell than from back here but if you do get your guys out you won't all fit in it. My guess is that Mandrick's already gone, anyway.'

Hank wasn't just frustrated because of his missing people. The flooding prison had also drowned his future. Everything he had worked for was about to be washed up on the beach and he knew who was behind it. He gripped the crank handle firmly as if it had become a weapon and hurried out of the room.

The controller faced Zack who was waiting for any changes to his orders. 'Get going.'

Zack walked into the airlock and with the controller's help closed the outer watertight door. He marched down the short connecting corridor and into the barge. 'Let's go,' he said and the nearby guards closed the inner door and screwed the cleats home, making it watertight. 'Everyone make sure you're secure in your seats. It's gonna be a bumpy ride.' Zack went to the instrument panel and turned several dials as gas hissed from pipes along the ceiling. He concentrated on a series of gauges as their needles climbed.

'Listen up. This is how it's gonna work. When the barge releases it's gonna float straight to the surface. Like I said, it'll be a bumpy ride. The barge might go up at an angle which is why you stay strapped into your seats. There's a drag cable on the bottom to stop it inverting – if it works. If you start feeling a little weird don't worry about it. When we hit the surface we're gonna remain at Styx depth pressure inside here. The barge'll expand a little but the system's designed to compensate for the pressure. Anyone starts getting pains, live with it. We got no medical aid for the bends on board. On the surface we wait for the emergency crews who should already be waiting for us. We've got enough air to last twenty-four hours. That's more than enough for the crews to attach a decompression system to that docking hatch,' Zack said, pointing to a hatch in the roof. 'We'll all stay in here, in our seats until the barge decompresses. We got a little water, no food, and a bucket latrine over there so sit tight and relax. Breathe easy. Any of you Talibutts speak English translate what I said for the others. You can also pass it on that if any of you guys wanna fuck around, try any of your suicide shit, I'll kill yer.'

'And you'll have a little help too,' said one of the burly white prisoners, eyeing the Afghans with a sour grimace.

'The emergency team'll be accompanied by armed guards,' Zack went on. 'So if any of you are thinking this could be a good time to make a break for it, forget it. They'll shoot to kill anyone trying to escape.'

Zack faced the panel and turned several wheels that allowed water to flood the short corridor between the outer and inner doors. One of the guards watched through a small glass porthole in the door. When the corridor was full Zack operated a gas-activated mechanism. There was a series of loud clunks and then the barge jolted heavily. This was followed by the sound of creaking as if the barge was stretching. Another massive jolt suddenly shook the vessel. Many of those inside feared that it signalled a disaster about to happen. A long silence followed, broken only by the gentle hissing of gas. One side of the barge started to rise and the water under the decking rushed to the opposite row of benches, drenching the legs of those sitting there. Zack secured himself into a seat as the barge levelled out before rising up on the other side. This time those sitting on the other row got a soaking. The entire barge creaked and groaned as the outside pressure reduced.

Zack stared at the main depth gauge on the panel. The needle dropped from the fifty-metre mark and speedily made its way to the forty-metre marker.

Stratton walked into the hospital to find Christine crouched over Doctor Mani who was lying on the floor on his back. Durrani was on his side not far away and Stratton went directly to him. He turned the Afghan over to make two immediate discoveries. First, the cut in his abdomen was open and the tablet had obviously been removed. Second: the man was dead.

Stratton looked at Mani who was barely conscious. Blood seeped from the dressing that both he and Christine were holding against his gut.

'We have to get out of here,' Stratton shouted above the sound of the klaxons.

Christine did not respond. Her hands were trembling and only then did Stratton notice in the poor light that her face was badly bruised. Her eyes were glazed and staring ahead as if she was looking at nothing.

'Hey,' he said in a softer voice as he touched her shoulder.

She snapped a look at him, her eyes filled with anger.

He held her gaze, trying to appear sympathetic. 'Let me take over,' he said, putting his hand on the dressing, hoping the offer might signal his friendship.

The gesture appeared to have the desired effect. Her expression softened as if she had returned from wherever she'd been and her eyes flickered as they moistened.

Stratton felt for a pulse in Mani's neck. The doctor's heart was beating rapidly, along with his breathing. The man was slipping away as his blood flowed from his body. He would not last long without a massive blood transfusion and surgery to close the internal injury. The journey to the escape barge would kill him even if Stratton could carry him all the way there. 'Can you hear me?' he asked him.

Mani's eyes flickered open and he looked at Stratton like a child waking up to find his father there, happy to see him. 'Is it bad?' he asked.

'You've lost a lot of blood,' Stratton said.

'I thought so.'

'Did you take anything from the Afghan's belly? Was it you who opened him up?' Stratton asked.

A frown grew on Mani's brow as he fought to collect his thoughts. He smiled. 'It was very small,' he said. Then he had a sudden thought: 'Was he a spy?'

Christine began to take an interest in the odd conversation.

'Where is it?' Stratton asked.

Mani started to slip away, his eyes glazing over.

'Doc . . . Is it here, in this room?' Stratton persisted.

Mani struggled to hold on to consciousness. 'Mandrick has it,' he gasped. 'I gave it to Mandrick . . .'

It was his last word. The air left his lungs and his muscles relaxed.

Stratton got to his feet, fighting to retrieve the map of the prison in his memory and see the warden's escape pod on it.

Christine withdrew her bloody hands, unsure where to wipe

them. As she got to her feet she realised that Stratton's clothes were soaked through. At the same time it became apparent to her that the cacophony of alarms was not inside her head but was real. 'What's happening?' she asked.

'We need to get out of here.'

She didn't move, wanting to know more. She was stubborn by nature and did not follow others easily, regardless of how obvious the reasons might be.

'The prison's flooding. Everyone's evacuating. If we hurry we might make it to the escape barges.'

Christine did not need any more information. Together she and Stratton hurried out of the hospital. When they reached the steps leading down to the main corridor, Christine paused in horror as if she had not quite believed what she'd been told. 'What happened?' she asked as she caught up with Stratton and entered the water that was thick with debris and seaweed.

'This is what you get when you play with electricity,' he said as he waded ahead of her through thousands of assorted ration packs and plastic cutlery.

Hank Palmerston made his way up the final stairway to level one and along a poorly lit corridor. At the end of it, around a slight bend, he saw Mandrick pulling on a wetsuit. The scene was illuminated by a bright halogen light from inside the hatch of a sophisticated escape pod its interior the size of a Smart car.

'Taking your time, Mandrick?' Hank called out as he approached.

Mandrick was surprised to see the CIA man but he quickly composed himself and zipped up the front of the suit. 'I'm in no great hurry,' he said, picking up his waterproof bag.

'This all your doing?' Hank said, closing the gap between them.

'I have to take the credit.'

'How'd you do it, cutting the power and bypassing all the safety procedures?'

'I used a virus program. It was far more effective than I expected. Cost me five hundred dollars from a hacker in Moscow. Well worth the investment.'

'So how's it all work from here? I'm curious. I mean, soon as you pop to the surface you'll get picked up along with everyone else. My boys'll be waiting for you when you open the hatch.'

'Forgive me if I sound smug but I had thought of that. This is a very sophisticated pod. It doesn't have to be on the surface to decompress. I can do it right here without leaving the dock. Like every good captain I'll be the last to leave my sinking ship.'

'Then in your own sweet time you'll float up to the surface – during the night, I expect.'

'A calculable risk.'

'Sink the pod and swim ashore,' Hank said, stepping closer while deciding on the best way to take Mandrick down.

'I think I can make it by daylight – or be well out of the area, at least.'

'I suppose you have enough to buy a nice little house in some far-flung corner of the globe?'

'A nice *big* house, actually.' Mandrick held up his waterproof bag. 'But you're right. I should get a nice little one at first – low profile and all that.'

'If we don't find a body, Mandrick, we won't stop looking for you.'

'That has been my biggest concern. But luck clearly favours the bold. At the very last moment – less than an hour ago, in fact – I believe I found myself a little insurance.'

'What kind of insurance?'

'To be honest I'm not entirely sure. Something we found stitched inside the gut of one of your Afghans – the one you interrogated about the helicopter he shot down . . . Durrani. Yes, I do listen to your interrogations.' Mandrick opened the waterproof bag, removed his minicomputer and lifted the flap to reveal the small card. 'I suspect it's what Gann believed Charon was after. It must be valuable . . . if not to the CIA then to someone else. It'll become clear once I find out what it is. It's going to be fun. Maybe it'll give me something to do during those long evenings in front of a cosy log fire. Or perhaps I'll go for the moonlit beach. I haven't made up my mind yet.'

'So do you wanna make a deal – right now?' Hank took a step closer, trying to figure his way through this. Mandrick was far too confident and, since he'd told him the essence of his plan it suggested that he did not believe Hank would get out of the doomed prison alive. Hank only had one weapon to stack a fight in his favour.

'You're not in a position to make any deals. Besides, there's only room for one in this pod. Sorry.'

Hank let his hand fall by his side. He still had the heavy crank key. He held it like a club and moved forward to close the gap between himself and Mandrick even further. 'You ain't going anywhere, my friend.'

Mandrick took the pistol from the bag and aimed it at him.

Hank stopped in his tracks. This was the closest to checkmate that he had ever been. He'd had a gun pointed at him before, but not by someone like Mandrick. He knew Mandrick's background. He'd been one of the South African's selectors. Hank took a step back and dropped the crank key. 'OK. You win. Get on your way. I won't try and stop you . . . We'll finish this some other time – if I ever get out of here, which is probably a long shot by now.'

'Sorry about this, Hank. But we'll have to finish it now. You might get lucky.' Mandrick pulled the trigger.

The sound of the shot was deafening in the small rock corridor. Hank staggered back, dropped to his knees, felt his chest and looked at the blood on his hands in disbelief.

'Look at it this way,' Mandrick said. 'I'm doing you a favour. You'd probably end up suffocating to death in some black freezing-cold air pocket all alone. It's better this way.'

Hank looked into Mandrick's eyes as he struggled to breathe. Mandrick pulled the trigger again and this round went through Hank's head, killing him instantly.

Mandrick placed the bag into the pod, paused to check that he had everything and climbed through the narrow opening. Halfway in he turned onto his back and with barely enough room to manoeuvre he sat up, grabbed the edge of a door that had a small glass peephole in it and swung it shut. He pushed down a lever and twisted it, securing the door before shuffling further back into the pod. He heaved himself into a comfortable bucket seat, a line of air bottles to one side and a small operations panel with various dials and gauges in front of him.

Leaning back, Mandrick pulled down the inner hatch, locked the seal and looked up at a waterproof instruction pamphlet attached to the bulkhead above him. He read the first-stage instructions and compared an illustration with the various valves and levers surrounding him. To begin the decompression sequence he pressed a button, starting a small electrical pump that began to remove gas from the pod to reduce the inside pressure.

Chapter 16

Stratton and Christine hurried past the access tunnel that led down to level five and the mine beyond and found the stairs further on that connected to the upper levels. When they reached the top Stratton stopped on a long gantry that headed in two directions. He pointed to his left. 'Head down that way. Follow the arrows to the escape barges. Good luck.' He moved off in the opposite direction.

'Where're you going?' Christine called out. She started to follow him.

He stopped, frustrated by her obstinacy. 'You're the type that never does as she's told, aren't you?'

'I like to know what's going on, yes. Why aren't you heading for the escape barges?'

Stratton gritted his teeth in irritation. 'I need to get what I came down here for. Now you know. Go.'

Christine grabbed hold of his arm as he turned to move away. 'Maybe I don't trust you. There's no cause worth dying for. Maybe you know of another way out of here.'

'It just so happens that could be true. I also think your chances are better if you go for the barges – that way.' Stratton pulled away and continued along the gantry. When he looked back she was still following him. He stopped and raised his hands to the heavens. 'What is your *problem*, woman? What is it that you are so stupidly suspicious about that you're prepared to die to find out?'

'Tell me where you're going and I'll leave you be.'

He looked into the young woman's eyes. Her expression was still determined. Time was running out. 'I have to find Mandrick. OK? Goodbye.' He hurried along the gangway and around a corner to a narrow staircase that led up. As he reached for the rail he realised she was still behind him. 'You've got to be kidding me. You said you wouldn't follow if I told you where I was going.'

'I didn't know you were going after Mandrick.'

'Go away,' Stratton said with a harshness of tone that unnerved her.

'I can't,' Christine said, suddenly overwhelmed by everything. 'I want to escape. I'm scared. If it wasn't for you I'd be running like a jackrabbit to the barges. My mission now is about getting to Mandrick too. But you're not running away. You're not scared. Maybe you know something I don't, maybe I'm all wrong about you but I don't think so. You're charging headlong into the fight with the battlements falling down around you. I always dreamed I would be like that if it ever came down to it, but I'm not. Not without you.'

'You want to work together on this?'

'Yes,' she said, gritting her teeth.

'Then go hold one of the barges. I'll get Mandrick and drag his sorry arse back and we can both have him.'

Stratton ran up the steps, leaving Christine watching him, her glare turning downright acid.

When he disappeared at the top she looked around at the crumbling prison. Sea water was cascading down walls, the dim emergency lights were flickering, the klaxons were fading as the emergency power grew weaker. In stark contrast a jaunty computerised voice announced the time. Remaining there a single minute more was madness.

Stratton scurried along the narrow corridor and as he turned the corner he saw Hank lying on his back, his eyes open, blood trailing from a hole in his head. Stratton moved past him to the watertight door at the end of the tunnel and he peered through the small porthole.

'We're too late,' Christine said, standing over Hank.

Stratton continued looking through the porthole. He considered ignoring her but decided that was clearly a waste of time. 'Yes and no,' he said. 'The pod's still attached.'

'Can we open it?'

'If we could the pod would probably jettison and we'd drown a second later.' He looked at Christine thoughtfully. 'We need to get to the surface.'

Something behind him caught her attention. Her mouth slowly opened. 'Is that an escape barge?'

Stratton turned to follow her gaze through the window. The massive, black barge was moving gracefully away, a huge drag cable trailing beneath it. It slowly tipped up at one end, levelled out, tipped a little the other way and then began to rise.

'There's still one more left. Let's go.' Stratton started to head off, pausing to pick up the crank key beside Hank before continuing along the corridor and down the stairs, Christine hot on his heels.

They ran along the gantry, reaching the entrance to the tunnel they had come along minutes before, and came to an abrupt stop. Sea water was pouring from it like a waterfall and cascading into the chasm below.

'Can we get through that?' she asked, addressing the question to herself as much as to him.

'We have to,' Stratton said. He leaned across the torrent to plant an arm on the edge of the tunnel. He reached inside and took hold of one of a stack of conduits bolted to the stone. A firm tug proved that it was secure. 'Go for it,' he shouted above the din of the rushing water.

Christine didn't hesitate, jumping past him to grab hold of the conduit. She pulled herself into the tunnel, fighting against the flow. Stratton leapt in close behind her and they headed into near-darkness as the emergency lighting grew even dimmer.

The going was hard. Their feet constantly slipped out from beneath them due to the force of the water. 'Watch out!' Christine suddenly shouted as she pulled herself tight against the wall.

Stratton did the same as several tables, carried on the flood, came bumping down the corridor at speed. Both he and the girl managed to avoid being struck.

Christine moved a few metres further on to a large bracket which she wrapped her arms around in order to snatch a breather. Stratton pulled ahead of her. 'Keep going.'

She grabbed a pipe as far ahead as she could reach and pulled herself along.

They rounded a bend where the light grew in intensity to discover that it was an emergency light illuminating a sign above a door across the tunnel from them: ESCAPE ROOM. Christine pulled herself opposite the door, wondering if they could cross the gap without being swept back the way they had come. Stratton made his way further up the tunnel. Without any hesitation he pressed his feet against the wall while holding on to a pipe and, as if he was starting a backstroke race, pushed off for the other side.

He turned onto his front as he reached the opposite wall and grabbed for a hold, moving with the water until he reached the door. Large metal brackets were fixed to the wall either side of it and he grabbed the first, pulling himself against the door that was in a small recess. He reached a hand out to Christine. 'Go for it!' he shouted.

She did not hesitate and threw herself across the gap to grab his hand. As she secured herself he banged on the steel door. The noise of their efforts seemed to be swallowed up by the sound of the rushing water. Stratton took the crank key that he had hooked inside the waist of his trousers and repeatedly struck it against the door.

He repeated the noisy assault as he searched for a way to open the door but there did not appear to be one. They feared the worst.

'They've gone, haven't they?' Christine said, knowing the answer.

Stratton stopped banging. 'I think you're right,' he said, searching in vain further along the walls to either side of the door for a manual-override slot to fit the key into.

'What about the ferries?' she asked.

'They're further on up there,' he said, pointing in the direction they had been going. 'But the doors into the dock won't operate without the OCR even in an emergency.'

A body lying face down in the water drifted past. Judging by the uniform it was that of a prisoner. It was a chilling illustration of the fate that lay ahead for them.

Stratton thought about his diving set outside the dock by the facility umbilical. But even if there was a chance of getting to it, which he could not see, there was only one set and he would have to abandon Christine. It didn't look like an option either way.

'Do we have any choices left?' she asked.

'Only thing I can think of is to find somewhere we can breathe.'

'You think they'll send a search team in here within the next six months, if ever?'

'It's possible,' he said, not believing it.

'OK, so let's go find somewhere we can stay warm, get three squares a day and breathe for the next six months,' she said sardonically. 'That wasn't aimed at you, by the way. This is all my fault. I held you up.'

'I don't think so.'

'I did and you know it. I'm a pig-headed bitch.'

'Listen. If you're going to be my best friend for the rest of my life you'd better stop whingeing.'

Christine looked into Stratton's eyes, unable to suppress a slight smile. Then something caught her eye as it floated towards her and she plucked it out of the water. It was a ration pack. 'We have dinner at least.'

'What is it?'

She held it closer to the light to read the label. 'Chicken supreme.'

'That's very good, you know.'

She appreciated his humour in the face of such adversity.

'I know where there's an air-storage chamber,' Stratton said. 'Might even be some electricity.'

'What are we waiting for?'

'Hold on to me. Let's stay together.'

'For the rest of my life,' she said as she grabbed hold of his arm and he let go of the door bracket.

They shot down the tunnel, fending themselves off the sides. They soon reached the metal gantry, spilling out of the tunnel onto it as the water plummeted to the lower levels. Stratton got to his feet and they hurried to the stairs and down them. They crossed to another flight of steps, scurried down them to a broad tunnel that was waist-deep in water that was not flowing as fast as in the previous one and headed past a sign directing them towards the hospital. Stratton was encouraged by the shallower water that suggested, for the time being at least, that the prison was not necessarily filling from the bottom up.

They reached the narrower access tunnel that led down to level five and the mine to find the water cascading down it more vigorously than before.

'We're heading down?' Christine asked.

Stratton nodded. 'Let's hope this one hasn't filled yet.'

He entered the tunnel and, holding firmly onto the side, made his way down the slope. Christine was close behind him in the near-darkness.

They reached the open pressure door with '5' stencilled on it and continued down the increasingly steep incline. The water became deeper as they descended and was chest high by the time they arrived at the larger corridor that led towards the scrubber room and the mine.

'This is good. I was worried this tunnel would be completely filled by now.'

'Yeah, this is really good news,' Christine said, feeling very cold and unable to hold back her cynicism.

They passed the battered bodies of the guard and prisoners who had been washed down the tunnel when the level five pressure door had burst open. The corpses were floating together in a recess.

Stratton arrived at the entrance to the scrubber and pump room where the engines were now silent, and climbed in through the doorway. The hissing had been replaced by a forced bubbling sound as the water only just lapped over the valve on the stack of huge air bottles that Hamlin had opened.

'This the place?' Christine asked as she moved inside.

'All the air you can breathe.'

'If there was a search team, you think they'd come this far down?'

'Sure. Might even be a priority. Probably more chance of surviving longer here than anywhere else.'

'I never tire of your optimism,' she said, looking behind the door and suddenly jumping back, startled. 'Jesus Christ!'

Gann was standing against the wall, his right arm gone at the shoulder, his face seriously charred. The flesh was practically burned away, exposing his teeth and cheekbone. One of his eyes was gone. He appeared to be dead at first but then he moved his head stiffly to face them, his one eye minus its eyelid moving in its socket. When he recognised Stratton he took a step forward, reaching out to him with his remaining hand. But he was so weak that he could barely stand.

Stratton stood his ground as Gann forced himself to take another painful step. He moved close enough to grab feebly at the front of Stratton's jacket with his charred fingers. He tried to say something, but his lips were gone and his throat was so horribly burned that he was unable to form a word. His knees suddenly gave way and he dropped face down into the water where he stayed.

'Was that Gann?' Christine asked.

'Yes,' Stratton said, turning away and wading over to the rack of gas cylinders. He reached into the water for the bubbling valve and turned it off.

'The lights are brighter in here,' she noted.

'I think there's a power line into here directly from the barge. What are your electrical skills like?'

'I can change a fuse, a spark plug.'

'Pity.'

'Why?'

'If we can find a power link to the barge we might be able to turn it on and off. Make a signal of some kind.'

'I like it.'

'The water will eventually stop rising – that's if there's nowhere for the air to escape in the roof. We put the air valve on trickle flow and . . . you know. Wait.'

Stratton climbed the rack to get out of the water.

Christine climbed up beside him. 'Hey, we're alive and breathing and in a while we'll be dry. That's way ahead of where I thought we'd be when we were outside the escape room.'

'I'm sorry it's not any better.' He was disappointed that he had been unable to get them out.

She put her hand on his and squeezed it. 'My name's Christine, by the way.'

'John,' he said.

'Where are you from? I guess we have no more need for secrets.'

'I'm a Brit.'

'I figured out *that* much.'

'I'm from a town in the south of England. Poole. Don't suppose you've even heard of it.'

She shook her head apologetically. 'England's on my list of must-see places . . . I'm curious as hell about you. Who do you work for? If you don't want to tell me I'll put it down to you being optimistic about us surviving and I'd probably be happier that way.'

'British military intelligence,' Stratton said.

She was surprised to find his timing and apparent lack of optimism amusing.

'We lost something in Afghanistan. The Taliban found it and it ended up in here.'

'Why didn't you just ask us? I thought we were the great alliance.'

'I understand it would've been embarrassing for our side if you guys found out what it was.'

'Oh.' Christine nodded. 'Bummer, you dying just to save someone an embarrassment.'

Stratton had to concede that one. 'What are you dying for?'

'Mine isn't much better . . . The White House wanted this place closed down and they needed evidence of the shenanigans going on down here. We decided to pool with the feds in the end but, well, you know better than anyone how that one ended . . . It was my stupid ego that killed me. I could've got out earlier but I had to go that one step beyond where I was asked to.'

'Yeah, that'll do it sometimes.'

'How'd you get in here without our help?'

'I didn't. My lot conned the White House into running a security exercise. We offered to test the prison – see if I could escape from it.'

'They bought that?'

Stratton put out his hands – he was the proof.

'So how's it going?'

'I'm still working on it.'

They both chuckled.

The lights suddenly went dimmer.

'The thought of Mandrick getting away with this really pisses me off,' she said.

'Maybe he won't.'

'I'd like to know it, though . . . I hope the lights don't go off completely,' Christine said, her fears momentarily getting the better of her.

'There's a box of candles in that room up there,' Stratton said, indicating the transformer room. 'We won't sit in the dark.'

She looked at him again. 'You're very comforting, aren't you? You been in this business long?'

'A few years . . . I always believed there was a solution, even to the most desperate situation. Somewhere, somehow there's one for this. Now, maybe it requires a much higher intelligence or strength than we possess to find it.'

'Or luck.'

'Or luck . . . But it's there.'

Christine noted that the water had risen several inches since they'd climbed the rack. 'I think we should head for a higher spot to sit or we'll soon have to swim—'

'Shh!' Stratton interrupted.

She obeyed, watching him, his brow furrowed, eyes searching the far wall for something.

Stratton had picked up on a sound that did not belong with the others. It came again. A single short ping, like metal striking metal, but muffled as if it was a long way away.

Christine heard it too. 'Others made it down here.'

That was a possible explanation but Stratton had another on his mind.

The noise came again. He jumped off the rack into the water that was now close to his shoulders, started to wade through it, then changed to the breaststroke and powered himself towards the door.

'What makes you think they're in any better situation than we are?' she shouted.

He ignored her and swam through the door. The lights flickered. Christine was suddenly alone.

'I'll check it out with you,' she called out. She jumped in and followed him.

She caught him up outside and he headed deeper into the main tunnel, the surface of the water now close to the ceiling. Stratton stuck to the side closest to the scrubber room, hoping to find an opening or a corridor that would lead to where the noise had come from. He considered the possibility of not being able to return to the scrubber room but he still felt compelled to find the source of the noise. He could never ignore his instincts when they were this strong.

Stratton came to the top of a door and glanced back to see that Christine was closing in on him. He ducked beneath the surface to feel if it was open.

It was slightly ajar and he heaved against it, wedging his body into the gap and pushing the door open wide enough to get through.

He broke the surface to find himself in a small room with a raised floor. A single emergency light provided some weak illumination. He pulled himself out of the water onto the raised ground.

Christine broke the surface and swam to the edge of the floor. After pulling herself out of the water she stood beside Stratton, rubbing her arms against the cold that was gripping her. Stratton put a finger to his lips. They were in a miners' storeroom. There were piles of picks, hammers and shovels, drill bits and chisels, mining helmets, harnesses and overalls. Stratton tested the light on one of the helmets. It worked and he left it on to provide more light.

The sound came again, still with the muffled effect that made it seem like it was coming from beyond the walls although now it was louder than before. Stratton put his hands on the wall as if trying to feel where the noise was coming from.

Christine looked back at the water rising above the top of the door they had just come through. She wondered if they would be able to make it back to the scrubber room.

The metallic tap came again. Stratton followed the wall to the edge of the floor where it disappeared under the water and he crouched to examine the spot. He climbed off the platform into the water and quietly sank below the surface.

Christine watched as the water was disturbed further along the wall.

A moment later Stratton surfaced. 'There's a way through.'

'Can you tell me why we're doing this?' she asked.

'Not exactly,' he replied.

She nodded. 'OK.'

'It's a hole, right below me, a metre or so down. I'll see you on the other side.' He ducked below the surface again and was gone. Christine did not lack courage and lowered herself into the water. The cold attacked her immediately. She was blindly following a man she didn't know into oblivion and was doing so without much of a second thought. It didn't feel like the wrong thing to do, either. She took a breath and ducked under the water.

Stratton surfaced inside a large natural cave that was brightly illuminated by a string of small halogen spotlights hooked onto the walls. There was a large rudimentary triangular metal framework made up of dozens of pieces of iron lengths welded or fixed together with clamps, bolts and cables. An acetylene bottle and gun leant against a wall. A pulley hung from the apex of the framework near the ceiling with a cable running through it, one end disappearing into the water, the other over a rocky plateau above him.

Christine surfaced beside him, wiped the water from her face and eyes and looked surprised at the contents of the cave.

Stratton climbed out onto the plateau to see Hamlin propped against a winch that was secured to the rock floor. He had a hammer in one hand and a chisel in the other. He looked as if he was asleep. Christine climbed out of the water as Stratton went to Hamlin's side and put a hand on his chest.

Hamlin opened his eyes and took a moment to focus on the face above him. 'Ahh, the ferryman,' he said, a smile forming on his lips. 'Come to take me to Hades? I do believe I'm finally ready.'

The end of the cable that came from the pulley at the top of the derrick-like construction was secured onto the winch drum which Hamlin had evidently been trying to free.

'How you doing, Tusker?' Stratton asked in a soft, friendly voice.

'Not too good . . . Gann screwed me up,' Hamlin said, releasing the hammer and chisel. 'I warned you he was a son of a bitch.'

'If it makes you feel any better he isn't any more.'

Hamlin nodded approval and as he took in a breath it was accompanied by a gasp of agony. Several of his ribs were clearly cracked or broken. He took a moment to concentrate on his breathing, keeping it as shallow as possible to reduce the pain. 'Getting' outta here is all I've ever wanted to do,' he said.

'You can still make it,' Stratton said, fishing for the 'how' of Hamlin's escape plan, wondering how lucid the older man was and if he would share whatever it was he had been coveting. Stratton had no doubt that Hamlin had hatched some kind of plan.

Hamlin shook his head in disagreement. 'Gettin' through that goddamned sump nearly killed me . . . You know how many times I've swum through there? Gotta be more'n a thousand.'

'How'd you find this place?'

'They let me alone for hours at a time to repair the mining

stores next door. I found it when I was snoopin' around one day. I flooded it so they'd never find it. Last two years've been the most enjoyable I've had in any prison. Maybe even beats some years when I wasn't . . . Building it a little at a time, day by day, gave me something to wake up to.'

'Building what?' Stratton asked.

'Gettin' all the right pieces was tough . . . especially the plates. Then gettin' 'em through that damn sump. That was as much of a challenge as puttin' it together.'

'You built it in here?' Stratton asked, looking at the derrick again.

Christine did not have a clue what either man was going on about but she sat back, listening intently.

'Piece by damned piece.' A spasm suddenly shot through Hamlin's body and he went rigid as he fought the pain. A moment later it subsided and he took a breath. He looked over at Christine. 'Wish I'd gotten to know you better, ferryman. Takes a special kinda guy to find a chick in a disaster at the bottom of the ocean.'

There was a distant rumble, followed by a surge of water from the sump. The level increased dramatically. Christine looked with concern at Stratton, fearful that they would not make it back to the air supply.

Stratton got to his feet, frustrated with the old man's ramblings, and wondered if he could figure out for himself what Hamlin had built. He studied the framework, noting the cable leading from the pulley down into the water with another, thinner cable coming out beside it where it was wrapped several times around a large rock to secure it.

Christine stepped beside him and kept her voice low, though even a gentle whisper echoed in the cavern. 'Should we try and get him back to the air bottles?'

'He won't make it,' Stratton replied, looking at the water where the cables went into it. It was separated from the sump by a natural wall of rock but there was something that looked different about it. He crouched and brushed the surface with his hand and the water that churned up was white as milk. 'This water comes directly from outside.'

'We're just above the seabed here,' Hamlin said. 'The opening down there is big enough to drive a truck through. It's what started me on the idea.'

Stratton crouched beside Hamlin again. 'What is it you built, Tusker?'

Hamlin looked into his eyes. 'First one was made two and a half thousand years ago.'

Stratton looked back at the water, the cable going up to the ceiling, the spacious cave, the entrance apparently big enough to drive a truck through, the metal plates that Hamlin had described. He looked back at Hamlin who was wearing a smirk.

'A bell?' Stratton asked.

Hamlin's smirk broadened before a painful cough wiped it away. 'Finished it a couple weeks ago,' he said, recovering. 'Took me a week to get it outside. I got pretty damn good at holding my breath.'

Hamlin's expression turned serious as he held out a hand. Stratton took hold of it. 'Take it up for me . . . prove to those sons of bitches that I could do it.'

The water level rose again, creeping up the rock and reducing the surface area of the small plateau they were on.

'Release that cable,' Hamlin said, indicating the winch. 'I don't have the strength any more.'

Stratton took hold of the hammer, glanced at Christine who was struggling to make some sense of what was taking place, and took a heavy swing at the bracket holding the cable to the drum. It snapped off and the end of the cable shot up through the pulley and down into the milky water where it disappeared. 'That other one too?' Stratton asked, indicating the thinner cable tied around the rock.

'No.' Hamlin said, waving his hand. 'You'll need that . . . You said you knew diving.'

'Yes.'

'Inside the top . . . a tap . . . your air. Rest you'll have to figure out,' Hamlin said, growing weaker.

The water trickled over the rock wall and into the milky pool. It slowly covered Hamlin's feet, rising towards his backside. 'Help me up, will yer?' Hamlin asked.

Stratton put his hands under Hamlin's armpits and pulled the older man to his feet. Hamlin winced but fought the pain, indicating that he wanted to stand on his own. Stratton let him go and Hamlin shuffled to the edge of the milky pool.

'That leads to the bell,' Hamlin said, indicating the thin cable. 'Good luck, ferryman . . . Race you to the top.' Hamlin dived into the milky water and disappeared below the surface.

Christine stared after him. Stratton tore his gaze from the place where Hamlin had dived into the water and looked at her.

'You want to take another dive into what could turn out to be nowhere?' Stratton asked.

'You really believe that crazy old man's built a diving bell? One that'll actually work?'

'I wouldn't stake my life on it under normal conditions.'

'You're serious?'

'One thing I *do* know. We follow him out there, we're never coming back.'

Christine swallowed gently as she looked around the ever-shrinking cave and back into his eyes. 'I've been following you into oblivion most of the time I've known you. Why stop now?'

Stratton nodded, lowered himself into the water, grabbed the cable and pulled himself below the surface.

Christine watched him go. Without wasting another second to

consider the wisdom of it she jumped into the milky water, grabbed hold of the cable, took a deep breath and pulled herself beneath the milky surface.

Hamlin emerged from the vast cloud of milky water that covered the seabed like an impenetrable mist. He took a final stroke towards the surface, eyes wide and looking up. Bubbles escaped from his mouth as he ascended, travelling alongside him like pilot fish. He maintained his composure as best as he could until the spasms of asphyxiation took hold of him and he shuddered as he drowned. His body went limp and the bubbles alongside him grew larger.

Hamlin's body gradually expanded, his clothes tightening around his flesh before they ripped open. His skin stretched and gave way as it tore in places. His eyes popped from their sockets and fluid escaped from his ears seconds before his skull cracked open. More bubbles escaped from his flesh and blood, his bones splitting as the rapidly expanding gases freed themselves from the marrow. A trail of human detritus floated from the wrecked torso, lengths of intestinal tubing swelling like a string of balloons. The heavier parts of Hamlin's body sank back down while thousands of smaller bits of him, buoyed up by gases, headed towards the sunlight. Moments later a million of his bubbles broke the sunlit surface and mingled with the air.

In the distance the prison's security vessel was moored alongside one of the escape barges. Suddenly, a hundred metres away, the surface erupted as if a huge whale was trying to reach the skies. It was the second escape barge, on its side. It had ascended at speed from its undersea mooring. It came out of the water several metres before its weight dragged it back down. When it next came up it flopped over onto its underside and levelled out, the water cascading off the flat roof and down the sides.

Chapter 17

Stratton pulled himself along the thin cable, unable to make out anything by its shape or shade. The cable continued down for several metres where he hit the jagged seabed with the side of his body, still unable to see anything through the white 'milk'. He pulled himself along the bottom, quickly reliving the nightmare of his recent near-drowning.

As his lungs started to complain of the lack of oxygen his head struck something metal. It was a piece of angle iron secured to one side of a large drum of some sort. The cable coiled around the drum, effectively coming to its end, and Stratton released it to feel his way beyond it. There were several more cables criss-crossing iron struts but the gaps between them were too small to crawl through. He was running out of air and suppressing uncontrollable thoughts of returning to the cave.

Stratton stretched out his hands in every direction to work out the shape of the construction and discovered that the struts formed a rough circle. He moved over the drum and through this circle to find himself inside a container, which he followed up into a narrow dead end. He was rapidly heading into oxygen deficit and Hamlin's words telling him to look for a tap echoed in his head. He found a small pipe that led to what was clearly a large metal gas bottle but without a valve at the connection. He quickly followed it in the other direction to find what could be described as a tap and tried to turn it but it wouldn't budge.

Something grabbed Stratton's leg and Christine climbed up

beside him. Her hands felt up his arms and to his hands and together they fought to turn the valve. Their lungs were bursting, both of them with only seconds left before they would involuntarily gulp in water. The tap suddenly moved and they could hear the hiss of escaping gas.

Stratton spun the tap open as quickly as he could and pushed his face into the highest part of the bell, pressing his lips to the metal ceiling in search of the gas. A pocket of air quickly grew and he gulped in a breath, at the same time pulling Christine up alongside him. She took in a lungful of air while choking violently. Now their faces were pressed together in the ever-increasing air pocket.

The water level gradually dropped and the bell, which had initially been leaning at an angle, moved upright as it became buoyant. Stratton felt around in the darkness in order to find out more about Hamlin's rudimentary construction and its operating system. 'You OK?' he asked.

'Yes,' Christine said finally after clearing her throat. 'I didn't think we were going to make it that time.'

'You get used to that.'

'Do you have a sense of humour apart from at times like this?'

'I'm best when I'm scared shitless.'

The bell started to ascend but it did not travel far before coming to a creaky halt as the cable below went taut.

Stratton felt around the bell's interior from top to bottom. 'I've got to believe Hamlin put some kind of light in here. He had good attention to detail.'

Christine helped him search. 'I've found a wire . . . it splits and there are clips on the ends.'

'Now look for a battery.' Stratton felt around the base of the bell where Hamlin would have put anything heavy to help keep the vessel from inverting. 'I have it,' he said.

She grabbed his arm, found his hand and put the clips in it.

He attached one to a terminal and as soon as he touched the other a small halogen light flickered on at the top of the bell. The tiny space was flooded with light.

Stratton secured the clip and looked at Christine who was staring at him. He smiled. 'Welcome aboard the *Nautilus*.' He pointed to an inscription scrawled on the bulkhead.

They proceeded to examine the bell and its contents. The outer shell was little more than metal plates fixed to struts of angle iron, some welded, other parts bolted together with rubber in between that acted as a seal. Struts also formed a bench that Stratton sat on to get a clearer perspective on his surroundings. Christine sat opposite him.

The cross struts gave the framework its strength and all in all Stratton was impressed. 'You have to hand it to the old man,' he said.

Two large gas bottles were lashed either side of the small chamber. 'These are our breather mixes – argon and oxygen,' Stratton explained, feeling the cylinders' cold metal skins. There was a smaller bottle lashed beside one of them with a valve on the end which he turned on briefly to check that it had gas. 'This is pure oxygen. We'll need that to increase the oxygen percentage as we ascend.'

A metal container was secured under one of the brackets and Stratton untied it to see what it was. It contained liquid and he removed a cap on the side, smelled it and put it to his lips. 'Water,' he said, offering Christine some. 'Just a sip.'

She took it from him and relished a mouthful of the refreshing liquid. 'I don't know how much sea water I've drunk,' she said, taking another small sip.

Stratton removed a plastic bundle from one of the struts and tore it open. 'Blankets,' he said, handing them to her. She took them eagerly and immediately wrapped one around herself.

A white plastic board was fixed to the bulkhead. It had two

columns of figures written on it in indelible ink. 'This looks like an ascent table,' he said. 'Just five stop numbers and a time beside each . . . Give me your watch.'

Christine screwed the cap back onto the water container and checked the timepiece on her wrist. 'It's broken,' she said, examining the broken glass.

'Hamlin wasn't wearing one. Check that box.'

She leaned down and opened a metal box tied to one of the braces between her feet. 'Pliers, screwdriver . . . and a watch,' she said, holding it out to him.

Stratton inspected it. It was a waterproof digital model and appeared to be working. 'You're not claustrophobic, I hope.'

'I've got too much else scaring the crap out of me . . . What's next?'

'We figure out how to head up.'

He looked down at the milky water surrounding their feet. 'This milk doesn't help any . . . I'm going to turn the gas off for a moment while we figure this out.' He reached up for the tap and closed it. The hissing ceased.

'Why's the water white?'

'A Gulf of Mexico phenomenon,' Stratton said, squatting down and reaching into the water to feel around the drum. 'Some kind of mineral washed down from the coast . . . The key to going up is obviously this cable drum . . . There's something clamped to the cable stopping it from unrolling . . . Hand me those pliers.'

Christine gave him the tool and he reached down to find the clamp and figure out how to release it. He felt a clip of some kind which he took a grip on before pausing. 'I can't feel how this clamp works.' He decided to pull on the clip which felt as if it was moving out of a hole in the block secured around the cable. The clip came away and the block opened and fell off the cable. The drum immediately started to turn.

'We're going up,' Stratton said, looking perplexed.

'That's good, right?' Christine asked, wondering why he appeared to be so concerned.

The drum turned easily, paying out the cable as they rose. Stratton checked the ascent table. 'There's no depth here.'

'How do we know when to stop?'

'There has to be a depth gauge.'

Christine quickly inspected the contents of the box. 'Nothing.'

'There must be something,' Stratton said, checking around the nooks and crannies of the small space with increased desperation. 'It's one of the essential factors in decompression.'

'What else could you use if you didn't have a depth gauge?' she asked, unsure exactly what she was looking for.

'I don't know. There must be something. Hamlin had to know the decompression stop depths.'

The white water around their feet disappeared and was replaced by clear water. The drum was suddenly visible as they rose out of the milk, rotating quickly as it paid out the cable.

'We've got to stop it!' Stratton said, lowering himself to apply pressure to the drum with his foot in an effort to put the brakes on. It had no effect and he stood on it with both feet. Christine jumped down alongside him and together they tried to stop the drum from turning. But the cable continued to pay out.

'This is not good,' Stratton said, looking around. 'We're missing something. The answer is staring us in the face.' No sooner had the words left his mouth when there was a heavy clunk and the drum stopped turning, bringing the bell's ascent to a halt.

They climbed off the drum and Stratton crouched to inspect it. 'You sweet and brilliant man, Tusker Hamlin . . . It's another clamp. And there are others attached to the cable around the drum. We don't need a depth gauge. The cable's pre-set for every stop.'

Christine slumped back down onto her cross-brace and pulled her blanket back round her. She offered one to Stratton who took it and did the same.

He consulted the table, checked the watch and hit a button on the side of it. 'Four and a half hours. Then we move up to the next stop.'

She exhaled noisily. 'Is it going to be this easy?'

'I doubt the decompression will be perfect. There's always risks even with the most sophisticated set-ups. It'll be a resounding success if we're barely alive by the time we see daylight . . . We're going to have to watch each other for any symptoms. There'll also be a carbon dioxide build-up. We'll have to flush the air every so often.'

'What are the signs?'

'Discoloration – the lips, for instance. Light-headedness. Talking crap.'

'I think I've suffered from it before,' Christine said, trying to match his humour. But there were too many fears for her to keep it up for long. 'Is there enough air for the two of us? Hamlin planned this trip for one.'

Stratton shrugged. 'My maths doesn't extend to cubic litres and oxygen consumption at partial pressures. Sorry.'

He decided to set the tap to a gentle flow of air. 'If these bottles are full we should have enough.'

'How come you know so much about diving?'

'Ever heard of the SBS?'

'You were a courier?

'A what?'

'SBS is a courier company – isn't it?'

'No, I wasn't a courier . . . It's like your navy SEALs.'

'Oh. OK. Makes sense,' Christine said, wrapping her arms around herself, feeling the cold.

Stratton moved to the end of his strut and lifted his blanket to make some room. 'Sit over here. We need to keep warm.'

'Not the old Eskimo ploy,' she said, moving across the bell to sit beside him.

'The lengths I go to to use that line.'

They pulled their legs out of the water, propped them on the opposite strut and adjusted the blankets. Stratton put an arm around the girl and they got as comfortable as they could.

'What happened to Durrani?' he asked.

'He killed Mani and I think he intended to kill me. But he hesitated for some reason. I guess he was in a lot of pain. Then the lights went out. I punched him in the chest with everything I had. He must've been in bad shape. When the lights went back on he was lying on the floor, gasping for air . . . I've never seen anyone die up close before today.'

'How'd you get so beaten up?'

'That bastard Mandrick.'

'What's the deal with him?'

'Works for the crooked corporation that owns Styx. They were making money from the mine, cheating Uncle Sam. Small potatoes. But a good enough reason for us to shut down the interrogation cell before it became an embarrassment . . . Mandrick kept all the dirt on a small computer. He liked insurance. It was all the proof I needed. But I blew it . . . Doesn't matter now, though. We got what we wanted in the end. At the risk of sounding mercenary, this works out pretty good for us.'

'Glad someone's happy.'

Christine looked at Stratton. 'He has what you came for.'

Stratton had not forgotten.

'He'll get picked up when he surfaces,' she said. 'The feds still want him.'

'That's not good for me, though. The feds'll get what I came for . . . But he knows they'll be waiting for him. That's why he's still down there. That pod's designed to decompress at depth. He'll surface when it's done . . . You have any idea what time it is?'

'It was around four p.m. when I went to see Mandrick. Dinner's at six but I wanted to see him a couple of hours earlier. It couldn't have been more than an hour after that when the alarms went off.'

'That means it'll be dark when we surface. He needs it to be dark. We're ten miles off the coast. Not a problem if you're wearing the right gear. He'll be miles out of the area by dawn. On the road by late morning.'

Christine had nothing consolatory to offer.

'Unless we're there when he surfaces,' Stratton added.

'He must've started his decompression long before us.'

Stratton had already thought of that.

She wondered what was going through his mind. 'Why do I get the feeling you're planning on taking another risk before we're even done with this one?'

'I want to finish what I came for.'

'I've been around special ops for a few years now and I've never met anyone like you before. What drives you?'

'I don't know.'

'Fear of failing? No. I have that but I'm not in your league.'

'I get as scared as the next person. I suppose I just don't know when to quit until I'm in over my head. Then I have to figure how to get out. So far I've been lucky.'

'You've solved one puzzle for me.'

'What's that?'

'I've wanted to be like you all my life. But I never made it because deep down I didn't really believe you existed . . . Thanks.'

'You hitting on me?'

'Could be my last chance. This is the new me. It's your fault. I see what I want and now I'm going for it.'

They chuckled together.

'We should relax and save our air,' Stratton said. 'Try to sleep. I'll stay awake.'

Christine rested her head comfortably against him, enjoying

the closeness despite the circumstances. He placed the palm of his hand against the side of her head.

She mused thoughtfully for some time but her eyelids soon grew heavy as the events of the day drained her. Seconds after closing her eyes she fell into a deep sleep. It seemed to her as though only a few minutes had passed before the digital clock chirped.

She sat up, wondering where she was for a second.

Stratton took the pliers and reached down into the water. He jiggled with the clamp and a few seconds later the drum began to roll and the bell ascended.

He adjusted the gas, adding some oxygen to the mix, breathing in and out deeply, hoping he might spot any dangerous symptoms before they incapacitated him. He had experienced decompression sickness before during a familiarisation exercise in an RAF decompression chamber before a week of HALO jumps with the SAS. The team had been inside a large chamber containing chairs and tables and had been invited to occupy themselves with a variety of games such as kit construction or drawing pictures. In Stratton's case he'd had to continually subtract seven from four hundred.

It was odd the way some had reacted differently to others. And at different periods of the decompression process. Some people had lasted barely a minute before they'd begun to act strangely, drawing wildly or becoming hysterical. One of the guys had started to do a little jig. Assistants wearing oxygen masks had been on hand to give oxygen immediately to anyone who showed signs of going under. Stratton had concentrated everything he had into subtracting his numbers and when the decompression had reached a dangerous level the pressure had been reversed and the exercise brought to a stop. When Stratton had reviewed his maths afterwards he'd found that he'd only made a couple of mistakes and had wondered if that was down to poor arithmetic or if he had started to succumb.

The bell came to a sudden stop and Christine tried to make herself comfortable against him once again but she was becoming fidgety. She chuckled to herself as she pulled the blanket down. Stratton was immediately aware of a change in her.

'Let's go for a swim,' Christine said, giggling.

Stratton reached for the oxygen bottle and turned it on, giving the bell a good burst to increase the partial pressure, hoping that was the right solution. Christine started to relax and although she was breathing heavily at first she calmed down to a normal level and lay quietly against him.

He offered her the water container that was getting light. She took a small sip. He elected to pass on his drink for the moment and replaced the cap.

The hours passed by slowly but the stop times became shorter until they reached the final one. Stratton set the digital watch. 'How're you feeling?' he asked.

'I'm OK. I was in and out of dizziness a few times.'

'You have any muscle pains . . . headaches?'

'My head's fine. I think I'm OK everywhere else, too. This isn't the most comfortable eight hours I've ever spent . . . except for the company, which I've enjoyed more than I can remember enjoying anyone's company before.'

'Do I need to give you a little more oxygen?'

Christine smiled. 'I'm not talking crap,' she said, looking into his eyes. 'You're a hell of a guy, whoever you are.'

Stratton looked a little embarrassed, unused as he was to compliments. It made him even more attractive to her and she kissed him gently on the side of his mouth. 'Whatever happens . . . thanks.'

'It was my pleasure.'

She rested her head on his shoulder again.

'We're ten metres from the surface, give or take whatever the tide's doing.'

Christine looked at Stratton in surprise. 'Only ten? You mean we've made it?'

'Only thing I remember about decompression stops is the last one is usually ten metres from the surface.'

'I don't believe it – I mean, I do. I just don't.'

'I can feel pins and needles in my fingers.'

'Me too. Is that bad?'

'We'll probably need a recompression. But I think we'll be fine,' he said, getting off the strut to sit opposite her.

Christine could see he had something on his mind. 'What is it?' she asked.

'Mandrick. I can't let him go.'

'What can you do about it?'

'I can be there when he surfaces.'

'You don't know when that'll be. He might wait down there for hours.'

'No. He has air limits too. He'll do around the same time as us. But if I'm down here when he surfaces I'll lose him.'

'Is it OK to skip this last stop?'

'It won't kill me. As long as I can get to a chamber soon after.'

'And if you can't?'

'There'll be one on board the rescue craft.'

'So your plan is to swim around up there, hoping he pops up right beside you?'

'You've got a better idea?'

'Yes. You've done your job as best you could. You nearly died, half a dozen times, trying to succeed. You said yourself it was only to save someone an embarrassment.'

'That's what it is to them. Not to me.'

Christine's expression softened. 'Why am I trying to argue with you?' She removed her blanket. 'OK – I'm coming with you.'

'No, you're not. There's the clock,' Stratton said, putting it in her hand. 'When it beeps get out and swim to the surface.'

She let the clock slip through her fingers. It plopped into the water and disappeared. 'Oops,' she said, looking at him.

'You're a stubborn bitch.'

A strange sound like a distant grating stopped them arguing.

'What's that?' Christine asked.

'No idea.'

The noise grew louder and the bell began to vibrate.

'A boat?' she asked, looking up.

'No,' Stratton said, looking down.

The cable was rattling where it joined the drum, the vibrations growing with each passing second. The bottom of the bell suddenly moved as if it was being yanked to one side. It started to lean over and they could make out something rising out of the gloom towards them.

It was Mandrick's pod, caught on the cable and coming up at them like a torpedo.

It slammed into the base of the bell with tremendous force, almost smashing the drum from its housing and tipping the bell onto its side. Water flooded in as the bell inverted.

Stratton and Christine were tossed around as if they were inside a washing machine. Then the bell stabilised and started to plummet.

Stratton grabbed Christine with one hand and the struts now above him with the other. The bars had twisted in the impact and the drum was threatening to block their escape. The bell sank rapidly as Stratton fought to pull himself through a small gap. He released Christine in an effort to free himself and when he'd got outside he reached back into what now felt like a cage for her. She was clutching him through a gap too small to pull herself through. Stratton reached in through the largest gap, grabbed her brutally and yanked her over. He pulled with all his might as his lungs cried out for air, suddenly fearful he might have to let her go.

Then, as if a door had opened, she popped through the struts and as the bell continued its journey back to the depths they headed up, swimming for their lives.

Stratton broke the surface, gasping for air. A second later Christine appeared beside him, fighting to stay on the surface as she too gulped for breath.

Stratton saw the pod only metres away as three large red bags inflated around it. There was a cluster of bright lights in the distance beyond, undoubtedly the rescue mission but probably too far away for them to see the pod unless someone was actually looking at it.

Stratton swam towards it as the hatch began to open. He tried to climb onto the pod but the large inflation bags made it difficult to do so.

Mandrick rose out of the hatch, looked towards the emergency crews in the distance and, satisfied that he was far enough away, began to make ready for his departure. He pulled out his waterproof bag and placed it on the side of the hatch. Then he removed a knife from his belt and stabbed the nearest inflation bag. As the gas escaped he slashed another and was about to slice the third when, to his utter amazement, he saw Christine on the other side of it.

'I don't believe it,' he said, stupefied. 'Christine. You have to be the most tenacious person I have ever known.'

'That's what my mother always told me,' Christine said, seeing the waterproof bag in Mandrick's hand.

Stratton surfaced behind Mandrick's back, took hold of the pod and eased himself out of the water.

'This is the end of the road, Mandrick,' Christine said.

'You must be referring to yourself,' Mandrick said as he reached down into the pod.

Stratton wrapped his arm around Mandrick's neck, the bone of his forearm across his throat. 'She was definitely referring to you,' he said, gripping Mandrick's hand that held the knife.

With his other hand Mandrick pulled a Very pistol out of the pod and aimed it at Christine. 'Release me or I'll put this flare through her head. Don't doubt it.'

Stratton froze.

'Take your arm away,' Mandrick shouted.

Stratton loosened his grip. 'You can't get away,' he said, his mind racing for a solution.

'For the last time, move away or she's dead,' Mandrick said.

As Stratton released him he noticed a strap hanging loosely from the back of Mandrick's life jacket. He hooked it over the hatch lever as he moved away. 'Whatever you say. Just don't shoot.'

'Only if I have to. I don't want to give away my position, now, do I?'

Mandrick buried the knife's blade in the remaining inflation bag. The pod quickly began to sink. Mandrick released the knife, grabbed his waterproof bag and went to climb out of the hatch when he discovered he was held fast from behind. He struggled to pull himself free as water flooded into the pod. His actions quickly became desperate as he thrashed from side to side in an effort to break his bonds.

Stratton and Christine floated in the water, watching as the pod filled and sank beneath the surface. In a final act of fury Mandrick wildly aimed the Very pistol at Stratton and fired. The flare shot across the water in a bright red light in the direction of the rescue craft and Mandrick disappeared below the surface.

At the same time, to Stratton's horror, Christine shot below the surface. He immediately thought that she had somehow become entwined with the pod, took a deep breath and was about to follow her when she surfaced, spluttering for air, beside him.

When she regained her composure she looked at him with a pleased expression on her face. 'Sometimes, when you want something bad enough the risks don't matter.'

Stratton was unsure what she meant.

She held up Mandrick's waterproof bag.

Stratton grinned. 'That's my girl.'

A boat powered towards them, silhouetted in the lights of the emergency crews behind it. It was a semi-rigid inflatable and a figure in the bows was shining a searchlight on the pair in the water. The engines clunked into neutral as the craft came alongside.

'I don't believe it. It's Stratton,' an Englishman called out.

Stratton recognised Todd's voice seconds before he saw his beaming face.

Paul came to stand beside his colleague. 'Christ! How the bloody hell . . . ?' he exclaimed. Then he hurried to help the pair into the boat.

They wrapped them in blankets and stood back looking at them in wonder.

'Before you do anything else,' Stratton said to Paul, 'our chip is inside that bag. The rest belongs to her.'

Paul took the waterproof bag while Stratton opened his blanket for Christine. She slid beside him and he wrapped them both up. 'Oh, and Paul? I think we might need a decompression chamber, and soon.'

Paul nodded to the coxswain who slipped the engines into gear and powered the inflatable towards the main rescue party.

'Do you think they have one we can use together?' Christine asked. 'I've gotten to like sharing confined spaces with you.'

'That's what I call risky,' said Stratton.

'It's my new middle name,' she said.